About th

Mark Ciccone is a science fiction and alternate history writer, based in Milwaukee, Wisconsin, USA. He holds a PhD in American History (Civil War & Reconstruction, a favourite period for his current and future alternate history work) from UW-Milwaukee. His other works include *Red Delta*, *Obsidian & Steel*, *For State & Country*, *Divided Worlds: An Alternate Space Race*, *Dillinger in Charleston* and *Dixie Curtain*. A lover of reading in general, and sci-fi and history in particular, he was first introduced to writing for pleasure and publication in 2010, with the online competition NaNoWriMo (National Novel Writing Month). Since then, he has competed in and won NaNoWriMo every year, and hardly a day passes for him without some kind of writing work. Nonetheless, he always makes room for at least an hour of reading a day, and the occasional relaxing smelly-sock tug-of-war with Maddie, the family dog.

Discarded

Mark Ciccone

unbound

This edition first published in 2021

Unbound

TC Group, Level 1, Devonshire House, One Mayfair Place, London, W1J
8AJ

www.unbound.com

All rights reserved

ISBN (eBook): 978-1-78965-124-9
ISBN (Paperback): 978-1-78965-123-2

Cover design by Mecob

Printed and bound in Great Britain by Clays Ltd, Elcograf S.p.A.

Super Patrons

Rhel ná DecVandé
John-Michael O'Sullivan
James Pierson
Michael Russell
Linda Schmeling
Ste Sharp
Brian Thompson
Renee Thompson
Tom Ward
Brigitte Zimmerman

Chapter 1

March 2056, 3:00am

The monitor beeped, signalling the hour. Tony Brant set aside his book with a grunt, and eased his feet off the console. He checked the holo-screens: nothing on the corridor cameras, those covering the outside compound area, or beyond the electrified fence. Hardly anything from the motion-trackers, either, other than a few whispers that pointed to rabbits or some other small wildlife.

He tapped at the glowing keys, acknowledging the time. Adjusting his utility belt, he stood up and started for the door, murmuring, 'Time is now 0100. Beginning hourly walk-through. Nothing to report yet.' The transparent sticky-mike under his lapel sent this on to both the servers in the building and those at ProShield Security HQ. That, combined with the cameras watching in the hallways, would satisfy the owners and his boss that he really *wasn't* sleeping on the job.

Not that the place would get ripped off or fall apart if I did. When he'd first taken the night shift here, six months ago, he'd

1

been surprised at the security laid out for the place. Nestled in the mostly derelict northwestern part of what had been Turmoil-era D.C.'s Military Zone, the site consisted of a single square office building, three floors above and one below. All his boss had told him was it had once belonged to some software company, which had gone belly-up in '46 and was now owned by the city – which exact agency, he didn't know, or care. The aboveground workspaces and computer labs were crammed with filing cabinets, plastic tubs and cardboard boxes, all of them overflowing with documents or computer parts. It was almost like the National Archives downtown, only neater.

Below ground, it wasn't much different. One small records room, protected by a vault door, and two basement garages that had been sealed off with concrete and earth – probably to turn them into more archive space. Tony had access to the records room but had been warned on his first day only to enter it when his boss or the building owner was present and ordering him to do so. He had no idea what was stored inside, or why there were so many sensitive yet discreet precautions around it and the building. He didn't mind not knowing, in any case – after his time in uniform, abroad and at home, he preferred the quiet bliss of not knowing much beyond a few simple rules or facts.

The overhead lights flickered just as that thought crossed his mind. As he looked up, they blinked again, and went out, plunging the room into darkness. He stiffened, then relaxed when he saw other lights from the city through a conference room window. Even with the 'Second Reconstruction' finally up and running after four years, the power grid in D.C. – and nationwide – was still spotty at best. The emergency generator automatically kicked in after thirty seconds, unless the blackout ended before then.

A faint *pop* sounded from somewhere above him. Clicking

on the flashlight at his belt buckle, he stepped closer to the window, waiting. Then he frowned, peering harder at the outside lights. The glow seemed too close for a local failure. Looking past the fence, he saw one or two old streetlights on, down the road. If *they* were still burning... He looked down at the luminous dials on his watch: 03:20. The generator should have kicked in almost a full minute ago.

Spinning on his heel, Tony speed-walked back to the door. Taking the stairs two or three at a time, he rapped out, '03:19. Blackout of unexplained nature; generators unresponsive. Moving to—' He caught himself. If both the grid and the generator were out, the servers would be, too, which meant no wi-fi, and all hardline links had been removed in the original security set-up, to avoid possible cyberattacks. He grabbed for the backup walkie on his shirtfront. It didn't have much range, but his company maintained another security post maybe three blocks away, and the blackout didn't look to have extended that far.

Reaching the first floor, he saw the lights were all down there as well. He headed toward the main office, thumbing the walkie's transmit button as he walked. 'This is Tony Brant, ProShield ID number 7556-80. Unexplained blackout taking place at my location; generator unresponsive. Please advise.'

The only answer was a harsh buzz of static. *That* was unsettling. The radio was practically clear-channel, and there were plenty of other users within range. He should be able to hear faint voices or codes, even if he couldn't reach or recognise them. *What the hell's going on?* He hit transmit again, to make the same call, when a new thought struck him. *That pop... right before the lights failed... No... It couldn't have been...* But nothing else fit. Which meant...

His hand dropped to the 9mm at his waist. In that same

instant, a faint waft of air seemed to swirl around him. Out of nowhere, a gloved hand closed tight around his wrist. He twisted instinctively... and then he was facedown on the carpet, pinned by someone's arm or knee, his gun hand wrenched up behind him. He struggled, trying to twist free, and drew in a breath to shout.

A sharp coldness pressed at his neck, just above the carotid. 'Quiet,' a voice from behind him murmured: a woman's. 'Cooperate, and you won't be harmed.' Keeping his head still, Tony allowed the rest of his body to go slack. The pressure at his back eased. 'Smart,' said the voice. A fierce jerk on his arm, and he was hauled upright, the knife still at his throat. The intruder spoke again. 'Ready?'

'Yes,' another voice answered – deep, and male. A shadowy figure moved into the weak beam of the belt-light. He was a full head taller than the guard's five-ten, dressed in grey-and-white running pants and jacket. A mask of some blue-black, shimmery fabric covered his face, except for his eyes and mouth. When he stepped closer, the guard saw gloves of similar make covering his hands, running up into his sleeves and down over his feet. It was like an all-over wetsuit, or some weird BDSM outfit.

With a few deft motions, the second intruder removed Tony's sidearm and ejected the clip, then broke the weapon down and tossed the pieces down the hall. Sliding the clip inside his jacket, he spoke two words. 'Let's go.'

Tony felt the hold on his arm vanish. Before he could even twitch, steel-like fingers clamped at the back of his neck. Speaking carefully, he asked, 'Where?'

'Downstairs,' the woman replied. 'You'll open the vault, we'll take what we need, and be on our way.'

'I can't. The power's down, and the locks are sealed—'

The grip on his neck tightened, making him gasp. 'There's a

back-up generator, separate from the one for the building,' the woman said, a touch colder. 'Runs all the time, protected from any energy spikes. But you already knew that, so don't waste our time – and yours.'

'Easy,' the man said, raising a hand. 'He's just a grunt, only told what he *needs* to know... and I doubt he knows anything beyond the door.' His eyes – blue-green, with an eerie glow of some kind, or so it looked – fixed onto Tony's. 'Like my partner said, we don't want to harm you. Comply, and we'll be gone in a few very short minutes. Don't, and we'll resort to other measures – ones we prefer not to use unless absolutely necessary.'

The knife pressed deeper into Tony's throat. He swallowed, carefully. 'All right... All right.' The man nodded once. The grip at his neck disappeared, along with the knife. Then a sharp prod at his back: *get moving.*

Unlike the doors opening onto the other three floors, which required just a swipe from his ID card, the one leading to the basement needed both that and a separate keycode. When he approached the panel, however, the keys were dark. The door opened easily when he turned the handle. When the three of them started down the stairs to the corridor beyond, the second intruder removed a small pin light from some hidden pocket, and attached it to the front of his jacket, throwing eerie shadows off the walls with every stride.

The corridor beyond was plain grey-white walls, with tan linoleum flooring. After maybe a minute's walk, they reached the vault – a single square stainless-steel door, with thumbprint scanner, keypad and ID swipe. Tony glanced over his shoulder, and saw both intruders watching impassively. 'If the vault's on its own power, it probably has a wi-fi link, too. Even if my bosses didn't get a signal from me, they might from the vault's system, and—'

'We're aware of that,' the woman replied curtly. She was dressed in the same running gear and all-over mask. Her black-brown eyes boring into him, she flashed the knife again—eight inches long at least, with a gleaming hairsplitter edge. 'So I suggest you get a move on.'

Trying to ignore his racing heartbeat, Tony placed his left thumb on the scanner, then swiped his card and punched in the code. A faint *beep* sounded, followed by a set of loud *clunk*s as the locks withdrew. The door popped open a foot, letting out a rush of pressurised air into the corridor.

Noiselessly, the man stepped past and grasped the edge of the door with one hand. In the poor light, Tony could just make out his fingers and upper arm tensing and flexing, pushing sharply against the metal. At first, he thought the other man hadn't correctly guessed the door's weight, and would soon try to wrench it open further with both hands. Then the thick slab swung away, as easy as if it were cheap plywood.

His jaw dropped. *What… What the hell…* Before he could speak, the woman stepped in front of him, knife at the ready, blocking most of his view as her partner stepped across the threshold. Keeping his gaze in the general direction of hers, he stole several quick glances over her shoulder. He spotted a single office chair standing against the far wall, facing an old-style solid computer monitor and hard drive. The secure storage boxes were interspersed throughout the room, miniature keypads brightly lit.

The man stepped up to the monitor. Even at a distance, the guard could see him reach into another part of his jacket, and pull out a matchbook-sized device, which he placed atop the hard drive. A faint whining note emanated from the machine, fading after a few seconds. His back still to the door, the man retrieved the device, holding it between two fingers as he moved closer to the storage wall. He rolled up the sleeve of his jacket, revealing more of the black skinsuit, or whatever it was. Ignoring a warning glance from the woman, Tony angled his head for a better look, and saw the man touch his thumb to the fabric at his left wrist. A holo-screen, about the size of a large notecard, shimmered into existence above the forearm sleeve.

Surprised at the door, Tony was flabbergasted now. As he watched, the man pressed the device to his sleeve, just below the screen. The image blinked several times, displaying several lines of illegible text. The man grunted, a single note of satisfaction, and looked around at the various boxes. 'It's here,' he said.

The woman nodded, not taking her eyes off Tony. 'Fine.' With no more warning than that, the pommel of her knife lashed out for Tony's face.

Reflex kicked in at once. Tony ducked, and rolled to one side as the blow struck the wall. Blade ready this time, the woman straightened, and charged. He crouched low on the balls of his feet, and sprang forward, catching her by the waist. She let out a startled 'Oof!' as they landed hard on the corridor floor, him straddling her chest. Not wasting a second, he raised a fist and punched her in the jaw, smashing her head against the floor. A spike of pain hammered up his arm, but his shout was drowned by the woman's scream – and the crackle of breaking teeth and bone. His smile was half exertion, half snarl; he'd gone through plenty of boxing in the gym and the Army, and he could land blows as well as any pro. The woman lay still, moaning. Even with the mask, he could see how misaligned the jaw was. He lifted his arm for the shock-cuffs at his belt, almost an automatic motion – just as the woman's knife hand came up.

Lights exploded in front of his eyes. He flew backwards, crumpling against the wall. Everything was spinning: the vault, the walls, the floor. Groaning, he looked up to see the woman getting to her feet. When she turned to look at him, he saw her jaw and mouth, what should have been a mangled, soppy mess of blood and teeth... already shifting back into place, as if by its own will. He goggled as the woman brought a hand to her mouth, wiping away a gob of red muck from her lips. Beneath, the gash from his punch was slowly fading, sewing back together – leaving unmarked skin beneath. Then a curtain of black crashed down over his eyes, and he knew nothing else.

At the sound from outside, Greg spun around. He was at the vault door in a blink, one hand reaching inside his jacket. Stepping out, he looked to his left in time to see the guard topple to the ground, dead or unconscious. Slowly, he fought down the gut reaction, and looked Leah's way. 'That wasn't necessary,' he murmured.

'More secure than tying him up.' Her voice was mushy, but understandable – the compound was working fast, as always. Retrieving her knife, Leah slipped it beneath her own jacket. A flap of the clinger suit immediately peeled free and closed over the blade, sheathing it.

'And if he dies in the next ten minutes?' he said, still quiet, but with a sharper edge. 'This isn't Pyongyang or Tehran – we can't leave bodies. Not here.'

Leah gave him an annoyed look. He met it with a stony one of his own. With an air of granting a great concession, she nodded, and bent to the guard's side. She put two fingers to his neck, and delicately peeled back an eyelid. 'Just out cold. He'll come to in maybe half an hour.' She straightened, and looked at Greg impatiently. 'Now let's *get moving*. Somebody's bound to notice an EMP going off in this city, no matter how small.'

Letting it go, Greg stepped back into the vault. He looked

over the walls again, until he spotted the box that had been indicated on the hard drive's records, set directly above the monitor. Taking the code-cloner out again, he attached it just below the keypad. The little device beeped once, twice, three times. Then the keypad's screen blinked on, a cascade of numbers flashing across it. After maybe five seconds, the access code froze on the screen: 776532846536. With a loud click, the box unlocked, and slid open.

Stepping around the terminal, Greg peered down into the compartment – easy, given his height. Inside sat a single metal cylinder, set atop a two-pronged metal mount. Roughly the shape of a large beer can, its only distinguishing mark was a small aperture, set just below the seal at the top – about the size and shape of the end of a human finger. With infinite care, Greg reached both hands into the compartment, and lifted the cylinder free.

A red light flashed on in the centre of the mount, followed by a low buzzing. 'Dammit,' Greg muttered. Gripping the cylinder in one hand, he trotted for the door, where Leah stood, knife at the ready. 'Must've tripped a weight sensor, or a backup alarm.' Leah nodded, as if she'd expected nothing else.

They jogged up the hallway, taking the stairs three at a time. When they stepped through the double front doors, Leah froze, holding up one hand. She sniffed the cold March air once, twice, and cocked her head in several different directions, before nodding all clear. They broke into a dash. As they bounded across the empty parking lot, Greg chuckled, 'I'll never understand that. All the tech and skills we got from the start in the Project, and you still make like some old-school tracker out of one of the Doctor's old movies.'

'Hey, it worked a lot better than *this*, plenty of times,' Leah retorted, gesturing to her clinger. They rounded the street corner without slowing, the air rushing around them. Their ride – a battered, twenty-year-old hybrid – lay a few blocks down, maybe a minute away. 'Besides, I was *trained* with stealth in mind. Relying on tech all the time would've been a waste, and probably gotten us killed in less than a second.'

They halted beside the car. With no trace of breathlessness, Greg answered, 'Well, after tonight, we have the means to make sure none of us have to face that again.' He held up the canister.

Leah nodded, sombre now. 'You're sure there's no self-destruct? Or something else to wreck the data if it's removed?'

'If there were, we'd have seen the results.' He lifted the canister up to catch the light from a nearby streetlamp. Pointing to the aperture, he said. '*This* is the hard part, as of this moment. Getting the treasure was easy – now we have to convince the only person who's bound to have the key.'

'You think that's gonna happen?' Leah inquired. 'Even if he's still alive, there's no guarantee he's still where it looks like he landed. Or that our surprise arrival won't make him react… unpleasantly.'

'Don't have a choice.' Greg flipped the canister to his other hand and pressed it against his waist. Two thin membranes looped around the object, securing it. 'We've been hunting for the truth about us since the Bomb: where we came from, and *whom*. This gives us some of it – but he's the clincher. Short of the Doctor coming back from the dead, there's no other way of convincing the world, and making sure we have a future.'

Sighing, Leah opened the passenger door and climbed in. As Greg got behind the wheel on the other side, she touched a slight protrusion at the clinger's throat. The edge of the section covering her face unsealed. She peeled back the entire mask, letting it fall behind her shoulders, where it slipped beneath her jacket and resealed against the back of the clinger.

Her reflection stared at her from the windshield: strong,

light-brown features, and black hair tied into a tight bun hanging partway down her neck. To any average observer, she was an average, young, lighter-skinned black or Hispanic woman in her early twenties. Until one saw the wrinkles around her vivid, glowing brown eyes, that is… and what lay behind the eyes themselves.

Glancing to her left, she saw Greg removing his mask, too. He scratched at his dark reddish-blond buzz–cut, as he buckled in with his free hand. He didn't even glance her way. She sighed. 'Look… I'm sorry, about back there. I'm just… sick of all this, and I want it to be over, same as you.'

Greg shifted in his seat, facing her. His pale, outwardly youthful face was set in grave lines. 'I know,' he murmured. He reached out a hand, laying it on hers. They stared at each other for a long moment. 'Ready?' he asked.

She squeezed his hand, tight. When she spoke, it was in a whisper. 'Since Seattle.'

The corners of his mouth quirked, in what might have been a smile. Turning forward again, he pressed the starter button. Quiet as a breeze, the car pulled away from the curb and disappeared into the ill-lit gloom.

Chapter 2

Noon, the Following Day

The corridor buzzed with activity. Four or five men and women in white lab tech smocks were running UV lights and other scanning devices over the vault door and interior, and doing likewise with the corridor floor and walls. Two men in blue overalls from ProShield's IT branch were huddled over a tablet computer by the door, checking the schematics of the building's wiring. Two other teams were combing the upper floors, looking for any other signs of the intruders.

Standing by the main staircase, Hargrove took all this in peripherally. He smoothed the front of his shirt, and adjusted the lapels of his jacket. No one who saw him would see any sign of his anger or impatience in his eyes or posture. The muscles in his neck pulsed, as if in speech, though his mouth remained closed. *Assessment?*

Several terse bits of text flashed across one lens of the silver-framed glasses he wore. *Connections to backup generator severed at crucial junction in first floor wall. Shaped charge, punching through from outside. Initial blackout caused by intense, localised energy spike knocking out landline connections. EMP device of Project design likeliest cause.* A short pause, then more words: *Local techs have situation in hand. Instructions?*

Hargrove's throat flexed. *Conclude examinations, and stand by.* Focusing his attention on the world around him again, he flexed his shoulders, and started back upstairs, to the main security office. None of the techs or guards paid him any notice.

Two men were already in the office as he approached. One, in a ProShield guard's uniform, was nursing his shoulder, and touching gingerly at a bloodstained bandage wound around his head. The other was older, in a dark suit and with silver hair similar to Hargrove's own sandy-white. He was gesturing at the guard in a mix of scepticism and fury. His words reached Hargrove's ears when he was near the top of the stairs. '—heard of anything like that, and I've been working with every kind of tech imaginable in the last twenty years.' Hearing new footsteps, he turned, and caught sight of who was standing behind him. He stiffened. 'Mr Hargrove! I wasn't aware you—'

'Never mind, Mr Rockford,' Hargrove cut in. 'I'm here to see how my property came through last night, and whether anything *else* is missing.' He surveyed the guard's injuries with a critical eye. 'Seems you had a rougher night of it, Mr...'

'Brant. Tony Brant.' The guard started to stand straight, but winced, and rubbed at his temples. 'It all started with the blackout. I went down to check the vault, as required, and these two huge bastards jumped me from nowhere. Don't have a clue how they got in; heard from one of the techies that they sliced through a window one floor above, right after the motion sensors went down. There's supposed to be a backup for the alerts built into the frames – guess the blackout took care of those, too.' His brow furrowed, making him wince again. 'They had some kind of weird tech with them – used it to crack the vault door in no time, and do the same with the hard drive, and whatever storage drawer they were looking for inside.'

'None of which, like I was saying, is even *possible*,' Kenneth Rockford cut in. The ProShield owner wiped a hand across his forehead. 'All-over smart suits, advanced code-cloners – and this crap about self-mending injuries, from the one you tussled with?' He glared at Brant. 'You sure they didn't deliver that hit a little harder?'

'I know what I saw,' Brant insisted. 'I don't how they had them, but they did. So you might wanna look into that before you start blaming the guy who's just supposed to make the rounds, and ignore the shit worth stealing – like the boss says.' He jerked a thumb in the direction of the vault.

Ken's face reddened. Hargrove stepped in before he could respond. 'I assure you, Mr Brant, no one blames you. From what I've seen at this point, you responded appropriately, and handled the situation as best you could.' Brant looked relieved, pathetically so. Hargrove turned to Rockford. 'The security systems look to have performed as expected, too, but my people'll want to comb through the data themselves, make sure there's nothing out of place that the intruders might've exploited.'

Rockford glowered. 'Nothing *is*, Mr Hargrove. We followed the specs laid out when your people and the city contracted with us. We can't prepare for *everything*, but we *were* prepared for any of the most likely break-in methods.' The ProShield boss let out a slow breath, bringing his temper down with a visible effort. 'Obviously, though, this wasn't one of them. If any errors resulting from poor procedures or precautions are found, I take full responsibility.'

'No need for that, Mr Rockford,' Hargrove said easily.

'While I'm certainly not happy about last night, so far I haven't seen any sign it was aided or made possible by negligence on your outfit's part. All we can do now is determine exactly *how* it happened, and take the next steps.'

Now both Rockford and Brant looked relieved. The anger flared in Hargrove's mind, just for a moment. If *he'd* been allowed to choose security for the place, or even known *some* of the details – putting that thought aside for the moment, he excused himself, and stepped back out into the hallway, moving to another unoccupied office farther down. He shut the door behind him, and closed his eyes, inhaling and exhaling slowly. *So close, and then* this.

He hadn't been *completely* thrown to the wolves, after the Seattle Bomb and the end of the Project. The original prototypes remained under his control, and whoever sat in the White House – or, more importantly, in the offices at Langley – knew they needed him around to control them, and to make more if needed. Nevertheless, the new government, shorn of the people who'd so eagerly backed his programme alongside the Project, hadn't come near him in the last five years. There were some benefits to this isolation: he was free to continue his work, with tacit approval and some support staff and equipment. And his reputation meant no one dared arrange an 'accident' for him. But he was still an outcast, kept at bay by the same people who'd benefited from *his* work, *his* success. Now, while he was just starting to earn a fragment of the power he had once held, *this* had happened – and those people would be on his back every step of the way, or trying to be.

He glanced into space. *Status?* he inquired.

The reply came in seconds, blinking across the lens. *No new developments. Standing by.*

Prep for return to HQ. He thought for a moment. *Maintain visual alert cues at all means of egress from Capital area. Asset J-003 reassigned to Union Station; other assets to remain in ready mode at HQ upon arrival.* He signed off without waiting for a reply and headed out the door. There was no need; his people would get the work done, without question.

The moment he came out the main entrance, two men in brown coats appeared from either side, falling in half a step behind him. They were tall, slightly above Hargrove's own height, but far from skinny; muscles strained at their sleeves, shoulders and plain khaki pants. Mottled red-white scars peeked out from beneath their shirt cuffs and collars. Their eyes stared into nothingness, through silver-framed glasses identical to his.

Across the parking lot, two more men of similar appearance waited by the pair of plain black sedans that had brought Hargrove and his team to the site. At his nod, three of the guards moved to the rear car, still unspeaking. The vehicle's struts creaked loudly as they got in. The fourth brown-coated man climbed behind the wheel of the first car. Hargrove climbed in the back, settling against the smooth leather.

The engine started up with a low purr. Hargrove looked out through the tinted window, at the decrepit office building. Both hands started to close again. If he'd been told that *anything* from Golem was here, he'd have claimed it for himself, Agency be damned. Now it was gone… and they'd be coming to him in hand for help reclaiming what should have been *his*.

He willed himself to relax. A little patience – that was all he needed. He'd been waiting for years already; what were a few more days or weeks? If he played his cards right, he might even get a hold of the canister before any Agency team was called in for the job. And once he had it –

He watched the building recede behind them, merging into the surrounding mass of warehouses and offices. His throat began pulsing again, relaying new orders. Text began flashing up before his eyes. Wherever the damned thieves were, he *would* find them. Of that, he was dead certain.

Chapter 3

3:15pm

A soft grunt of displeasure came from the bathroom of the dingy motel room. Seated by the front window, Greg looked up from his street vigil. Leah was standing before the mirror, studying her reflection with a critical eye. There was no scar from last night's scuffle, and the broken jawbone and teeth had healed perfectly, as expected. Still…

She stuck her head around the corner. 'How's it look?' she asked.

Even with the poor light, Greg had to fight hard against a smile. 'Depends. You planning on sticking with it?'

She snatched up the bottle of dye from the counter and hurled it at him. He caught it with a fast jerk of his hand and set it on the table in front of him. 'I'll take that as a no,' he said, deadpan.

'*Definitely* no.' She stepped out of the bathroom. 'It'll do for today, though. Same in your case, for which the world would thank us.'

Greg clutched his chest, mock-mortified. His humour faded as his fingers traced a section of raised, bumpy flesh on his left pectoral: a near-perfect circle surrounded by a splatter pattern of scar tissue. *One souvenir from Karachi I could have done without. If I hadn't been among the first ones picked to test out the clingers, those explosive rounds would've ended it, ARC or no.* The compound was capable of healing almost any non–lethal wound, but every now and then it left marks behind, for who knew what reason. He preferred to see it as a warning, a caution against ever believing he was invulnerable. *Although the first few missions rammed that home pretty good – and others, later on.*

From Leah's solemn look, her thoughts marched with his. Turning away, she began packing up the last of the toiletries they'd bought at the block's pharmacy earlier that day. 'You're sure about the time for our exit?'

'Sure as I can be,' Greg replied. Standing, he moved to check his duffel for a last time, one of the two on the double bed. He hefted the canister in one hand, then returned it to the duffel. 'We should reach the station in ten minutes, barring any surprises, and be on the *Limited* in the same amount of time. Twenty minutes, and we'll be en route to Chicago.'

'Unless they stop us somewhere along the line – or in the station,' Leah replied gravely. She came out of the bathroom, setting the toiletry bag by her duffel. 'Either'd be easy to arrange nowadays. What then?'

'They won't,' Greg replied. 'Remember the set–up at the archives. We've got what we need, and they want it back, bad – but they won't do anything that risks us, or the canister, coming to light. Push comes to shove, they might try the standard "terrorists with WMD" claim – it's worked often enough before, especially the last ten years – but then they'd have all kinds of questions coming their way from higher-ups who weren't ever told about us, and that'd be even worse than having the public breathing down their necks.'

Leah considered this, then nodded. 'Fine. Car's taken care of?'

'All prints wiped, and parked four blocks away. Somebody might get curious after a day or two and call the impound, but it'll probably be stolen before then, which'll just add to our cover.'

He zipped his bag duffel shut again. Apart from the canister, all it held was two changes of clothes: additional camouflage for the clinger suits. The jackets and pants they'd laid out already would serve until they were well out of D.C., at which point they would change, or ditch the outfits altogether, like they'd done from last night.

Putting on his jacket, he looked up as Leah let her towel fall to the floor. Standing naked by the bed, she picked up the clinger with one hand and rummaged through her bag with the other. Greg turned to one side, trying not to seem obvious. From Leah's mild chuckle, it wasn't working. When he allowed himself to look her way again, she was zipping up the clinger, bringing it just shy of her neck. The amusement in her eyes dimmed a little. 'Is it still weird, for you?' she asked. 'The reactions?'

'A little.' Greg picked up his own bag, slinging it over one arm. 'The inhibitor withdrawals are supposed to be extreme, what with all the years we were given them, to keep our skills fresh. But it hasn't been for me – so far, anyway. It's more not knowing what to do when it's done, that's the problem. What with how the Doc and the others kept us isolated, even between assignments, I guess it was inevitable.'

Leah nodded in perfect understanding. After pulling on her own outerwear, she slung the duffel strap over one shoulder.

A tiny smirk came to her lips. 'In that case… we'd better start learning the ropes, shouldn't we?'

Smiling back in the same semi-hesitant way, Greg extended his arm. She wrapped hers through the crook of his elbow, interlacing their fingers. They stepped out onto the second-floor balcony, and headed for the stairs after a careful glance in all directions. No point locking up – the keycard reader was busted, anyway, and they'd paid enough in new paper cash to shut the landlord up, at least for a few more hours.

Greg's eyes kept roving as they walked up the street. They weren't drawing any obvious attention, but that didn't stop him. His clothing – boots, jeans, grey shirt and black leather jacket – let him look like half the other locals in sight, and warm enough that nobody would wonder at his wearing them in the chilly afternoon weather. He patted at his now-golden buzz-cut. *Maybe I'm just nervous about the blond messing with my IQ.* That was a joke he'd heard often when younger, though he still didn't fully get it. Then he glanced at Leah. *Could be worse, though.* Her get-up was likewise unremarkable: boots, khakis and a white blouse over the clinger, all covered by a grey wool raincoat. Her hair, however, was now lengthened by temporary extension curls, and dyed a mess of red and midnight black. *One can argue it's so weird, it's actually* normal.

They arrived at the stop just as the bus pulled up – a rattling, wheezing hybrid model at least twenty years old. The elderly driver didn't give them a second glance as they waved their fare cards over the bus's scanner, and took seats near the front. The neighbourhoods they passed through alternated between partly torn-down office complexes, dilapidated housing projects, and half-finished 'revitalisation areas.' On their ride into town, Greg and Leah had heard plenty of grousing about the cities being essentially left to handle housing, energy and food crises on their own, while the bulk of 'Second Reconstruction' money and manpower went to favoured spots in the rural areas, or just into private hands. Having seen much of the country in the last few months, the two of them knew the truth: there simply wasn't enough to go around.

They're not calling it the 'Turmoil' for nothing. Compared to their circumstances five years ago – and that of a lot of other places nowadays – most Americans these days were in hog heaven: enough food, reasonably stable energy, reliable transport and medicine. Still, it was plain the slide from self-proclaimed superpower status wasn't sitting well with a lot of the country. *Somebody should've told them that twenty years ago, or forty.*

His reverie was broken by the bus's automated, monotone alert. 'Mass Avenue! Union Station!' Picking up the duffel, Greg moved to the front of the bus, Leah right behind him. A massive white pile of a building, with connections branching all over the country, Union Station had been one of the first targets for reconstruction after the Pulse, and the subsequent riots. Heading up the front steps amongst the other afternoon commuters, Greg noted fresh plaster over a line of bullet holes and shrapnel gouges above the main doors, and scaffolding on the roof that hadn't yet been taken down. The main entrance doors were new bronze and glass, gleaming in the late afternoon sun.

Just beyond these, a sprawling security checkpoint had been set up, taking up what had apparently been a restaurant. Greg took in the whole arrangement: the mobile X-ray and body scanners, the wafer-thin metal detector stations, the pat-downs for random travellers. His grip tightened on the duffel strap. They were prepared for the usual sweeps, but there was always the chance the canister's former owners had agents in the crowd, or among the usual guard details.

Can't be helped. We want out of town today, and fast – just have to run the gauntlet. Squaring his shoulders, he fell into the nearest line. Out of the corner of his eye, he saw Leah merge into the one to his left: backup, in case the guards stopped him.

When he reached the head of the line, the guard, a stocky, middle-aged man, tapped at his tablet checklist with one finger. Not bothering to look up, he intoned in a bored voice, 'Afternoon. Please place all luggage and other items on the scanner bed, and proceed through the imager.' He poked at the tablet again. 'Next, please!'

Greg did as he was told. The clinger's fabric would shield their knives and .32 pistols from any scanners – not that whatever metal detectors or body imagers they passed through would pick up the ceramic-carbon polymer the two were composed of. The canister was another matter. Outwardly, to the untrained eye, it looked like any other external hard drive. *But how many of those are on the job today?*

He stepped into the imager, willing his heart rate to slow down. The blue scanning rays dropped rapidly down, then back up, followed by a cheerful beep. Nodding to the woman at the control screen, he moved forward a few paces. To his relief, the duffel slid down the belt moments later, unopened. Looking to his left, he saw Leah going through the imager, and flashed a smile, which she returned.

Past the checkpoints, the station was a madhouse. Throngs of people were coming up and down the escalators, congregating at the few shops open on the street level, or moving to the ticket machines at the far end. The rumble of footsteps, passing voices, and occasional announcements all blended together in a harsh mix, only abating in a few small areas when roving groups of security personnel passed through, with portable bag scanners or decked out in quasi-military fast response gear. Greg carefully turned his eyes away from one such group, looking straight ahead. Leah, at his side once more, did the same.

The ticket auto-counter's screen blinked on at their approach. The blonde AI clerk's image flashed them a bright smile. 'Hello! Destination?'

'Chicago,' Greg replied.

'Purpose of visit?'

'Business.'

The smile never wavered. 'Please place your payment and valid photo ID in the requisite scanners, and await printout of ticket and receipt.'

Now comes the next *hard part.* The driver's licence and cash card Greg pulled from his inner pocket were technically valid; the former had his image, the latter had real cash on it, and multiple tests by Jorge and the other tech savants out West had assured him the verification tags for both were authentic. The problem was the picture itself. He'd been photographed any number of times while in the Project, but those images had either gone up with Seattle, or been wiped by the Pulse – or so he'd been told. If some random pic was still floating around somewhere, they wouldn't get far.

The machine buzzed, spitting the cash card and licence back out. As he collected these, a thin strip of paper dropped into the receptacle below the scanners. 'Thank you very much for choosing Amtrak! Have a pleasant ride!' the AI chirped.

Greg scooped up the paper and moved aside for Leah. Her cards passed muster as well. Ticket in hand, she moved close to him, unsmiling. 'We good on time?'

Greg looked at his watch, then at the departure board hanging overhead. 'Yeah. Next one leaves in ten minutes, and they close up at five.' They started for the gates, as he continued, 'Everything clear on our exit from Chicago?'

Leah nodded. 'Change trains for Milwaukee, then bus up to

Green Bay. Once there, we change again, and grab a rental or hitchhike to the last stop.' Her walk slowed. 'You're sure we can't bus it the whole route? Rentals in those parts might be suspicious enough to pass the word along about two tall strangers with plenty of cash.'

'Same rumours would start flying if we went the Greyhound route,' Greg replied. 'Once we hit Green Bay, we'll be farther off the radar, and much closer to the target than if we took the long way around, through the Twin Cities. We can't expect to stay under forever, not if we want in and out fast.'

Leah nodded, still not looking convinced. Passing the Amtrak police office, they came into the main waiting area, just short of the gates leading to the tracks. The place was packed: families in worn and rumpled clothing, swamped with kids and weather-beaten luggage; a few individual men or women in a wide array of flashy, expensive attire; and a small reserved section of elderly folk, in all kinds of passé outfits. Two squads of soldiers sat or stood in a group nearest the far right-hand gate, resting or talking amongst themselves; a few of them passed around half-and-half smokes – Cuban tobacco and Denver weed, by the smell. They were decked out in full combat gear, dyed in forest camo patterns, and which bore the marks of recent, heavy usage. *Must be from the pacification zones in the lower Appalachians,* Greg mused. *Probably off to deal with the few, scattered militias left in the Dakotas or Montana, given the route. And D.C. being what it is these days, they're probably heading straight out again, after no more than a couple days' rest.* For Golems, it wouldn't have mattered, or very little. For these men – and teenagers, a few of them – it was taking its toll, by their haggard expressions and languid movements.

After a little searching, they found a pair of seats two rows away from Gate B, their departure point. Greg kept his bag on his lap; Leah set hers on the floor. An instant later, she had to snatch it out of the way as two kids – a boy and girl, brother and sister by the look of them – raced past them, giggling and shrieking as they chased each other through the crowd, leaping over feet and luggage. A haggard, middle-aged woman with greying black hair followed several paces after them, mixing mumbled "Scuse me's' to those she stumbled over with shouts at the two kids.

Leah clicked her tongue sympathetically. 'That's not going to stop any time soon.' She let the bag drop to the floor again, this time between her feet. Her face became more pensive, and faintly morose. 'I wonder if *we* were the same, before the Project. If whatever families we had – our real ones, or the adoptive or foster ones the Doc said some of us came from – had to wrangle *us*. Or if we were more the rare, quiet types.'

'We'll find out soon enough,' Greg said, setting a hand atop his bag. *Hopefully* lingered unspoken. There were no guarantees about what the canister contained; they'd known that before setting out. All they knew with any certainty was that it came from the Project, which made it priceless all on its own. Once they could get it open…

They sat quietly amid the hubbub, their outward calm belying their readiness. After a bit, Leah hesitantly broached another question: 'Do you think it's true? What the… tests said, before we left?'

'No idea,' Greg replied solemnly. He was staring straight ahead. 'We thought it was impossible for the inhibitors to wear off. But it happened, and is happening, to everyone.'

She leaned closer, brushing his arm with her fingertips. He didn't react, at least not in any obvious way. 'If they're…' She hesitated, then forged on: 'If the preliminary tests we ran *are* right, what would you want to—'

26

Before she could finish, Greg's arm wrapped around her shoulders. He pulled her closer, and pressed his lips against hers, hard. She stiffened, startled. He broke the kiss, shifting so that they were nuzzling cheek-to-cheek. 'Tall guy, behind your left shoulder,' he murmured. 'Black hair, brown overcoat. Standing by the old Starbucks spot, holo-reader in right hand.'

Leah's hand tightened on his lapel. 'How long?' she murmured.

'Since the bus, maybe longer. Then four spaces behind you in line, and twenty yards behind at the counter.'

She moved back a little, gazing into his eyes as she stroked his cheek with her left hand, joining him in character. Her right reached into her coat, closing on the grip of her pistol. 'Any others?'

'None in sight.' He placed his free hand on her wrist. 'He could just be a scout, or a suspicious Fed. Whatever he is, he won't make a move here.'

'And if he's got friends? Or jumps on the ride?' she whispered, letting some of her anxiety show.

'Too many around us, if he does. And it's two against one – even the Pentagon wouldn't send a solo agent to face two of us. And they won't risk derailing a train to stop us... except if it was a ride built for two.'

Donning a bright smile, Leah gripped the hair at the back of his head. He winced at the fingernails digging into his scalp. 'So we keep going?' At his nod, she let go, still smiling. To anyone else, they were just another young couple, stealing a kiss before the long ride.

Above them, the loudspeaker suddenly blared. '*Now boarding, Capitol Limited, with service to Chicago, and intervening stops. Please have all luggage at hand, and ready for storage if requested. In accordance with the National Emergency and Defense Act of 2035, all items and persons boarding may be searched as demanded by Amtrak personnel, and—'*

Tuning this out, Greg got his feet, looping the duffel strap across his body; Leah did the same. Discreet manoeuvring brought them near the head of the column, just a few spaces down from the seniors and soldiers who were being given first passage. Passing through the doors, Greg looked up at the polished metal of the gate's arch. The brown-coated man was in line, holo-newsreader tucked under one arm and a small suitcase in his left hand; camouflage, or additional weapons. The reflection was warped and distorted, but he could just make out the man's black hair, day-old stubble, and visor-like silver-framed glasses. Two deep, pale scars ran up both sides of his neck, ending just below his jawline.

Since they had tickets but no seats reserved in advance, Greg and Leah headed toward the rear cars—'cattle loaders' was the term, nowadays. Before stepping up onto the car's stairwell, Greg cast another look around. No sign of Brown Coat. *Probably picked another spot, waiting for us to separate or otherwise go lax.* At Leah's impatient tug on his hand, he climbed up the steps.

The seats were arranged three to a row on the left, two on the right; they picked the latter. Seeing that Leah was taking the window seat, Greg held out his bag to her. 'Better that we switch,' he murmured, still wearing the happy expression. 'A little extra protection.' She nodded, and took it, her smile becoming more strained.

After one last look up and down the aisle, he sat down. Without taking his eyes off the door at the far end, he unzipped his jacket and pulled his shirt free. Reaching underneath, he grasped the knife hilt. The clinger came loose at once, and he twisted the blade under his wrist and up his jacket sleeve. One jerk of his arm, and nine inches of pure murder would sprout from his hand. At his right, Leah made the same preparations, and stuffed the bag between her armrest and the window. She murmured. 'So we stay here, for the full trip?'

Greg nodded. 'He comes in here, we move past him – there's no other way – and head to the lounge car. Short of jumping off mid-stop, there's no sure way of avoiding him, in the Chicago station or anywhere else. So we stay in the spots with plenty of people, and arm space.'

She nodded, a single dip of her chin. Then she surprised him with a soft snort of laughter. 'Good thing I hit the bathroom before we left.'

Their hands brushed together. A keening whistle note sounded from the loudspeakers, followed by the fainter shout of 'All aboard!' from the conductor at the end of their car. Leah settled back in her seat, eyes half-closed as she stared out the window. To anybody else, she looked to be falling asleep – but if there was even a hint of danger in the car, she would be up and moving in less than a second, weapons or hands at the ready, same as him. *And not all that's from the genes or training,* Greg thought, with a flash of smugness.

That flash disappeared, almost instantly. *And it wouldn't be needed, if we'd led normal lives. But the Doctor kept that from us – him and all the rest at the Facility. Now the last of us are left wandering the country – hell, the world – after being left for dead, for God knows what reason, and being hunted by shadow-men: again, God knows why.*

Leah's hand slipped into his again, jerking him out of his reverie. Looking her way, he saw she was still staring at the now-moving urban landscape, that half-asleep expression still on her face. He smirked. *She always did have me dialled in, and knew how to cool me off.* Squeezing back, he sank more comfortably into his seat, watching the far-end door, and the one behind them through the window reflection. Eight hours to Chicago. *After that seven-day 'meditation' outside Urumqi in '35 with Hiroshi – to name just one – it shouldn't be hard to sit through one train ride.* He squeezed the hilt of his knife. *I hope.*

Chapter 4

4:00pm

Somewhere Outside D.C.

The car braked, wheels squeaking. Hargrove opened the door and stepped out. The building in front of him might almost have been a twin to the one in the District – nearly the same exterior, and close to the same layout. The parking lot was packed with cars. People in everyday clothing were streaming in and out of the double glass doors at the front.

The lobby was unremarkable, with a few blue-cushioned chairs and couches arranged before a wide reception desk emblazoned with the old Advent logo: a merged capital A and T, set against a dark blue circuitry hologram and flanked by two double helixes. A small number of office workers were clustered around the bank of elevators at the end of the room, or moving between the offices on either side. At the sight of Hargrove, these people moved back or retreated into various rooms, giving them a wide berth. Some stared, either at Hargrove or the thickset guards. Hargrove only smiled, nodding politely to those he passed. He'd been in de facto charge of the place since the Pulse, and a power before then. Even without the Agency's recognition, *he* was the boss, here.

He stepped into the closest elevator. The two guards moved in behind him. The ride down was uneventful for the first few minutes. Once or twice the doors opened, and one or more workers would start to board, but immediately pull back when they saw who was already aboard. Hargrove just kept smiling, enigmatically. On the display above the doors, each floor ticked off. Lobby. Basement. Sub-Basement. Garage. Auxiliary Garage.

When the last faded from the screen, the car came to a sudden halt. All the buttons went out. Hargrove pressed his thumb to a square light box above the main panel. A faint *beep* sounded, and the light recessed into the wall, sliding up to reveal a keypad and microphone. He typed in a code, and spoke slowly and clearly. 'Simon Hargrove. Specialist.' Another beep, then a loud thunk. At once, the car resumed its descent, much faster this time. No floor names or numbers appeared on the display.

When the doors slid open, a huge, two-floor room was laid out before them. The lower level was packed with desks, holo-terminals, servers and other machines. A dozen offices and conference rooms made up the second floor, accessible by a metal walkway curving in either direction along the wall and coming together in a wide staircase in front of the elevators. The air was a low buzz of murmuring voices, humming hard drives and the occasional whir of printers. Slinging his jacket over one arm, Hargrove motioned for the guards to wait, and started down the walkway. Here and there people looked up to glance at him, then looked back to their work, as though they didn't want to meet Hargrove's gaze for too long.

He finally halted before an opaque glass door, at one corner of the room. Stepping up to the terminal beside it, he lowered his glasses. When the retinal scanner blinked green, he punched in a five-digit code, leaned closer to murmur his name once again, and put his thumb to another scanner surface below the pad. The tiny needle below it poked his flesh, and he withdrew his hand, wiping it on his pant leg. Mildly painful, but the extra biometric security layer more than made up for the constant sampling needed whenever he was away from this floor.

The office inside was as understated as the upstairs lobby. Grey-white walls, a glass-top desk, holo-terminal, two plain black office chairs, a wall safe and a pair of filing cabinets. Stepping behind the desk, Hargrove waved his hand over the terminal sensor. The screen and keyboard flickered on at once. He sat down and tapped at the keys. His eyes flicked over the several different windows that appeared. No reports in yet from any of his assets, here or inside the city. No noteworthy calls intercepted, and no sightings worth following up. Current assessment was the targets were sitting tight, waiting for contact, or a window to leave.

Not much else they can *do*, he mused with a scowl. *It's the U.S. capital, for Christ's sake; there're probably more cameras, mikes and satellite coverage than any other city on the planet.* And if a contact was waiting for the canister, or for them, he doubted it was in the city, or anywhere near it. So they needed out after a maximum of twenty-four hours. *Half of which they've probably already used to throw off any tails, and prep for departure, if they haven't already done so.*

Either way, all he could do was wait – and prep for the Agency grilling him soon. He tapped at his keyboard again, calling up a new set of files. No better time to confirm his suspicions and knowledge, and gauge how much the Agency *really* knew.

The first file was the oldest: details on the successful test of what was later termed ARC – Accelerated Regeneration Compound – that had taken place in 2023. Bottom line on that: for the first time, there existed a means of providing regeneration of lost or damaged human tissue. If a kid broke his arm falling off a bike, the compound would fix him in an hour, maybe two, without any need for a cast. If a firefighter came out of a job with third-degree burns, the compound would eliminate the damage within forty-eight hours – if applied fast enough. A year after this test, the incoming administration had sent an envoy to the two doctors overseeing the tests, and offered substantial federal backing and funding... if they agreed to continue their work under the supervision and advice of the military. Outwardly it was all about finding new treatment options for the Veterans' Administration – but the President and the Pentagon wanted something more. Something that would give the country an edge in the crises starting up around the world, back then. Enhancements for soldiers in the field – or a completely different kind of soldier, made from practically nothing, like the Golem of myth. Hargrove allowed himself a sardonic smirk. 'Seems nobody *does* learn from history,' he muttered.

At the time, the compound's effects had still been only partly known, and the powers had accepted that there wouldn't be any real progress on the 'enhancement' issue for years, if not decades. Also, the lead doctor on the project – Richard Garrett – had turned out to be reluctant to enter into a partnership with the Army. He'd just wanted to continue studies, learn more about its impact on the human body as a whole, before he moved on to higher-level testing. Inside of two years, though, he'd come around, in a way. By '28 the compound was ready for use among military-age humans – and even from the start of life itself.

'And thus was born Project Golem,' Hargrove murmured. The most ambitious military and covert operation ever undertaken, by the US or any other nation. The most successful, too, by all accounts – up to a point. In the spring of '32, Dr Garrett succeeded in implanting the ARC into a human subject. The files didn't have much more until '35, but they did indicate that the subject – a boy, mid to late teens – had been altered in such a way that he matured extremely rapidly in just over three years, per the Project's estimate – and still retained the ARC. When the Colombian Intervention failed, just at the end of that period, a White House memo had come out indicating that Garrett had unveiled the subject – and at least four others of similar creation – in a private audience with the President and the Joint Chiefs. Apparently, Garrett had still had doubts about using them as soldiers, but the Pentagon and the White House were gung-ho for it. All part of the 'Measured Response' strategy, as they saw it – trying to appease a public sick of putting boots on the ground all over the Third World.

The records covering the next several years were still spotty – not surprising, with the Pulse and everything else. The first confirmed Golem exploits were in Pyongyang, in '36, not long before the DPRK went under. Then it was all over the map, literally, for the next few years: Pakistan, Ukraine, central China, right up to the real start of the Turmoil, in '39. After that, almost total silence. Every one of them had gone dark, most right before the Pulse. A fair number – maybe as many as half – have been confirmed dead in various parts of the world, and here, but there're still plenty unaccounted for. They were officially listed as MIA in Agency reports, but…

'But we all know what those're worth, nowadays,' Hargrove said, smirking again. So, for all anyone knew, there could be dozens, maybe hundreds of these creations still running around loose. *Two of which practically walked into the vault last night, and walked out with the most crucial records on the people and methods that created them.*

He leaned closer to the screen, studying the files more intently, and calling up what his team had already gleaned from the site. Even with all their talents, the intruders would've needed significant help in locating this place, as well as maintaining their equipment. The evidence indicated a localised EMP burst to fry the primary grid; that was a standard tactic on many Golem insertions. And judging from their reaction to the guard, it seemed they'd changed tactics – they were no longer simply disposing of obstacles. All this pointed to new developments among whatever survivors there may have been from the Project. Some form of re-grouping, perhaps around a new leader or governing body, with a new agenda – which involved what was taken from this site.

Hargrove tapped at the holographic keys again. A single human figure appeared, with text and graphs scrolling on readouts to either side. He studied the image, nodding unconsciously as he read. All the Golem subjects had grouped together in five-person teams, with individuals bringing specific traits to the table. Some were altered and trained with speed, dexterity, and tracking prized above the rest – those were mostly women, by all accounts. Others were made with an emphasis on brute strength, and tolerance for pain – primarily men. But all of them shared a few common traits: high intelligence, excellent general athleticism, outstanding marksmanship, six-foot-plus height – and the ARC. Ideal soldiers, from the Pentagon's standpoint. Based on Brant's report, they'd carried their typical mission gear. The EMP burst was most likely caused by one of the experimental grenade launchers they were sometimes issued with, during more perilous actions.

He pressed a single key. The revolving central image shifted, displaying the human figure decked out in a black all-over suit, its pattern shimmering and changing under the light. A hood of similar material seemed to grow out of the back of the garment, and extended to cover the figure's entire head, turning it into a seamless black statue. This was the crown jewel in their skill trinity, above any gear and even the ARC: the Advanced Combat and Infiltration Garment. The Golems typically referred to it as a 'clinger,' based on the one or two battlefield reports he'd dug up. Designed first by the Defense Advanced Research Projects Agency (DARPA) in 2030, before it was snapped up by the Project. The exact design was still classified, but Hargrove had a vague idea of the core component.

He pressed another key. The image zoomed in on the figure's torso. A new window opened, showing a black multi-limbed circular object. Tiny traces of circuit pathways shimmered at its centre. 'Nanotechnology,' he murmured. A tiny flare of anger rose for an instant, before he managed to tamp it down. With this, the 'clingers' were basically an all-in-one set-up. *His* people had never determined the exact makeup – the Project folk had made sure it was sealed tight. Short version, the nanotech was encased in supposedly bulletproof and blade-proof fibres, and programmed to repair damage, redirect to strengthen the armour where hits were most likely – the chest, upper arms and legs, and so forth – and coalesce at hands and feet for added force and impact in empty-hand combat. He zoomed out, showing the entire suit. Several 'patches' on the chest and waist, designed to wrap over weapons and tools as needed. What were supposedly called 'field terminals' in the left sleeve: holo-display computers, used to keep in touch with others in the field, translate any written or spoken language, and, with a few accessories, capable of hacking any computer system in existence.

With an air of mild disgust, he punched another control. The image disappeared, reverting to the initial background. 'The perfect tool, for the perfect weapons,' he growled. If it was just the two Golems from last night – which he doubted – then he'd have a much easier time tracking them down, since they wouldn't have any of the old support systems in place. But if the other three members of their original team were backing them up, then they were probably halfway across the country by now. And if there were even more of their breed, hiding out somewhere, passing on instructions and equipment…

Text began to flash along the bottom of his left lens. He stopped, pulsing his throat several times. *Hold. Send to personal terminal.* A vidchat window popped open at once, filling the whole holo-screen, showing a brown-haired, serious young man in a plain tailored black suit and blue tie. His light brown eyes were calm, with outward friendliness – a look that couldn't hide his poised, probing body language. He seemed boyish, but Hargrove could see the lines around his eyes, and the tiny trace of silver at his temples. Wherever he'd been, it had aged him fast. 'Morning, Mr Hargrove,' the man said. There was little trace of pleasure in his tone.

'Good morning, Agent…' Hargrove trailed off.

'Ben Costa, Special Activities Centre.' The man's fingers tapped away below the screen, likely verifying the connection's security for the millionth time. 'I've been assigned as the primary agent for the investigation of the… incident at the records repository, and as your liaison. Given the circumstances, and your familiarity with the technology and other factors involved, you'll be allowed to take point on any new developments in the matter, though no unilateral action will be taken without clearance from the Director.'

'I see,' Hargrove said, letting some tightness into his voice. 'How nice to still merit such care and attention.' Costa didn't answer. Hargrove went on, 'I'm assuming the Agency still considers my arrangements with them valid, then?'

'When word came about the break-in, and *what* was taken, some of my bosses wanted the place scrubbed altogether, along with everything else related to the contents of the stolen item.' Costa's expression made it clear what *everything else* entailed. 'Cooler heads prevailed, however, and it was ultimately agreed to maintain the Agency's relations with your endeavours, with the goal of recovering the item before it's delivered into the wrong hands.'

Hargrove smiled, without humour or pleasure. 'By any means necessary?'

Costa nodded, with a grudging air. 'Within reason. If we're dealing with the sort of people the Agency suspects, some collateral damage is expected, but we don't want bodies or buildings dropping all over the place. I'm not cleared for the specifics – yet – but obviously the Project, wherever its HQ *once* was, has to stay buried. The new administration may have signed off on your helping to do so, but they're edgy enough about cleaning up the shit brought on by the last administration. One slip-up, and we're all out – feet-first, probably, in certain cases.'

'So I've known for some time,' One of Hargrove's hands opened and closed a few times, the only sign of his anger. Turmoil or not, he'd damn well *had* the perfect solution to the ailing Project, perfected after two decades of work, sweat and not a little blood. When the Seattle Bomb had gone off, he'd been at the peak of his power and influence. Even with the Pulse that same day, he'd managed to stay in business. Then within a matter of days, his finances, facilities and people had gone on the chopping block of the new 'reconciliation government', destroying any hope of expanding his work. The next batch had been decommissioned before any had been close to ready, and he was barred from government work, with the Army, the Agency or anyone else – blacklisted, in other words. Now he was being lectured by the errand boy sent to watch over him, to make sure he didn't spit on the sidewalk.

A soft alarm began to beep from the computer. He punched up a new window, studying the few lines of text that appeared. He tried not to smile. *Saved by the bell.* Meanwhile, his throat pulsed some more. *Route to main surveillance team, then board and pursue to destination. Additional assets en route.* He scrolled through the last line, then stood up. 'You'll have to excuse me, but there's been a development. I'll be in touch shortly.'

He cut the connection before Costa could reply and strode out of the office. The two brown-coated guards fell in beside him. He descended the stairs, two at a time, and came to a stop before a terminal at the far end, where a woman in plain office dress was tapping at the holo-keys with one hand and swiping through multiple windows on the screen with the other. 'What is it?' he demanded.

Not looking up, the tech answered, 'Possible confirmed sighting of last night's targets, based on descriptions from the security guard and information from existing files. Sighting was at Union Station, two minutes ago, boarding Capital Limited for Chicago. Report came from Asset—'

'Yes, yes,' Hargrove interrupted. 'Any sign of others with them, or any incoming or outgoing calls?'

'No, sir. Sole activity was the ticket purchase. Booth cameras recorded the targets' images and hints of their equipment. These were again noted by platform devices just prior to departure.' She typed and swiped some more. 'Should I alert military authorities along the route, or signal for interdiction?'

'No,' Hargrove replied at once. 'Our man in place has his orders, and will execute them at the earliest – and most discreet

– opportunity.' He squinted at the screen – best to keep up appearances. 'Signal all other stations of this sighting and instruct them to remain on standby in the event the targets deviate from the assigned route. I'll inform Upstairs and prep the extraction team. Take–off from Andrews the moment our operative reports having secured the targets.'

Ignoring the tech's murmur of assent, he spun on his heel, and marched toward the elevator. As he got in, he tapped at his smartwatch, calling up the vidchat with Costa. 'We've got something,' he said without preamble, and relayed the gist of what he'd heard.

'Good,' the agent replied when he was done, still monotone. 'We'll stop the train once it's out of the District. Won't be hard to make up an excuse – bad tracks, faulty engine, something. Then we cordon off a wide radius, and—'

'Not an option,' Hargrove replied. 'It'd take too long to convince Amtrak, and to communicate with the train, much less avoid scrutiny for stopping a line full of civilians. If we did, our targets would be tipped off, and vanish into the sticks, for good. But once they reach the end of the line, they'll be a lot more complacent, and we'll be in the best position to cut them off from whatever their destination may be.'

'We'll still have to notify the Army, though,' Costa said. Hargrove looked at him sharply. The agent elaborated. 'The route they're taking passes through any number of martial law zones. Chicago's the worst headache: plenty of troops and checkpoints, but there's any number of back ways out. The garrison's prepped for threats, but those of the conventional bomb or other terror activity, ones that affect specific sites. For something like a manhunt, they need warning, advisement on checkpoint placement—'

'No,' Hargrove interrupted. 'This isn't a typical manhunt. These are augmented targets, with intimate knowledge of all the Army's tactics, and the Agency's. What's more, we need the item they stole, intact. The Army gets involved, they'd have to level half a city block at least to bring the targets down for certain – something I'm sure your bosses would frown on.'

Costa glowered but said nothing. Hargrove continued, softening his tone microscopically. 'Still, we'll need to give a heads-up to the Chicago commandant, and those in the other urban zones, with the proviso that they keep it under wraps until and unless the targets show in their areas. Once they do, we can move within minutes – and our assets'll have plenty of advantages, when they go head-to-head.' He smirked, reassuringly. 'We'll bring these two down – and we'll do it quietly.'

Costa's nod was wary. 'There's only one thing that's bugging me – *us*, I should say.' Hargrove arched an eyebrow. The agent continued. 'We know all this: the Project's origins, the specifics on the Golems themselves, their operations – enough for two or three life sentences, or worse. If the break-in was to leak all this, it'd cause problems, but the Agency can handle the fallout, no matter what the White House says. There's no evidence pointing to the Russians, any European agencies, any of the bigger terror groups, or what's left of the Chinese. And if Golems were behind it, they'd know the whole story anyway. So: Why?'

Hargrove bit down on a chuckle. He'd suspected Costa was naïve enough to go looking for that kind of answer. Or was there some other reason – a hope of picking his brains some more, or trying to? Arranging his face into solemn lines, he said, 'We'll have to ask, when we find them.' The agent nodded, looking far from convinced.

Chapter 5

He was standing in a clearing, ringed by dark evergreens. The air was dewy and cold, but the sun was chasing away the last of the rainstorm. He looked down at himself. He was in grey shorts and T-shirt, and barefoot. Both were soaked clean through. Water was dripping off his arms and from his hair.

'Gregory?' He turned. A man's form, dressed in a white lab coat, loomed out of the murk. His face was a dripping blur, with an edge of brown hair. He blinked once, and the man was inches from him – all he could see now was an expanse of white fabric. 'Come inside, Gregory,' the man said. The voice was calm, worldly, inviting. His hands appeared, holding a syringe in one and a trio of pills in the other. 'You'll catch cold – and you need your medicine.'

No, *he tried to say.* I don't wanna. I wanna stay outside. *To his dismay, the words sounded like a child's – high-pitched, plaintive, pleading.*

The hands folded together. When they opened, the syringe and

43

pills were gone, replaced by a strip of grey cloth. Holding it in both hands, the man moved closer. He tried to move, to run, but his legs wouldn't obey. His vision went grey as the band fell across it, then faded to black.

He was in another place, lying on his back on a slab of cold metal. His head, chest, arms and legs were held down by cloth straps. He jerked against them, but they didn't yield. The walls around him were a dazzling pure white, with soft light shining down. He could hear the faint beeping of machines, and thought he could see screens of some sort to either side. Human figures moved in and out of sight – ghostly white suits, without faces.

One of them approached from his right, a syringe at the ready. He quailed. Please, *he said silently. His voice was deeper, but broke like a teenager's.* Please, no more. What is all this for? *Then the syringe slipped into his arm, and black slid over his eyes again.*

He was lying on his side, on soft padding. His body was free, but aching horribly: in his bones, his muscles, his skin. Even a twitch brought sharp, stabbing pain all over. The room was pitch-dark, but he could just make out another, childlike form, lying on a pad a few feet in front of him. There was soft sobbing, coming from here and there. A soothing voice – a woman's *voice – was singing tenderly, somewhere above him:*

'Sleep, my child and peace attend thee,
   All through the night
   Guardian angels God will send thee,
   All through the night
   Soft the drowsy hours are creeping
   Hill and vale in slumber sleeping,
   I my loving vigil keeping
   All through the night.'

He longed to raise his arms, to reach out to the voice. It was hopeless; the pain was too great. The moaning around him worsened; perhaps the others yearned for the same.

A shaft of harsh light fell across his spot. He angled his eyes toward it, bringing spikes of agony at his temples. Another white figure appeared, face hidden by opaque, gleaming metal. Behind it stood two others, in the same attire. Squinting, he could see the wheels of a gurney behind them. They began to approach, pulling the gurney in. He tried to curl up, to moan, to hide – to do anything. But his arms were locked, and his legs. They came closer, hands outstretched…

Greg sat up, breathing in hard, short gasps. A light sheen of sweat coated him, absorbed fast by the clinger. He wiped his face, then twisted in his seat, gazing up and down the aisle. No sign of their fellow traveller. A quick glance at Leah: she was leaning against the window, eyes closed. The bag was tucked in the crook of her left arm. Her right was cocked beneath her, in just the right position for the blade to drop into a waiting hand.

Nice to know somebody's *on the job,* he thought, in self-reproach. The 'meditation' tricks he'd had drilled into him should've lasted longer, allowing him to rest while staying awake. Most of his generation could last a full forty-eight hours without sleep and still stay alert; some for seventy-two. Maybe the constant movement and adrenaline ever since their departure from out West had taken more of a toll than he thought.

He leaned carefully over her, straining to see out the window. They were inside the city limits, but despite his well-adapted eyes, the late-night darkness, combined with the carpet of urban lights, made it near impossible to spot any landmarks, much less the approaching station. He sat back, shaking his head a little to clear the last of the sluggishness. *Haven't had any of the dreams since a little before we started out. The night we decided, in fact.* He still had only guesses about them: childhood fears, old memories from training, a mix of both, or something totally different. He shook his head again. *Doesn't matter. Can't have them distracting me now.*

The brakes began to grind. He turned to shake Leah awake, only to find her already sitting up, eyes clear and coat unbuttoned. She looked carefully about the cabin, toward the front and rear doors. 'Any sign of our friend?' she whispered.

Greg shook his head, deciding not to let her know about his dozing off. 'Not for the whole trip. If he *is* tailing us, he'll wait to make a move until we're clear of the train, probably even outside the station. Too many chances for us to slip away in the crowds – and for collateral damage, if he goes loud.'

'Well, then.' Leah reached beneath her shirt, grasping the butt of her pistol.

Greg grabbed her wrist. 'Not yet.' At her questioning look, he said, 'Security might be lax in some areas due to overstretch, but Union Station isn't bound to be one of them. We'll wait to make any moves until we're past the cordon. And I'm fairly sure our fellow traveller plans on the same.'

Looking doubtful, Leah removed her hand. The train decelerated further. The car's loudspeaker crackled, and then the driver's voice announced, softly, '*Ladies and gentlemen, we are approximately one minute away from our final stop at Platform 10, Union Station. Due to the heightened threat level at this time, I must inform you all that—*'

Greg ignored this, and stood up, slinging the bag's strap over his head. Around him, the few passengers in the car were getting up as well, pulling their bags from beneath seats or from the overheads. Most of the seats had emptied the closer they came to the perimeter of the Martial Law Zone covering nearly all of northeastern Illinois. Other than the Eastern Seaboard, there was no place more patrolled or observed in the states east of the Mississippi – hence their plan to be on the way to Milwaukee in no more than an hour. *No chance for the trains anymore, though; buses are too easy to stop, too. We'll need a car, one which won't be missed for a while or draw more than a cursory glance on a police report.*

He turned to face the rear door. Leah was standing a pace behind him, bag in hand. As the train inched toward the platform, she muttered, 'Straight off the platform, and up to Adams Street?' Greg dipped his head. 'And if blocked, then the Great Hall and Clinton exit?' He nodded again. 'Then?'

'Then we keep moving,' he whispered back. 'We find a lot, minimum of six blocks from the station, grab a car, and get out of the city by the best route available.' He tapped Leah's left sleeve. She tapped back in acknowledgement. The train came to a complete stop with a loud, chuffing wheeze. The doors at both ends of the car opened, as did the exits just beyond them to both sides. Silently drawing in breath, he started forward.

Out of nowhere, a figure in blue and red conductor's uniform stepped forward to block their path. Greg tensed, but the other man just smiled. 'I'm sorry, sir, but you'll have to wait a little longer. There's a group of soldiers disembarking, and we've been told to keep all civilian travellers aboard the cars until they've been deployed.'

'I see.' Casually, Greg let his free hand drift to his belt, close to his holster. 'Any idea why they're deploying *here?*'

The conductor shrugged. 'Word on the wire is the threat level was being raised for today, at this site only; most likely it's a drill, or a false alarm. It shouldn't be more than a few minutes, then you'll all be allowed to disembark.' He moved back a little, half-closing the door in front of him.

'Thanks.' Stepping back a pace, Greg leaned up against the nearest seat and crossed his arms, as if he were mildly impatient but accommodating. Catching Leah's eye, he twitched his chin imperceptibly, toward the window. *Check.*

Nonchalantly, she bent over and began feeling around the seats, like any traveller looking for lost keys or a wallet. After a few seconds, she straightened and moved to stand next to him. Her right hand opened and closed rapidly, five times: *Twenty-five.* That accounted for all the soldiers they'd seen in Washington. He made a C with his left hand: *Combat ready?* His teeth gritted at her tiny nod. His hand shaped into a pistol. *The tail?* She gave back a minute shrug; no sign. *Which could mean that there really is a drill or other alert in play. But what are the odds that a tail latches on in D.C., and two squads get pulled off assignment to guard our exit?*

For maybe five minutes, Greg, Leah and the other half-dozen passengers in their car sat or stood where they were. A few of their fellow travellers were muttering to each other or into phones, complaining about the hold-up. They just stared at the door, or into space. Finally, the conductor stepped back inside. 'All right everyone, I'm told we can begin disembarking. If you'll please move in an orderly fashion—'

Greg and Leah were the first in line, but they allowed a few of the others to fall in ahead of them. No point making it obvious they wanted off. The cavernous platform area was brightly lit and filled with noise: the hissing and clacking of trains, and a steadily milling crowd of arrivals and departures, their voices mingling into a discordant mass.

Stepping down first, Greg looked back and forth down the crowded walkway. A few Amtrak security men were mixed into the crowd, but there was no sign of soldiers or other security – or the Brown Coat. He let his left hand fall and twitched his two main fingers sharply: *Follow. Close.* A brush against his left shoulder indicated Leah's assent.

They moved toward the north end, staying in the thickest part of the crowds. When they had gone maybe twenty feet, Greg slowed his pace, grabbing Leah's arm with two fingers. Three soldiers stood at the base of the escalators, assault rifles at the ready. His eyes flicked to the elevator: two more in position, relaxed yet prepared. The others were probably deployed to the other exits or waiting for them outside.

Keeping up the steady stride, he angled to the left, so that he faced the baggage claim. A good chunk of the crowd was heading in that direction, so they still had some cover. Leah moved closer to his side. Donning a smile, he looked her way, gesturing with his free hand as he muttered, 'Keep left, then left again, straight through the Hall to the street.'

She nodded, her smile belied by the intense gleam in her eye. 'Anybody following?'

Greg glanced at the wall to their left, which was plated with silvery metal. The camo-clad men weren't moving, but there was one blurry shape, maybe twenty yards behind them –

He stiffened, but stayed in motion. 'What?' Leah asked, keeping up the false cheer.

'Brown Coat, closing fast.' Her hand tightened on his arm. The crowds had thinned around them; only a couple dozen other travellers were in sight, wandering or standing in small groups. They were within sight of the Great Hall. No cops or soldiers milled at the entrance, or at least none that he could see. Greg risked a glance back. The Brown Coat was striding towards them, gliding easily through the crowd with unusual grace. He looked to Leah. 'If he gets within ten paces, we go flat-out for the door. If—'

A sharp stabbing pain struck his left side, above the waist. He flinched, his stride faltering. He grabbed at the afflicted spot – and felt a tiny metal dart, pierced clean through the clothes and clinger suit.

Leah clenched his sleeve with both hands. 'Greg? What's wrong?'

Fighting to keep his pace and breathing steady, Greg yanked the dart out. Leah's eyes widened. A cold numbness was beginning to spread, over his pelvis and down toward his hip. 'Left-hand door,' he ground out. 'Just keep moving.'

Before she could respond, Leah flinched and gasped. Halting, she reached up to her left shoulder. She stiffened. 'Oh, *shit.*'

Without a second's thought, she wrapped her free arm around Greg's, and broke into a brisk trot. Even as they moved, he could see her whole left side was already starting to loosen and droop, as if she'd had a stroke, or been given a muscle relaxant or sedative. *Tranquiliser? Stun round? Paralysing agent?* They were supposed to be immune to all three, and more; plenty of experience had proved it. *What the hell is this?*

They were at the exit inside thirty seconds, drawing a few puzzled glances from other travellers along the way. *Better that than bullets,* Greg thought sluggishly. *Speaking of* – Looking behind, he saw Brown Coat, roughly fifteen feet away. A tiny pistol of unknown make was just visible beneath the right cuff of his coat.

He and Leah put both shoulders to the door. It took all his effort – and hers – to keep from doing a face plant on the street outside.

The night air was frigid. Only a handful of street and building lights were lit, casting the sidewalks and surrounding edifices in deep shadow.

Breathing hard, Leah pulled herself fully upright, still clinging to him. 'What now?' she gasped.

Greg looked about desperately. The buildings all around them were high-rise offices, most looking empty and neglected. No checkpoints or sandbag nests at any of the corners. Then he turned his gaze southward and beheld a massive layered pile of white concrete: a parking garage. He fought to raise his right hand; the numbness had reached his entire chest, and his upper legs. 'There. Inside.'

They hobbled and stumped down the street, like three-legged racers. Few passers-by were on the street, most not even bothering to glance their way. In the far distance, Greg thought he could hear sirens, and the sound of a loudspeaker voice. *Probably sealing off the block, under the whole 'drill' excuse. Gives our friend a better sightline.* He cast another frantic look over his shoulder. Brown Coat was emerging from the door, gun now in plain sight.

They were nearing the ramp for the fenced-off outdoor lot when the numbness suddenly seemed to slow. Surprised, Greg flexed his left arm. The feeling was coming back, sloughing off as though he were pulling the limb out of ice water. From her mystified look, Leah was experiencing the same change. Heart hammering, he pulled her even closer, leaning heavily against her shoulder. 'Keep like this,' he whispered. She nodded, exaggerating her limp.

The main driveway into the garage loomed to their left. Both security booths were empty: another lucky break. Nearly tripping over every other step, Greg pulled Leah through the entryway, moving toward a couple of empty lots just inside; she mimicked his pace. The numbness was almost gone from his legs now, and his chest. *Perfect timing.*

When they were out of sight from the sidewalk, Leah released her grip, and shook out her limbs. She pulled off her coat and shirt one-handed. The clinger suit shone dully in the light from outside. Wordlessly, she put a hand to her pistol and knife. He pointed to the latter. *Can't risk drawing* more *attention.* Leah smirked, and yanked the blade free. He did the same, and motioned for her to move behind the nearest car across from them, a battered blue sedan. When she had done so, he locked gazes with her, put a finger to his lips – and dropped to the ground, going limp with the bag underneath him, knife clenched in an outstretched hand.

Leah's mouth opened in shock. Before she could speak, the sound of approaching footsteps reached them. She dropped farther back behind the car, knife ready. Greg held himself still, as the steps came closer. *Come on. Come on.*

The first thing he saw was a boot: Army-issue, brown and battered. Then a pair of legs, clad in khaki trousers. He kept his eyes staring into the distance, breathing in short and tiny gasps. If Brown Coat thought the trank or whatever was still working, he'd probably expect him to be still breathing, but also immobilised.

The boots came to a halt, a few paces away. He heard a faint grunt, of either satisfaction or surprise. Letting his eyes dart up, he beheld the man's face. Blocky features, with dark green, strangely blank eyes behind the silver specs. Mottled white-red scars on his neck stood out garishly in the overhead lights. His chest bulged against the white shirt he wore – either body armour, or Herculean muscle. The man raised his hand, bringing the pistol to bear on Greg's face.

Greg snapped to his feet, knife slashing at the extended arm. The coat sleeve parted, spurting blood. Brown Coat grunted again, the pistol falling from his hand – but sprang back with the same speed and agility. Greg advanced, slashing left-to-right, and back again. The other man ducked the cuts and back-flipped out of reach, toward the driveway. Coming to an abrupt halt, he whipped both arms out to either side. Two paper-thin blades, almost as long as his forearms, dropped from his sleeves, the hilts sliding into his hands.

Before Greg could do more than blink, Brown Coat charged, whipping both knives in front of him. He ducked low to avoid a slash to the face, then had to roll to one side to keep from taking another in the guts. Coming to one knee, he swiped at the man's legs. With a dancer's grace, Brown Coat crouched and leapt, so that the knife slashed only air, and swung his left fist down at Greg's head.

The impact knocked him flat on his face, almost shattering his jaw on impact. The knife skidded across the pavement. His head and ears rang shrilly. Gasping in pain and blinking blood from his eyes, he looked up to see Brown Coat standing above him, both blades raised in a scything swing. He groped for the pistol, but his hands were wobbly.

Suddenly Brown Coat jerked and grunted. Twisting around, he swung the blades at the air behind him, hacking and slashing. Clumsily, Greg rolled out of reach. He forced himself upright, and managed to draw his pistol, clasping it with both hands. Vision refocused, he saw Leah leaping back and around Brown Coat's attacks with gymnastic skill. Her knife protruded from the attacker's back, buried to the hilt almost centre on his spinal column. He should've been paralysed – dead, even, if the blade passed through to his heart. Greg hefted the pistol, searching for a clear shot.

Brown Coat lashed out with his left blade. Leah dodged, right as his other weapon came up in a reaping arc, aimed at her stomach. Her stifled scream grated at Greg's ears. Barely avoiding another swing, she dove and rolled to the right behind the car once more, one hand clutching at a gaping red tear in her clinger. Brown Coat stepped toward her, blades raised.

Steadying his arm at last, Greg squeezed the trigger, four times. The shots rang out like cannon blasts through the garage. Brown Coat spasmed, gouts of red bursting from his back. Moving in sharp lurches, he turned to face Greg. The next four hollow-points struck him dead-centre in the chest, blasting little bloody chunks in spatters across the asphalt. He staggered, but stayed on his feet. A thin, jeering smirk crept across his face. He lifted the blades again, and began to stride towards Greg. Greg ejected the clip, pawing at his waist for another. *What the fuck is this guy? Even we can't stand after that, not so damn fast! How –*

A loud revving cut through the air. Startled, Greg spun to his right. The blue sedan was leaping in reverse, lights glaring. It slammed into Brown Coat at the waist, bending him over the trunk, knocking his blades and glasses away. Tyres screeching, the car smashed into the far wall, pinning the bulky man against the concrete. Greg winced at the sight and sound of crunching metal and bone. As abruptly as it started, the engine died, ticking loudly. Silence slammed down over the garage.

Greg slapped in the new magazine, and hobbled toward the car, coming around to the driver's side. Leah punched open the door, almost knocking it off its hinges. Another punch deflated the airbag. Legs wobbling, she grabbed the doorframe with one hand, and pushed herself free of the seat with the other. The jack device fell from her other hand, a mess of cuts and dislocated digits. She was covered with blood from the waist down, and more dripped from a broken nose and several facial cuts, but she seemed no worse than stunned.

Greg grabbed her arm – gently – to steady her. She blinked hard a few times, before she finally seemed to register him. Her teeth were streaked with blood when she smiled. 'Just needed a bigger club, huh?' she ground out.

Despite the receding pain, he let out a bark of laughter.

'First one big enough to win a gun fight, anyway.' Sober again, he looked over at Brown Coat, still jack–knifed and motionless. They'd picked the Walthers for concealment, not stopping power, but not even *they* could shrug off eight mushroom rounds. And he wasn't wearing armour, or not that Greg could see—

His analysis broke off. Through the ringing, he could suddenly hear new sounds. Sirens, and the drone of a deuce-and-a-half engine. 'We gotta go, *now*.' He moved around the front of the sedan. 'There was a four-by-four in the outside lot. If we hurry, we can—'

'Greg!' Leah shouted. He spun around. She was pointing to the rear of the car, a half-dumbfounded, half-terrified look on her face. Looking that way, he heard a hoarse grunting, and saw Brown Coat's arms starting to twitch. The man's eyes flashed open in the same instant. His arms jerked and flopped, hands clenching at the sheared plastic and metal pinning him to the wall. When his fingers clawed against it, Greg could see deep gouges in the metal – and no blood. The deep cuts on his face, from flying glass or metal shrapnel, were already starting to close.

Very slowly, Greg stepped away from the car. He picked up his bag, keeping his eyes locked on the gruesome sight before them. 'Come on.' The sirens were louder now, pounding at his aching head. He took Leah's arm again. She was still staring at the other man, her face transfixed and uncomprehending. 'He's not going anywhere for now. And we won't be either if we stick around.'

That shook her loose. Nodding, she started after him, then halted, and picked up two objects: Brown Coat's pistol and glasses, the latter now mangled and cracked. She wrapped them up in the remains of her shirt, then picked up her duffel and continued after him. Greg nodded in approval; whatever the hell this guy was, they needed intel on him, and damn quick.

Less than a minute later, they were speeding out of the outdoor lot. Their luck held – the military hadn't yet thrown up any roadblocks to cordon off the shoot-out area. In a matter of minutes, they were on I-90. Thanks to the traffic restrictions, it was easy going, but crowded enough that they were soon lost among the Army transports and other civilian cars.

Changing lanes, Greg looked over at Leah. She was leaning back in the passenger seat, dabbing at the wound in her chest with bits of gauze from her bag's aid kit. The gash was healing even as he looked; it probably wouldn't even leave a scar. He grimaced. The blade had cut a long slit clean through the clinger suit, from the right side of her waist to just below her left breast. Another inch or two deeper, and it would have gone through her sternum into her heart, and hewed off bits of both lungs. Regeneration might still have been possible then, but no amount of ARC had ever brought a Golem back from a sure killing blow.

The clinger, on the other hand, was taking longer to close. He could see a few of the nano-fibres lacing back together, but at a slow pace he'd never seen before. *These things can turn away almost everything: bullets, knives, stun rounds – even grenades, as I know firsthand. Only our blades could cut through them, and that with serious effort. So what the hell was* he *carrying that could do it easily –* and *arrest repair?*

Glancing up from her work, Leah noticed him watching her. She smiled. 'I'm OK,' she said softly. 'Just making sure this is going as expected.' The smile faded. 'Who was that, Greg? Who the *fuck* was that?'

'No idea.' He looked back out at the road. His hands were

starting to tremble on the wheel – from adrenal crash or remembered dread, he couldn't tell. A tiny edge of fear crept into his voice. 'When that bastard took so much damage, and kept standing... and that trank, whatever the fuck *that* was—' He couldn't finish. 'That was the first time I thought that... that we wouldn't...'

Leah's hand closed on his arm. Keeping one on the wheel, he clasped hers with the other. Little by little, the surge passed. He pulled himself fully upright in his seat. 'Whatever he was, he'll be off the field for a while – long enough for a good head start.'

Leah nodded, all business again. 'We'll need to ditch the car before too long. Even if they don't have descriptions, or count on us getting out of the city so fast, they're bound to send out alerts for suspicious cars – or just a suspicious couple.'

He jerked the wheel, shifting lanes again. The sign above the road now read I-94. 'We've got until Glenview, or the state line, before anybody picks up on either. By then, we'll have switched, and be off the main roads, away from the denser urban areas. The Army's always hated moving out into the 'burbs and boonies, so they'll rely on local cops to do the leg work, but we'll be well out of range before any tips come in.' He looked ahead, to the mostly deserted stretch of highway now before them. 'Before today's over, we'll be at the site – and closer to the answer.'

Leah's smile was thin and satisfied. She leaned back in the seat once more, her hand still laced with his. Very little was said for the rest of the drive.

Chapter 6

Hargrove bent down and picked up a piece of debris, not much bigger than his thumb. Holding it up, he recognised it as part of a car's taillight. He rubbed at it with thumb and forefinger, then tossed it back on the ground by the wreck. The entire rear of the car was crumpled like tinfoil, reducing its size by nearly a third. That, combined with a deep, spiderweb-crack depression in the far wall, pointed to something being slammed between it and the concrete with terrific force, like a body. The bloodstains on the car metal and the spatters of dried gore on the garage pavement all pointed to a serious firefight, and possibly hand-to-hand combat.

'It's the craziest damn thing I've ever seen.' He turned, and saw an older man in Army grey with captain's bars standing just a few paces away. A few other Army techs were packing up their CSI-gear, sending puzzled glances now and again toward the four new arrivals. Both bodyguards were in position near the entry ramp, their backs turned to the scene. 'We got here inside of two minutes after the first shots were reported. But all we found was this goddamn mess – and him, half-dead on his feet.'

The Army officer pointed to the security booth. A third

brown-coated man was seated there, sans glasses, and ignoring the two nearby Army sentries who were trying and failing not to stare at his ragged, bloodstained clothes. 'We were just bringing up the med team when the call came in about the rest of his – ops team, was it? – coming to retrieve him, and that we were ordered to wait until they did.' He gestured again, taking in the entire garage floor. 'We sealed off everything within two blocks of this place, and doubled our roving patrols, but nothing popped up. If we'd had satellite clearance we might've caught them before they cleared out of the city or went underground, but—'

'Thank you, Captain Myerson,' Hargrove interrupted, holding up a hand. 'No need to apologise; you and your men did their best, under the circumstances.' His gaze swept over the lot. 'Please inform General Briggs that his assistance – and discretion – has been extremely helpful, and that we'll be in touch if our investigation turns up anything.'

The captain nodded, still looking confused and unnerved. Hargrove walked over to the bedraggled guard. The man looked up at him, not speaking. From the splattered gore on his shirt, coat and face, it was difficult to tell where his wounds were, or if they existed at all. That suited Hargrove fine.

He reached into the pocket of his jacket, bringing out a fresh pair of silver spectacles. Glowering, he held them out to the guard. 'How're you holding up?' he asked, his tone that of a concerned partner, or parent. The bloodied man grunted what might have been words, as he slid the glasses down over his nose and ears. 'Yeah, thought as much,' Hargrove said. 'Anything you picked up on where they're headed?' His throat pulsed, once: *Status?*

Another grunt. Text blinked at the bottom of Hargrove's lens: *Green. Target IDs confirmed. Ultimate destination still unknown.* A moment's hesitation. *Suspect one target seized original MCSD.*

'Damn,' Hargrove muttered; *that* he could say aloud. The loss was a problem – but there was another to deal with now, far more worrisome. *Was the compound successful, in any way?* he pulsed back.

Unknown. When Hargrove glared at him, the guard went on. *Confirmed hits on both targets, prior to entering garage. Targets appeared lethargic and near collapse, in keeping with compound's anticipated effects. Upon entry, both were still active. Likeliest explanations: Suits impenetrable to compound delivery system, or compound is not as effective as believed.*

Blood thundered in Hargrove's temples. Stiffly, he said, 'Well, that's… too bad. We'll have to get details the hard way, then.' *Understood. Continue recovery, and rejoin main team. Await further orders.* The guard nodded, still expressionless.

Hargrove spun on his heel, and marched back toward the wrecked car. He eyed it for a time, gathering his thoughts. Finally, he punched up Costa's number on his smartwatch. The agent's face appeared at once. 'What's the situation?' he demanded right away.

'Stable, for now,' Hargrove replied. He relayed what the third guard had said. 'My man's still out of it; might be a little while before he gets all the details together. Based on what he *did* say, and the reports we've gathered, it's safe to say the hunt remains low-key, and thus off the radar for anyone else who might be watching. Won't be hard for the Army to keep this part under wraps, and for us to maintain overall security.'

'Maybe,' Costa said, not sounding as if he believed it for a second. 'And I'm having a hard time seeing how your man could just walk away from a firefight with two types like you described, with only a couple of flesh wounds.' He glanced to either side of the screen, then continued in a lower voice, as if that could keep him from being overheard. 'Considering this mess, these "Golems" were packing enough to do serious damage – bullets, knives, cars, doesn't matter. So how exactly is one of your GI Joes supposed to have survived this, let alone given more than a scratch to the two we're supposed to be bringing in alive?'

Hargrove met his gaze levelly. 'My people are prepared for any and all contingencies, Agent Costa. That includes dealing with the type of people we're pursuing. You'll have to be satisfied with that, unless the circumstances change.'

He stepped closer to the car. Kneeling, he dipped the first two fingers of one hand into one of the blood spatters along the car's side door. One of the brown-coated guards was at his side in a heartbeat, a palm-sized lab scanner in hand. Hargrove brushed the blood against the scanner's surface, and waited. The device beeped twice. Two spiralling DNA strands appeared on the screen, along with a small scrolling column of text. He looked up at the other guard. *Target origins confirmed,* he pulsed. *All assets be ready for departure, five minutes at most.*

The guard moved away, almost without noise. Hargrove stood up and pulled a bleach-wipe from a small packet in one of his pockets. 'Seems that my man *did* give our targets more than a scratch, Mr Costa.' He wiped the device clean, and held it up to the watch's face for the other man to see. 'ARC-positive blood: The scan confirms it. Based on the impact there' – he angled the camera in the wristband at the garage column, and the crumpled trunk—'it appears one of them took a serious hit, enough to knock them out of the fight for some time – and maybe their journey.'

'That what your "asset" states happened?' At Hargrove's nod, Costa continued, 'So he managed to get into the car, hotwire it, and damage one or both of the targets – all with just a few scratches.' He let out a low whistle, in mock admiration. 'Must be some impressive training they hand out, wherever these boys of yours come from.'

Hargrove slipped the scanner into a coat pocket. He raised his arm, so that their faces were only a few inches apart. 'If you have something to say, Agent, say it.' His voice was calm, but there was no mistaking the cold anger beneath it.

Costa was equally stoic. 'Like you said: there're some things I – and the Agency – have to "be satisfied with", for now. But you know that my bosses came to you solely because of your past experiences with the Golems, or so I was told. If there's anything you're not sharing in this operation, for whatever reasons, I can damn well guarantee they'll be the least of your problems, in short order.'

He gestured at the screen – past Hargrove, toward the bodyguard in the shack. 'You said it yourself: these "Golems" are practically untouchable with clingers, and their skills. So it stands to reason that your men have something that nullifies both of those enough to let them get close, making it easier to keep everything out of the spotlight. Whatever it is, it wasn't among the facts I was read into. I pass that along, it can make some people Upstairs nervous. Enough to take this hunt over, and pull the plug on whatever science fair shit you've been stuck with since the end of the Turmoil.'

Hargrove didn't flinch. He stared at the agent, hard. Finally, he let out a little sigh. 'You're right, Mr Costa. When a person spends so long out of the spotlight, like you said, it can lead to him becoming a bit paranoid about sharing anything. My apologies.'

Costa nodded, his expression still vaguely suspicious. Hargrove straightened, putting on an appearance of briskness. 'In the interest of cooperation, then...' He motioned for the black-haired guard to approach. When Hargrove reached out a hand, the guard drew a silver pistol from inside his coat and laid it in Hargrove's palm. He worked the action, popping out a single round, and held it up to the smartwatch screen. Unlike a standard bullet, this one had the appearance of a dart, sans tail or feathers. The point was elongated and looked sharper than the average syringe. There was no external casing – it was meant to be fired with compressed air, or a charge that didn't require additional protection for the round.

Staring at the dart, Hargrove spoke in a professorial tone. 'When the Golem Project really got off the ground, there were, of course, security concerns. All that training, all that firepower and all those innate abilities bestowed on several hundred individuals, from birth – let's just say it made some people a bit nervous. But any alteration in the process, to make the batches more compliant or controllable, would've required months if not years of reworking, and had a greater chance of backfiring. So it was decided that in the event any of them went off the reservation – whether alone or en masse – there would be an ace in the hole, ready for use at a moment's notice. That's where my people at Advent came in, again.' He held the dart out to the Agency man. 'Thus was created the Pax Contingency.'

Costa squinted at the dart's point. 'What's its purpose, exactly? Some sort of magic bullet to turn Golems to dust, instead of a cleric's ramblings, like the old legends?'

Hargrove smiled thinly. 'Something like that. The science is beyond me – a mix of tranquilisers and tailored neurotoxins; my R&D people could explain it better. But it boils down to this: the compound in this dart is strong enough to dope a full-grown elephant for two days – or a Golem, for a maximum of thirty-six hours. They'd be alive, and conscious, but effectively immobilised – like a coma patient. Combined with a prototype metal sharp enough to pierce even clinger fibres, it was supposed to be the ultimate tool in ensuring the Golems never got to the point of endangering themselves, their comrades or ordinary Americans. Only a handful of Project personnel and vetted officers were supposed to have them. Although ultimately there were no incidents that required their usage, the fear never went away. Therefore, Advent was tasked with retaining a small stockpile, at the request of President Daniels. Not enough, probably, for long-term pursuit or full-scale engagements, but certainly for the immediate future.' Popping the clip, he slid the dart back atop the others.

'Interesting,' Costa said. He glanced to the silent guard. 'So when your man tracked the two targets to this spot, he managed to stick them both?' Hargrove nodded. 'What happened, then? The compound expire, or the round not penetrate?'

'That's still unclear,' Hargrove answered. His eyebrows furrowed a tad. 'From my operatives' statement, both targets were sluggish and ill-coordinated for the duration of their encounter. That argues for the compound's effect. Yet based on past lab results, both targets should have been paralysed, save for breathing.' The frown receded. 'It doesn't matter, in the long run. We know now it slows them down long enough for severe damage, which is nothing to sneeze at in this situation. What matters right now is tracking their next move.'

He motioned at the two bodyguards. 'My man couldn't get a look at their getaway ride, but they won't risk using it for long; they may not get reported, but locals are still certain to remember strange cars passing through. So they're back underground, for the next little while, and in one state, which makes it relatively simple to force them into a corner.'

'So, what, then?' Costa demanded. 'We all know what happens to cornered animals – and people. If we're forced to pin them down in a populated spot again, it'll turn bloody damn fast.'

'Then we make sure we don't – and get to a higher vantage point.' Hargrove snapped his fingers. Both the entryway guards appeared beside him in a blink, freezing into statues. 'There's a permanent garrison at Fort McCoy, in Wisconsin. Also a Ranger contingent, if I remember right. Correct?'

'Yeah, part of the Rural Rapid Response Teams set up during the Turmoil.' Costa's eyes narrowed. 'What are you suggesting? Until now, you wanted to avoid the Army, for reasons I – and the Agency – still don't fully—'

Hargrove waved the question away impatiently. 'We set up shop there fast, we'll be sitting astride all the routes our targets might use, and have quick-response personnel ready to assist if necessary.' Seeing Costa's dubious expression, he waved again. 'The Agency can handle the clean-up here. As for discretion, the garrison commander isn't going to let anything slip that might make Chicago seem unsecure, now will he?'

He signed off, and made for the exit. The guards moved ahead, brushing past the few soldiers and techs still present. *All assets converge on me. Destination: Fort McCoy. Prep for long-distance travel beyond.* Glancing to his right for a moment, he saw Myerson, reflected in the security booth window. The officer stooped to check a last piece of debris, before tossing it aside and moving to speak with one of the techs. Hargrove allowed himself a quiet snicker. Everyone else was always one step behind. The entire Agency already was, so that was no great surprise. He strode out onto the street, guards in tow. Soon enough, everyone would be brought up to speed – and *he* would have the pleasure of doing it personally.

Greg turned the key. The pickup's engine died, with a shake

and clatter. *Been a long while since I had to use one of these old rides. Even in most of the Third World spots, I never had to. Although, to be fair, such was never part of the usual assignment.* He slid the keys into his jacket. *And it looks like it'll be the same here, too.*

With the engine off, the silence was almost complete. Before them, and to either side, loomed a dense tangle of second-growth forest. Towering elms, maples, birches and pines mixed together with thick brush and thickets in a dark mosaic, much of it decorated with late, melting snow. The only sounds came from both sides of the gravel roadway: grass rustling in the wind, the chirping of early-arrived birds and the occasional rustle and snap as a rabbit or other small animal crawled and bounded through the underbrush. Save for the road, there was almost no trace that man had ever set foot here.

Beside him, Leah was taking off her jacket and khakis. 'You're sure this is the only way to go about it?'

'Unless we want to head back to Phillips, or just walk right up to the spot,' Greg returned. 'I'd vote the first – maybe we'd even get our 'rental deposit' back on this junkheap. That guy in town who owned it was *real* happy to see new cash in these parts, though, so it might be hard.'

She punched him in the arm. 'I'm serious. If what we're looking for is *here*, isn't going about it black-ops style just going to spook the target – or just get us killed?'

'If it *is* here – and has been for as long as I think – we won't have to worry about it. There's only so far the target can go, if he does get spooked.' His face hardened, just a little. 'Besides, we *were* literally *made* for tracking.'

'So was he.' Leah returned. She sighed. 'But if we've come this far, we may as well take the risk.' She patted at her chest and sides, checking weapons and armour strength. 'I'll take point. Signal every twenty-five metres, from opposite ends of approach.' When he opened his mouth to object, she put a finger to his lips. Her dark eyes were calm and even. 'Like you said, I was made for this.'

That much was true. Still, Greg hesitated. 'If we go together, close proximity—'

He got no further, because Leah was already pushing open the passenger door. Muttering under his breath, he shed his jacket, and jumped out as well. Looking ahead, he could just make out Leah's slim, dark-clad form disappearing into the brush. Drawing his knife, he plunged it into the mud, making sure the blade was well-covered. Plenty of men, and Golems, had been brought down by the split-second gleam when unsheathing for the kill. He sucked in a breath, then pulled the mask-hood over his face and took off at a steady jog.

His feet made hardly a sound amidst the undergrowth. Every so often, he would pause to gently push aside this branch or that set of bush leaves or ferns. The clinger's black exterior made him stick out like a moving oil slick – the versions he and Leah had chosen hadn't been programmed to include winter camo – but he was fast enough to never show more than a flicker of darkness against the trees and snow.

After twenty-five metres, he halted. Almost at once, the thin, rolling note of a female hawk-owl reached his ears. He made the reply whistle, and resumed moving, more slowly now. He was coming to a stop again farther on when a new scent reached his nostrils. Wood smoke – and roasting meat. He froze, eyes darting in all directions. Not sensing anything else, he moved behind a nearby elm, knife hand against his chest. Keeping his breathing steady, he peered around the trunk. Maybe a hundred yards away, he made out the peak of a thatched roof, sitting in the middle of a partially cleared ring of brush. A few wisps of smoke trailed from a slim chimney at one end. Greg's hackles flared. *This is too damn easy.* He crouched low, shaping his lips to make the signal call.

A shadow fell over him. Before he could fully turn around, something hard and unyielding smashed into his right temple. As he fell, head spinning, he lashed out with his knife, aiming for where his attacker's leg should be. A second blow – a bladed hand – cut the move short, snapping his forearm just above the wrist and knocking the weapon from his hand.

Fire streaked up his arm. Pushing it aside, he swung his left fist in an uppercut, aiming for the assailant's sternum; one punch would shatter it like glass. A rush of expelled air rewarded him – but no crunch of bones. Greg dropped to all fours, rolling over his bad arm to get clear. A massive hand closed on the calf of his left leg. He felt himself being dragged back like a rag doll. Pawing at the front of his suit, he yanked the pistol free and twisted onto his back to take aim. Another blow smacked into his wrist, swatting the weapon away. Then he was lifted into the air, and slammed back to earth, facedown. Winded and gasping, he looked around, and saw his knife, protruding from the snow a few inches away. His left hand darted out to grab it.

A tremendous bulk crashed onto his back, pinning him to the ground and driving out the little breath he had. Almost delicately, a hand closed over his left fist, and pulled the knife free. 'Easy now,' the rough voice murmured. 'No point doing yourself more damage.' In one sharp flick, the blade was at his throat. 'How about we call in the rest of the guests?'

Another hand closed on the back of Greg's neck, pulling the mask-hood free. A sharp tug brought him back to his feet and up against his captor's chest. The man had to be at least six inches taller than Greg, making him past seven feet. The smell of wood smoke, animal fat and human sweat was thick in his nose.

The other man marched him around the tree in a few long strides, coming to a halt in a small space partly covered by bushes and fallen branches. He jerked to either side, testing the stranger's grip – with one bad arm, he couldn't yank himself free. He felt the cold blade at his neck again, and desisted. 'Good move,' the voice grunted. Then it changed into a ringing bellow:

'Hello out there! I have your friend here with me! You have fifteen seconds to come out, hands in the clear! If not—' He didn't go on, nor did he need to.

The echoes faded. Not even the birds seemed to make a sound. Greg held his breath. *Come on, Leah. Don't do anything stupid.*

'Five seconds!' The blade pressed deeper. A dribble of warmth ran down Greg's neck. He held still as he could, ready to move if he saw the tiniest chance.

Just before the final second, a *pfft!* sound reached his ears, off to the right. At almost the same moment, his captor let out a grunt. The knife hand was withdrawn, and he felt the grip on his clinger loosen. He yanked himself free, swinging his left leg out in a wide sweep. The stranger made a crouching leap, avoiding the strike, but his move was sluggish. Instead of bringing his other leg or good hand up for a strike, Greg back-flipped away from him, landing in a combat crouch. Looking about wildly, he spotted a rock twice the size of his fist, and snatched it up, clenching it tight in his good hand as he wheeled to face the stranger.

To his surprise, the other man was stumbling backwards, crashing through the brush. He was gurgling loudly, as if trying to form words. His left hand was clamped over his right upper arm, which hung limp. Staggering and lurching like a world-class drunk, the giant finally crashed onto his side, crumpling a wide patch of undergrowth beneath him.

Breathing hard, Greg let the rock drop. Cradling his busted arm, he turned to his left at the sound of crackling twigs. Leah emerged from behind two bushes, and stepped into the clearing. In one hand she held her silenced pistol. The other clasped the strange gun picked up from Brown Coat. Both were aimed unwaveringly at the huge man lying prone before them. Without taking her eyes from the still form, she asked, 'You all right?'

'I've been better.' He let out a short hiss – the bones in his arm were resetting themselves. Looking at the silvery new weapon, he remarked, 'Smart move. Didn't think it would work on *him,* though.'

She flashed him a smirk. 'Honestly? Neither did I.' She pressed the second weapon against her waist, letting the nano-fibres close over it while she kept her pistol at the ready. 'Given how it turned out with *us*, felt like a safe bet it would again – particularly on *him*.' Her face clouded, just for a moment. 'Last time we get to make it, though – there was only one round left in the clip. If whoever *that* was back in Chicago had something strong enough to trank us, you'd think he'd have backups.'

'We'll worry on that later,' Greg said. He studied the mammoth, crumpled form. 'Right now, let's just worry about *this*. If he dies—'

As if in denial, the stranger groaned. His legs began to twitch. Whatever the trank might be, it was wearing off. Leah unsheathed her knife at once, tossed it to Greg, and trotted over to stand above the stranger's head. Drawing her gun, she aimed at his temple.

Up close, the stranger looked much less immense and animal-like. His clothing was rough flannel and wool, decorated in homemade civilian woodland patterns. He wore battered, heavy work boots, which should've given him away at the smallest step – but hadn't. His face was both angular and muscle-bound, with dense, close-cropped brown hair and beard. His eyes, a startlingly light green, were flicking in every direction, looking for escape or a weapon, or both. When Greg stepped closer, those eyes fixed on him. The man's jaw champed fiercely, as if chewing gum. At last, he forced out, 'Who – are – you?'

Sharing a long glance with Leah, Greg pressed the release at his throat, letting the clinger suit peel away down to his waist. He held out his right arm. In the crook of his elbow, just barely visible in the morning light, was a tattoo, written in black-blue ink: *G-250/228.*

The stranger's eyes went huge. Greg crouched beside the stranger, taking his limp right arm in both hands, pushing back the sleeve of his coat and shirt. In the exact same spot, a tattoo in similar colours was inscribed: *G1.* Solemnly, he said, 'We're family – Cayden.'

Chapter 7

A fire crackled merrily in the hearth. A pot of venison stew hung suspended above the flames, steaming and bubbling. Cayden dipped a long metal ladle and poured out three large bowlfuls with practiced care. 'Sorry for the lack of variety,' he grunted. 'Other than the occasional night-time trip to Lac Court Oreilles, I get all food from the forest. Sounds hokey, but in this case it's true. All the leftover New Age types'd probably run screaming back to the suburbs, if they had to live it.'

'No complaints here,' Leah answered. She took her portion in both hands. 'Way we've been travelling lately, hot food of any kind's a luxury.' She nodded at their surroundings. 'And after yesterday, a place like this was just the kind of "off the grid" we were looking for.'

The room around the three of them was small, but comfortable. Although the exterior of the cabin was rough-hewn logs, the inside walls were smoothly planked, except for the door and the small solitary window looking out on the clearing. There was a secondhand card table in the far corner with two folding chairs, all of them bearing ancient Park Ranger labels. A shabby armchair and coffee table sat near the fireplace; a couple of tattered paperbacks rested on these. Another opening led to a much smaller bedroom, with a handmade down mattress and pillow resting on a rough-carved frame, and a handful of clothes hung on wooden hooks.

The only decorations in sight were a handmade quilt, and a pair of wolf skins. A thin strip of wood jutted out over the fireplace, on which rested a single photograph in a cheap, dented brass frame. The image was of a man's face: light brown hair, black-rimmed glasses, and a grave expression, as if he were incapable of smiling in any way.

Cayden's features were set in similar lines. 'Until today, I thought it *was* – which is why I reacted the way I did. We *may* be "family" in the sense that we shared the same background, but you haven't convinced me yet not to torch this place and move on – with you two in it, if necessary.'

Leah slurped nonchalantly at the stew. 'Then it's a good thing we brought a little unexpected backup.' She patted at her chest, with her free hand, where Brown Coat's gun was attached.

Cayden still didn't smile. 'Another reason why I should be long gone.' After a perfunctory sip, he set the bowl down, and faced Greg. 'There're plenty of questions to ask, but I think the first one's obvious.'

Greg met his gaze. 'And easily answered.' He set his bowl down, too. 'Leah and I heard the Doctor mention this state plenty of times, mostly when he talked about his hiking trips up north, in this area. Given the closer ties you had with him than the rest of us – and your last mission before the Seattle Bomb, not too far away – it wasn't that much of a stretch to assume you'd be holed up nearby.'

Cayden grunted, in what might've been acceptance or scepticism. 'It wasn't a mission – at least not one needing Golem attention. But Upstairs insisted.' He stirred his soup. 'Some backwoods loners had been sniping at National Guard convoys moving from Eau Claire to the Twin Cities. Took me less than two hours to paint them for the airstrike, then strike out on my own. Heard about the Bomb a day later, and rumours about the supposed clean-up of the Project not long after, from some hacked Army reports. That's when I went underground, and made my way here.'

He gestured at Greg's clinger. 'But *you'd* probably already know that, given how you just happen to have the last suit model made for the Project before it folded. And the weapons, and whatever that compound is you used on me?' He looked from one to the other. 'From here, it looks like a sweeper operation. Better late than never?'

'It's not,' Leah said bluntly. 'We came by the suits and other gear legit – more or less. The compound – that's a different story. Which, from all we've learned, can only be answered with your help.'

The taller man's brow furrowed. 'How's that?'

By way of answer, Greg stepped over to the armchair, where the two duffels sat. Reaching inside his, he pulled out the metal canister, and held it out. 'You ever see anything like this before?'

Cayden took it cautiously in both hands, looking it over from every angle. He shook his head. 'No. Where'd it come from?'

'From the archives vault at what used to be an office for Advent Tech – one of the main military contractors for the Pentagon during Daniels' time,' Leah answered. 'They also worked as part of certain side projects—'

' – Like Golem, yeah,' Cayden interrupted. 'They designed the first nanotech for the clingers, and the earliest battlefield versions, too. Then they backed out, to work on other projects, while the Project continued working on it with off-the-books funding. We all knew that from the start – the earlier generations, anyway. I can't speak for yours.'

'Then you'll probably also know how close and how often the Doctor worked with the Advent design teams,' Greg said. 'He was always fretting over the clingers, trying to personally make sure they weren't just functional, but protective. Like a helicopter parent on steroids, at times.'

Cayden's face was rigid. 'Yeah. He was like that a lot.' He hefted the canister. 'But what's that got to do with this, or Advent?'

'A couple of weeks before Seattle went up in smoke, we were called back to the States, after a job in Indonesia,' Leah said. 'We were given an assignment a lot like yours: in the Rockies, not far from Boise. Before heading out, we were refitted at the Project labs – ARC booster shots, clinger tune-ups, the usual process.' Her voice became flat. 'At one point, I went to talk to the Doctor in his office, and found him in the middle of a file dump from his main terminal. He told me it was a back-up precaution for a few crucial files, in case of an attack on the lab's energy sources and connections to the outside world, or even the lab itself. When I asked him what the likelihood of that was, he just smiled, and said he wasn't sure, but that he wanted to be prepared, even if it meant keeping the data somewhere he wouldn't have come within miles of before. At the time, I didn't make much of that. But when I remembered his dealings with contractors – including Advent – they were the only possible candidate. And *this* was the only way the files would've been secure enough for him.'

Greg cut in. 'Two weeks later, we're partnered up with three others, and sent off to comb for a cell of Aryan crazies supposedly camped out in the mountains. The word from On High – meaning the Pentagon, or the Project, which amounted to the same thing – was one of these groups might have stolen a suitcase nuke two weeks ago, and had plans to set it off in one of the camps taking in refugees from the militia attacks on Denver and other towns further east. For almost a week, we saw nothing – just trees and rocks. Then, the same night the Bomb goes off, we find the encampment, just south of the border with Idaho… '

A tiny fragment of light showed through the branches and undergrowth – almost a thousand yards distant, give or take a few. Greg halted and raised a fist, dropping to one knee at the same time. The other four Golems – Yelena and Akande to his left, Samir and Leah to his right – mimicked him, silenced XM10s up and tracking for any threats. Greg squinted. The lenses in his clinger's hood automatically compensated, zooming in and focusing on the light, night-vision filter dropping in. The trees and brush were still thick enough around the clearing to hide most of the light source, but he could nonetheless see enough of its outline. A prefab mobile home, two or three rooms: closest thing to the camp's HQ, probably. He held up two fingers, pointing first right, then left. His teammates silently fanned out, still in pairs, to sweep the perimeter and position themselves. With Greg approaching from the south through the thickest brush, the camp would then be covered from three sides, and the easiest escape paths on the northern side cut off.

Greg moved forward, clinger-clad feet hardly whispering over the mulch and foliage. More of the campground came into view as he wove through the brush: a half dozen dome tents, two slightly larger, square four-corners. No lights, other than those behind the shaded windows of the prefab. Two heavy pickup trucks parked between the prefab and the four-corners. No one in view yet, either, near the tents or walking any sort of beat in the enclosed area. Not uncommon with small insurgent groups, especially in areas like here in the Idaho panhandle, where they had considerable support or presence. Still –

A figure stepped out from behind a tree, twenty or so paces ahead. Greg immediately pressed himself against another; the darkness and the clinger's camo function concealed him at once, or so they were meant to. The figure gradually coalesced into a blocky, bearded man in woodland-pattern fatigues and cap, combat boots and too-small bulletproof vest, an AK-74 slung carelessly over one shoulder. Greg could smell the booze, cigarette smoke and sweat on him even from a distance; the clinger hood's filters couldn't keep *those* out, or not quite. The sentry – undoubtedly what he was *supposed* to be – ambled in a vague zigzag in Greg's general direction, NV-goggled gaze wandering disinterestedly over the forest. He stopped to hawk and spit into the nearest bush, then grunted and reached for his fly – turning and bringing himself face to face with Greg's tree.

Greg was moving before he could finish the motion. The sentry had time for one startled grunt before the Golem's hands grasped his head, snapping his neck with not much more effort than a typical human would have turning a stove knob. Greg caught the man as he fell, sitting him against the tree. He could've stayed hidden, even let him finish taking a leak – the clingers were shielded against night vision, and *that*, too. But if there was one, there could easily be more – and he and his team had to eliminate the targets fast already, before one raised an alarm and the whole group decided to go out in a blaze courtesy of the cargo they'd stolen.

Bringing his weapon up again, he moved to the very edge of the clearing. Other than some mild snoring, and the normal background buzz and rustle of the forest, he didn't hear anything, from the surroundings or his team; they wouldn't break radio silence, in any case, even if each of them was tangling with a whole squad. He blinked twice, then twice again. The filters shifted, to the multicolour of infrared. Two human-shaped forms were huddled in each of the tents; two more in one of the four-corners, and four in the last. Five – no, six – were clustered in the prefab, around an electric heater; probably the higher-ranking ones. One of these last sat a ways apart from the rest, in another section of the prefab: the "commander", most likely, or whichever semi-military title this bunch preferred. He risked a quick look at the – dimmed – map on the holo-screen on his arm. The four green dots of his team's transponders blinked, all in the appropriate positions. He closed the screen and raised his arm, letting the sensor attached to his wrist do its work while he pressed a control at his mission gear belt. A low crackling filled his ears: the Geiger counter. The sound grew strongest when he aimed it towards the prefab. *Smart* and *stupid, to keep it so close.* The level also seemed a bit low, for the type of cargo in question. Maybe they'd improvised shielding for it, since reports indicated the original had been left behind with the convoy.

He brought his weapon up and sighted on the nearest tent. First the men in those, then the rest around the prefab. Then Yelena or Akande would enter the prefab and deal with the last half-dozen, up close; they couldn't risk shooting into the place and setting off the triggers on the cargo. Then secure the cargo itself, sweep the area one last time, and radio for extraction. Smooth as clockw –

The door to the prefab opened the same instant he squeezed the trigger. Another man in fatigues, this one with a sparse pencil moustache, stepped out onto the prefab's tiny front porch, yawning and stretching. The bullet snapped cleanly through the tent, taking out the first man with an audible slap-punch of tearing fabric. Tired though he might be, the second man was alert enough to catch *that*. 'What the hell?' he muttered, reaching for the pistol at his belt. He hadn't even unsnapped the catch when two more shots from Greg punched into his chest. With a strangled shout, he dropped, thumping facedown over the trio of porch steps.

A babble of raised voices and shouts rose from inside the prefab. *Shit*, Greg mouthed; silence mattered above all, even when a task went south. He shifted aim again, firing once, twice, twice again, then twice more. All four tents were dealt with by the time another figure appeared in the doorway. As Greg shifted aim, however, he ducked back inside, and his round punched into the doorframe. The shouts became even louder. Behind the shades, more figures dashed about, taking up defensive positions; they knew they'd be vulnerable outside.

Of course, the prefab was no defence, either. Switching back to infrared, Greg made out two men crouched low beneath the main window, another behind a couch on the opposite side, rifles in hand. A fourth man was upright and moving to the rear of the prefab with a shotgun. The fifth and last man was flat on the floor, apparently unarmed – and appeared to quail, when the fourth stood over him. Greg dropped the shotgun wielder with a quick three-round burst through the thin aluminium wall, then targeted and picked off the two by the door with equal speed; he saw blood splatter against the window shade. The man behind the couch rapid-crawled to the door and sprayed a volley out into the darkness, maybe to give him cover to roll out and make a break for it. Two or three of the rounds passed within a foot or so of Greg. He didn't flinch, only fired a pair of shots, dropping the shooter.

No more shouts or shots rang out. Greg stayed still, waiting and scanning the camp. On the infrared, the sixth man still lay on the floor: breathing, yet barely moving – and still near the cargo hotspot. Not the commander, then, unless he'd already been wounded somehow, since Greg hadn't done it. A hostage? That made more sense – except the report of the convoy attack hadn't mentioned any taken. Some other prisoner, or a snitch? The unknowns were beginning to pile up. This wasn't unfamiliar, in itself – but they *shouldn't* be, in an assignment this routine.

He slammed the door on the speculating. The cargo was first; everything else, secondary. He made a final heat sweep of the camp, checking all the now-cooling bodies. When nothing moved or changed, he pressed at his arm, sending out the converge signal, and advanced.

The other four team members moved into the campsite at nearly the same moment he did. They probed each of the tents, checked all the sightlines, coordinating with a few hand signs and not a word spoken. Only after that did they move to the door of the prefab: Akande and Yelena moving through and fanning out, Greg behind them, Samir and Leah taking up watch to either side.

The inside of the prefab was filthy, even without the sprays of blood decorating the walls and floor: decrepit furniture, ripped-up muddy carpet, cigarette burns and gouges in the walls and all over the cheap wooden kitchenette. A small pile of empty beer cans sat in one corner; other than this, though, there wasn't much litter. There were plenty of guns and clips, however, laid out on the "living room" table, on the couch, and on the kitchenette counter, every one of them clean and well-maintained. A tiny hallway, no more than eight paces long and two wide, lay past the kitchenette, with a bathroom on one side, a tiny space that had probably once been a closet, now a bunkbed compartment, on the other – and a sliding fake wood door at the very end, almost fully open, giving onto a larger room, with two beds against either main wall.

The Geiger's crackling reached a crescendo when Greg

aimed his sensor towards this last. Yet the emissions still felt weak, even close up. A soft moan emanated from the room. He tensed; Akande and Yelena took aim in its direction. He motioned to Akande: *Move up*. The other Golem fell in behind him; Greg went into a half-crouch, to give him better aim. Gun at the ready, he stepped into the room. The sixth man still lay between the beds, his back to the door. Greg checked the corners, then moved to his side. In the shaft of light from the hall, he saw the man wore a uniform: Type IV naval working garb. When he turned the man over, he made out the bars of a captain at his collar. No name tag, but a tape strip insignia above his breast pocket, and another at his upper arm: a trident, wrapped in the symbol of the atom. A nuclear weapons security officer.

He ran the sensor over the man. The Geiger readings matched, and there were slightly stronger traces nearby in the room. A hostage, then, who probably worked close enough to nukes – and might've been exposed to the stolen ones, here in this room – that the radiation still clung to him. *Very* close, judging by the patches of blonde-brown hair beginning to fall from his scalp, and the first burns and blisters of serious rad poisoning on his hands and face. There were multiple bruises over his face as well, and a slight giving sensation when Greg probed carefully at his side indicated bruised or broken ribs. He took in all this in a couple of seconds, trying to fit what it meant with the report. No hostages from the convoy, and none of the team had turned traitor. A deserter from another unit? Maybe – yet it seemed too much of a coincidence. And again: where was the nuke *itself*?

The man moaned again. His eyes fluttered, struggling to open. Greg put an arm under his neck as a pillow, lifting him up a bit, then looked to Akande. 'Take Yelena and search the rest of the camp – check if the weapon was moved.' His

teammate nodded and left the room without a word. The
man coughed harshly several times; flecks of blood were clear
amidst the spittle. Greg lifted him a little higher, to a more
reclined position. He groaned again, then finally seemed to
come awake, or close to it. He looked up at the Golem, gaze
still somewhat unfocused. 'Wha... who're you?' he forced out.

'Special Forces, sir,' Greg replied: the standard answer.
'You're safe; the rest of the group holding you has been dealt
with. We're signalling for evac now.'

The officer coughed again; more blood showed on his lips.
He managed to bring his arms beneath him, propping himself
up without Greg's help, and looked around. His face, already
pale, lost even more colour, making his injuries even starker.
'Where... Where is it?' he whispered, the panic clear in his
voice. 'The case... they dumped it in here, along with me,
right after we got... Where *is* it?'

'We're searching now, sir,' Greg replied. Reasonably good
news: if the nuke had been here, it couldn't be far; they'd had
the camp under surveillance for two days, and the bomb had
gone missing only a day and a half prior. He paused, then
decided it was better to know, given everything else that was
still *unknown*: 'What's your name, sir?'

'Drew... Drew Barsamin.' Another coughing fit forced the
officer back to the floor. Greg turned him on his side again,
to help his breathing. When the fit passed, Barsamin rolled
over and looked his way again, red now trickling freely from
his mouth. His gaze, however, was much clearer, like he was
focusing all his strength into it. 'Wait... ' His eyes, a pale green,
went huge. 'You're... You're a *Golem*.'

Greg went rigid. Before he could decide whether to answer
yes or no – or make the normal, reflexive move and snap
the man's neck – Barsamin grabbed his wrist, with sudden,
desperate energy. 'You need to get the nuke... and get back,'

he gritted out through the pain of the wounds and irradiation. 'The convoy... the nuke was from Seattle. Two of 'em... stored after a *Project* mission... in China... Xinjiang.'

Yet another deep, hacking cough paralysed him. He spat out a mouthful of red and black, and collapsed on his back. Greg moved to help him, but he pushed the Golem back, feebly. 'No... no point.' He took several shuddering breaths, whispering raggedly in between: 'When... when the Turmoil hit the fan, not far from us... I gave the order... move to Livermore. Two convoys... different times. First one... then the second, another route.'

His voice dropped further, until it was almost inaudible. 'Crazies hit us... just outside Medford. Knew we were coming... had to. Killed some, grabbed me... and the package. Dirty nuke, stuck me with it... didn't keep it shielded. Pounded on me when I... ' He coughed again, or rather gargled. More blood flowed, noticeably blacker. 'Heard one say they were watchin' for the second... don't know if... '

He lowered his head, words trailing off. Greg put a hand to his shoulder and beneath his neck, shaking gently. 'Sir... *Captain.*' Barsamin's eyes opened a slit. He wasn't going to last much longer, but *any* intel he had was essential – especially with the Project involved. 'Captain... did you see or hear where they might've moved the package?'

'N... no.' This came out as barely a whisper. 'Something... the sale... went wrong. Said they kept me... ransom, or just hostage. Mighta hit the jackpot... if they knew...' A tiny twitch of his mouth; he was trying to smile. 'Or woulda just shot me... save you the trouble, or my peo—'

He broke off, doubling over and retching. His whole body shook with the pain and effort of the spasm. Greg turned him over and started to call for Leah – she was carrying what meds they had – when Barsamin let out a final, choking gargle, and went still, slumping on his back a final time. His eyes were blank and staring, his chin and mouth dripping blood.

Greg put a finger to the man's throat. No pulse. He studied the body for a moment or two longer, then closed its eyes – a gesture he'd picked up from Caswell, one of his trainers, though he wasn't quite sure why – and stood up. Turning, he saw Akande standing in the hallway, his hood pulled back. The other Golem's dark brown face was the same unsmiling mask Greg's likely bore. 'He's gone?' he asked.

'Yes.' Nothing more needed to be said – at least not until the after-action report. Especially that last from Barsamin, about "my people" – who, by implication, also knew about the Project. He pulled back his hood, and checked and reloaded his XM10, as much out of precaution as to keep his mind on the mission at hand. 'Anything in the compound?'

'Plenty of small arms and ammunition, and a pair of Stingers with a case of warheads for each. No sign of the package itself – or hints that it ever *was* here, apart from the radioactive traces in this structure and a few footprints elsewhere.' Akande also checked his weapons, then walked back out into the main living area. The dead militiamen were all gone, bloody drag marks leading to the door. 'The others are checking the tents and laying out the bodies for the clean-up teams. We're ready to signal for evac once they're done.'

'Good.' It wasn't, not until they'd recovered the bomb. The main threat was neutralised, however, and their next steps were clear. 'See if you can find any sign of recent departures, and check any computer gear they may have. Long shot, with backwoods paranoids like this type, but they had to have left *something* pointing to where they moved the package, or sold it.'

Akande nodded and began tossing the room. Greg went back outside, jumping down from the porch. Leah and Samir, hoods off, were standing over a row of bodies – some in fatigues, others in underclothes – in the centre of the campsite. Yelena, also with her hood back, was just emerging from one of the two larger tents. Even in the near-darkness, her frown was plain, making her round, pale Slavic face and buzz-cut black hair even more severe. Something had to be off, and badly, to give her that look. She held an object in her right hand: a satellite phone.

She came up to Greg. 'Only real comms gear in the place,' she said tersely. 'Found it on the body of the first target out of the prefab. Other than this, no laptops, no cellphones, no radios except a crude civilian model in each truck, without much range. Not completely off the grid, but close enough – which makes this even stranger.' She held up the device for Greg to examine. 'Phone has scramblers built in – professional work, military or government, beyond anything this cell could put together with what they've got, or likely steal given their reach. Their one sure means of communicating with any group beyond this site, basically – and they shouldn't *have* it, with their isolation and available tech.'

'Understood,' Greg replied. One more unknown, to add to the list. Keeping this to himself, he finished: 'Make a last sweep of the camp's eastern side, and I'll send the evac signal. Jorge should be able to break the scramblers, once we're back.' Yelena nodded and trotted off, sticking the satellite phone to her belt. Greg watched until she was out of the weak light, then called up the holo-screen on his arm. Two sharp taps brought up a red button symbol: the evac call. He let his finger hover above it, contemplating everything from the mission, then pressed it, firmly.

Samir and Leah came up to him as he closed the screen. 'Last targets accounted for,' the other male Golem said. He was nearly Greg's height, making him among the taller men in the

Project, with black-brown hair a couple shades lighter than Yelena's and a swarthy, Mediterranean-Middle Eastern cast to his face. He didn't ask about Barsamin; he could tell there was no point. 'Four of them had mild burns and other evidence of irradiation, though not severe enough to be fatal. They must've handled the package more than the rest, or been in closer proximity to it; we've tagged them for special examination.'

'That's about ten minutes out, as of now,' Greg said, indicating his arm. 'Facility chopper will bring us out; clean-up team's right behind it. They'll tell us how long this bunch had the package, which'll point to where and when they stashed or sold it. After that—'

'Hold it,' Leah interrupted. Her head was tilted toward the west, listening. 'Something's coming in.' At first Greg didn't follow her – then he heard it himself. The humming whine of jet engines: F-35s, by the pitch, and approaching fast. Low-flying, too, like they were avoiding radar, or –

The whine swelled to a hissing roar. Three aircraft streaked by over the northern end of the campsite, almost too fast to see. Greg yanked his hood on; the lenses could track them better than the unaided eye, even a Golem's. In the greenish night vision, he saw the three fighters – now many miles away, by the clinger's automatic measurement – bank and turn, bringing them back around towards the campsite. Two of them split off from the centre craft, on almost diametrically opposite courses; the third kept boring in. There was a flash of something at its underbelly, and an object fell away. Greg could see what it was, no matter the distance and without the lenses. A JSOW – Joint Standoff Weapon, among the most powerful surface-to-ground bombs.

His legs were already breaking into a sprint as he registered this. Samir and Leah were hardly half a step behind him. Even as he ran for the trees and brush ahead, though, he knew it was close – too close for a sure escape from the blast radius. But they had to try –

The JSOW detonated. At first, there was no heat, or shockwave; just a total smothering of all sound. Then a surge of fire and energy slammed into his back, propelling him off the ground like he'd suddenly grown wings and spinning him crazily about. He caught a glimpse – almost a snapshot – of Yelena, both legs gone, spiralling back down into the explosion's inferno. Then he struck one tree with a snap of breaking ribs and arm, bounced off another, then ricocheted again to the ground, rolled and buffeted about. His other arm and both legs broke in this; by then he was almost too far gone from the pain to notice. Flames danced across his clinger; this kept them from his body, yet the heat was still strong enough to make his skin bubble and blister beneath it.

Abruptly, he crashed into a boulder, breaking several more bones – but he stopped rolling, smothering the fires on him. Fighting through the agony, he propped himself against it. The once-quiet forest was now engulfed in flames, from root to branch. His breath tore out of him in ragged bursts, knives digging in his lungs with each one. The clinger's filter barely kept out any of the smoke and stench. The ARC was already kicking in, thankfully; he could feel his arms and legs resetting, and the chest pain grew less, second by second. The burns would take longer; he'd seen it before – and, now, was again.

At that moment, though, he contemplated this only in a very distant, clinical way. Had he been even a second slower… A heavy object crashed through the blazing branches, landing with a jarring thud several yards away: a human's upper body, one arm gone, the waist a torn, smouldering edge. Greg didn't need to see the face – charred beyond identification – to recognise Akande's build. Him, and Yelena: both gone. And Samir, and Leah –

A new shape loomed out of the smoke and fire in front of him. He reached painfully for his knife, or his sidearm. Both were gone, along with his rifle. The shape came closer, finally resolving into two figures, one carrying the other draped over their shoulder – and both dressed in clingers. He slumped against the boulder, too weary and dazed to try to get up. His two teammates. One had their hood still back, showing a head scorched completely bald, crimson white burns over the entire face, healing by inches. Even through this, however, he could make out Samir's eyes, glazed with agony. His helper – Leah, he realised laboriously – halted a few feet from Greg, and let him slide gently to a patch of clear earth. The wounded Golem moaned – stronger, this time – and lay still, chest slowly rising and falling. Leah gingerly pulled his hood on, and sealed it, then looked Greg's way. Her eyes didn't quite have the thousand-yard sheen to them, but they were close. *What now?* they asked him, or maybe no one. And for the first time in his life, Greg didn't know...

Greg paused. Cayden said nothing, showing only professional interest. Greg's voice became flatter. 'Samir made it, though it took a while. After we'd healed enough, we holed up in an old mineshaft not far from the campsite, to wait out the blaze – and any follow-up strikes. Soon as the fires were low enough, we got to a town about fifty miles south, and found transport. It was then we heard the reports on the Army net of the cloud over Seattle, and the expected fallout. At that moment, we knew the assignment had been a set-up... and that the Doctor and the Project were dead. So we went underground, to wait out whatever came next.'

'Until now,' Cayden finished. There was a strong edge of doubt in his voice. 'So, if I've got this right... you think whoever was running the Project – D.C., the Pentagon, whoever – was behind the Bomb, along with the attacks on you, then and now? Why would they take out their best? And during the Turmoil?'

'We don't know, not for sure,' Leah answered. 'All we *do* know, or suspect, is that even with the safeguards in place, the Doctor was so afraid of losing the Project's data that he moved it to some external storage unit before the lab was destroyed, and that he had some kind of connection to Advent. It wasn't much of a lead, but it stands to reason that he found some way of getting his info to a place or person he believed was safe. Once we dug up enough info about the Project's early dependence on Advent, it was easy work to find their old offices in D.C., and determine which ones had the most security – and drew the least attention.'

The other man still looked sceptical. 'Sounds like a lot of guesswork and hunches.' He held up the canister again. 'Plus none of it explains why you came *here* – or what *this* has to do with *me*.'

Greg opened his mouth, but faltered. Looking Leah's way, he saw her staring calmly back at him. He tilted his head. *Should we?*

Her chin dipped, infinitesimally. *No choice. If he didn't know before, he has to now – no matter what comes of it.*

Drawing in a breath, he looked Cayden's way again. 'When we were digging for the records, we weren't just looking for technology or contacts. We wanted to know *where* we came from: who gave us up for adoption or put us in foster care before the Project picked us up, like the Doc and everybody else told us. *We* sure as hell don't remember; either we were infants when it happened, or we lost the memories somehow, thanks to the ARC or some other way.' His voice tightened a bit. 'We didn't find anything on that – but we *did* come across a fragment of an older file, buried in an online storage site used by the Pentagon that had been almost totally fried by the Pulse – almost. It was a list of the original five-person team of Golems the Doc presented to Snyder and the Pentagon brass. At that time, he'd adopted the serial number set–up, so there weren't names for all of them – except for one.' He paused. Cayden just stared back at him, unmoving and silent. 'Yours was that one – as team leader. You, and the other four, you were the first of us… and yet he picked you as the prime example.'

'So?' Cayden asked. His voice was hard and suspicious now. 'If you're wondering why that was, join the club. I never learned the reason, and the Doctor wasn't exactly the sharing type.'

Greg shared another look with Leah. 'After we found that list, we kept digging. It took a while, but we finally found a reference to the Advent archives, in an old Langley communique right before the Bomb. A snippet about a "sensitive item" being brought in from Washington State, to be stored off-site and marked "Eyes Only", for the sender. There was also a phrase about "personalised security measures": a lock system designed by the sender himself, supposedly with a very specific type of biometrics – one that had only been on drawing boards at the time, for the government and probably the whole private sector.' He pointed to the small aperture on the device. 'It was the kind that only one person, presumably the sender, could open – or somebody with a bio-signature like his. We're still not sure – but there's only one way to come close.'

Cayden looked the canister over again. His scruffy features showed only confusion. 'What are you saying? If the Doctor *did* code this thing to *him*, then why'd you—'

He stopped. His eyes went wide; the light green irises almost seemed to disappear. Both hands clenched around the canister, vibrating with the effort. Greg stepped back, keeping his hands in the clear; Leah did the same. If the other man's shock was strong enough, he could tear down the entire room in seconds, and them with it.

Instead, after two agonising minutes, Cayden moved away from the fire. He sat in the armchair, canister in one hand. He stared at it, eyes narrowed in surprise, anger, disgust, horror – or all four. When he spoke at last, his voice was the harsh, rough tone from earlier. 'You're sure?'

Greg moved to his side. 'You tell us.' He pointed to the canister.

After a long pause, Cayden laid the canister on his lap. Extending his right index finger, he pressed it to the aperture. A faint click, and he drew his hand back. A tiny drop of blood beaded at the tip of his finger. There was a snap of separating metal, and a puff of depressurised air, as the top seal came undone. Still silent, Cayden took hold of the cap, and twisted it free. Lifting the canister to the light now, he peered inside. Delicately, he reached into it, fingers bent into tweezers. Greg realised he was holding his breath, and let it out in a soft rush. *One bit of proof, at last.* And if it was for real, that *had* to mean all the rest – their origins, the source of their amnesia, the reasons for *both* – was out there to be found, at long last.

Cayden withdrew his hand. Clasped between his thumb and forefinger was a slim, touch-connect flash drive, roughly the size of a human pinky finger. Strands of tensile fibre hung limply from it – adhesive suspension webbing, preventing it from rattling around the interior and risking damage to the data. Cayden held the device up to the light, not saying a word. Greg stepped closer and extended a hand. The other man looked his way, his face a solemn mask. Finally, he handed the drive over.

Peeling off the webbing, Greg extended his left arm, and pressed the wrist activator with his other hand. The holo-screen sprang into existence, covering half his forearm. He touched the drive's connect surface to the suit's interface, just below the screen itself. Immediately, row upon row of random text, numbers and symbols began to cascade across the screen. After several seconds, the image froze. Four empty spaces appeared, and a single word flashed above them: *PASSWORD*. 'Shit,' he muttered, without much anger. *Figures there'd be another wall over whatever's on this thing.* He held out his arm to Leah. She said nothing, but the disappointment was plain. Cayden just stared at the now-empty canister in his hands, not moving a muscle.

In a whisper, Leah asked, 'What now?'

Greg didn't answer, not at first. He looked at the screen once more, then at Cayden. Carefully, he shut off the interface, and peeled away the drive. Stepping to Cayden's side again, he wrapped his hand around the canister, tugging it free of the other man's hands. Cayden didn't even seem to register his presence. With similar care, he dropped the drive back into the canister, and closed the cap.

Drawing himself to his full height, he looked to Leah again. He held the canister out to her. 'Our suit systems don't have enough processing power to break encryption like this,' he said in a low voice. 'But if we get him back out West, the Sanctuary will have the right people and equipment, and then we'll be ready for the last part of the plan.'

She nodded. Greg turned back to Cayden, who was sitting ramrod straight, still staring blankly. As quietly as possible, he moved in front of the armchair. 'Cayden?'

The other man didn't appear to notice him. His face was

blank and passive, like a wax dummy. Slowly, he stood up, joints cracking. Even with the poor light, the new, growing determination in his eyes was clear and strong. Stepping up to the mantle, he took down the photo, cupping it in one massive palm. He stared at it for a long time. At last, he lifted his head, and met their gazes. When he spoke, his tone was firm. 'All right.'

The last of the sun's rays were stealing through the trees, casting a soft grey-gold light over the clearing. Looking up from a last once-over of the pickup's engine, Greg saw Cayden emerge from the cabin. He'd changed into a heavy leather jacket, green and blue plain flannel, dark jeans and work boots. The black gleam of his clinger was just visible beneath the shirt collar, and extended over his hands. His beard was gone, and his face was scrubbed clean, courtesy of the creek a mile away. A minor bulge at his chest showed where his own knife was sheathed; another, larger one at his waist outlined a 9mm. In one hand he held a small green canvas bag, with *US Army* still stamped in faded grey letters. The other held a sealed tinfoil package – or, at least, *looked* like tinfoil. Standing in the door, the taller man looked intently all around him, plainly trying to soak everything in one last time.

Leah came up beside him. She'd scrubbed all the dye and styling out of her hair, as he'd done. 'No sign of any other visitors,' she murmured. 'We keep on the back roads, we'll skirt the reservation, and hit the main highways to the Twin Cities without leaving any signs. We'll have to head north for a while, and jink around to throw off any obvious possible pursuit, but it should be clear driving. After that… it depends on him.' She looked Cayden's way. 'You sure he's ready for the saddle?'

'No,' Greg said. Leah looked at him, surprised. Watching the other man, he finished, 'But as long as he's with us, we've got both halves of the answer. Right now, we need to get back home, and he's our best bet of getting there.'

From her expression, Leah wanted to disagree. Nonetheless, she held her peace. A loud ripping sound drew their attention back to the cabin. Cayden had torn off the top of the packet. With a dispassionate air he flung his hand out, sending a clump of great sand-like material flying into the air. It spread in a fine mist over the cabin's walls and roof. He did the same three more times, from the rear and both sides of the cabin, then crumpled the packet up, and stowed it in his jacket.

He hadn't gone more than half a dozen steps toward the duo before a loud *crack!* ripped through the clearing. Another followed, then a steady staccato of cracking wood and crumbling plaster and dirt. The roof of the cabin sagged, and then dropped into the cabin in a cloud of tiles and dust. The walls and windows collapsed inward not two seconds later, crumbling away like a sandcastle in high tide as the deconstruction compound did its work. Within two minutes, all that remained of the cabin was an irregular, grey-stained rectangle. That would disappear soon, too, leaving just a large patch of dirt and disturbed snow.

Never could get used to how fast 'Tacitus' works, Greg mused. He slung his duffel over one shoulder. *Better than risking a forest fire by torching it, though. Plus the compound self-destructs fast enough to not leave any real trace, or so we've been able to guesstimate.*

Aloud, he said, 'Let's go.'

Chapter 8

The Following Morning (8:00)

The ops centre was packed and busy: aides running in and out with computer printouts or holo-tablets, techs seated or standing before radios and satellite connections, and the individual officers or group of them standing before digital maps, outlining the day's actions for their units. Hargrove stood near the centre of the room, over a darkened 3-D table map display. Two of his bodyguards stood not too far away, dressed in dark green coveralls devoid of insignia. On the opposite side of the table stood a tall man with silver-streaked dark blonde hair, dressed in plain woodland fatigues, with a colonel's eagle insignia and a tiny nametag: *Patrick.* Costa observed from a nearby screen. There were dark shadows under the agent's eyes; he probably hadn't slept since Hargrove had left D.C., only catnapping here and there. By contrast, Hargrove felt perfectly fine – energised, in fact.

'My men are ready to assist at a moment's notice.' The colonel's voice was low and cool. 'Unlike the reservists down south'—his lip curled a little—'we've been patrolling and keeping the peace in the upper Mississippi Valley and northern Wisconsin for the whole length of our tour, the last five years. If the two individuals you're after are sighted anywhere within 500 miles, we can have an interception force on site within an hour – at best, thirty minutes.'

'And as I told you a moment ago, Colonel, this matter won't remain low-key if we start dropping in Rangers at every potential sighting,' Hargrove answered. He kept his tone patient – no point to irking any more people, given the recent chat with Costa. 'Your men may be trained for covert ops – tag-and-bag on normal insurgents and militia groups, among others – but you don't have the slightest clue what you're dealing with here. Which is why we must avoid displays of force, and let the targets come to us until we have enough intelligence and advantage to bring them down quietly. Discretion is an absolute necessity.'

Patrick's jaw ground back and forth. 'Then, may I ask, Mr Hargrove – why *exactly* are you here? What info Agent Costa provided makes the level of clearance you have perfectly clear. But if you wanted an off-the-books staging area, I'm certain Langley or the Pentagon has plenty still available. Based on what I've seen of your men, you don't lack for effective response if the targets do turn up, and so wouldn't have to risk anything classified being revealed to me or my personnel. In short, sir: you could be operating from much more suitable circumstances, instead of wasting my time, my men and my resources on some bullshit whack-a-mole chase.'

'Simplest reason in the world, Colonel,' Hargrove answered smoothly. 'Your facility is the largest and most well-equipped between the Twin Cities and Milwaukee. The two individuals we're after were last sighted on a direct northbound route out of downtown Chicago. At some point, they'll eventually have to pass within this field's operational radius. If we want any chance at bagging them before they leave the Mississippi Valley, this is the place to observe, wait and operate from. All we need is space, and some equipment to assist in monitoring the likely routes and frequencies used by our targets.' He paused. 'Of course, if you'd care to take this up with those further up the chain on the handling of this "chase", feel free.'

Patrick went a faint shade of grey under his tan. The Ranger officer wasn't a coward – Hargrove had seen his record en route to the base. But he also had to know what it meant to have a defence contractor and his Agency watchdog dropping in unexpectedly. Since the Camp David Coup, the Army was on hair trigger alert for any crisis or turf war that might endanger it. Even an innocuous query about a routine operation – or what was described as such – might well lead to the White House coming down on the colonel like a landslide in short order, for 'overstepping his authority'.

Clearing his throat, Patrick said, 'Very… very well. If all you need is space and equipment, Mr Hargrove, we can oblige.' He nodded toward the back of the room, where a set of holo-displays and hard drives sat in one corner, darkened and unoccupied. 'What sort of intel should be forwarded to your terminals?'

'Any reports dealing with suspicious vehicles, persons, or events within the scope of your patrols, aerial and ground.' Hargrove said. 'We'll handle all satellite info. I realise it's a lot to go through, but we can set aside the field reports that don't lead anywhere in a matter of minutes and catalogue the rest almost as quickly.'

Patrick nodded. Turning to Costa, he asked, in a more cautious tone, 'Can we count on any assistance from the Agency, if we require additional processing power? Our equipment's up to snuff, but it's isolated from the Net save for very limited bandwidth connections to the Pentagon, to avoid or easily trace hackers or taps. Up till now we haven't required anything else, but it might – no, *will* – put us out of our element to work with more complex data.'

'Shouldn't be a problem,' Costa replied. He shot a glance Hargrove's way – did he expect the other man to override him, or try to? Hargrove said nothing, only watched politely. The agent went on, more ruefully, 'As for being out of element, I can sympathise. Only connection I had with any operation like this was a few incidents during my time in the Tenth Mountain, pre-Turmoil. Mostly smash-and-grab work in Pakistan and the Taurus, with a few other jaunts in the Middle East and Iran before I came back for "peacekeeping" work here.'

Patrick's dark blue eyes widened a bit in respect. 'Went through a few of those myself, in the Caucasus, before and after the Russians did their stop-and-start bit in Ukraine.' His gaze hardened. 'Never thought I'd end up pulling the same duty here at home.'

Costa nodded, in perfect understanding. Hargrove moved to the display table. He tapped at the holo-keys, calling up a topographical map of the main search area: Wisconsin west and north of Madison, Minnesota east and south of Minneapolis, and a small corner each of Illinois and Iowa. Another flurry of tapping, and the main highways and state-county road systems lit up, glowing a soft green. Addressing the colonel, he said, 'We know they can't risk air or train travel. Foot's too far below the level of speed needed to avoid surveillance. So it's reasonable to assume that they'll stay on the roads, whether freeway or back-country, until they believe they're clear. Therefore, we need to maintain roving Humvee and chopper patrols along the main north-south routes in this state – I-90 and I-94, and county roads 51, 61, and 93.' A tap of a key, and the chosen routes turned red. 'I can probably wrangle access to a Predator, but it would be short-term, and only effective if we managed to get visual confirmation of the targets, or their vehicle.'

Costa cleared his throat. Hargrove looked up, mildly annoyed. 'Yes, Agent?'

'Just a thought: What if the targets really do have someone they're trying to reach in this region? I'm not talking another part of an extraction team, or supposedly dead comrades – like we already discussed, they'd draw attention from *somebody*, even underground. I mean somebody else on the Pr – who was higher up in the organisation that trained them. Not the top man, but someone close to him, maybe.'

Hargrove frowned. What was the kid driving at? 'The organisation, and what's left of it, has been under a microscope from Day One. That means the foot soldiers like our targets, all the way up to the top man and his closest people. We've even got dossiers on the cleaning crew, courtesy of the few files your superiors handed over. Even with the post-Pulse problems, I doubt we'd miss anyone.'

'Doesn't mean it's not impossible,' Costa returned. 'We may have confirmation that the organisation's main site was destroyed, but that sure as hell doesn't mean all the personnel – doctors, technicians, trainers, whatever – died at the same time. Something as big as what we're dealing with can fragment with no trouble, without leaving a trail. Some members die, others join similar groups – and plenty more just leave whole hog, trying to find something quieter.'

He typed something on his own board. The map zoomed outward, showing the entire upper Mississippi Valley. 'There has to be someone in this area who was part of the organisation in any of those capacities. All we need to do is narrow down which ones had connections to any part of the region prior to the Pulse or Turmoil, and who worked the longest at the organisation. They'll be the ones our targets had the longest and most enduring connections to, and therefore'll be the first to be approached for safety or transport. We find those people, we find the targets.'

No one spoke for a stretch. Hargrove's eyes moved from the map to Costa, and back again. Was there something that the agent already knew, about the Project or its people – more than he'd showed so far? If there was, what *else* did he know? Did that mean – He forced the train of thought aside. 'Very perceptive,' he said. He gestured to the enlarged map. 'With that in mind, perhaps you'd like to enlighten us as to the starting point?'

Costa ignored the sarcasm. Looking at Patrick, he asked. 'What's the first character any new recruit runs into, whether he's a soldier, terrorist or wannabe gangster?'

The colonel smirked. 'A mentor. Weeds out the weaklings, makes sure only the serious and hardcore stay in.'

'Right. It wasn't just the advantages these targets had going into the organisation that gave them the edge. They still needed years of training before they were ready for work in the field. And for the type of work involved, they needed the best of the best for trainers, to hammer them into the ideal members in just a couple of years. Which means the trainers had to be part of the organisation themselves, from the start and for the long haul, probably to the point that they came to see the recruits as family.'

Costa pressed a few more keys. On the map, the Twin Cities changed to a yellow, irregular splotch. 'We know the targets were heading north-northwest at their last sighting. They have to know we're watching the border with Canada a lot more closely than pre-Turmoil, even in the remote spots. So no matter how far north they go, they'll have to at least brush by Minneapolis or St Paul. And if they want any chance of getting out of this general area without being sighted by our surveillance or a suspicious patrol, they have to know someone who can hook them up with the means to keep on the move. Transport, weapons, food – whatever they need at a second's notice.'

Hargrove studied the image. Reluctantly, he nodded, and picked up a wafer-thin tablet from one corner of the table. He tapped three times at its screen, and held it out to the agent. 'These are the files from Advent and your bosses, on the target's known regular contacts during the period that corresponds to their training. Don't get too excited, though. Most of them only include names, and no mention of activities. And it was standard practice to give false names or info in organisations like these, so—'

'I get it.' Costa said with some annoyance. 'But it beats just sitting around with thumbs firmly inserted up our asses. From their behaviour so far, we should assume this to be a race between us and the targets – no idea what's beyond the finish line, but we damn well better make it across before them.'

Smirking, Hargrove nodded again, tapped at the screen once more to send the files on to Costa, then turned away to study the terminal, both guards in tow. That let him hide the tiny shudder of relief. If Costa was following *this* type of lead, he wasn't filled in on the parts of the Project that *really* mattered. That meant his superiors weren't either, or hadn't passed it on to a junior agent out of inertia, fast-tracked clearance or not. Either way, his position was still secure.

Behind him, he heard Costa speak again. 'Colonel Patrick. Can you explain this number here?'

Hargrove turned around. The Ranger officer was peering at his own tablet. '18Z-G... That's a military designation for a senior sergeant, in the Special Forces Branch. The 'G' doesn't make any sense, though. Might be a typo, but I doubt it. Why?'

'The man holding this rank, F Caswell – he's listed as a "training consultant", from the start of the organisation's existence, with no end date listed.' Costa's vidfeed shrank, allowing the file he'd called up to fill much of the screen. 'No date or place of birth. Nothing about his past operations – not much of a surprise there. Just a couple of references to his specific training: Recon tactics, empty-hand combat…'The agent stopped. 'Airborne assault techniques, including pilot certification.'

'You think he was the main trainer for these targets?' Patrick asked.

'No sign of anybody more qualified in the rest of the files,' Costa replied, with growing confidence. 'Somebody had to give them the right edge, alongside their tech and whatever other abilities they had from the start. Who better than a Green Beret? And who else would have the know-how to stay underground for years at a time?'

'A Ranger, for one,' Patrick countered. The humour in his tone took the sting out. Serious again, he pointed to the entry. 'Anything listed as to relatives, other ties, last known whereabouts?'

Costa skimmed the screen again. 'Just a fragment. Something about an old family farm, about fifty miles south of Minneapolis. You recognise the coordinates?'

Patrick's features darkened as he read. 'Yeah. That's at the heart of what used to be a TRZ – Temporary Relocation Zone. A couple hundred thousand people swarmed out from the Twin Cities during '44, migrating into the suburbs and farmlands. Right away they ran into local "security forces" who weren't exactly thrilled to see their city brethren.' His grip tightened on the device. 'We actually had something close to a handle on the situation before the Pulse – but the whole region was burned, bombed, and generally torn up to hell when we finally left.' He coughed roughly, and handed the tablet back. 'So if this guy did end up going back there during the Turmoil, it's a sure bet there's nothing left of him or his place.'

Before Costa could answer, the doors to the Ops centre banged open. Three men in Ranger fatigues strode in. All three men wore full combat kit and still carried weapons, both of which bore the signs of frequent field use. Ignoring Hargrove and Costa, the trio stepped up to Colonel Patrick, coming to a stop with sharp salutes. The foremost man – a sergeant – was first to speak. 'Sir. We just completed our sweep of the northern counties, and… we found something unusual. Something we felt you should see personally.' With one hand, the young officer drew out a small plastic bag, one-third full of grey-white powder. Hargrove stiffened at the sight. His hands started to shake, before he willed them to be still. It was all he could do not to reach out and snatch the bag away. If *this* was still out there –

Colonel Patrick held it up to the light, puzzled. 'What exactly is this, Duncan?'

'No idea, sir. We found it during a flyover of the southern end of Chequamegon Forest; one of our spotters noticed a clearing where an old park ranger cabin was supposed to be. Given concerns about possible gunrunning, I ordered the team down to investigate.' Duncan's face was impassive, but the bewilderment was plain in his attitude. 'When we hit the ground, all we found was a rough patch of this grey material, like ashes. But there was no sign of any burning in the area. And someone would've reported the smoke plume, even with the snow and damp.'

Patrick peered more closely at the bag's contents. 'Doesn't look like burnt wood or any other flammable compounds,' he mused. He closed a fist around it. 'Where *exactly* did you find this?'

The sergeant stepped up to the map table. He touched a finger to the display, which immediately focused on a green swath in northern Wisconsin. 'Right here, sir. There were some footprints in the area; they're in the video and photo records we turned in before coming here, as per procedure. No tyre tracks that we could detect leading in or out of the forest – the nearest community is around thirty miles away, and there was no evidence of any substantial traffic from any direction, by car or off-road. To be perfectly frank, sir, we have no idea what went on in that clearing.'

'I see,' Patrick replied, staring at the marked region. 'Thank you for bringing this to my attention, gentlemen. You'll be notified if any other information or action becomes necessary.' Duncan saluted once more, as did his men; Patrick returned them gravely. When the three men had departed, he turned to Hargrove. 'Well, sir? What do *you* make of this?'

Hargrove held his hand out for the bag. He looked it over for a time, turning it over in both hands. Long training kept his face calm, and his movements sure. Despite this, he felt a slowly growing thrill of pleasure. He had to fight not to smile. It *was* what he figured. Which could only mean that the targets were getting close to wherever they were heading, or desperate, or both. Either way, things were starting to look up at last. When he looked up at the colonel and Costa again, his gaze was intense and focused. 'Gentlemen, we may have just caught a break.' He swung his gaze to Costa. 'You find anything else in the files?'

'Maybe.' The agent's vidfeed expanded again. 'Given what's not in the files, it's barely enough to go on... but there's nothing else in a thousand miles that comes close to the kind of contact our targets need.'

Hargrove glanced at the tablet, then the map, and back again. The hungry smile appeared, in full this time. 'No… there isn't.' He stabbed the off button, tossed the device onto the map table, and stuffed the bag into one pocket. Then he tapped the map display again, bringing up the Twin Cities and the surrounding suburbs. 'Colonel, I need two Ospreys fully equipped and ready to depart in ten minutes. One to carry my associates, the other a squad of your best, for back up if necessary; I'll follow by in the chopper we arrived in. Ground insertion, rapid deployment; two hostiles, possibly more—'

'Wait, wait, wait,' Costa interrupted. 'You want a full insertion? What happened to staying low-key?'

Hargrove took a deep breath, letting it out with exaggerated patience. His voice held the same. 'We've tried that, and with the best team for the job.' He jabbed a thumb at his two guards, who were watching the scene with their usual impassivity. 'Chicago showed how easily the targets can slip past our *discreet* methods, with an entire garrison literally waiting to pitch in. This time, we're going in with full support.' He glanced sharply at the colonel. 'All of which will of course remain as under the table as possible, however.'

'If you want as much "under the table" as that, Mr Hargrove, you'd do better sticking with your own men,' Patrick replied. 'Rangers aren't exactly the discreet type.' He looked down at the image. 'Still, we can provide the machines and manpower. There've been plenty of reports of possible smuggling in the area, and the garrison in St. Paul has been on the horn for more support recently. My men can be presented as such, if the need arises.'

'I'm glad to hear it,' Hargrove said, keeping most of the scorn from his voice. He touched the display once more, focusing on an area northwest of Minneapolis. 'From our records, this is the only site where our targets can find fast, below-radar transport out of state. Based on our knowledge of this Mr Caswell, we can assume resistance, so your men should be prepped accordingly. Non-lethal takedowns if possible, but weapons-free clearance is granted if necessary.'

'What exactly *is* the site?' Costa pressed. 'And why Caswell in particular?'

Hargrove tapped at the highlighted area, bringing up a dark square patch. Two minuscule text columns appeared beside it. 'Monticello Airfield. An abandoned site at the start of the '40s, it was reopened as a private field in '45, by some local air freight magnate.' He looked slyly at both men. 'Apparently the Army has arrangements with the owner – a Peter Caswell, formerly of Faribault, Minnesota – to deliver aid stocks to sites across Minnesota, the Dakotas and Montana. But he rarely manages the actual deliveries, or even coordinates with the local military authorities. That's handled by the manager and security chief for the airfield itself… except there's no name listed.'

'And you think it's the same guy?' Patrick inquired.

'Or a relative.' Hargrove pulled himself upright. 'Doesn't matter either way. What matters is we have a bona fide destination for our targets, and a window to snatch them that's closing every second we stand here chatting.'

He glanced at the two guards. *Load up. Non-lethal preferred, but prep for otherwise.* They nodded and started for the doors. He looked back to Costa and Patrick. 'My associates will precede us in the move on the airfield. The targets might've gotten lucky just facing one, but by the time we and Colonel Patrick's men land, mine will have them – and the item – wrapped up and waiting for pickup.'

'You're sure that's wise?' Patrick asked. He stared after the departing men, both evaluating and uneasy. 'My men have the most experience in rapid insertions of any branch, in this part of the world. I'm sure yours are well trained, but if the targets are as dangerous as you've indicated—'

Hargrove waved a hand, smiling. 'Your concern is appreciated, Colonel – but unwarranted.' The predator's smile returned. 'The targets have only seen *one* of my men in action, and barely escaped. Now we'll see how they deal with three – and on *our* terms.'

Chapter 9

Monticello Airfield, Outskirts of Minneapolis

The car came to a halt in the first vacant space, just inside the entrance to the lot. The tyres spat bits of gravel and crumbling asphalt. Leah killed the engine. Greg's hand tightened on the duffel bag's straps. 'You're sure he's here?' he murmured.

'No other place is likely,' Cayden replied, in the same tone. The older Golem leaned forward in the backseat. 'He was never the type to push paper from up high, or from some back-room office. So the official HQ for his operation might as well be right here.'

'There's a comforting thought,' Leah said, with no trace of humour. 'Next question: How's he going to react to *you*, of all people, walking through the door? And what if he's already marked by–'

She got no further than that, for Cayden unlocked his door and stepped out. The car's springs squeaked and groaned with the motion. Rising to his full height, he started off, his stride sure and unafraid. Leah and Greg shared a look, before getting out as well.

In front of them was a large aircraft hangar, flanked by

offices and storage rooms. The entire complex was composed of reinforced concrete and a metal roof and double doors; one glance told Greg they'd been strengthened against anything short of a Tomahawk missile. The main building looked as though it could hold a squadron of F-24s and all their accessories, or house a full infantry company without making them bump elbows. Keeping the duffel close, he set off after Cayden. Leah was a half a pace behind.

When the taller Golem was within a dozen steps of the door, a low buzzer tone went off. Greg reached beneath his jacket, but Leah grabbed his arm. Cayden came to a halt, hands hanging at his sides. The double doors began to slide back, throwing up the occasional shower of sparks from the concrete. Peering past Cayden, Greg could see the silhouettes of several ancient prop aircraft, one or two that looked like two-seater jets – and a single human figure, approaching at a steady walk from the other end of the building.

The doors halted with a jarring thud. Bright morning sunshine spilled through the entrance, reflecting brightly off the various aircraft within. Stepping into it, the figure revealed itself: a stocky, grey-haired man, dressed in a white, oil-stained jacket and khaki cargo pants. Despite a pronounced limp in his left leg, he carried himself like a soldier.

Halting, the stranger surveyed the trio. His eyes narrowed at the sight of Greg and Leah. His hand drifted towards the small of his back. Then he looked towards Cayden. For a moment, he seemed turned to stone. At last, his lips parted. 'Christ… it really is you.' His voice was croaky, but strong.

Cayden stepped closer. One arm came up in a solemn, rigid salute. 'Yes, Sergeant.' The older man returned the gesture, then held out his hand. Cayden clasped it, tightly but carefully. 'Good to see you again, Frank,' he murmured.

'Likewise.' The older man stepped back a little, looking him over critically. 'Never thought I'd see one of the original Five still walking around. Doc must've put a little somethin' extra in your formula.' He gave Greg and Leah another careful once-over. 'Who're these two? Later models?'

Greg wanted to bristle at that, but found he couldn't. He extended a hand, giving his name; Leah did the same. The older man shook, his grip strong yet still cautious. 'Frank Caswell, Special Forces.' He jerked a thumb at Cayden. 'Used to work with this punk when he was still in diapers – in mental years, anyway. Stayed on as a "consultant" when my carcass picked up a few too many fractures and tears, which is probably why I never worked with anybody in your generation.' He turned back to the taller Golem. 'What brings you out from whatever rock you crawled under?'

'They dropped in on me yesterday, with some info about the Project,' Cayden replied. If any of the earlier turmoil over the 'info' still churned in him, he didn't let it show. 'Seems they pissed off a few people getting it, too, and need to get out West.'

'So you figured some help was in order,' Frank finished. He looked hard at all of them once more. 'How'd I draw this particular honour?'

One corner of Cayden's mouth twitched, in the barest hint of a smirk. 'I knew you used to live south of the Twin Cities, and I felt like a reunion was in order. Besides, let's face it: a Green Beret quitting to work at an airfield? That's bound to raise flags.'

'It's my cousin's operation,' Frank said, mock-indignant. 'I'm more security than maintenance. I handle the planes, he handles the paperwork – which thankfully means I rarely have to deal with *him*.' The seriousness returned. 'If somebody's after you on account of the Project, you're gonna want to stay deep under – and that means getting out of *here*. They're gonna mark down and watch anything that can get five feet into the air, if they haven't already.'

'Normally we would,' Leah said. 'But cars are too easy to track, and we can't go incognito in crowds anymore in this area. Much as I loved the hikes in training, I'm not in the mood for a literal cross-country run.'

Frank's eyes crinkled in what might have been amusement. 'Good to see they kept the techniques straight, at least.' To Cayden, 'In all honesty, this place is as good as flagged anyway.' He waved toward the planes. 'My cousin's had some difficulties with keeping his birds in parts, much less in the air. So he's been bringing in goods from certain folk across the border. Folk who've had plenty of run-ins with the Twin Cities garrison, and the Rangers out of Fort McCoy.'

'Chance we take,' Cayden answered. He eyed his old trainer. 'If this place *is* flagged, they'll be coming for *you*, too. Since we're still out of sight, they'll switch to looking for Project contacts. How long until they connect the dots to this place?'

'Let them.' Frank set his jaw. 'I've been on the receiving end of a lot harsher shit than any desk-bound spooks can dish out. They come here, all they'll get from me is name and rank, same as they did when it all folded.'

All three Golems looked at him. 'What do you mean?' Cayden asked. His voice was neutral, but Greg sensed the tension beneath it.

Caswell grimaced, as though wishing he'd never opened his mouth. 'Before the Bomb, the Doc had us packing up all our crucial gear, and torching or erasing any files we had on the – training programmes, outside of the main archives controlled by some AI system. Said it was a precaution, what with the riots in the suburbs, and the troops being posted downtown. Everything was going according to plan, until he shows up in the main complex, day before the detonation, half-out of his mind. Says we need to scatter, and go underground if we had to – all the trainers, the engineers, the nurses and support staff. Said that there was a good chance we could be hit inside of a week. When I asked him why, all he said was that "people" were working to shut down the Project, possibly Hiroshima-style. I thought he'd gone nuts, but I kept up with the evac. With what we were sitting on, we couldn't risk doing anything else.

'The next day, right as I'm driving across the Portland bridges, there's this crackling boom to the north. My comm link with the lab goes dead in the same second. Ten seconds later the satellite radio goes nuts, saying there's a mushroom cloud rising from Puget Sound, that radiation's blanketing the whole southern half of the bay, heading south and east. Then the Pulse hits – and it's lights out across the planet.'

A haunted gleam appeared in the old soldier's eyes. 'I kept going; eventually made it to a military camp in an abandoned business district south of the city. Far as I knew, my ID and everything else tying me to the Project went up smoke, leaving me as just one more soldier stationed in the Northwest, looking to report in. Nobody asked too many questions, giving me time to plan my next trip – wherever I could decide *that* would end.' The gleam hardened. 'Then, four days after the blast, this creepy bastard from D.C. shows up. Had a couple of big guys in brown coats with him; I pegged them for covert ops, of some kind. Says he's with the DHS, that they're debriefing all the personnel they can find that got out of Seattle before the Bomb, and—'

'Wait,' Greg interrupted. His blood ran cold. 'The guys in brown? What'd they look like, exactly?'

Caswell's brow creased in thought. 'Can't remember their faces. They never talked either – that was what set off alarms for me from the start. They all had glasses, that I know –

and some scars on their necks, like from surgery. Thought the bigshot might've been a relative, matter of fact; he was bulked up, and I thought I could see a couple of the same fresh scars on his hands.' He looked suspiciously at Greg. 'You know something about them?'

'Somebody with that same get–up – maybe even the same guy – tailed us from D.C. to Chicago,' Leah said. 'He had Golem strength, maybe more – and ARC-ability, only better. And he had something that sedated us, or tried to, when he got close enough to use it. We barely made it out – and he was still alive when we did.'

For a moment, Caswell looked dumbfounded. Then calculation returned to his face. His tone was quiet. 'We went into this office building, beyond the base perimeter. His two boys stayed in front, on lookout. We chatted for a few minutes – low-key stuff, mostly dealing with my posting, any intel I had about the area in the path of the radiation, any suspicious sightings, etc. I told him I was a spec-ops trainer, providing advice to the Seattle garrison about counter-insurgent warfare in the Olympic Peninsula and north of the city – mix in a little truth with the cover.

'Near the end, he asks me, real casual, why I was heading out of the city when it blew. I say I was given a new assignment by the garrison commander, outside the city – true enough, and the real man was ash by then, along with all his files. The guy thanks me, makes a note, then stands up to shake my hand and escort me out. Just when I'm opening the door, I see him pulling out the silenced pistol.

'I dodged the shot, and started wrestling with him. Managed to get a punch in that put him out of it for a second, grabbed the gun and bolted. The guards didn't spot me, though Christ only knows why not. Didn't know what was waiting at the base, so I snatched a car from the refugee lot and headed south.

Took me ten months, but I finally made my way back here, thinking I was free and clear – or at least not worth coming after.' His mouth turned down. 'Seems I was wrong.'

Cayden stepped closer to the sergeant. 'The "agent" – what was his name?'

The old instructor frowned. 'Name stuck 'cause I knew a kid with the same first name in boot camp; same hair, too.' The frown deepened. 'Shaun something, with an H, I think. But if he was high enough on the spook food chain to know about the Project, and to have clean-up orders for any survivors, he probably changes names like he does shirts. Why?'

The older Golem shook his head a little. 'Might be nothing.' His features crinkled. 'I remember the Doctor mentioning somebody he'd tangled with in the military over the Project – somebody who'd supposedly helped with the original ARC tests. Can't remember his name – but yours rings a bell, somehow.' The wrinkles went away. 'If he *was* one of the brains, or just a gawker higher up—'

Beneath his heavy tan, Caswell turned pale. 'Jesus,' he muttered. 'If *he's* after you, then it's a lot goddamn more than just a clean-up. Whoever's handling all this – him alone, or whatever bunch he answers to nowadays – they're not after you three for the usual reasons.' He looked hard at his former student, then at Leah and Greg. 'You must have something this guy wants, for himself and or his bosses – and I'm bettin' on the first one.'

Leah started to speak, but Caswell waved her to silence. 'Don't wanna hear it. Less I know, the better, same as before.' His hawkish gaze fell on Cayden. 'So I'll just repeat what I said a moment ago: *Get Out.*' He motioned dismissively to the hangar. 'Forget flying. Forget the Project. Forget whatever jaunt you're on, and just go under again – *deep* under.'

'We're *trying* to,' Greg broke in. 'If we had any better options, we wouldn't be *here*. There's no other way we can stay ahead of whoever's behind all this. How long would we last if we kept hoofing it, or swiped some other ride? You've been around the same block as us enough times. You probably know to the second when they'd find us, and bring in the Boys in Brown – or a Predator.'

'Besides,' Leah added, 'what makes you think it'll stop with us? You said yourself: this isn't a sweeper operation. Whoever's working the levers isn't going to stop with what the Project turned out. They're coming after *everyone*. We leave here without help, they'll find us – and they'll scoop you up as a bonus anyway. You help us, and go under yourself, there's at least the chance we can all stay out of the dragnet. But either way, you stay here, you'll end up the same way we will.' She set a hand on the old man's arm. 'Help us, and we can help you—that simple.'

Caswell didn't answer. He looked at Greg and Leah, and at Cayden, who regarded him silently in turn. He turned and stared at the hangar. His shoulders sagged, almost imperceptibly. He let out a deep sigh, and looked down at the tarmac. When he lifted his gaze back to the three Golems, it was hard and direct. Making an abrupt about-face, he started back inside the hangar, motioning for them to follow. 'What do you need?' he asked tersely.

'Fast, low-radar profile, and space for three,' Cayden answered, in the same tone. 'Doesn't matter if it's jet or prop-powered, but range is essential. At least to the Rockies, maybe more.'

The older man's mouth twisted. 'I've got something, but no guarantees about quality.' He came to a slow halt in the middle of the hangar, studying one plane after another.

His eyes fell on a craft in the far-right corner. It was a single-engine prop, wings folded vertically and tucked in the shadows well away from the door. At first Greg thought it was simply painted dark, but when he stepped closer, he saw that the hull was in fact *soaking in* much of the light. Not enough to render it completely invisible, but plenty to obscure the lines and original white paint exterior of the craft.

'C172V,' Caswell said. His tone was part wistful, part annoyed. 'Unofficial name is *Grey Witch*. Still technically a prototype – one its makers love to hate. Runs on long-term batteries, with two backups, and solar chargers in the wings. Maximum cruising speed 400mph, but I've hit 500 for an hour at a time – at the cost of the entire battery. Ceiling just shy of 15,000 feet. But even with the chargers, you'll have maybe four hours – five at most – before the main batteries crap out, and the backups are iffy, to put it mildly.'

He laid a hand on its engine. 'Hull design absorbs light, like you can see. Also keeps out radlevels to the tune of 10,000 rems, though thankfully nobody's had to test *that* yet. Shape and material also renders it almost completely radar-invisible – a little personal touch, added by a disgruntled engineer friend of my dear cousin. Emphasis on the *almost*, by the way – some poor sap flying this thing on Pete's orders got spotted by trackers every time he flew "special assignments" over the border, and only managed to lose them by gaining altitude and practically gliding for long stretches.' The sour grin told them exactly who that sap was. 'Haven't had to fly her in a few months, so there's no guarantee on maintenance, but she should work for the distance you got in mind.'

Leah moved closer as well. She brushed the propeller with one hand, looked through the cockpit windows. 'Saw a couple of these on the Mexican border in '49. The cartels loved them for running 74s and other gear to the Southwest militias. Even had the chance to fly one once. The end wasn't pretty, though.'

'Nor was the camp you flew it *onto*,' Greg said, deadpan. 'Still, you're the designated pilot among us, so I suppose we can make do.'

She flipped him off and continued her circuit around the craft. Greg turned back to Caswell, serious again. 'You're welcome to join us, you know. Where we're headed, you'd be in a lot more demand than here.'

Caswell smiled thinly. 'Thanks, but no. Way I see it, you're taking this bucket at gunpoint from some old man. They'll rake me over the coals to say otherwise, but I've been well-roasted before. Best I can do is make them waste time here.'

'Doubt they'll be in the mood to,' Leah cut in. 'You might be good, but you haven't seen what they're throwing at *us*. If there's nowhere else you've got secure enough to go under, there're plenty of people where we're going who'd welcome somebody with your skill-set.'

'No.' Casual before, Caswell's voice now had the snap of command. 'I'm through running. If they want to end me here, fine. Shady work aside, this place hasn't been a bad retirement spot, and I'm not leaving it easy.'

To that, Greg could only nod. Caswell nodded back, his features solemn and proud. Turning to Cayden now, the older man hesitated, then stepped forward and wrapped both arms around his old trainee in a tight bearhug. Cayden returned the motion. Separating, both men shared a long, unreadable look. Caswell stepped back a little, coughing gently. 'Come on. Let's roll this sucker out.'

Greg started to speak, but Cayden's hand shot out, gripping his shoulder. 'Hold it,' the older Golem rumbled. His head was tilted, in the direction of the field. 'What's that?'

'What—' Greg stopped, as a new sound reached his ears. He

strained to listen. Then he heard it: rotors – at least four. Cold fire lanced through his veins. 'Choppers.'

He flung the two duffels to Leah. She dumped them through the side window of the plane onto the rear seats. Together they grabbed one of the wing supports. A quick glance showed Cayden doing the same with the other. Caswell ran to the other end of the tarmac exit, and tapped furiously at the door controls.

The two metal slabs began sliding open, an inch at a time. Caswell worked the keypad again, then slapped the control box, muttering a curse. Greg pulled, the muscles in his arms and shoulders bunching and swelling. Compared to the vault door in D.C., the plane was almost as light as a mountain bike, but still unwieldy, and there was little room for quick manoeuvre. The metal itself was also slippery, maybe from the stealth material.

Despite this, they had the plane's nose lined up with the doors by the time a sizeable gap had appeared. Changing position, Greg readied himself to push alongside Leah, when the sound of rotors outside rose to a crescendo behind him. He looked up through the gap in time to see two planes appear above the building, flying at a slow clip toward the end of the north-facing runway. They were ungainly grey craft, with large bellies and no visible armament. Two sets of massive rotors blurred at the end of either wing. *Ospreys*.

Crouching low, he shoved at the craft with all his strength. Leah and Cayden matched the effort. Wheels rumbling, the *Grey Witch* rolled out maybe twenty yards, its tail just clearing the exit. 'One more, and you're good to lower the wings!' Caswell called out.

Whipping his gaze back toward the runway, Greg saw one Osprey bank away, following the perimeter of the field in a wide arc to the southeast. The second made a sharper turn, angling to face the hangar, exit ramp lowering. *Dropping the first half of the circle.* Its altitude dropped like a meteor – one hundred feet, then seventy-five, then fifty. At this range, the thunder of the engines was titanic. *No time for a last push – gotta get in the air* now.

The Osprey roared directly over the hangar, missing its roof by mere feet. Three man-sized objects dropped from the bulky craft's ramp. Greg ducked reflexively, half-deafened. He grabbed the wing support and pulled himself upright. The objects struck the tarmac, feet first; the impacts rattled through his boots. A cloud of dust rose from each. All three were crouched and hunched over, like men at prayer.

After one or two heartbeats, they unbent at the knees and waist, rising to their full six-foot-plus height. The closest one – the tallest of the three, with buzz–cut black hair – extended his arms to both sides. Foot-long blades dropped from his sleeves. Where he stood, it wasn't hard to make out the pale, nearly-healed scars on his face. The other two – one blond, the second brown-haired – held .45s. All three eyed the group with relaxed alertness.

Letting go of the strut, Greg reached for his own weapons. A hand seized his jacket: Leah. She jerked her head, towards Cayden's side of the plane. He looked in that direction to see the older Golem, sans jacket, stepping purposefully toward the trio. His knife flashed in one hand – an older, extendable version of theirs, almost a machete like that of his opponents'. Every line and movement in his body exuded calm, and total awareness.

The trio let Cayden approach. When he was a few feet away from the lead man, he came to a halt, knife hand hanging limp. They stared at each other. A hint of scorn was plain beneath the leader's silver-framed visor glasses. Greg willed his legs to move, to rush out and help, but found he couldn't. Leah's tiny sips of breath beside him told him she was in the same state.

A deafening blast rang out to Greg's left. He was crouching low, gun and pistol ready, before the next two shots rang out. The blond Brown Coat staggered backward and crashed on his side, three gaping, bloody holes in his shirt. Twisting around to track them, Greg saw Caswell standing halfway around the door's edge, a smoking old-model .45 clenched in both hands.

The other two Brown Coats burst into motion. Black Hair charged Cayden, a spinning blur of flashing blades. Brown Hair ducked and rolled to his right, gun tracking toward the door as he came to one knee, in front of his fallen partner.

Without a second's thought, Greg pushed off hard from the floor, back-flipping through the exit. Bullets sparked and whizzed past him; one tugged at the back of his jacket, like someone trying to get his attention. He came to a halt on both feet, halfway behind the door. His pistol barked, once, twice. Brown Hair went flat, firing back as the shots passed over him. Ducking, he glanced to the other side. Leah was already behind the *Grey Witch*'s tail, gun and knife in hand.

Watching her movements, Greg almost missed Brown Hair springing to his feet again. The other man broke into a sprint around *Grey Witch* for the left-hand door, firing a shot with every second step. Two rounds snapped past Greg's head, and he dove to the left. A line of fire traced itself across his right thigh, making him hiss in pain. He looked down to see a neat tear in the pants and clinger fabric. *First blades, now bullets?*

He landed on all fours, handspringing forward to get clear of the gap. Two bounding strides brought him up against the door, just behind Caswell. The old trainer cast him a grim look, not saying a word. He didn't need to. With those three blocking the tarmac, it was a matter of seconds before their partners in the other Osprey landed and swarmed them from behind. Pistol in one hand, knife in the other, Greg crouched for the roll back out to the tarmac, ignoring the pain in his leg. *Fast and slick, straight to the plane. Then –*

Shots rang out, from the other side of the hangar. Turning, he saw Leah dashing for the cockpit, Walther blazing. Lightning-fast, a trio of shots answered her, but she was behind the plane's body by then, and the bullets bounced off the bulletproof windows. Her head ducked out of sight, then reappeared in the pilot's seat, headset on. She waved frantically at him. *Come on!* she mouthed.

Before he could make a move, Caswell made it for him. With a primal grunt, the older man pushed off from the door and charged for the plane, twisting at the waist to level his weapon. Brown Hair sprang forward, knife carving for the ex-sergeant's face. The .45 bucked and roared. The shot punched into Brown Hair's gut dead-centre, and he pitched over backward like he'd been struck with a sledgehammer. As he fell, his own gun discharged. Caswell grunted in pain, grabbing his shoulder. The .45 clattered to the floor. His loping stride turned into an awkward shamble.

With inhuman agility, Brown Hair pushed off the ground with both hands, landing on his feet right between Greg and the plane. Blood dripped copiously from the chest wound, but he didn't seem to notice. Scowling, he raised his gun hand, aiming for Caswell's head.

He got no further than that, as Greg lunged out from behind the door. Brown Hair whirled, knife flashing, but the Golem was already ducking below the swing. He slashed up and left, ripping a long gash through the top of Brown Hair's shirt, and cutting clean through his jaw. The follow-up slice parted both cheeks and tore away several teeth and a hunk of nose.

Blood spurted in every direction. Brown Hair roared in pain, staggering backward with his gun hand clapped over the wounds. When he lowered it, the ragged Maltese cross made by the cuts was plain to see. Snarling like a wounded wolf, he started to lunge forward again, as Greg took aim. Without breaking stride, he dove low, smashing his head and shoulders into the Golem's gut and toppling him to the floor.

'*Whuff!*' Greg grunted. His attacker pinned him in a scissor hold with both legs, and clamped his now-free hand on Greg's left wrist, shaking the gun away with brute strength. Several floating ribs cracked, sending jolts of electric fire through his chest; he gasped and choked at the pain. His knife hand lashed up, but Brown Hair's fist crumpled his forearm, sending the blade skittering across the floor.

Grinning grotesquely, the taller man raised his own dagger then jerked once more, almost dropping the blade. He leapt off Greg, and spun around, moving rapidly out of sight. Dazed, Greg could see the hilt of a knife – *his* knife – protruding from the attacker's shoulder. Looking to his left, he saw Caswell slumped against the plane's tail, one arm still extended in a throwing gesture. Brown Hair was striding toward him, knife raised.

Greg lurched up, seizing his fallen pistol. Aiming as best he could, he twitched the trigger, again and again. Four of the bullets tore into Brown Hair's upper back. His twist around was cut short by the next three smashing into his arm and both shoulders. The last struck him near the back of the head, exiting in a vivid spray of red and bone. With a hitching grunt, he toppled. A twitch or two, and he was still.

Coughing, Greg sat up higher, awkwardly getting his feet under him. Looking Cayden's way, he froze. Black Hair was dancing a lightning circle around the older Golem, blades darting in and out like scorpion tails. Cayden was ducking and jerking with an artist's grace, avoiding nearly every cut, his own knife blurring in only occasional jabs or slashes. Black

Hair's clothes were rent with every strike, and his face was a mask of blood from innumerable cuts. Cayden's were barely touched. Droplets of red sparkled in the air like rain, but the bulky attacker kept coming. A new motion to the left caught Greg's eye. Blond Hair had pushed himself up to one knee, one hand reaching beneath his jacket. As Greg watched, he drew a silvery pistol – twin to the one he'd carried in Chicago – and took careful aim at Cayden.

Greg leapt forward, yanked his knife from Brown Hair's back with his good left hand, and hurled it underhanded. The blade plunged into Blond Hair's neck, burying itself almost to the hilt. The attacker let out a gobbling shout, red spraying from his lips. He crumpled to the ground once again, clawing at the knife with his free hand. The other squeezed the trigger – as his partner stepped into the line of fire.

Black Hair jerked. A glint of silver was visible against his back. In that split second, Cayden ducked a last swing, and plunged his knife into his opponent's gut. Blood exploded over the older Golem's face and chest, giving him a demonic look. Solemn and unblinking, he pulled the blade free, grabbed the other man's jacket, and swiped it across his throat with surgical speed. When Black Hair staggered back, the gash yawned like a toothless second mouth, dripping red. Choking, the attacker fell face first to the tarmac, a dark puddle already forming beneath him. Within moments, all was quiet.

Greg half-limped, half-trotted to Blond Hair's side, fighting away the agony in his chest and arm. When he tugged his knife free, he saw the unconscious man's carotid was still moving, feebly. The gunshot wounds were still open, but starting to close and heal over. Shoving his dismay aside, he placed the knife tip at the man's temple. His free hand formed into a fist at the butt of the weapon. *Gotta make sure... if that's even possible with these bastards.*

A bearlike hand closed on his healing arm, bringing him up short. He turned to see Cayden's bloodstained visage. 'No time,' the older Golem said tonelessly. 'Contingent of Rangers is landing at the far end of the field. They'll be here in less than a minute.'

Greg cast another look at Blond Hair. Slowly, he took the blade away, wiping it on the fallen man's jacket. He paused. For just a moment, at the angle he was kneeling, there seemed to be something strange about the man's face, beneath the new injuries and old scars. Something familiar –

Somewhere far behind him, he heard shouts, and the clomp of running boots: the other half of the Osprey contingent, now landed. He shelved the thought, and stood up, looking back to the hangar. Cayden was already by the *Grey Witch*, bent over Caswell's crumpled form. Moving closer, he saw the two men clasp hands, before Cayden picked the older man up like a child and carried him to a spot by the edge of the door. Face still expressionless, the older Golem trotted to the rear of the plane, placing both hands on the tail. A sharp grunt of effort, and the craft rolled the last few necessary yards. Greg looked Caswell's way, and saw that he was sitting calmly upright, one hand clenched against his shoulder. The other held a small, square metal device. He had just enough time to register it as a remote when the old sergeant closed his fist.

A whooshing roar of flame billowed out from behind either of the hangar doors, engulfing the corners of the structure. Seconds later, another blast erupted, this one from the two Cessnas. Within ten seconds, the entire space was ablaze. *Incendiary bombs,* Greg realised belatedly. *Probably had them in place for when and if the Army or the Feds ever showed.* Now it would delay the rest of the strike force and deny them any readily available transport beside their Ospreys.

Watching the inferno, he noticed Cayden out of the corner

of his eye, trotting back to Caswell's side. The two men stared at each other, not saying a word. Caswell extended a hand. Cayden took it, pumping once in a firm handshake. Pulling gently away, he jogged back to the front of the plane.

Greg was at his side a moment later. Climbing inside, the older Golem murmured, 'Said he wasn't in any shape to fly, that he'd keep them occupied. No point arguing, not with *that*.'

He jabbed a finger at the last word. Turning, Greg saw Blond Hair was groggily pushing up to all fours, coughing and spitting red. The stab to the neck was already healed, and the chest wounds closed. A few seconds more, and he'd be fighting ready.

'Greg. Greg?' He shook himself, and met Leah's gaze. She held out the copilot's headset. Without a word he took it, ducking and rolling under the plane to reach the other side. The engine started up with a soft cough and buzz as he climbed in, and they began taxiing before the door fully closed.

The cockpit itself was surprisingly roomy. There was a sizeable gap between his and Leah's seats, almost as large as that in a sedan. The rear seat could accommodate two, rather than the typical one. Cayden was staring fixedly out the window as he strapped in. When they swung onto the main runway, Greg could see the burning hangar in full. Two massive figures in brown were standing over a third limp form, the glint of their blades plain to see. Just beyond, he could see several tinier forms, in light grey uniforms, moving at a fast walk from either side of the building.

The engine rose to a loud hum. Acceleration pressed him back in his seat, wrenching his gaze away. A faint lurch, and they were clear of the ground, gaining speed and altitude by the second. He stole a glance back at Cayden. The older man was sitting ramrod straight, staring at nothing.

Unsure what to say, Greg sat forward. When the craft

banked, turning westward, he looked out the window again. The grey-clad specks were fanning out, likely to search the entire complex. The attackers were still standing over their fallen team member, completely motionless. Two new figures – one in a brown jacket like the attackers, the other in uniform – approached them. Their handlers? Or something else altogether?

The plane banked again, causing the hangar to drop behind them. Greg turned away from the window. They'd find out soon enough – all too soon. He glanced in the rearview. Cayden hadn't budged an inch. His eyes shone, with tears or anger. Plainly, for him, the next time couldn't come soon enough.

Chapter 10

The fire in the main hangar was already starting to die down, thanks to the backdraft from the chopper and the Ospreys. Hargrove's eyes smarted from the smoke. He hawked and spat to one side, trying to clear the taste from his mouth. Three Ranger techs in HAZMAT suits were combing over the less-damaged plane wrecks, checking for more explosives or other, salvageable evidence. The hangar itself was only lightly damaged, but the aircraft were all write-offs.

He studied the scene for a few more moments, taking in all the devastation. Then he pivoted and strode toward the building a few yards away: the main security office. Two of his guards – one blond, the other black-haired – stood by the door, .45s out. Their clothes were torn and bloodied beneath the coats. Both of their faces bore ugly, jagged gashes, still not fully closed. And all this had been from *one* of the targets – a new one, by their reports. The third guard – the brown-haired one – had already been carried back to Hargrove's chopper; there was nothing to be done *there*.

He fought the urge to punch the office door as he halted before it; with his tightly bottled anger, he'd probably take it clean off the hinges. More than twenty years of gruelling

work, and now he was a man – an immensely important man
– down. *Status?* he pulsed, almost biting the word off.

Prisoner secure, Blond Hair replied. *Minor injuries; no
likelihood of escape. Personal wounds significant, but recovering;
likewise those of J-003.* A second or two, then a last line: *M-002
confirmed KIA.*

Hargrove gritted his teeth. He knew *that*, of course. *Prep for
departure, estimate ten minutes,* he pulsed back. His jaw worked
back and forth. On top of the decrease in manpower, every
second here was another that could be spent tracking the craft
– a hard enough job already, with the stealth plating noted by
the Rangers during take–off. *All other assets—*

Trotting footsteps from behind cut him short. He swivelled,
and saw Patrick approaching. The officer's field uniform was
smeared with smoke and grease. 'My men are all in place
around the compound,' he said brusquely. 'Agent Costa's
already provided the explanation, if needed. Far as anybody's
concerned, this was a foiled attempt by a local militia group to
steal Red Cross supplies earmarked for the Dakotas. We were
able to drive off the thieves, but they succeeded in torching one
or two of the aircraft before escaping in their own ride.'

'Good story,' Hargrove said, not smiling. 'Just the right
amount of success to keep people happy – and enough failure
to keep them edgy. An old trick, but I'm sure the Agency's
never cared for public opinion.'

'Yeah, well, there's plenty to be edgy about now.' Patrick
glanced at the office door. 'Anything from him yet?'

'No. Not expecting anything, either – not soon, that is.
Even without his ties to the Project, he's old-school. Probably
went through the wringer on an hourly basis all through the
Turmoil, and came out with barely a shaving cut. Based on
that, any methods the Agency has up its sleeve would take too

long, or not work at all. So it may be better if the questioning were left to me, and my associates.'

Eyeing him warily, Patrick nodded. Hargrove motioned with two fingers. The two guards moved away to either side, staying in easy voice range. Without looking Patrick's way again, he flung the door open, and marched inside.

The prisoner was seated in the office's main chair, erect and proud. His thighs and lower legs were swathed in reddened gauze. More was wrapped around his left shoulder and upper arm. His arms were wound behind the chair, tied at the wrists with grey plasticuffs which ran to similar bonds around his ankles. When he lifted his head at the door's opening, Hargrove saw only dull, burning defiance.

He began pacing a slow circle around the bound man. 'I'll come straight to the point, Mr Caswell,' he said, formally. 'You helped two – excuse me, three – targets of a national manhunt flee this location. That alone earns you a lifetime pass to Leavenworth, nowadays. On top of that, you've aided in the transport of extremely valuable stolen property – and we're not talking about the cross-border jaunts done at your cousin's behest – along with directly participating in an attack on federal personnel.'

Caswell didn't speak, only continued to watch him. Hargrove went on, 'All this, of course, doesn't even consider your previous association with the targets, and your involvement in their organisation. Even without it, I'm well within my rights to arrange a solitary cell for you, for the next two centuries… and that's the kindest option.'

He halted. 'But the nice thing about my line of work? There's always plenty of room under the rug.' He leaned closer, though still out of arm's reach. 'Even with your prior connections, I doubt the targets divulged anything about their eventual destination. Probably they wanted to keep their dear old comrade and teacher out of trouble. Or maybe it was just out of habit. Still, I'm sure they passed along some hint about their eventual plans, and how they came to add a third member to their trip.' He looked at his watch with exaggerated patience. 'Share that with us, and we won't need to break out the body- or mind-altering methods. They're counterproductive, anyway, in my view.'

The old man turned his head away, in clear contempt. With one foot, Hargrove hooked Caswell by his left leg, spinning him so they were face-to-face. The prisoner winced, but remained silent. Hargrove finished, 'One little bit of info about either of those, and you can start *real* retirement. No guarantees on Florida, but you'll at least be watched over and cared for, like anybody else in their golden years.'

Caswell didn't answer at first. He looked from the guards to Hargrove, and back again. Without a change in expression or any other hint of warning, his left knee shot up, aiming for Hargrove's crotch. Given the prisoner's strength and speed, it was easily strong enough to rupture something, or break some crucial bone. In nearly the same moment, his good arm yanked free of the cuffs, snatching for the other man's throat.

Hargrove was quicker, though. A neat sidestep, and he was standing beside Caswell again, one hand clamped around the prisoner's free wrist and twisting it back behind his head. His smile became cold. 'Very good, Staff Sergeant. I can see the Pentagon's money was well spent.'

He yanked down, hard. There was a loud *pop* as Caswell's shoulder dislocated, and the grotesque sound of tearing muscle. The older man let out a sharp bark of pain, before clamping his jaw shut, hard, short breaths hissing between his teeth. Hargrove released his grip, and stepped in front of the prisoner. His other hand shot out, clamping over the sodden bandage on Caswell's left leg. The prisoner groaned, and tried to shift away, but Hargrove held him in place. Blood seeped through his fingers. He leaned in again, voice soft as a lover's. 'Tell me what you know, and this'll end well for everybody.'

Caswell's glare was scorching. 'They'll be over the mountains by dinnertime,' he growled. 'Whatever you wanted from those three, it's long gone.' His teeth flashed in a death's-head grin. 'Do what you want with me. You would've last time, so let's not waste any more breath.'

Hargrove squeezed the wound, eliciting another gasp. He studied the bound man, with a calm, almost affable air. Then he let go and stood up. 'Thank you, Mr Caswell.' In a flash, he stepped behind the chair. 'You've been most helpful.'

Before Caswell could react, he grasped the man's head in both hands. His wrists flexed, like screwing open a pickle jar. There was a sickening crunch. The older man's feet drummed on the floor, then went still. Tenderly, he released his grip, letting Caswell's head droop against his chest – with blank eyes staring up at the ceiling.

Hargrove took a packet of cleanser wipes from his jacket, wiped his hands clean, and tossed the reddened wad in a nearby trash can. He didn't smile, but eagerness sparked in his eyes. *Still behind in the race – but now I know* exactly *where the finish line lies.*

Without another glance at the body, he walked out. Passing between the two guards, he pulsed *Prep the body for transport, and stand by for departure.* The two men stepped into the office, one reaching beneath his jacket and bringing out a folded length of black plastic-like material. He took a deep breath, and stared down at the ground, sorting his thoughts. The canister was still out of reach. And there was a new player in the game – unknown, and with *Golem* abilities. His men had given plenty of details about the man, but nothing had come up in the files he'd gathered on the Project. Nor could he ask Costa, not without running into more questions or Agency stonewalling.

The thieves were desperate; their coming here made that plain. Ordinarily, that meant they would make more mistakes, enough to hang them before long. But Golems worked best under the gun; it was what they were *made* for. It *would* be easier to track them now that they were airborne, even with stealth in play, but there were still few guarantees of forcing them down without destroying the canister. It was fairly clear *where* they were headed – but that made things worse, not better. More questions loomed, from Costa or Langley, the further west they went, and more unknowns. Either or a combo of these would scuttle everything before he was in a position to set it all in stone. He lifted his head, chin set in firm lines. He *had* to keep up the chase, and find the damn canister. There was no other option.

'Mr Hargrove?' He turned to see Colonel Patrick standing nearby, XM10 in both hands now. 'We've secured the whole airfield, and quenched the worst fires. You get anything from—' The Ranger colonel cut off, looking over Hargrove's shoulder. Both brown-coated men had emerged from the office, carrying a black body bag between them. Patrick's lips thinned in suppressed anger. 'What happened in there?' he grated.

'What was necessary,' Hargrove replied. He smoothed the front of his jacket. 'I'll need you and a team of his top people to join us for our next flight. Fairchild Air Force Base, TOD twenty minutes.'

Patrick's glare was scorching. Ignoring it, Hargrove walked toward the far end of the main runway, where the Osprey that had brought his team waited. The main issue – where to go next – was resolved, or on the way to it. Now it was time to investigate the latest one – potentially the most troubling of all.

The craft stood alone on the tarmac, separate from the others that had landed Patrick and his Rangers. All four brown-coated guards stood by the entry ramp. *Keep watch.* They moved a short distance away, eyes moving ceaselessly. He stepped up into the rear bay of the craft. Two man-shaped forms lay on the floor, wrapped in body bags.

Kneeling by the closest one, Hargrove pulled the zipper halfway down. The empty, lifeless eyes of the brown-haired guard stared up at him. He grimaced as he took in the damage. The wounds didn't shock him – he'd seen just as bad, if not worse. The cuts on the guard's face yawned wide, two or three inches deep and still glistening red. The wound on the left side of the dead man's head was a gory crater of blood, bone and brain matter. When he pulled the zipper down further, he saw the three entry gunshot wounds, and the four exits. Hollow points, without question – and from pistols, not rifles or SMGs. Not powerful enough to stop the guard on their own, but no laughing matter. Same with the appalling facial cuts.

The headshot, on the other hand... He reached up, turning the body's head for a closer look. Spotting a first-aid kit nearby on the wall of the craft, he pulled it down, extracting and donning a pair of latex gloves. Thus garbed, he probed at the entry and exit wounds to both temples, peering carefully into the gruesome mess. He grunted. The round had torn clear through the cerebral cortex and shredded a good deal of other grey matter. With such an injury, the guard wouldn't have recovered.

Hargrove straightened, stripping off the gloves. All this only confirmed what the other guards had already told him. Golems could die from headshots, as could any human; all the records said so. But his men were different, in more ways than the obvious. Therefore, it had been logical to believe they couldn't be brought down the same way. The corpse in front of him said that had been an error on his part. Such a mistake, however, could be corrected – and he would damn well make sure it was, the next time around.

The same was less true of the other, unsettling wounds he had seen earlier, on his other associates. He touched a finger to the frames of his glasses. A tiny video image appeared on the right lens. The footage showed his view of the airfield, looking out one of the Osprey's viewports as he had made his approach. His lips shaped a phrase: *Fast-track*. The image blurred, speeding through the landing, the first sweeps of the burning structures. *Stop*. It froze, displaying his first look at the three-man strike team. The black-haired leader was standing near the middle of the shot, hunched over, both hands covering the dripping wounds to his face and throat.

Resume, One-Quarter Speed. The footage began to play, much slower. Hargrove squinted, focusing on the wounds. Even allowing for the slowed playback, they seemed to be closing less quickly than should be normal – a lot less. But that was impossible for these men, as he well knew. That left only one option. And if it were true…

Allies approaching appeared on the left lens. Casually, he set the gloves by the body bag, and mouthed *Close*. The video vanished at once. He stepped down the ramp, in time to see Colonel Patrick walking towards the Osprey, his stride brimming with purpose. 'I've informed Mr Costa of our next destination,' the colonel said stiffly. 'All that's needed is a last sweep for any remaining evidence, then we leave an Army cordon in place and take off. I've already selected a squad of my best, and prepped the transport for departure in ten minutes. Naturally, they're concerned about approaching the Seattle CZ, but we'll have MOPP gear. Anything else that's needed, they'll pick up at Fairchild.'

Tension seeped into his tone. 'Since we don't have time for the paperwork, I'm holding off passing on the details of our time here to Langley. Once we've finished the job, though, you can damn well believe they'll get chapter and verse – and have a *very* strong need to sit down and chat with *you*.'

'Can't wait,' Hargrove replied evenly. 'Been too long since I heard from my friends back East, anyway. I was starting to think they were ignoring me.'

'Can't imagine why.' Patrick's face was like stone. 'From that little show back there, though, I imagine there's a reason.'

Hargrove's face went rigid. Nevertheless, he kept his voice calm. 'Whatever impressions you might have, Colonel, I take no pleasure in my action. Given our time constraints, we had no other options. Mr Caswell *might* have yielded information, true – but we had no guarantees of its validity, or how soon it would have helped. It would've taken longer to get the *true* intelligence – much too long. We've been behind the targets at every turn in this chase, waiting for them to pop up, or arriving minutes, hours too late. Caswell wasn't going to tell us anything, certainly not fast enough to improve our chances. So I acted to elicit a sliver of information, before his worth to us as a source expired.'

'What information?' Patrick demanded. 'If we're headed to anywhere within 500 miles of the Seattle Zone, I think I should know *that* much.' The sarcasm came off him in waves.

'He pointed us west,' Hargrove answered. '"Over the mountains": the Rockies, maybe as far as the West Coast. It's enough for us to go on, and suitably vague to let him reveal something so that we would ease off – I've seen the trick before. Now we can focus our efforts—'

'Where, exactly?' Patrick interrupted, letting more of his anger show. 'Heading to the Coast barely shrinks our pursuit area. Hell, it just gets *bigger*. They could still be planning to duck over the border, north or south, or get out onto the ocean.'

'True,' Hargrove allowed. 'But they can't make it across the border by air. Every radar station between Alberta and the Rio Grande will be watching for the slightest blip, even without bulletins from us. Plus, our military presence is *much* bigger in the West Coast than anywhere else; they'll be watching the skies just as closely. Sooner rather than later, they'll pop up on somebody's screen.'

Patrick's face was the picture of doubt. 'Perhaps. But there's one question I'm still waiting on.' The colonel moved a step closer. 'You might have leeway when it comes to certain parts of this assignment, but *I'm* Langley's military point man for this, per Costa's instructions. That means *all* decisions – over leads, tactics, or prisoners – ultimately go through *me*. So when exactly did *you* get carte blanche to run this operation like some damn pet project?'

Hargrove sighed. Inside, he was seething. He'd hoped to avoid this moment; if he played the card meant for it, the situation would only get more dangerous. Still, if it would shut the bastard up, and maybe give him time to stay out in front – He smiled, bitingly polite, and reached inside his jacket. 'Since you asked so nicely…'

He withdrew his hand, holding a slip of paper, and held it out to Patrick. The colonel unfolded it, still suspicious. His eyes went huge at the header symbol: an eagle clutching an olive branch and cluster of arrows. He rapidly scanned the rest of the document. When he was finished, he looked to Hargrove again. The surprise was gone, replaced by wariness. 'This is a—'

Hargrove's nod was slow and careful. 'You asked about carte blanche?' If he felt like grinning, nothing in his face showed it.

He pointed to the document. 'I'd say a presidential pardon is about as *blanche* as one can get. I'd hoped to avoid using it, save in special circumstances. Clearly, the lack of understanding between us falls under that category.'

Patrick darted his eyes back to the page. He skimmed further down, gaze alternately narrowing and widening at what he read. Hargrove kept his smile hidden; the list was extensive. Coming to the bottom once more, Patrick stiffened. 'This has Snyder's signature – from the start of his first term.' He stared at Hargrove, bafflement mixing with suspicion. 'How in Christ did you get *this*?'

'*How* doesn't matter,' Hargrove said. He plucked the paper from the agent's hand and returned it to its pocket. 'All that *does* matter is, now you know exactly which people I ultimately report to – and what leeway *they've* given me, as opposed to the Agency.' When Patrick's expression darkened, he added, 'That *doesn't* mean, however, that I'm doing any of this half-cocked. So I suggest we get back on track, and continue with the hunt as we've been doing.'

Patrick studied him, jaw muscles working. Hargrove could guess what he was thinking, near enough. The colonel might not be up to speed on how much power *really* lay behind the kind of permission slip Hargrove had – especially coming from the Snyder days. But he would know that the current government was edgy about leaving those quasi-legal permissions in place, 'reconciliation' or not. One phone call, and Hargrove could be in a black site inside of an hour. At the same time, that kind of call wouldn't help the current case, and might in fact worsen it, by tying up the one resource – Hargrove, and his team – that stood a chance against the kind of targets the Agency was dealing with.

At last, the other man bit off, 'Fine.' He tugged at the collar of his uniform. 'I'll check that my men are ready for departure. Once *this* is settled – we can discuss all other matters.'

Hargrove smiled. 'Looking forward to it.' He motioned to the bodies in the Osprey's rear bay. 'I'll see to the bodies, make sure they're airlifted out to D.C. at our next stop. In the meantime—'

Patrick held up a hand, cutting him off. 'Hold on.' He brought the other to one ear, turning away. 'Say again... When? You have the coordinates? Good, we're set to take off. Call your team together, and we'll rendezvous at the other end.' He faced Hargrove again. 'NORAD's radar picked up an unidentified blip heading westward, roughly northwest. It's going in and out, and hard to lock onto, so the Mountain sent out a discreet alert to all branches. Possible smuggling aircraft, they're calling it.'

'What's the nearest major facility, along the plane's route?' Hargrove demanded.

Patrick frowned in thought. 'Fairchild Air Force Base, if I remember right. It's the hub for all operations in the Pacific Northwest, and specifically for the Seattle Contaminated Zone.'

'That's where we head, then, as planned.' Hargrove's body went taut and eager. This proved it. There was only one place where the targets could be heading – one that he knew *quite* well. 'You fill in the pilots; I'll get my people outfitted. We'll have to coordinate with the Fairchild people en route, see if we can get eyes on the targets while they're still in the air. Hopefully we can force them down before they reach the CZ, intact as possible.'

'Right,' Patrick replied, all business. He trotted to the front of the Osprey, throwing a last, cagy look back at Hargrove. When the colonel was out of sight, Hargrove turned to the four members of his team. *Board and stand by*, he pulsed.

Continue monitoring of signal from stolen comms device. Prep for aerial insertion, non-lethal takedown. Silent as shadows, the men climbed into the back of the plane. Taking seats on the hard benches affixed to the walls, they froze into immobility, hands on their knees.

Hargrove climbed in as well. Glancing back once down the ramp, he reached into another pocket, and knelt beside the body bag of his 'associate'. The baggie of grey powder glinted dully in the overhead lights. He peeled it open, and dipped it forward. A fine dust descended over the 'associate's' corpse, from head to toe. Almost at once, there was a soft crinkling sound, like paper being crumpled. Hargrove quickly resealed the baggie, then zipped the body bag shut and moved away. He'd seen the effects himself, but it was smart not to be too close to the stuff regardless. If all went according to design, and the amount he'd used, there'd still be a body, or most of it – and no sign of anything special, unless someone performed a full blood and DNA workup, *and* knew exactly what to look for. Given how fast events were moving, there wasn't any worry of *that*, not until he'd dealt with the situation at hand.

The Osprey's engines came to life with a thrumming roar. He tucked the baggie away, and sat down on the bench, opposite his men. A minute or two later, Patrick climbed in, wearing a pilot's headset and ear mufflers. He handed a second pair to Hargrove, and then moved to a seat farther up front, keeping his distance from the four men in brown. For once, Hargrove didn't need to hide his smile. Clearly the colonel was even more uneasy, working around him. But if it motivated him to pass word of the pardon on to Costa, or ask more questions that Hargrove couldn't answer... His hand found the baggie again. It wouldn't come out, not unless absolutely necessary. But that time might come – and soon.

Chapter 11

Above Mt Rainier National Park, Washington State

Four Hours Later

The landscape below was striking, despite the heavy cloud cover. From his window on the right-hand side, Greg could see a muddled carpet of grey and white, broken every so often by jagged contours of black stone soaring up in a squat pinnacle. Here and there, patches of tiny evergreen pinpricks sprouted towards the sky; otherwise the entire crumpled landscape was bare of vegetation for miles. If he craned his head forward, or backward, he would just be able to make out the even greater stretches of green and brown that made up the rest of the Park's range. Directly to the northeast, the line of the Cascades stood out in sharp contrast to the valleys of melting snow and brown-grey mud.

Five years after the Seattle Bomb, basically the whole of Washington west of the mountains was still considered contaminated and uninhabitable, left to the elements and whatever looters or bands of stubborn residents felt like chancing it. Even the rest of the state was a toss-up – the radiation cloud hadn't stayed in the Puget Sound area for more than a few hours before drifting south and east, forcing yet more evacuations, and knocking the region's and the country's economy for another tailspin. All this, combined with increasing temps and worsening weather, meant yet more ruination to what had once been one of the few truly 'wild' areas left in the continental United States.

He turned away from the window. Leah was making minute adjustments at the controls. Cayden was seated in the rear, face and clothes wiped almost clean, staring into the void as he'd been doing since Monticello. It was clear he wasn't just reliving the fight, or bottling up the adrenaline. The few cuts he'd taken at the airfield were healed, without even a hint of a scar; they'd closed up within bare seconds of take–off, instead of the few minutes it normally took for Golems of Greg and Leah's generation. *No question – he was more than just a prototype.* Greg's gaze fell on the two duffels, for the hundredth time. *And if what we saw at the cabin was right, I've got a pretty clear idea how—*

A faint coughing sound broke the silence, from the engine compartment. Fully alert, Greg looked to Leah. 'That what I think it is?'

She nodded, without taking her eyes from the cockpit window. 'Charge is dying in the main batteries, and the backup – not enough sun or UV at this altitude. Going higher to find it'd just drain the reserves faster.'

Cayden leaned forward, looming over the two of them. 'How much time do we have?' he rumbled.

'Half an hour – forty-five, if we don't push it.' She glanced at the GPS monitor. 'We're about a hundred miles from the old Fort Lewis range. If we keep this speed, we'll hit the perimeter in maybe twenty minutes, and the meet in forty. Dicey, but we—'

A sharp buzzing sound cut her off. She flicked her eyes from gauge to gauge, until they settled on the tiny radar screen. Her knuckles whitened on the controls. 'Radar scan from unknown source,' she said tonelessly. The buzzing sped up. 'Gaining on us, too – couple thousand yards, and closing fast.'

Greg fought the urge to glance out the window. 'Any ID? Civilian or military?'

'Just the lock. Nothing on the transponder yet, but—' She stopped, squinting at the radar again. 'Oh, *shit*.'

A harsh buzzing reached Greg's ears, growing steadily louder. A grey, winged object shot past the *Grey Witch*'s port side, travelling a good several hundred yards before looping around approaching from ten o'clock high. The outline of the object was all too clear. He gripped the sides of the seat. 'Predator.'

'Yeah.' Leah peered out the window as the craft zoomed past again. 'Can't tell if it's armed, but it's a safe bet that's a yes, in this area.' One hand on the steering controls, she pressed a few buttons on the panel. 'No problems with the stealth shielding. Maybe they're chasing the ghost of our profile.'

As if in rebuttal, the radio crackled. The noise quickly resolved into monotone speech. 'Unidentified Cessna, this is Recon Patrol Drone 4484. You have entered restricted airspace. Identify, and state your course and purpose.'

'So much for that,' she muttered. Pressing the transmit control, she put on a cheery tone. 'RPD-4484, acknowledged. This is Golf Whiskey 8, carrying medical personnel and supplies bound for Longview Airport.' That was the furthermost Washington town within the scope of the Columbia River Resettlement Area. Greg had heard there were some refugees still camped there two years ago, but had no idea if there were any of them left now. 'We appear to have suffered a glitch in our primary guidance system, hence our drifting into this area. We will correct this momentarily.'

The voice was frosty. 'All craft found in violation of quarantine line are to be escorted to Forward Operating Base Yakima, for further evaluation at Fairchild AFB.' A wink of light off metal: the drone was beside them again, to their right. 'Stand by to adjust course accordingly.'

The drone drifted closer. Greg could see the minigun under its nose, but no sign of missiles. *Must not be expecting anything needing that kind of ordnance – not that that helps right this second.*

Letting a bit of panic show this time, Leah thumbed Transmit again. 'Golf Whiskey 8, negative. We are carrying crucial supplies for the Longview camps. Deviation at this time would result in further needless delays, and possibly deaths. Request permission to correct course for intended destination.'

'Request denied.' Icy before, the voice was pure robot now. 'Either adjust course, or prepare to be forced down. You have thirty seconds to comply.' A loud *click*, and the voice went off. At the same time, the drone drifted out of sight, towards their rear.

Greg cursed under his breath; Cayden only watched silently. Greg looked Leah's way. 'Any ideas?'

She said nothing at first, eyeing the various screens again. Suddenly, she smiled. 'Maybe.' One hand lifted to the headset again. 'Golf Whiskey 8, acknowledged. Making course correction now. Be advised: our engine levels are low, and falling by the second. We may require an emergency landing prior to our arrival at FOB Yakima.'

She clicked off before the controller could answer, and tugged at the rudder, putting the *Grey Witch* in a gentle turn northeast. Seeing Greg's puzzlement, she pointed to one of the readouts, at the top of the dashboard. 'Geiger says there's a strong fallout plume blowing from the deposits in Seattle, settling over this whole area. Even the latest Predators aren't rad-hardened enough for the levels it's putting out. We get low enough, it'll screw with the drone's link to home base, and maybe the guidance system. It gets thrown off, maybe enough to crash, or just to leave it wobbling all over the Park—'

'While we keep heading west,' Greg finished, smirking. 'What about *our* exposure?'

'Counter's not showing enough to penetrate the hull. The plume looks to be staying above close to a hundred feet, and our clingers should keep out the residual ground levels, at least until we reach the perimeter.' They were facing directly northeast now, the sun glinting off the flaps. Checking the radar again, Leah frowned. 'Our escort's hanging a bit close, isn't he?'

Greg peered at the radar. Sure enough, the drone was within 200 yards of their tail. The angle of approach was off, too. Almost like—

He seized the rudder controls, yanking hard to port. The plane twisted, turning almost on its side. A line of tracers streaked past the starboard wing. Grasping the controls again, Leah throttled back, cutting speed and altitude. Still spitting rounds, the drone shot by overhead, going at least a thousand yards before banking in a slow turn. 'I'd say we're made,' she said, breathlessly.

The drone completed its turn, accelerating head-on. Leah put the plane in a downward corkscrew, diving below the next spray. Greg clenched the edge of his seat, fighting back g-force and nausea. Cayden held himself in the middle of the rear seat, hands and feet pressed against the hull. The drone streaked past again, at slower speed. Another bank, and it would be on them in seconds, with a much shorter range. 'What now?' Greg said through clenched teeth.

Leah spared a glance out the side window. 'Puyallup River's to our right, maybe a mile off. Best spot for a landing, unless we want to become evergreen kebabs.' She twisted the plane to the right again, twirling it through another barrel roll. The Geiger was buzzing now, instead of the sedate clicks from before. 'We're in the middle of the rad plume now. They want a clear shot, they'll have to get close.'

The plane's nose dipped, pointing itself at forty-five degrees. A ribbon of white-blue was visible to the right, winding through the forest. The trees became bigger and clearer; Greg could almost count the branches. Leah jinked right, left, then back, dipping the tail and nose at random. 'Almost there,' she muttered, squinting at the river. 'Come on, just a few more—'

Four rounds struck like hailstones fired from a giant's blowgun. 'Fuck!' Leah cursed. The *Grey Witch* lurched right, nearly turning over. Thrown against the window, Greg spotted two holes the size of a human hand punched through the starboard wing. Smoke and hydraulic fluid were already trailing from them.

Still turning the craft this way and that, Leah scanned the gauges. 'Main batteries are gone; reserves barely registering. Nothing from the starboard controls.' She pushed against the controls with all her strength. 'Hang on, this isn't going to be subtle!'

The plane dropped like a stone. Greg's stomach leapt into his mouth, before he forced it down. The river was directly below them, gaining with every second. He could see frothing rapids, and rocks protruding every few yards. Another volley of tracers zipped overhead; Leah ignored them. Her hand shot out and grasped his, fingers clenching tight enough to snap ordinary bone. He clasped it equally hard in return. Still staring ahead at the rushing water, she began counting. 'Seven... six...' Greg closed his eyes, pressing back against his seat. 'Four... three... two... one...'

The belly of the *Grey Witch* struck first, caroming off the river's surface at 100 mph. The landing gear sheared away with a screech of tortured metal. Greg's seat catapulted upwards. He threw his arms up against the ceiling panels, snapping both forearms like matchsticks. A microsecond later, the plane hit again, dipping hard left and down. The propeller struck the edge of a jagged boulder, tearing all three blades and twisting backward toward the cockpit. The craft heeled hard right, slicing the starboard wing through the water. Chunks of metal ripped away, pinwheeling in all directions. Momentum yanked them forward, nearly sending the plane twirling end over end – which would have shoved the engine back into the cabin and crumpled the entire frame, killing or severely maiming them all despite the ARC. Instead, the nose ground itself into the riverbed, throwing up a torrent of silt and spray. The port wing plunged into the current, digging deeper into the bed and bringing the tail up like a grave marker. Groaning piteously, the rear of the plane dropped hard on the rocky shoreline, breaking off the rear flaps and tearing off bits of the hull.

Hacking and wheezing, Greg pulled at the straps. His arms felt doused in tingling fire. When he spat, bits of pink froth landed on the controls. *Punctured lung.* Already he could feel the ribs retracting, and the internal wounds closing. Both legs were still working; it felt like there might be a double sprain, but those were healing faster than the rest. Still, it would be a minute or so before he was stable, let alone combat-ready.

Beside him, Leah was sitting up, too. Blood dripped from a gash on her throat and another on her forehead, but she seemed only stunned. She held out her hands. Both wrists were bent almost completely back, the fingers gnarled and mangled. She winced, once, as they began resetting, twisting and rotating back into place. 'You okay?' she rasped; the cut must've hit her vocal cords.

'Yeah, sort of.' He started to turn. 'Cayden? You—'

The older Golem loomed up between them. His shirt and coat were ripped even more from flying debris, and there were several deep, already-healing cuts on both his cheeks. 'I'm fine,' he murmured. 'We need to move. Drones won't wait around too long to confirm the kill in this zone, but that won't stop this one from strafing us again.'

'Right.' Greg glanced out the window but could only catch a sliver of the sky; the wing was buckled almost ninety degrees. He turned his gaze to the riverbank. 'Current's strong. We jump out, let it carry us clear of the wreck, and break for the treeline.'

'No,' Cayden said flatly. 'The drone'll rip us to shreds before we get a hundred yards.' Reaching to his waist, he drew his pistol. His right arm moved out of sight, reappearing with the dark green duffel from the forest. Unzipping it, he yanked out a few random bits of clothing and small gear. Eventually he pulled out what appeared to be a standard sniper scope, arm-length metal barrel, and attachable rifle butt. He snapped all of these onto the pistol, in a matter of seconds. Slinging the duffel over one shoulder, he hefted the weapon, looking gravely at them both. 'It'll be tight, but I can make it.' He kicked hard at the door with one foot, breaking it clean off. Modified rifle in one hand, he yanked himself through the hole, dropping with a loud splash into the water.

Greg tugged at the straps, then, exasperated, tore the buckle free and wiggled out of them; Leah cut her way free with her blade. He wrenched his door open, and dropped feet-first, feeling the river rise to his chest. Being mostly snowmelt, the temp had to be near zero, but the clinger kept most of the chill out. Fighting against the current, he waded to the western shore, grasping boulders here and there to keep upright. Splashes behind him said Leah was clear of the plane, too.

Clambering onto solid ground, he spotted Cayden several yards upstream, down on one knee and scanning the skies through his weapon's scope. The sound of the Predator's engine reached his ears in the same moment. A muted buzz this time, with the faintest hint of a stutter. *Must be the fallout, or some glitch made worse by it.* Which meant—

He whipped his gaze further upstream, to the west. A glint of metal flashed at him, maybe 600 feet high, and a quarter mile off. A short burst of speed, and the drone would have the easiest shot in the world.

His movements smooth and confident, Cayden brought the weapon to his shoulder, and chambered the first round. Exhaling, he froze immobile, peering down the sight. The drone's buzz grew louder. Greg could see its low-slung profile, dropping with every second over the valley. Any moment now, and it would have them lined up.

Cayden squeezed the trigger. A single blue tracer spat out, rocketing towards the Predator. The colour told Greg everything, in the millisecond before he ducked his eyes behind one arm. Bright white light stabbed at his eyelids, before the hood's filters dropped. Winking away tears, he heard the drone's engine sputter twice, and cut out altogether. The sleek, agile craft wobbled, before tilting into an awkward glide for the eastern shore. Its wings snapped off against the peaks of several dead pines, causing it to spiral. Then it smashed into the main trunk of another tree, almost punching clean through. A gorgeous ball of sparks, fire and smoke erupted. The nearest trees went up at once, adding to the drone's pyre.

Vision back to normal, he looked towards Cayden. The older Golem had unslung his bag and was coolly repacking the various parts of his weapon. Leah had moved closer, eyeing him with new caution. 'EMP rounds?' she ventured.

Cayden nodded soberly. 'A little upgrade I designed, to replace the more cumbersome rockets we were issued. Caswell showed me how.' A dark look crossed his face, before it returned to its normal blankness. He stuffed the last component away and zipped up, sticking the pistol back in its clinger guard. 'We've got maybe three hours of real daylight left. Assuming our watchers are on the ball, they'll have another drone in this area in half that time – and they see far better in the dark than even we can.' He met Greg's eyes. 'You two have the more recent experience in this area. What's our best route to the "perimeter"?'

'Depends.' Greg looked southeast, towards the headwaters. He drew a map in his mind, drawing from the countless times spent checking and re-checking the GPS against the landscape out the window. 'We're in the last southern curve of the Puyallup – maybe six or eight miles from Rainier. We keep following the river, we'll hit the old dam in Electron by 7pm, or a bit past that. Nobody's been there since the Bomb, not even us on patrol, and it'd be easy for another drone or whatever else our trackers have handy to sight us along the river's course. We'd eventually find *somebody*, but no guarantee as to when, in that direction.'

He faced southwest. 'If we rough it straight from here, we'll reach Eatonville and the 161 road inside of the same time, assuming the forest isn't too thick and the trackers don't have anything to cut us off with. Still not likely our friends'll have sentries out in that area – they don't stray much beyond the old Fort Lewis reservation. But we'll be in spitting distance of home, and have a nice, warm, glowing spot to shield us from the hunt for one night.'

'Straight it is, then,' Cayden's voice brooked no argument.

He stood up, re-slinging his bag, then stopped, and went on more guardedly. 'Where exactly *is* home, in all this?'

Greg could see where he was going. 'Not... the Facility. Another site, one that a few of us set up in the second year after the Bomb. It's isolated, but not completely. Enough for us to stay off the radar, and clear of the worst of the fallout.'

Cayden's shoulders sagged, almost unnoticeably. 'So none of you found—'

'No – nothing.' He peered at the other man. 'You've been having them, too, haven't you?'

Cayden's face turned to stone. 'Don't know what you're talking about,' He turned away, and started stomping toward the line of evergreens. 'We're burning up clean air and sunlight. Let's—'

'Pine forest?' Greg cut in. Cayden halted. 'Constant rain? Quiet, sterile halls? Guys in surgical gear, holding blindfolds or knockout shots? A woman's voice, always talking, from right above you?'

Slowly, Cayden turned around. Greg pressed on. 'We've been having the flashes, too – sometimes in dreams, sometimes in broad daylight. They were always there, even when we were in uniform – but they started to hit harder, after the inhibitors began wearing off.' He thought he saw a flicker of confusion in the older man's look at that, but couldn't be sure. 'They're all from the Facility, from the Project – that much we know. Maybe from between assignments, maybe from our early days. We know they can't be from our old lives – we all came to the Project as infants. But we still have no idea where it all was.'

He took a breath; easier, with the ribs completely reset. 'That's why we were looking for you. Because we need answers. If we're going to survive, let alone make our plan stick, we need to find the Facility – and whatever truth it holds for us.'

Cayden stood motionless, staring neutrally at them both. After a lengthy silence, he spoke, in much in the same tone, 'What sort of "plan" are we talking about? How does it involve me – or the canister?'

Greg's lips parted, but he found he couldn't speak. *We can trust him – but can he handle it?* After his reaction at the cabin, and given his 'detachment' since, there was no guarantee.

Leah spoke up, to his relief. 'The kind of plan we can talk about once we're *there.*' Nimbly, she tossed one of the other duffels to Greg. Catching it, he felt the canister through the fabric. She looked ahead, peering through the branches and underbrush. 'The forest's regrown since the Bomb, but a lot's died off, too. We'll have plenty of cover, but that won't stop thermal imaging, at least out here.'

She switched on the Geiger counter, salvaged from the plane. The device began clicking away at once, like sped-up Morse code. 'The fallout's still hanging over us. Wind's dropping fast, too, which means this whole area's going to be glowing in the next hour – possibly beyond even what our clingers can handle.' She paused, letting the implication sink in. *Don't need any reminding,* Greg thought. *Not after spending half a month on my back, pumped full of antirads, when the job in Lake Balkash went south in '44 – and after seeing what happened to Taylor.*

He tried to hide a shudder. The other Golem had been a new addition—'fresh off the line', in Project jargon, an expression he still didn't really understand. While he'd been skilled at explosives and tech in general, he hadn't anticipated just how much shoddy work and neglect had gone into the Kazakh nuclear plant's auxiliary reactor and power grid. Instead of only collapsing the wall needed for his exit to rejoin Greg at the recon site, the blast had torn clean through to the reactor's pile itself. In a matter of seconds, Taylor, Greg, the smugglers they'd been tracking, the would-be black marketers among the staff, and the entire complex had been doused in radiation. Only the plant's state-of-the-art suppression system – a first for the ailing country – and the lower-than-expected fuel reserves had prevented a combined Chernobyl and Fukushima.

Greg had managed to get them both to the exfil point, but not soon enough. Within a week, Taylor had died, languishing in hideous agony the entire time. Even the ARC hadn't been enough. *Hell, it just made it worse, wearing out his system by constantly kicking in. And the burns and scars, reopening every time from the isotopes.* Greg had been lucky, in more ways than one: after several more months' recuperation and retraining, he was back on his feet, and partnered with Leah. But he'd never forgotten his last glimpse of Taylor, wheeled out of the ER with his few remaining tufts of blonde hair falling out, and the scars and sores still open over his body and face, struggling to close…

Shaking his head, he refocused, and realised the other two were staring at him. Pulling back his damp, ragged shirt cuff, he punched up the sleeve holo-interface. When the screen blinked on, he swiped to the GPS. A risk, given the likely taps on the few remaining satellites, but the masking programs *should* still be functioning even after dousing the whole suit.

He pointed west, at a slight angle from their position. 'Straightest route to Eatonville's this way. Nothing showing up on the scan other than trees and random wildlife, so barring another visit from On High, be it an assault team or more remote-control death' – he gestured to the wreck of the Predator, barely evident through the smoke and flames consuming the isolated stand of trees—'we'll have nothing but a smooth fast-march to the Sanctuary.'

Cayden nodded, apparently willing to let the previous issue pass for now. 'Is there any way for you to reach this – Sanctuary, or its patrols, before we hit its perimeter? Might shorten the march.'

'Fallout screws with our comms, same as anyone else's,' Greg answered. 'It's less of a problem in most of the Sound's coastal areas – a lot of the deposits get blown around or sent eastward. But anything beyond that is a crapshoot on the best of days. You'd have to climb a tree to even get a whisper, and that's if there's no cloud cover.'

'Hm,' Cayden turned away and strode toward the nearest tree, a near-dead evergreen. When he was about fifteen feet away, he broke into a sprint. At five feet, he bunched his legs under him and launched into a flying leap, landing with a sickening *smack* against the trunk. Without pausing, he shimmied out on the thickest available branch, crouched, and sprang out into space. His hands closed on branches of another pine. Using the half second before they snapped, he pulled his body forward, wrapping his arms in a death grip around the trunk, and sliding down to a halt on a thicker bough. He looked down at them with no sign of breathlessness or fear. 'Then we'll want to speed things up, and get that whisper.' Not waiting for a reply, he crouched and sprang again, landing on another trunk further into the forest. A short pause, then another leap, with the same speed and grace.

Glancing at Leah, Greg could see she was equally surprised. *All the talk about us being the 'next generation' – and yet some things are still elemental.* Adjusting the duffel's strap, he sucked in a breath, and charged for the first tree. The crumbling bark rasped under his fingers, lacerating both palms. A sharp gasp said Leah had landed smoothly, too. Gripping the trunk, he began to climb toward the thickest branch, ignoring the blood seeping from his palms.

Chapter 12

Fairchild Air Force Base

Outskirts of Spokane, WA

The conference room was quiet. On one end of the table stood Hargrove, Patrick, the blond and black-haired guards. On the other, a tall man with white-streaked black hair, in grey woodland camo with a colonel's shoulder insignia and Air Force wings above his breast nametag: Flynn. Costa was watching from a screen as usual, though with a different, more austere background: a secure room that made SCIF look like an open school locker, maybe. The air was close and hot, made more so by the sunlight streaming in from the room's single wide window. Outside could be seen the base's main runway, the three main landing pads on the eastern side, the handful of personnel moving about prepping this or that jet or chopper, and the two lines of other such craft standing ready for launch or maintenance.

Hargrove kept his voice low and calm. 'When we first spoke, Colonel, it was my understanding that you were clear on the nature of my assignment to your jurisdiction, and that discretion was an absolute necessity.'

'That's correct, sir.' Flynn replied. He spoke robotically, with no sign of fear or apology. 'I likewise made this clear to my staff, and those responsible for—'

'And I was given to understand that any suspicious sightings within your jurisdiction – prior to and following my arrival – would be reported promptly, with all decisions also passed on within moments of being made.'

The colonel dipped his chin. If the interruption bothered him, it didn't show. 'Yes, sir.'

'So when you detected the aircraft whose specifications matched those my people passed on to you from Minnesota, what was your first impulse?' Almost meditatively, Hargrove began examining the fingernails on his left hand. The sleeve of his shirt receded, exposing the ends of a trio of pencil-shaped scars on the back of his hand, stretching up past his wrist. Noticing Costa eying them, he shifted his arm, letting the cuff fall back into place.

'To ascertain whether the craft in question precisely matched those specifications.' Flynn replied. 'Most of the regions immediately south of the Contaminated Zone – chiefly those around Portland and throughout the Oregon Cascades – are still dependent on regular aerial deliveries for essential supplies: medicines, tools, rations, clean water. It would have endangered many lives had we destroyed the target without first endeavouring to confirm its course.'

'But you were rapidly made aware of the target craft's purported course – or lack thereof?' Hargrove inquired.

'Yes.' Flynn's tone now carried a hint of irritation. 'And it was rapidly proven false. At which time my team followed protocol – ultimatum, warning shot, then interception.'

'True.' Casually, Hargrove stepped around the table, to the

colonel's right. 'And under normal circumstances, you and your command would be receiving commendation for your careful maintaining of the CZ perimeter, and of procedure intended to interdict any potential smuggling or other black–market activity in this area. But as I already explained, both during my flight and here, these are far from normal circumstances.'

He studied his right hand, letting it curl into a loose fist. 'You were instructed – clearly and repeatedly – to force the craft down, preferably without altogether destroying it, and corralling any occupants and cargo into a relatively small zone for pickup. However, your chosen course led to the craft's destruction, and that of the drone – the only one within close enough range to track any survivors.'

He swung his fist down on the table with a bang. When his hand came away, there was a circular dent in the bare metal. The table, once rock-steady and anchored to the floor, sagged incrementally in the middle. He'd pulled the punch; no point to showing off, and better the table than any of the idiot faces around him. But oh, the temptation was so strong.

Costa's eyes went large. Patrick backed up a pace, one hand close to his holster. The two guards just watched, silent as ever. Hargrove ignored them all, stepping closer to Flynn. In a low growl, he finished, 'Which means you've lost them.'

Flynn's legs shifted, leaving him ready to run or fight. He looked Hargrove straight in the eye. 'We were unable to corral the targets per your instructions. But they've been brought down, and are now limited to foot travel – assuming they survived the crash. If they did—' He studied the map again. 'It'll take time to bring in reliable satellite coverage, or another drone, but we *will* soon be able to track them again, and easily pinpoint where to—'

'All of which does us exactly jack shit, Colonel,' Hargrove

cut in. 'You had one task, and you failed. As a result, any survivors that we might recover will have taken steps to destroy the vital cargo you were also informed of, the second we come across them. Which leaves you – and whichever glass-eyed imbecile was piloting that drone – shit out of luck, as far as I and my superiors on the East Coast are concerned.' He stabbed a thumb in Costa's direction, making the agent start. A cold smirk flashed across his lips. The agent wanted full Langley control over this mission? Let him have it, then – on the face, at least.

Flynn's eyes sparked. 'If I may be perfectly frank, sir, I've been made aware of the previous difficulties your team has had in its pursuit of the individuals and cargo in question. Given those, I think there'll be more than enough blame to spread around for any failures.'

Hargrove's smile was colder than Arctic wind. 'We'll see.' He stepped back a pace, putting on a less confrontational air. 'In the interests of minimising said blame, Colonel, what intelligence do you have regarding the crash, and possible survivors?'

The colonel eyed him. With a few crisp motions, he stepped up to the chalkboard-sized smartscreen on the wall behind him. Touching a control, he cleared away the default image of the base insignia, then removed a thumbnail drive from his breast pocket, and slipped it into the reader slot. A map of the Cascade Line appeared, focused on the Mt Rainier region. 'Based on the drone's last satellite coordinates and video feed, we can say with certainty that the target craft went down in this grid, approximately ten miles east of the abandoned town of Eatonville, on the western bank of the Puyallup River,' the Air Force colonel intoned. A bright red dot appeared over the location. 'The evidence is spotty at best, but still shots from the drone's last moments do indicate the possibility of at least one survivor – no information as to which one from the profiles sent to us in advance of your arrival.'

Another dot materialised, this one green. 'The drone was brought down on the eastern side, roughly 300 metres away from the crash site. The radiation levels may have damaged its systems, though my technicians are still working on that. The persistent fallout from the Seattle Bomb – from the epicentre or other drift sites – is often dispersed by prevailing winds, throughout the Puget Sound area and into the mountains. This prevents deep recon of the entire zone, save by satellite, and the technologies we have are incapable of highly detailed shots – mostly very low-resolution images, compared to pre-Turmoil. This also means that we can't send in a clean–up crew to safely recover any bodies or cargo, until the local radlevels decrease. Best case, midnight tonight.'

'Unacceptable,' Hargrove said flatly. 'Any survivors – and there are, I assure you – will have made their way deep into the CZ by that time, along with their cargo. If we're to have any chance of recovering either, we—'

Flynn cut him off this time. 'Mr Hargrove, you're telling me what you need. I'm telling you what we have, and how it can best give you that. My people are the best and most experienced in this area, but they and their equipment have limits. I cannot in good conscience send them out in pursuit of any material or persons within the area in question, even in full protective gear. To do so would only waste valuable personnel, and not bring us one inch closer to retrieving the targets.'

'What about conducting aerial surveys, by chopper or Osprey?' Patrick asked. 'My boys could conduct the sweep; we've got all the necessary gear and transport, and the search wouldn't have to wait until more arrived from FOB Yakima or elsewhere in the Northwest.'

'A good thought, Dave – Colonel. But also not workable.'

Flynn pressed another control below the image, panning out to include the Puget Sound area. Another press of a button, and a multicoloured plume appeared: mostly red, with thin areas along the edge fading to orange and yellow, and stretching from the Kitsap Peninsula all the way to the fringe of the old Yakima military range. 'The fallout from the Seattle area is staying some distance above the ground, primarily due to wind conditions. Your birds could fly higher and still make their sweeps, but they wouldn't be able to pursue or recover anything. Plus they'd run the risk of more serious exposure if the wind shifts, which happens way too damn often around here. As for using the F-40s on station here, or additional craft from other Northwest or Plains bases, they're needed for other missions – and even with them, we'd still have the same rad problems, and poor resolution.' Flynn's forehead creased in frustration. 'Basically, they're asking me and my men to stand guard over Fukushima with a slingshot, and giving us maybe half a dozen stones to do the job.'

Patrick nodded sympathetically. He moved closer to the map, peering at the radiation plume and the two crash sites. 'If we can't come at the targets from behind – why not the front?' he mused aloud. Seeing Flynn's confusion, he pointed to a spot below the plume's southern edge, a few miles north and west of Mt St Helens. 'We refuel the Ospreys, and head south and west, to the Columbia River.' His finger traced a route across the screen. 'We follow it as far as Portland, then cut straight north, setting down or taking station just east of Tumwater. That puts us within range of any route the targets might take to the Sound, and minimises fallout exposure.'

'Like I said, though, we don't have definitive recon capability or fresh intel on the region,' Flynn replied. His tone was still professional, but there was an undercurrent of beseeching now. 'Plus, our estimates of the fallout's path are based mostly on past observations, due to patchy satellite coverage. It could shift south at a moment's notice, and cook your detachment in less than an hour.'

'Not to mention the time constraints,' Hargrove broke in. 'Your plan has merit, but leaves too much of a window for the targets to disappear deeper into the CZ – and perhaps slip past whatever cordon you set up. We need the direct approach at this point, no matter the risks.'

Patrick faced Hargrove, practically coming to attention. 'If that's the case, Mr Hargrove, I'll go with that approach.' His features were solemn and controlled. 'Rangers lead the way. One more time won't be any different.'

Hargrove donned a smile, broad and false. 'I admire your spirit, Colonel.' He gestured out the window. 'Have your men in protective gear and ready on the landing pads in twenty minutes. My team and I will—'

'Just a minute,' Flynn cut in. He stepped closer to Hargrove, perceptibly holding back his temper. 'I've already explained the danger – three times, now – and yet it seems you're still having trouble.' He pointed at Patrick and Costa. 'You may have brought the colonel and his Rangers here under yours and Agent Costa's auspices, Mr Hargrove, but *I* am the senior officer in this region. These men are the finest currently serving, and they are under my purview. I will not allow you to send any of them off into the glowing wilderness, after some runaways who're probably cooked by now, just to satisfy some goddamn timetable!'

Hargrove looked balefully back at him. 'It seems you're forgetting yourself, Colonel. This is my operation, and I will see it finished, by any means. You don't have the slightest idea how vital—'

There was a loud knock at the door. 'What?' Flynn and Hargrove barked in unison.

The door opened, admitting a slim, bespectacled man in grey. Coming to attention, he held out a tablet computer. 'Colonel. Latest reports just came in from the weather people. Given the deviations mentioned, I thought it best to bring them to you personally.'

'What deviations?' Flynn demanded. He took the device, flipping through the images one after another in rapid succession. Finally, he stopped, staring at one page. With controlled formality, he handed the tablet back. 'Thank you, Lieutenant. Send this on to FOB Yakima and the other Line stations, highest priority tag. And get a satlink prepped with our counterparts at the Commonwealth base in Penticton. They've probably seen this as well, but we'll need close contact to coordinate action.'

The young officer saluted, and departed, closing the door behind him. 'Care to enlighten us, Colonel?' Hargrove asked.

The Air Force officer glowered. 'According to our latest data, the prevailing winds from the Pacific have shifted north-northeast, due to an expected thunderstorm sweeping in off the ocean. While it doesn't offer a precise course, the report indicates that the fallout plume will be shifting along a similar trajectory, putting it on track to drop over the northernmost Cascades and over the Canadian border. Night's still expected to settle it in general over its usual spots, but a whole lot of territory that's been barely touched by the stuff in years might be exposed – hence the need for international cooperation.'

Hargrove's smirk was chilly. 'Mother Nature's giving us a little help, then. We can proceed with the eastern approach, and have a better chance at overtaking the targets; my men and Mr Costa will—'

'No,' Flynn interrupted. 'If anything, this calls for more recon, or the alternative route Colonel Patrick suggested. The situation has changed, and the fewer lives we risk in sorting it out—'

'I have a suggestion.' Costa said, cutting through the argument. All eyes turned to him. He spoke equably, with no trace of a wobble. 'What if Colonel Patrick and a small, select group take a slightly different western route, still below the plume, and probe a limited area around the crash site?' His hand moved at a control or two off-screen, and the map changed, panning out to the wider view of the mountains and Puget Sound. 'They follow the I-90 interstate, flying southwest through FOB Yakima's range, and swing below Mt Rainier, coming from the Goat Rocks Wilderness. Mr Hargrove's team can join them and remain on standby at Yakima if anything goes sour, or more of Colonel Patrick's men can load up in the Ospreys for rapid insertion at our signal.'

Patrick studied the map. 'Maybe,' he conceded. He traced a line on the map. 'Angling in a steady northwest arc, we'd come to a stop somewhere right outside this town here: Eatonville.' He marked the spot emphatically with one finger. 'We sit on the place for an hour – two hours, max. If nothing shows, we set up camp further south, out of any likely fallout range, and keep waiting. If something does show, we mark the spot, and call in the second team to approach from the east, closing the other half of the trap. If it turns out a bigger response is needed, Colonel Flynn can monitor and support us from Yakima – assuming he's willing to accompany us, to give more on-the-spot assistance.'

Flynn didn't respond. He studied the agent, and the map. 'Wind's still chancy, like we just learned, but we'd be able to adapt to that much more easily with fewer people, and react more adroitly to any change in the targets' course once we spot it. It keeps risk to personnel at a minimum, gives us a fifty-fifty chance from either direction of bagging the targets, and has the possibility of ending this chase by nightfall.'

The room went quiet once more. Again, Hargrove was first to break it, addressing Costa. 'Well – your approach is certainly better than the others we've heard so far.' He cast an acid side look at Flynn. 'Unless there are any objections?'

Patrick shook his head. 'Don't foresee a problem, given our experience – and your team's training. Provided, of course, that they stay in the supervisory role for the mission; my men have enough to deal with if these targets are as advanced–trained as I've gathered. Any unneeded action – generally called heroics – would only make it worse.'

Hargrove remained patient. 'Very well, Colonel. I suggest you and Colonel Flynn discuss the particulars as to personnel, equipment and weaponry, and prepare the Ospreys for departure. Mr Costa and I will finalise arrangements for my men and for transporting the targets to D.C. – and backup options in the event of failure.' His tone left no doubt about who would be to blame if that occurred.

Scowling, Flynn moved to Patrick's side. They huddled together above the tablet, speaking in lowered tones. Hargrove switched Costa's call and vidfeed to his smartwatch, then headed out the door. Both brown-coated guards followed half a step behind.

When he stepped onto the elevator, Hargrove waited until the doors closed, then brought the watch up, opening his mouth. The agent beat him to the punch. 'It's in the Sound area, isn't it? The HQ for Project Golem.'

Hargrove stopped. Behind him, the guards shifted, hands vanishing beneath their coats. He raised two fingers; they subsided. He touched a couple of buttons on the watchband, making sure the link was secure, and the audio routed to his earpiece. 'What makes you think that?' he asked in a nonchalant tone.

Costa looked steadily back at him. 'Nothing else makes sense. Everything you told me about these targets, stands to reason they'd only fall back to someplace they knew, in every possible detail. They're not just running around the CZ trying to lose us. They're running to the one place they know they can drop out of sight. Somewhere they've known their whole lives. Which can only mean the original site where they were altered, and trained.'

'Very astute,' Hargrove replied. 'I presume you also remember the level of discretion we're still operating under?' He waited for Costa to nod, reluctantly. 'Then I should give you a friendly warning. If this operation is endangered again in any way, whether through failure in the field, or an 'accidental' whisper to an unauthorised person on the way back, you can expect a visit, once I return to D.C.'

Costa's eyes grew wide, for a split second. His voice was tight. 'So that's it, then?'

Hargrove nodded. 'You've known from the start the dangers that came with working alongside people in my area, Agent.' He lowered his arm a bit; the point was made. 'So I suggest you keep any assumptions you might have about the ultimate nature of our assignment to yourself. Unless, of course, you'd like to sample some of the Agency's "enhanced interrogation methods" from a different perspective. A word or two in the right ear, in the right white building – and you will.'

The doors slid open with a loud ding. Beyond was the exit to the tarmac, a pair of wide, bulletproof glass doors. Hargrove ended the call, and donned a confident smile. He had no illusions of the consequences if *he* failed; hell, they only drove him all the harder. But Costa was still labouring under the idea that he and his bosses held the reins – and that he was still able to manage the mission without risking his own hide. In a way, then, Hargrove was doing him a favour, by warning him of the mission's *real* stakes. Working under the gun was far easier when you could spread the pressure around.

He stepped out from the building, into a cold, blustery wind. The sun was shining brightly overhead, with hardly a cloud in the sky, but the temp was typical March, for the Northwest. Several hundred yards across the way, two late-model Black Hawks were being prepped for take–off on the main helipad. From the make of the rotors, and the alterations to the hull itself, Hargrove could see they were the most current 'quiet' design, intended for far stealthier insertions than all previous models, and nearly radar–invisible.

Colonel Patrick emerged from the base building a few minutes later. He was in full battle dress beneath one of the new, paper–thin NBC suits, the hood and respirator thrown back. Eight other men in like garb followed immediately behind, as did two men in pilot coveralls, and Colonel Flynn. They passed by Hargrove in a few long strides. Patrick, however, halted and faced him again. 'I'm assuming you'll be ready to fly at a second's notice, if something happens to *my* team?' he asked with forced calm.

'Of course.' Hargrove inclined his head toward the two guards, standing further back. 'My men have had a few… mishaps along the way here against our targets, I'll admit. But that's largely due to tactics – they're unaccustomed to low-key, low-manpower assignments. When we find whatever spot the targets've gone to ground, they'll be more than ready.'

'*You'll* be accompanying them, then, like at Monticello?' Patrick pressed.

'Possibly, in an observer role.' Hargrove kept a damper on his smile. 'I'm not exactly at the stage in life to be roughing it in the woods anymore. My associates will handle any and all operations, should the need arise. I'll just be the directing brain, as before.' He glanced pointedly at his watch. 'Now, as to the job—'

Nodding, Patrick shook hands – carefully – and strode to the nearest chopper. He turned back toward the base building, locking eyes with Hargrove for the briefest of seconds in a final gauging, suspicious stare. Then he faced forward again, rattling off a stream of orders to his team.

One of the fliers and the four rearmost soldiers broke away, trotting to the second chopper. The rest followed the Ranger officer up to the first craft. Patrick spoke to Flynn for a few seconds, saluted and shook hands, which turned into a short but tight hug. Then the Ranger broke away and joined his men, clasping hands with one of them as he climbed into the chopper. Hargrove could see their lips moving, but the sound of the rotors starting up drowned them out. Flynn moved several yards away, watching the preparations.

The Black Hawk lifted off with a humming whine, angling up and westward. One of his associates moved to his side. Text appeared on Hargrove's lenses: *All team members present and prepped for departure. Signal from team member's confiscated comms device still readable, but fading – expect failure or discovery within three hours. Intended target?*

No target as yet, Hargrove pulsed back. *Possible interference in mission expected, from Agency liaison. Proceed to standby point, and observe Ranger insertion. If successful, land and assist in guarding targets and package on return to Fairchild. If unsuccessful…* He moved closer to the guard. His right hand darted out and back, dropping a small baggie into the guard's jacket pocket. *Further orders to come as situation develops.*

The guard stepped back, signalling to his partner. Hargrove watched them and the other two make for the Osprey they had arrived in earlier. The smile came back, colder and hungrier. Before too much longer – a day, maybe two – everything would fall into place, at long last. And if it took a certain body or two to help the process along, it wouldn't be the first time.

Chapter 13

Outskirts of Eatonville, WA

The sun was low in the west, throwing long pale shadows through the trees and brush. Crouching amid a half-dead bush, Leah abruptly raised a fist, and then flattened it. Twenty paces behind her, Greg and Cayden halted, and went prone. He moved his hand toward the Walther. The Geiger's clicks had been slowing for the last mile – he'd heard it on the closed-band link between their three suit hoodsets – so it couldn't be that she was worried about. They were nearing a gap in the forest, a clearing or the actual border.

Leah's hand came up again, making a V-shape with two fingers, and jabbing to either side of her. Leopard-crawling, Greg came to a halt a few metres to her left, just shy of the clearing's perimeter. Cayden stopped on the right. Drawing her pistol, Leah took several crouched steps forward. Left leg extended in front of her, she moved out from the treeline, staying low. Greg dashed silently up behind the nearest tree, peering out into the clearing.

Just in front of them was a low ridge, covered in tall grass. Several hundred yards further on, the outline of a deep gravel quarry crater was visible, with more grass and even a few saplings pushing up through the grey piles. Other than the half-collapsed processing towers in the centre of the crater, and a pair of rusted semi-truck cabins by the quarry's edge, there was barely any sign of human presence.

Coming erect with slow grace, Leah raised two fingers again, twitching them forward. Pistol at the ready, Greg stepped forth into the clearing, looking right and left. Cayden followed last, likewise alert. They moved at a steady walk, soon reaching a slight, overgrown rise between the main pits and rock piles. A long, paved road, cracked and uneven, meandered to the south, past a vacant parking lot and a collapsed building that might have been a warehouse or garage. The only sound was their breathing, an occasional bird note, and the rustling of the evening wind through the tree boughs.

Cayden came up beside them. 'Is this the place?' he murmured.

'Almost,' Leah whispered back. She pointed down the road. 'That leads to the outermost suburb of Eatonville, and past the local airport. The Sanctuary sometimes has patrols in these areas, but not for the last few months – not enough manpower, and it's easier to operate out of the Fort Lewis area, closer to home.'

Pulling back her sleeve, she activated the holo-interface, calling up a map and the motion detector. 'Nothing that looks like unwanted company – and any scouts of ours would show up, even in clingers. Rad count hasn't changed since we checked a half-hour ago, but it's still enough to mangle long-range comms.' She clicked the screen off. 'It's another fourteen miles to the edge of the old reservation. Figure another hour, maybe two if obstructed. We can hole up in the old airport tonight, and start again at dawn, or keep going through the dark. Riskier, but acceptable.'

Cayden didn't reply. Crouching, he scooped up a handful of dirt and gravel, sniffing at it like a dog checking familiar scents. Leah looked a question at Greg. He glanced around the quarry again, and down the road. 'I say we hole up,' he said at last. 'If anybody from the Sanctuary's in range, they'll find us soon enough, or vice versa.'

Leah nodded, then winced, and flexed her wrists and shoulders. The crash injuries had healed as expected, for all of them, but the afternoon's 'walk' hadn't helped the general soreness and adrenaline crash. 'Seems we could all use a rest, anyway. I'll—'

In a flash, Cayden was on his feet, clapping a hand over Leah's mouth. She stiffened, raising her pistol, but arrested the motion when he raised a finger to his lips. He pointed to the sky, twirling one finger in a circle. *Choppers.* Holding up two fingers now, he jabbed them southward, in the direction of the road. At first, Greg thought he was being paranoid. Then he heard it, too. The faintest disturbance in the air currents – and a low-pitched humming.

He jammed a hand inside his duffel, pulling out the canister. He slapped it against his belt, engaging the nano-clasp; better to have it close at hand. Catching the others' eyes, he pointed to the far side of the quarry, and the treeline just beyond. They could fall back into the trees behind them, but if they *were* being tracked, the choppers would set down on the first open clearing wide enough to accommodate the craft, and they couldn't risk being cut off.

With a brusque nod, Leah bolted. Leaping a good five metres off the rise, she tucked and rolled into a sprint, angling to the right. Greg started to bolt left, but stopped when he saw Cayden standing still, staring up at the sky. He motioned frantically. *Come on!* The older Golem didn't even seem to notice. Gently, he set down his duffel beside him, then straightened, still gazing into space.

The humming grew louder. The air around the two men began to shift and whisper. Greg made one last, desperate wave. Cayden gave no sign that he saw this, or cared. With a snarl of frustration, Greg took off running. Less than ten seconds later, he was crouching low behind a fallen log, out of sight. Poking his head above the decaying pile, he saw Cayden hadn't moved an inch. He hadn't drawn his pistol, or his knife. To any watching eyes, he seemed like a normal, everyday traveller, lounging at the local bus stop or sticking his thumb out on the highways.

A rustle in the leaves and branches beside him: Leah. Her face was pale with anger and fear. 'What the *fuck* is he doing?!' she hissed.

Before Greg could answer, the humming rose to a crescendo, pressing at his eardrums like the wings of a Cessna-sized hornet. He pulled the clinger's hood over his head and stabbed the sealant button at his collar; Leah made the same move. The sound dropped, but the air vibrations increased, stirring dust and dirt everywhere. He slackened his jaw to keep his teeth from rattling and dropped the eye screens on the hood.

Metal flashed in the lowering sun, to Greg's right. Whipping around, he saw two choppers emerge from over the southernmost trees, bearing for the quarry. *Black Hawks. 'Wraith' upgrades,* he assessed unconsciously. *Mostly used for insertion work. Rarely armed, given the risks of breaking stealth cover, like with the* Grey Witch *– but that doesn't mean they don't have deployable rotary cannon in either bay.*

One slowed, coming to a hovering halt – the command craft, judging by the two dulled yellow bars painted above the cockpit. The other kept moving, making a slow loop around the quarry's length, before swinging back over the main pit, stopping above its lip. Chunks of gravel and dirt spiralled all over, coating Cayden's poised figure. The older Golem didn't even twitch, looking serenely back and forth at the two craft.

Foot by foot, the command chopper dropped, coming to a rest on a patch of bare earth thirty yards away from Cayden. The bay doors slid open. Four men in NBC suits and mask scrambled out, fanning out in a wide semicircle. Each one held an XM rifle, trained on Cayden's face or chest. Greg zoomed in on him with the eye scanners, and saw that he was smiling dimly, like a housewife or chef who had an excellent spread laid out. *Why the Christ is he doing* that? *They've practically slapped the cuffs on, and we're just sitting…*

His mental train halted, with a screech of imagined brakes. At first, he was too dumbstruck to do anything but stare. Then his lips curled in a bemused smirk. *If he can pull that off – well, he* is *the first.*

Shifting a little, he ejected the clip from his pistol and tucked it away. Leah glanced sharply at him. Behind the screens, her eyes were wide and confused, even more so when he pulled a new clip from another pouch, one with a white tag near the top. Slotting it in, he whispered, 'Trust me.' She looked at him in confusion for a moment, then dipped her chin, and followed his lead.

He brought the pistol to bear on the scene, staring down the sight. Two more figures had descended from the landed chopper, also in NBC gear. One was an officer, upper echelon by his bearing and attitude, carrying a pistol. The second man was unarmed, so far as Greg could see, and had a similar military posture, but it was clear he was an outsider. *Must be the requisite spook, making sure of the capture.*

One of the other soldiers barked at Cayden. The older Golem went to his knees and clasped both hands behind his head, that tranquil smile still on his face. The crescent of soldiers moved closer to him, keeping several yards between him and themselves.

The officer and the spook came up behind the line. The former kept his weapon trained on Cayden. From the set of his mask, he was speaking to the spook out of the corner of his mouth. The spook muttered something back. Strangely, he seemed less eager than the soldiers to approach Cayden. That was a first, for Greg. *All the spook types we dealt with before, they're the type to shoot or cuff first chance they get – including whatever the fuck those things were at Chicago and Monticello. Might be a noob – except all the rest before were professionals. Doesn't fit.* He frowned.

The two men seemed to come to an agreement. Still keeping his weapon trained on Cayden, the officer waved to the team's sergeant. The man slung his weapon back over one shoulder. With his free hand, he pulled a pair of thin metal loops from a belt pouch, connected by an even slimmer wire. 'Clinchers', in standard jargon. Built similar to the shock-cuffs used by civilian cops, these were a blend of steel cable and nano-fibre, strong enough even to resist Golem strength.

Cayden angled his head toward the NCO as he approached. His smiling face was still fixed, but now there was a hint of something more. Mirth, as at a good prank – and, to Greg's surprise, a kind of sadness or resignation. It was as if he longed for the cuffs, but knew he wasn't meant to wear them. Watching for any twitch, the sergeant stepped behind him, and cautiously extended the first loop around his left wrist.

A sharp *pop!* rang out, echoing though the quarry. A blue-lit object the size of a baseball erupted from the woods to Greg's north, zipping high above the two choppers. Greg's eye screens dropped three more filters, blocking out most of the white flash of EMP. Looking down the sights again, he saw the hovering chopper shake and wobble, the engine hurling sparks and flame as it shorted out. The four soldiers, the officer and the spook were cringing and hunched over, moaning and shouting to one other. Less than two seconds after, the craft struck the ground, crumpling the landing gear and shearing off its rotors.

The whole scene dissolved into a haze of sound and motion. Even before the crash, Cayden was up and moving. He seized the sergeant's arm with both hands, pulling him over one shoulder and slamming him to the ground with a crackle of breaking bones. Leaping to his feet, he seemed to blur, reappearing several yards away, behind the two nearest soldiers. Two short jabs, and the men collapsed, gasping for air through cracked ribs.

By this time, the officer was moving himself. Without hesitation, he swung his weapon toward Cayden's back. At once, Greg's finger jerked. The pistol spat twice, striking the man in the chest and sides. He jerked and writhed, before collapsing. Greg winced; the stun bullets were powerful enough to knock out full-grown elephants, even in the lower-charge rounds he'd chosen – or fully-suited Golems. The two soldiers left upright spun to face the trees. Two shots from Leah took down the furthest of them, but the second opened up on full auto.

Half a dozen slugs punched into Greg's chest, shoulder and head. He tumbled flat on his back, dizzy, ears ringing. Leah's gun barked twice more, followed by a muffled shout. He blinked and turned his neck several times, checking for new damage: aside from the 'healing' indents in the fabric, none. Thanking the clinger's designers for the thousandth time, he pushed himself up on his knees, scanning the field again. All five soldiers from the first chopper were on the ground now, groaning in pain from cracked bones, nerve shock, or both. The pilots were still in the cockpit, huddled over their instruments. The spook wasn't in sight; he'd either ducked flat or was hiding in the chopper.

To the left, Cayden was emerging from the wreck site of the second bird. He carried an NBC-clad soldier by the collar in each massive hand, holding them almost a foot off the ground. Delicately, he laid them flat, ignoring their moans. Stalking back to the crash, he returned moments later with two more soldiers, placing them beside their comrades.

Still wary, Greg stood up. Beside him, Leah imitated the motion. 'You all right?' she asked. Her features were hidden by the hood, but the worry was plain.

'Yeah.' He stretched and wiggled his arms. 'Nothing a couple hours *away* from gunfights won't cure.' She just looked at him, not speaking. He sighed, and cracked his neck. 'I'm fine. Really.'

Out of the blue, a new voice crackled in their hoods. It was female, hard as granite. 'Getaway, calling Lockpick – repeat, Getaway calling Lockpick. If you are receiving, acknowledge and authenticate at once.'

Greg and Leah shared a surprised look. Pressing a finger to his earbud, Greg looked northward, where the EMP shot had come from. 'Getaway, this is Lockpick, acknowledged. Authentication: Golf-Lima-Delta-Charlie-314.' A simple code – their initials, their target and date of departure – but the signal was close, and it'd be scrambled beyond outside detection by the fallout.

There was a pause. Then the voice returned, a bit softer. 'Authentication confirmed. Report as to mission outcome.'

Greg looked out again, at the multiple bodies and two wrecked craft. Cayden reappeared, this time carrying the two pilots from the crash, and with two XMs slung across his back. Unlike the soldiers, these men were flailing wildly, trying and failing to break free. Ignoring this, the older Golem walked past the row of unconscious bodies, set them down, and cuffed each man over the head with one hand – not enough for a knockout, but plenty to rattle them. Picking up the clinchers from where they'd fallen, he laced them around the pilots' wrists. Moving to the side of the fallen sergeant, he removed several more clinchers, using them to bind the other eight together in pairs. Most of them were too out of it to notice; those who weren't earned a smack of their own, before desisting.

A flicker of motion, by the intact chopper. The spook was standing up, both hands empty. Cayden spotted him – and then he was beside him. Before the other man could flinch, the older Golem smacked him across the back of his head, causing him to go limp, then lifted him bodily by the back of his suit with one hand. With a final warning gesture at the assembled bunch, he started for Greg and Leah's spot. The spook squawked in pain, but didn't try to break away.

Taking all this in, Greg pressed his ear again. 'Outcome is Sigma, Papa Foxtrot Alpha. Repeat: Sigma, Papa Foxtrot Alpha.' *Success, Pending Final Action,* in the parlance they'd decided on before departing. *Not just here, either.*

The pause was longer this time. When the voice returned, the undercurrent of pleasure was easy to hear. 'Acknowledged. Extraction team is incoming, to the north. Stand by to confirm.'

Stepping out from the treeline, Greg spotted four human-shaped figures emerging above the quarry's northwest end. Zooming in, he saw all of them were garbed in clingers, their exterior patterns mimicking the surrounding forest. They moved at a steady, unhurried walk, aiming weapons toward the wreck or the trees around the clearing. He sucked in a long, relieved breath, and retracted his hood.

Cayden halted, dumping his prisoner at his feet. The man moaned, turning over on his back. Ignoring him, Cayden stared hard at the approaching party. 'That's our pickup?'

'Yeah.' Pulling her hood back, Leah looked shrewdly at the older man. 'You knew they were waiting, didn't you?' She held up her console arm. 'Only camo patterns on other clingers can hide the wearer from the types of scanners we're equipped with – but *you* knew anyway.'

The ghost of a smile appeared on Cayden's face, for the first time since they'd met him. 'You should know most of all that there's more to tracking than tech, or even your eyes and ears. *Everything* tells – smell, texture, the slope of the ground, the resistance to wind.' He kicked at the ground, throwing up a small cloud of dust, and inhaled. 'The prints were covered, but the disturbance was even more obvious than the trail. There were depressions in the bushes and gravel piles at the far end – no need for zoom-in to see them. And clingers have always had a faint odour, whether in the field or at the Facility. Something artificial, almost metallic – I suppose it's part of the creation process.'

'And that whole "lone bait" charade?' *Plus the look on your face, just before the EMP shot. Wonder what that was all about?* Greg held back the question, though it wouldn't go away soon.

'The rotors said everything,' Cayden said, in the same pedantic voice. 'If they were out for blood, they wouldn't waste their time with the stealth modifiers. All I needed was to stay in the open, and they'd come to me.' His tone became darker, more serious. He kicked the prone man before them in the leg, hard enough to hurt without breaking. The spook yelped, but held still. 'Plus, it's beyond time that we got a better idea of who's chasing us, and why.'

By this time, the four new arrivals were a few yards away. One broke off to check the wreck and collect the Rangers' weapons. Two others moved to stand guard over the prisoners, and look over the disabled intact chopper.

The fourth figure stepped up to the travellers. One hand pressed the hood button, and yanked it back, exposing a feminine face – white and youthful, with a short bob of pale blond hair. Her eyes, electric-blue with deep lines, roved over the three of them, and the group of bound soldiers. When she spoke, it was with the same hard voice as over the headset. 'See you picked up some extra trinkets on your D.C. jaunt.' She gave them another once-over. 'So you've got it?'

Delicately, Greg unclasped the canister, and held it out. Megan's expression didn't change, but he could sense the relief in her tough, wiry posture. She looked to Cayden, her gaze wary and calculating. 'And he's the one who can open and decode it?'

Cayden stared back stoically. 'To an extent. Seems there's another layer to get through – and I was curious enough to see what was so important beneath it to drag you younger types out after me.'

'Good.' Megan straightened, and gestured to the road. 'We don't normally patrol this far, as you know. But when Jorge's system picked up the drone crash, we figured you couldn't be far off, so we extended the range. We've got transport waiting by the old town airport – two Spectre-modified Humvees, full charge as well as backup gas.'

'So Overwatch is up?' Leah asked, pleased. Greg was, too. Jorge had been working round the clock since his own arrival at the Sanctuary to develop just the right all-encompassing software to piggyback on the world's sparse satellite and other surveillance networks – and mask it appropriately, no easy task with the NeoNet upgrade, and watchdogs on almost every access point. If it was working at last, the Sanctuary stood a much better chance of taking root – and guarding itself against anybody with the military equivalent of pliers and weed killer.

'Yep, two days ago. He isn't a hundred per cent on its range beyond the Cascades, but as long as there're satellites in place, anywhere in the world, the program'll work fine.' Megan glanced up at the steadily darkening sky, and the clouds forming to the east. 'Weather's supposed to take a nosedive overnight, which'll limit any satellite coverage. And the rad-count ought to mask any thermals.' Her eye cast critically over the prone figure before them, and the prisoners, now sitting close together and watching their captors closely while they ministered to their comrades' minor wounds. 'Which, if you're expecting us to lug this bunch along, are going to draw more patrols and drones like a gazelle carcass draws jackals.'

'We're not taking all of them.' Greg pointed to the man at Cayden's feet. 'This one has all the markings of a spook. Doubtful that he's the brains, but whoever's directing this wouldn't send anybody he didn't trust to handle a sweep like this.' He thought he noticed the captive shift at this, but ignored it. 'And unless I'm mistaken—' he waved at the group of prisoners '—there's somebody high-ranking in charge of *them*, more than just a typical front-line officer. Either one of them might have intel on exactly *who* it is that's been after the three of us. And if it comes to it, it'd be smart to have some bargaining chips.'

'And the others?' Megan moved a hand to the hilt of her knife, as if she expected the answer.

Would've been the one for me too, not all that long ago, Greg thought. *Still the same gut reaction in all of us, I guess. And she's always been more in favour of it, after her time in the Caucasus, and in Ukraine.* 'We collect their heavy weapons, ground the last chopper for good, and leave them. Any transponders they've got are fried, but they've got the suits, rations, and medkits.' He squinted eastward. 'Somebody'll be around soon – and I have a pretty good idea who.'

Leah's grim nod said she caught his drift. She looked at them questioningly, but she didn't push the subject. Instead, she brought two fingers to her mouth, and whistled sharply. The other three in the patrol trotted over. With their hoods up, Greg didn't recognise any of them, but that wasn't too strange. The Sanctuary's numbers had been growing by ones and twos every week or so for a while, and plenty of the old hands spent most of their days on the perimeter – in full gear, without tags – so it was easy for faces to lose familiarity.

Megan relayed Greg's suggestions to the patrol in a few terse phrases. Not bothering with salutes, they set to work at once. One – a woman, by her stature – climbed into the surviving chopper, and began yanking the controls and panels free, throwing up small geysers of sparks and smoke. The other two – both men, one stockier than the other – focused on the prisoners. The taller one gathered up all the spare ammo clips, holding them under one arm as he lifted each of the XMs by the strap with the other. The stockier man went over each man's cuffs, checked the seals on their suits, and ensured that every one of them had at least a knife – no worries about their trying to cut or shoot their way free. A few tried to struggle, but were swiftly quieted by their own comrades.

Activating her sleeve interface, Megan called up a map. At Greg's glance, Cayden strode over to the captives, undid the cuffs on the officer and marched him back to the throng of Golems. Up close, even through the suit, it was clear the man was a long-haul leader. He held himself erect, looking over each of them. No doubt he was searching for any weaknesses. His gaze lingered briefly on the other suited prisoner among them, whom Leah had pulled to his feet by that point, clinching his arms behind him. The two men's eyes met, but neither said a word. *Some other connection there, beyond the professional*, Greg concluded. *Have to chat it over, back home; might prove useful, and increase 'chip value,' once we're clear on* who it is we've got.

When the last of the patrol had rejoined them, Megan slid her hood back on. Greg and Leah did likewise; Cayden just stood, waiting. 'Good work, all of you,' the patrol leader said. Her voice softened, fractionally. 'By the way... welcome home.'

Chapter 14

Forward Operating Base Yakima, Eastern WA State

Colonel Flynn scowled at the map display. 'Nothing,' he muttered. 'Not a single word, in the last hour. Patrick would've signalled by now, rads or not, and no matter how the operation turned out.' He turned, aiming his glare at Hargrove. 'There a reason why *you're* still here, instead of holding up your end of this asinine plan?'

'Trust me, Colonel, I want to be out there as badly as you do,' Hargrove said. He kept his voice calm – soothing, even. He pointed to the map, which was focused on Eatonville. A wide streak of orange was imposed over the image, darkening intermittently to red in certain spots. 'But until the fallout clears, or drops to acceptable levels, we can't risk sending a search party. Your men have MOPPs and all other necessary gear, but the radiation counts out of the Sound are a guess on good days. If something *is* wrong with Patrick and Costa's team, there's no point throwing more men into the hot zone after them.'

Flynn's scowl deepened. He stomped away from the wall, looking out a nearby window. Outside, there were no personnel in sight. Thunder sounded, not far off, but no rain had fallen yet in the area. Per CZ procedure, the base was buttoned tight against any fallout that seeped across the Cascades: all patrol choppers and other vehicles stored, every building pressurised and pumping recycled air. There was little chance the active radioactivity would reach so far, but the precautions had kept contamination to a minimum since the base's creation.

The colonel studied the view, not speaking. When he faced Hargrove again, some of the temper had left his face. 'Where's your team holed up?'

Hargrove zoomed out the map image. 'Here: a little town called Packwood. It's the best possible spot, given the terrain and expected drift. They can be in the air in seconds, once we hear or see sign of the team.'

'There's no fallout bound for that area?' Flynn asked.

'Not from what the ground sensors say, and those are generally more reliable than the satellite forecasts. The bulk is sifting to around Rainier, running in a stretch from Easton to Randle, and pockets to the southwest. They're right on the edge and may pick up a light dusting at the worst, but they can deal with that.'

Flynn nodded. 'Tough bastards, then. Some point, you'll have to tell me where you found them.' Hargrove said nothing, only waited. The colonel sighed and looked to the window again. 'Just have to hope David and his people are tougher.'

'You worked together before?' Hargrove asked, as he sensed he was supposed to.

'South Korea, in '36. I was an F-40 pilot; he was part of the Ranger contingent added at the last minute, when the North Koreans were about done massing north of the DMZ. Turns out we weren't needed, not after those "covert ops" or whatever they were tearing up the DPRK from inside. Ran into each other in a bar in Seoul after de-mobbing, got to bragging about who would've racked up the most points if there *had* been any – one thing led to another pretty fast.'

The colonel smiled, rubbing his jaw reminiscently. 'Three years after that, we're both sent to Luzon, to go eye-to-eye with the Chinese after the Hong Kong dirty bomb and the cyberattack in Shanghai. Turns out he did a tour as a de facto Peacekeeper in Pakistan, after Karachi got nuked in '37 and that whole country went to the shits. Said he heard some damn weird stories in the refugee camps: all about "giant demons in black" stealing nukes, destroying weapons caches for the Islamists and other factions. Supposedly they knifed most of the leaders, too, which pushed the rest to the table.'

'Really?' Hargrove kept his face impassive. 'He believe those stories?'

'Not really – but he didn't rule it out,' Flynn said. 'Said it was probably some gung-ho glory boys: the SEALs, or some burn-even-before-reading CIA crap. He joked that if they were real, they'd have their work cut out for them in China... after they caught up to the Rangers, of course.'

The humour faded from the colonel's face. 'Three days later, I'm up in my fighter, eyeballing the PRC fleet hovering between the Philippines and that big artificial island base they built back in the teens. One of my squadron drifted too close to the picket line... and inside of two seconds, we were all dodging SAMs and long-range flak. We got away with no losses, and the Seventh Fleet launched a couple salvos, making the PRC pull back. With the occasional airstrikes and cruise missiles being traded over the next four days, I was sure World War III was bearing down fast. Wasn't for the intel pinning the attacks in China on that Xinjiang group, *we* probably wouldn't be talking now – along with God knows how many other people.'

'No arguments here,' Hargrove said, emphatically. The emotion wasn't wholly fake. If war *had* broken out in the South China Sea, his infant operation would have gone up in smoke along with D.C.. Instead, both sides had stood down – and then started imploding from the first events of the Turmoil. The following twelve years had been plenty of time to finalise his team, put them to the test, and win the right backing. A hand closed into a fist beneath the table. If just *one* part of the whole process had gone off *exactly* right, without any hitches…

He shelved the thought, focusing on Flynn's words again. 'Barely a month later, we're both called home, to deal with insurgents and riots in our own backyard. Patrick went down to LA, and I was posted to Lackland AFB. Quiet duty, for the most part; the Army kept the lid on in Dallas-Fort Worth and other cities, and the cartels and border warlords never got outside Brownsville or El Paso. Thought at times I'd be able to serve out my term without squeezing the trigger. Even had plans laid out for a reunion: Patrick, a few others – and my brother Eddie, after he finished his tour at Fort Lewis, around the start of '51.'

Hargrove's focus had been waning, in the face of the colonel's chatter. All at once, it sharpened. 'Fifty-one. So he was—'

Flynn's head went up, then down. 'He was a pilot, same as me.' The colonel's eyes became a touch brighter. 'Talked to him the day before the Bomb – professionally and personally. Turns out he was flying the same kind of patrols I was, keeping the skies clear above Sea-Tac and the other bases in the area.' The brightness grew, from anger or pain. 'He said it was dull, but worthwhile, although he wouldn't have minded seeing *something* happen, so he could show off his skill.'

The colonel pivoted away again, staring unseeing at the window. Wisely, Hargrove said nothing. Inside, he felt a touch of satisfaction. So there *had* been something off, with the delivery. Not that it helped much now, of course, but it didn't hurt to know. *Only goes to show what still happens way too often, when you do things remotely.* He picked up his jacket. 'If you don't mind, Colonel, I think I'll beg some coffee from the cafeteria here. My personal link to my team is still in place; if something comes in while I'm gone, I'll be back in a heartbeat.'

'Very well.' Shaking himself a little, Flynn cleared his throat, and studied the map again. 'Still no real change in the plume's direction.' His features turned thoughtful. 'Maybe once night comes, the wind will drop enough for a recon flight. Ground would still be too hot, but we'd have the chance to get a fix on Patrick's team. Long shot with the usual weather in this area, but—'

'Not a bad idea,' Hargrove said, nodding. 'I'll send word to my people, have them ready to lift off the second they see any shifts.' Hesitantly, he waved to the window. 'Might be they'll need backup; it's a lot of a ground to cover, even with the fallout. My people can handle the rads to a degree, but I can't order any of yours to—'

'Not a problem,' Flynn said firmly. 'We've been camped out here long enough to know *all* the risks – and to never leave anyone out to face them. Any help that's needed, we're ready.'

With a polite nod, Hargrove left the room. Starting down the hall, he pulsed, *Report.*

Text appeared at once: *Ranger landing site located. Two choppers – one destroyed, one damaged beyond repair, based on closer observation. Evidence of localised EMP detonation, as with Predator shoot-down. Recon of area still limited, but signs point to targets gaining ground transport from nearby ghost town, deeper within CZ. Tracker signal from comms device terminated at 1805; reason unknown, but suspect critical damage, resulting in loss of power. No indications as to Target's ultimate destination. Count eight survivors – four Rangers, four flight crew. No evidence of any distress signals having passed through jamming measures. Standing guard over survivors now, and awaiting instructions.*

Hargrove hid a smile, even though he was alone. Patrick and his team had poked the nest, then. Odds were they'd been stung to death before even knowing where from. Speaking of... *Status of colonel?*

A short pause. Then: *Status unknown. No indication present at landing site.*

He stopped dead. *None? No body?* With all he'd seen and knew of the targets, it'd been reasonable to assume they wouldn't leave survivors, the better to reduce their trail to whatever hideout or group backing them. They never had before, when working under legitimate orders; why should they have stopped after going underground?

Confirmed. Suspect individual was removed by Golem strike force, based on remarks from survivors. Another pause. *Remarks also indicate another individual present; description matches that of Agency liaison.*

Hargrove's vision flared red. He took several deep breaths, flexing his hands over and over. He hadn't anticipated this. The tracker had been a slim hope at best, but it had pointed him in the right direction, and there was no sign the targets had suspected it. But this – and now *Costa*? How *he'd* snuck out West to join the Ranger team, Hargrove had no idea – but evidently, he'd managed it. The Golems must have pegged him for a spook at first sight, and decided to grill him. Or he'd made some sort of deal to save his own ass, probably promising some sort of boon the targets and their bosses wanted from

Langley. Whatever the reason, the bastard was headed straight for the heart of the Project. When he got there, and if he started poking around its ruins...

Gradually, the anger died to a low burning in his chest. The chase was coming to a head any which way. Tonight's events only forced him to move up the timetable. *Understood,* he pulsed. *Conclude local area recon.*

Confirmed, came the reply. *Orders regarding survivors?*

The survivors – Hargrove paused. A little smile came to his face. Maybe there *was* a silver lining in this screw-up – one that he could thank the targets for, no less. He'd considered it when Costa and Patrick had first left, but had held off on the decision, until he knew *exactly* what the situation demanded. Now he did. *Execute Clean Sweep protocol. Return to Packwood once task completed, and resume monitoring of all frequencies and other energy spots within CZ until 0700. Will inform Fairchild commander at that time, and organise next insertion – possibly into Seattle area.* The tiniest pause. *Also prep for water-based action. Locate likeliest spots for water transport prior to my arrival.*

He signed off without waiting for a reply. When he resumed walking, there was the slightest bounce in his step – more anticipation than any kind of pleasure. All wasn't right with the world, or his plans, but he was coming out on top in the end. Of that, he had no doubt.

A soft alarm note pinged from the room's console. The man seated before it jerked out of sleep. 'Hmm?' He sat upright. 'What is it?' he asked groggily.

The holo-screen blinked on, showing a rough map of Puget Sound, and several scrolling data columns. A bright red dot appeared in the right corner of the map, inching toward the Sound.

Rubbing at his eyes, the man peered at the screen – and stiffened. He spoke into the ether. 'Are you sure?'

'Yes, Richard,' a voice replied – female, soft and melodious. 'The transponder was detected five seconds ago, passing within the border of my scanning range. All queries to determine authenticity and security have returned one hundred per cent. Current progress and course indicate the drive will reach the area designated as the "Sanctuary" within one hour.'

The man squinted at the map. 'Is there any way of determining exactly *who* is carrying the drive? Or whether it's being monitored by other parties?'

'No, Richard – I'm sorry. Due to our mandated isolation, I am unable to access any drone or satellite surveillance networks in the vicinity. Queries show, however, that the biometric security measure was cleared approximately twelve hours ago, though the password shield remains unbroken. This would seem to indicate Subject G1 is in possession of the drive, and seeks to access its full contents.'

Slowly, the man stood up. 'My God,' he whispered. Recovering, he pressed a control. The image winked out. 'Continue monitoring the transponder signal, as well as all frequencies out of the Sanctuary. Also reconfirm all eyes and ears along the outer perimeter.'

'Yes, Richard.' There was a second's silence. 'All requested measures are in place. Is there anything else that you suggest be done?'

'Yes. Please confirm all safeguards are in place here.' He adjusted his worn, faded white coat, in a show of preparation—or resignation. 'Looks like we'll be having a family get-together, very soon.'

Chapter 15

Old Evergreen State College Campus ('The Sanctuary')

A low buzzing reached Greg's ears. He sat up at once, tapping at his sleeve to shut off the alarm: 7am. Then he lay back down, passing a hand over his face. After reaching the Sanctuary, twelve hours before, he'd been too tired to do anything but mouth a few hellos, and shake a few hands. In minutes, he'd headed straight to his room, still in the clinger – and that was the last he remembered.

He kicked away the bedsheet and sat up again, blinking away the last vestiges of sleep. Even after nearly five years, the room was still drab and spartan. Once one of several modular units for student housing, it was now a shared spot for Leah and himself. The two separate beds that normally took up the room had been pushed together, secured with a few planks and nails. The walls were bare, except for a few tatters of ancient, torn-down posters. On the cheap, chipped wooden desk beside the bed rested a pen-sized holo-console drive, and several new printouts. A cursory glance showed them to be routine reports on the Sanctuary's perimeter, stores, and links to the outlying posts. Looking out of the room's one window, he could see sun-drenched ferns and bushes, dewy with the night's rain.

A shaft of light fell over the hallway floor: the main door opening. Instantly, he stuck a hand under his pillow, bringing out the pistol. Unsheathing his knife with the other, he moved next to the bedroom door with barely a rustle. Soft padding on the creaky floorboards, halting well before the door. A voice whispered, 'Greg? You awake?'

He relaxed. 'Yeah, come in.' Sheathing his weapons, he stepped out from the room, and saw Leah standing in the kitchen's entryway. Her clinger gleamed in the overhead lights, patterned to mimic the rainforest-like setting outside. 'How'd you sleep?' she asked.

'Not too bad.' He stretched both arms, turning his head back and forth. 'You?'

'Same. I stayed up a little when we got here, in case something changed. Finally hit the sack around ten.' Was there a hint of disappointment in her voice? If so, it was gone fast, replaced by her usual cool professionalism. 'Jorge called me in about an hour ago. He wanted to go over the latest patrol reports with us once you were up; I left them on the desk.'

He moved back into the room, picking up the thin stack of sheets. 'Anything critical?'

'Update on the population, for one: we're at 300 even, as of two days ago. The rest of Megan's patrol, they brought the numbers up: two from the Sahara, and one each from Colombia, Afghanistan and southern China. Didn't get their names yet, but we'll all know soon enough.' Looking over his shoulder, she pointed at several passages. 'Also got word on the fallout plume: came down as expected, and the few posts we've got in its path all hunkered down in the hardened shelters well in advance. Sensors were blinded by it and the storm for about an hour, but we had observers ready in the non-affected areas, and they saw nothing coming our way from the east, or anywhere else. Megan's out with another patrol now, checking for tracks or other signs of any visitors. Haven't heard from Hiroshi yet – Jorge mentioned he was out in the field, too, but couldn't tell me exactly where.' That was the fifth Council member, and their agreed-upon leader.

'The two we brought in?' Greg inquired.

'Jorge's taking care of that. He's got them in the central area now, under guard. Once the whole Council's back on campus, we can decide on what approach to take.'

Greg nodded. 'Cayden?'

'He's keeping watch over them.' She hesitated. 'He hasn't said anything since we arrived. I checked in on him before coming here, but he was just sitting outside the room, this quiet look on his face. I tried to talk to him, but he just ignored me. Far as I know, he hasn't left the building all night.'

He didn't stick around for the greetings, then, Greg pondered. *We were all tired, including him – but he volunteered for guard duty right off the bat. Didn't seem curious or suspicious about this place at all, either. Maybe he's hanging back, observing the most obvious threat – our two 'guests' – while he evaluates* us. Putting that thought aside, he refocused on Leah. 'What about the canister?'

'Jorge's hooked it to the main servers in the Library. From what he told me, the drive's first security layer's still open – we won't need Cayden to donate again.' Her eyes told she knew how much of a can of worms *that* was going to be. She cleared her throat. 'No idea yet if he's broken the password, or found anything else in the canister's design that might help.'

'Then we'd better see if he needs *our* help,' Zipping his clinger up fully, Greg patted at his chest, double-checking the weapons, and picked up the reports in one hand. A bit clumsily, he took Leah's hand with the other. Her smile said she didn't mind.

The air outside was fresh, overlain with a thick scent of forest decay. Beneath that smell was something else – a kind of ashy, metallic odour, like the leftovers of a campfire mixed with melted-down batteries. The Geiger counter at Leah's belt began ticking. *Fragrance of the Bomb*, Greg reflected darkly. The campus hadn't been in the direct path of the detonation, its aftershock waves or the initial fallout, but there was still plenty hovering around the Sound, often deposited by storms like last night's.

Nearly all the old dorm buildings they passed along the way were deserted, boarded up or otherwise closed to the elements. To their left, the athletic fields had been left to grow wild; there were plans to turn them to cropland this year, if enough manpower and tools could be pulled together for the job. Per Council decision, there were only a few dozen people allowed to live full-time in the Sanctuary's zone, the better to avoid overcrowding, resource exhaustion – and a possible missile strike eliminating the entire community. Smaller outposts of five to twenty had been set up all along the perimeter, from the southern outskirts of Everett to the border of the abandoned Skokomish reservation. They served as lookouts for any trouble out of the clear zones, and entry points for the few smuggling routes they'd been able to establish; Greg and Leah had used one to slip out of the CZ at the start of their mission. Anyone observing the outer edge of the campus would assume the place was still abandoned, or at best being occasionally picked over by looters.

The core area was different. Two heavy machine gun posts were concealed on either side of the walkway, immediately past the freshman dorm – concealed to non-Golem eyes, that was. Greg waved gravely to the clinger-clad gun crews, and received a few like gestures. Passing the Rec centre and the Activities Building – the latter of which served as the Sanctuary's main armoury, canteen and radio facility – he noted the rooftop snipers and light mortars at each corner. The offices and Comm Building beyond these had also been fortified and converted to temporary housing, additional storage and vantage points.

All the entrance points to Red Square, the main gathering area, were also sandbagged and guarded. Beyond these, the square was a subdued hive of commotion. Two dozen or so Golems in clingers, military overalls or salvaged civilian get–ups moved about in all directions, on all manner of tasks: manhandling supply crates, heading to or from sentry posts, handing out weapons or other necessities, poring over documents or sleeve readouts. All of them moved with dancer-like grace, even when burdened with easily 500 pounds or more of gear or other goods. Though differing widely in skin and hair colour, they all shared the same traits: calm, sculpted features, lithe athletic forms, and cool, collected attitudes.

More sentries paced along the edges of the Library roof, and atop the clock tower and the old lab buildings. There were hardly any vehicles in sight: the number of usable ones they'd recovered or stolen, civilian and military, was still pitifully small, and reserved for patrols or long-distance courier runs between the outposts when the radios were down. Three or four Spectre-plated Humvees – so called because of the radar-invisible plating which also reflected and projected the vehicle's surroundings – were grouped together near the chemistry section. A half-dozen men and women were tinkering with the engines, and checking the heavy machine gun mounted atop each one.

By contrast, the Library was quiet, almost tomblike. Just a few people were present in the ground-floor computer lab

– a few holo-terminals, and two entire walls of servers and memory banks – or moving about in the medical and storage areas that had been established in the second floor offices. Greg and Leah made a beeline for the former, exchanging a few polite greetings and nods along the way.

A lone, black-haired man sat at the nearest terminal, poring over line after line of data on the screen before him. The canister sat to his left, opened, the thumb drive plugged into the console. His features were tanned and swarthy, pointing to the Central American ancestry his file indicated, and to a lifetime in the field in every climate imaginable. Jorge had been among the most talented engineering and technical experts in the Project pre-Turmoil, and the foremost in both fields among all others in their mutual 'class'. Now he was the primary logistics man for the Sanctuary, and, like Greg and Leah, a member of the five-person governing Council.

Typing a last command, Jorge grumbled and stood up, disconnecting the drive and sliding it into a belt pouch. Stretching, he turned around, facing the two of them. His eyes, heavily shadowed and lined, lit up. 'Ah, Greg!' He stuck out a hand. 'You doing okay?' His voice was relaxed yet concerned.

'Closest to it since we left, anyway,' Greg replied, shaking hands. 'Sorry I wasn't able to drop by the Library when I arrived; we had to take care of our guests, and—'

Jorge waved his words away. 'No need for excuses. Anybody could see you were wiped out.' His smile was brilliantly white. 'After three near-miss deaths, plus a plane crash, anyone would want a little quiet time.'

'True.' Greg frowned. 'With the way things are right now, though, I doubt we'll have *any* of that for a while.'

Jorge nodded, all business once more. 'We've set the prisoners up in the Comm Building, in one of the side rooms. Guards outside all the entrances, and your friend by their door.

None of the outlying posts've reported sighting any more choppers, or drones of any kind. Nothing coming by ground or sea, either, according to Overwatch. There was a blip on the radar around eight last night, not far east of Rainier, but that disappeared almost as soon as we spotted it. Nothing else's been seen from any likely approach in that area.'

'What about the patrol we left behind?' Leah asked. 'Any sign this blip might've been a search craft?'

'I scanned the area where you left them through Overwatch, just a few minutes ago. The fallout and cloud cover were still a problem, but the satellites responded fine, now that the program's fully inserted.' Jorge's features turned grave. 'No sign of the patrol, except for the two choppers – they'd been torched, it looks like. A pro job, too. Maybe someone managed to pick them up while the storm and the fallout left us temporarily blind, but there's no indication that the blip came anywhere near the site, if it was in fact S&R. Megan and her team headed out at 0500 on a general perimeter run, and will sweep the area again, if the fallout permits. She'll report in the second she's done.'

'Where's Hiroshi on all this?' Greg asked in turn. He hadn't been present to greet Greg and Leah's party, but that wasn't unusual. Being leader, he seemed to believe it was essential to be everywhere at once, and so was often gone from the Sanctuary except for scheduled meetings.

'He's finishing a sweep on Kitsap, between Bremerton and Belfair,' Jorge answered. 'I spoke to him before coming here – he said he was coming back via Case Inlet. Should be here by eight at the latest; probably closer to seven-thirty, depending on the fallout and his pace.'

One of Greg's eyebrows rose. 'Why Bremerton? We swept that place for anything usable practically the first day after we got here, mostly around the old shipyard. Wasn't much left after the Bomb's tsunami, and even less after everything else: the fallout, refugees and Navy demolition crews.'

'I said the same thing. He said he'd had some vague memory of there being a stockpile of material in the area. How he remembered, I have no idea.' Jorge frowned, more confused than displeased. 'He also mentioned picking up traces of a possible energy source, somewhere not far away. No real clues about its nature; only that it wasn't obviously nuclear, and that it seemed to get stronger as he moved further east. But the more he moved towards the Sound, the higher the radcount climbed, so—'

Greg nodded, understanding. 'He say whether he was able to mark where he first detected it? Or maybe guess the location?'

'East and north, by several degrees. That pointed him towards Bainbridge Island – and Seattle, of course. He got as far as the outskirts of Gorst, before the count edged into the upper levels.' The confused frown grew. 'Strangest thing of all, from what he hinted, it didn't appear to be an aboveground source. Closest he could come to a location was somewhere northeast of Navy Yard City, before he had to pack it in. He went on to say he didn't believe it constituted a near or serious threat, but given your return, and the hunters right behind you, he suggested we increase our alert stance. I've already devoted a portion of Overwatch for constant monitoring of the area – all frequencies, all levels – and sent warnings to our post in Belfair.'

'Fine. When he gets back – and once we've dealt with the situation here – we'll talk about further measures, maybe an exploration party.' Greg looked around the room. 'Meantime, let's keep our attention mainly on the south and east approaches. Whether somebody put that patrol back in circulation, or airlifted them out under the storm's cover, they're probably looking to establish a base camp within striking range, and soon.'

Jorge and Leah both nodded. Squaring his shoulders, the engineer motioned to a nearby door, behind the main reception desk. Taking the hint, Greg and Leah followed him through it, to a small office and break room. Once the door was closed and locked, Jorge reached to his belt. Holding out the thumb drive in one palm, he lowered his voice. 'Now – what do *you* suggest, as to our next move?'

'We need an idea of what's on *that.*' Leah pointed to the canister. 'We only had vague ideas about it, and its possible contents, before we set out – just that it contained files from the Project, maybe even a backup of its core data. Classified by any standards, and certainly somewhere up in low orbit in this case. Cayden was enough to get us past the first layer of security – something we'll need to get into later with him, I can tell – but the second one we couldn't break, not with the equipment we had. Whoever's after it is pulling out all the stops. Drones, Rangers – and those guys in brown, with abilities and weapons only *we* were supposed to have, and a few things we didn't. There's no way D.C. or whatever agency's working the strings would waste all that on trying to recover just *any* encrypted files.'

'*Still* encrypted, too.' Jorge's hand closed over the drive. 'I got to work as soon as you handed it over last night. It isn't only password protected – there's a type of firewall that I've never seen before, shielding the password algorithms. I tried using some custom-made virus programs to breach it, and the code just spat them back out. Worse than that; I had to crash the console each time to keep the viruses from infecting *our* network. Any security program can be made that *blocks* intrusions, but this one corrupted my attempts, and turned them on me.'

The other man stared at his closed fist in frustrated bewilderment. 'It was like the code was partially sentient, in some way. Like an AI, but with far more capabilities than any of the pre-Turmoil versions. That's the only explanation that comes to mind – but it's absurd. No AI – and that's what it would have to be – has ever been made that could fit on something this small. There've been theories, of course, but—' He trailed off, turning the drive between his fingers.

Greg broke the silence. 'Putting all this aside, we have two men from Outside sitting under guard here – one soldier, and one likely spook. Either of them could shed light on who's after this drive, and what those things were in Chicago and Monticello. So we need to get them talking, before we make any more attempts to breach – and possibly lose – the drive.'

'What do you mean, *things*?' Jorge asked. 'You mean the spec ops team Leah mentioned?'

'They were sweepers, or amped-up agents. Leah smashed one of them with a car after we got off the train, when whatever trank he used on us wore off. Inside of ten seconds, he started healing up almost the exact same way ARC does. Cayden and I slashed two of them almost to shreds in Minnesota – and they were up and moving as we took off. Only thing that appeared to work was a headshot, through the temple or back of the head; shots to the body or anywhere else just pissed them off.'

Jorge went rigid. 'You… you think they were Golems?'

'Not from what I saw. They had the same regeneration ability – but it was faster, and a lot less neat. Plus, they had old, deep scars on their necks and hands – serious surgery, at a guess. None of us ever had those, not even after the worst training periods, or post-mission recovery and operations. Plus they all sported the same equipment. Short swords, those trank pistols, silver glasses. None of it was anything like what we carried.'

'I may have an answer on that last – maybe.' Jorge beckoned them to another terminal. The frames Leah had picked up rested atop a mini-scanner, beside the keyboard. One lens had a jagged edge where a tiny section was missing; the other was cracked all the way across. A thin wire ran from the terminal to a tiny port in the frame, above the cracked lens.

Jorge picked up the glasses, balancing them in his palm. '*These* were easier to figure out, compared to the drive or the pistol – though I might have something on the second, too, with some time. You remember those 'smartglasses' that were all the rage for a short time, back in the late '20s?' When Greg and Leah nodded, he went on. 'Well, even the most advanced versions on the market were bulky and difficult to use under the best circumstances. They were supposed to do everything: email, phone or text conversations, record video, take pictures, play music, and handle any number of activities on the old Internet. Instead, they were so constantly hit with bugs and other software problems – and lawsuits, mostly after accidents that happened when people tried using them in cars, or almost anywhere else – that the companies behind them all but stopped production. They went back to making smaller versions of all the devices they'd slapped onto the glasses: Cameras, phones, everything.'

'But the "smartglass" didn't flame out completely?' Leah asked.

'Right. My searching's been limited – we don't have a lot of files from that period, and the NeoNet is still mostly closed off, per our decision.' He set the glasses back on the scanner. 'But I dug for a little while and found a couple of old Pentagon memos that mentioned *this*.'

He typed away at the keyboard. A new window opened, showing an image of an intact pair of silver glasses. 'I haven't yet been able to find the exact manufacturer. The only hint is a passage mentioning "an independent contractor, anonymous for security reasons". Typical cover for the Pentagon's covert research operations – or something else, maybe.'

Greg and Leah exchanged looks. Staring away in thought for a moment, Jorge missed this. Returning to his spiel, he said, 'The official name is Multi-platform Communications and Scanning Device. The nickname, which took a little more digging, is AllSpec – for "all specifications", or "all spectacles".'

Jorge pressed a key. The image began rotating, allowing every angle of the glasses to be seen. 'Multi-spectrum camera in each hinge, similar in make to the ones in our clingers. Continuous wi-fi connection, hardened against hacking or disruption; that's disabled now, from the damage and my own work. A hint of what *might* have been a commercial GPS tracer; the circuitry for it, if that's what it was, was shot to hell a while ago, so there's no risk of a signal to anyone else. Hands-free text, video, audio and Internet commands. Vibration speakers in the temple tips; microphone in the bridge, also vibration-sensitive.' He pressed another key, freezing the image. 'In short: the ideal, casual communication device. At least from the perspective of whoever designed it.'

'We might have some idea who that is,' Greg said grimly. At Jorge's confused look, he elaborated: 'We knew that Advent Tech was behind the designs for our clingers, at the start of the Project. They cut ties with the Doc long before we came around, but I doubt they just closed up shop.'

Jorge frowned. 'You think *they're* behind this work?' He studied the image. 'I don't see how. Everything I found on Advent before you started out – it all said they'd downsized drastically. Cutting staff, closing facilities, to the point they were doing more *consulting* than manufacturing. I don't see how they could have built this, without all that.'

'They wouldn't need to,' Leah put in. 'Something as vital as the Project, *nothing* gets thrown away.' She looked to Greg. 'Cayden mentioned Advent backing out not too far into the Project, and going to work on "other pipe dreams".' She pointed to the glasses.

Greg let out a long, slow breath. 'If it was, then it's a safe bet the rest of the gear we saw on those brown-coat types was designed by them, too. Which means—'

'This isn't a simple manhunt,' Jorge finished. His expression was the darkest either of the other two had ever seen. 'Whoever's turning the wheels behind the chase for you, they had – or still have – access to Project materials, and the tech spawned or inspired by it. The blades, these glasses – even the ARC. And they're not just after the canister, whatever it contains. They're looking to track down *everyone* the Project turned out.'

The three of them stared at each other, and the glasses. Greg found his voice first. 'We need to get the Council together, *now*. I'll tell Cayden to meet us at the Longhouse.'

'I'll alert the outposts, have them on watch for anything bigger than a hawk crossing the CZ,' Leah added. 'The weather's clear, and the radlevels at a minimum for now – easy viewing in all directions.' She turned to Jorge. 'What's the timeline for cracking the canister drive?'

Jorge looked unhappy. 'As I told you, I have *no* idea. If I had access to the original specs, even part of them, it might be possible. Until that or some other miracle happens, I'm restricted to trial and error.'

Leah sighed. 'Fine. Once we decide on a plan, stick with it.

Sooner we break the encryption, the sooner we know exactly *what's* on the damn drive, and maybe *who's* after it.'

Jorge dipped his chin. 'Right. We'll also need to—'

The rumbling sound of engines cut through the conversation. Looking to the lobby entrance, Greg saw two Humvees come to a halt, bare inches from the doors. The occupants began piling out before both vehicles had completely stopped. Their clingers and weapons were soaked and mud-spattered.

One of the lead vehicle's riders pulled back his hood, revealing Megan's face. She spoke and gestured at the other patrol members; one by one they peeled off, XMs and other weapons at the ready. After the last had gone, she pushed through to the lobby, moving at a swift walk toward the three of them. Her face and hair were sweaty and dishevelled, and her breathing came in sharp puffs, as if she had run all the way to campus instead of driving. In one hand she held her XM by the muzzle. The other held some sort of helmet, one Greg didn't recognise. He trotted up to her, Leah and Jorge following. 'What is it?'

Megan halted. 'We have a *serious* problem,' she growled. She lifted the helmet up for all to see. On closer inspection, Greg saw it was the same headgear the Rangers had worn at Eatonville. There were several small, deep dents at the sides and rear, and a crack through the drop-down visor. A spatter of dried blood ran from the brow to just above the left ear. A name was inscribed on the right temple, in white block letters: *DUNCAN*.

Jorge took the helmet, turning it over in both hands. 'Where did you find this?'

'Not where we left it,' Megan slung the XMs over her arm. 'We arrived at the site, as planned – no ambush. At first it looks like there's nothing but the torched choppers, until we find marks from one, maybe two other craft, bigger than the two our Ranger guests arrived in. Then we find four sets of new footprints, moving to where we left the patrol and their pilots.' She fished around in a belt pouch with her free hand, bringing forth a camera memory card. Activating her sleeve interface, she held the card against its surface. The screen blinked, then coalesced into a chain of miniature images. Megan pressed one, enlarging it to the entire screen. 'That's where things got messy.'

Greg, Leah and Jorge crowded closer. The image was of a stretch of overgrown grass and weed, heavily trampled, and flattened in a rough circle in one area. Small bits of glinting metal were visible in one or two spots. Shell casings; Berettas and H&Ks, at a glance. Another zoom-in showed a few dark, glistening splotches here and there, splattered about the flattened areas. Nobody needed three guesses as to what it was.

'That's just the start,' Megan warned. She skipped ahead several images. 'There was a smaller blood trail, leading to a smaller clearing about a mile to the north. When we got there, the blood trail came to a stop in the heart of another quarry pit – but we didn't find any bodies. Only thing we found was a couple of piles of ashes, along with a few scraps of what we soon determined to be military-issue fabric.'

The three of them exchanged puzzled looks. 'You're saying someone found the patrol, then executed them and burned the bodies?' Greg asked.

Megan shook her head. 'That was the obvious answer. Until we realised there weren't pyres, and our clingers didn't detect any accelerant present. What they *did* find was this.'

She fished a tiny vial out of another pouch, holding it up to their eyes. 'Best we can put together, somebody landed to pick up the Rangers, then jumped them all, bashed their heads in, dragged them off site – and dissolved the bodies with Tacitus powder.'

Silence dropped over the little gathering. Leah's strained voice broke it. 'This kind of stuff was restricted to us alone – the Doctor designed it himself. The only remaining stocks are what we had on us before and during the Turmoil, and at the Facility; God knows where that is, or if it still exists. All the packs we carried are kept here, under five or six different locks. So unless one of our teams went rogue—'

'Wasn't one of ours,' Megan replied at once. 'I was in touch with all the outposts, and the few other patrols we had out starting at 0500. None of them came within miles of the site. And I've made a point of checking on the general stockpile almost on the hour since the two of you left. Every grain of the stuff's accounted for. We even asked Cayden to hand over his, and he agreed. It *might* be possible that someone else got hold of a sample from what you say he used in Wisconsin, but—' She trailed off, clearly not sure what to believe, then handed the vial to Greg.

'Whoever it was, he's a new player,' Jorge said. He looked from Leah to Greg, and back again. 'You say the teams sent after you *all* had similar qualities and skills to ours? ARC-like recovery, the upgraded blades, the AllSpec?' They both nodded. 'They were on you starting from D.C., with assistance from the Rangers – and the Fairchild garrison – only after your encounter in Chicago?' They nodded once again. Their comrade stared pensively at the helmet, and the vial. 'If these hit teams *were* based on ARC-related technology, then the best answer to all this is that somebody, well-placed within the covert ops branch, gained access to the Project, and buried the canister and its contents, long before the two of you volunteered to recover them. Maybe before the Bomb, or the Turmoil.' His expression became longer, and grimmer. 'Maybe even someone who was once part of the Project from the beginning.'

Leah sucked in a breath. Megan's mouth thinned even more, but she held herself to a nod. Greg felt coldness spread from his neck to his groin. It was all he could do to keep from crushing the vial into even finer powder than its contents. Once again Leah was first to speak. 'Even... Even if *that's* true, if it's the same team after us, and they have the powder, why'd they waste it getting rid of a couple of Rangers? They could just as easily bundle them off to some out-of-the way post, separate from each other to avoid the word spreading. We saw plenty of that with some of the units we were attached to, if they happened to see us in action. It would've been pointless to eliminate anybody who did – and too noticeable.'

That jarred Greg back into speech. 'Whatever these things are, they can't be completely on the level, with D.C. or whoever's supposed to be running them.' He took the helmet from Megan. '*They're* not afraid of being seen on the job – *we* saw that at Monticello. What they *are* afraid of, or seem to be, is anybody learning too much about *us*. Our skills, our speed – most of all, our plans, whatever they think they are.' He lifted the helmet to his eyes, staring at the cracked visor. 'When the Rangers saw us in Eatonville, the main worry for the brains behind the chase wasn't that we got away – but that we left witnesses. So they disposed of the patrol, probably with some suitable excuse for its commanders, and whatever families there might be. Now they're either waiting for new orders, or watching the CZ, waiting for *us*.'

Their eyes turned to the doors, staring through them to the square – and the wilderness beyond. Finally, Megan broke the silence. 'Well, for the time being, we don't have a way of finding out for sure. We have the canister, but the only person who can open it is dead. There's *somebody* out there with ARC-enhanced fighters, and that's a definite threat. But until whoever it is makes a move against the outposts, or the Sanctuary, we can't even get an idea of how many there are, let alone who they answer to – or what they're carrying.'

'Then maybe we should,' Greg answered. The others looked at him, confused. 'We've got a Ranger officer and a covert agent sitting right here on campus. Types like that don't disappear without *somebody* noticing, or signing off on his being part of any covert operations – that's what they're trained for, after all. And while the agent probably wasn't kept in the loop about *every* aspect of the hunt for us and the files, he'll have seen whoever's really in charge, or gotten their name in passing. So if we show them *this—*'

'They'll be more inclined to open up about the specifics of their mission,' Jorge said. 'But if they're already expecting that outcome for them and their counterparts, why *should* they tell us anything?'

'There's that,' Greg allowed. 'But we don't have time to spend sitting around waiting for them to talk – or for their "friends" to drop in. So if there's a chance they'll talk *now*, once they know what happened, I say we take it.'

Leah nodded. After a second or two, so did Megan. Jorge sighed. 'All right. But we should wait till Hiroshi's here, too. Then we can vote as a full body on our next course of action.' At those words, his clinger interface lit up with a soft beep. Lifting it to his eyes, the engineer smiled. 'Speak of the devil. He's landing on Eld Beach right now. I'll send word to meet at the Longhouse.'

'Good.' Greg called up his own interface, typing a quick message. 'Cayden'll bring our guests over shortly. Once everybody's all together, we can at least *try* to get a handle on all this.' The others nodded, their faces a mix of eagerness and apprehension. The group broke up: Jorge started back to the computer lab, to collect the drive and canister; Megan headed out the door and called over several men from her patrol. No doubt she was arranging extra security for the campus proper, and prepping reinforcements for the perimeter outposts.

Leah moved to his side. She set a hand on his arm, gently. Her voice was low and concerned. 'You sure about this?'

'No,' Greg confessed. 'But like I said – there's no other options. Not good ones, anyway.' His grip closed over the vial. 'We need a break, badly. And this – plus our two guests – might be the only chance we have at finding one.'

Chapter 16

FOB Yakima

A vein throbbed in Flynn's forehead. With great deliberation, he set the tablet down on the conference table, and walked to the window. Outside, last night's clouds had nearly cleared, revealing a vivid, orange-yellow sunrise, tinged with rainbow colours: a regular sight in the region, courtesy of the Seattle Bomb.

By the set of his body, Flynn was a hairsbreadth from matching that explosion. When he turned to face Hargrove again, his expression was still calm – but there was a murderous tint in his eyes. 'You're *absolutely* sure?' he ground out.

'I'm afraid so,' Hargrove replied. He gestured to the two men who stood in silence by the door. The forest camo they wore was stained and rumpled from hard use outdoors. 'My people found the wreckage a short while before heading back here – and the remains. They assumed at first that some critical system failed in both craft – a rad spike affecting the computers, maybe, or some other fault the maintenance crews didn't find. When they didn't find any bodies, they widened the search area – and found that.'

He pointed to the tablet. Its screen showed a single picture: three piles of grey-white ash. On closer inspection, it was possible to see fragments of green and brown fabric, mixed into each mound. That had been a nice touch, he admitted to himself. 'We're still not certain when the team was brought down, or how – or *what* the hell was used to dissolve the bodies once that happened. But judging from this, it's clear the targets didn't want any survivors.'

'Tracks?' Flynn bit off the word.

'A few, jumbled together. No clear idea how many attackers there were – maybe three or four, possibly counting the targets. There were tyre tracks by a quarry near the crash site: heavy-duty vehicles, no more than two. We weren't able to tell how far out they went, or how long they might have been there.'

A low growl rose in the colonel's throat. His hand darted out, picking up the tablet again. He swept through each of the images Hargrove's team had taken. When he had gone through all of them, he set the device back down, with exaggerated care. he looked to Hargrove again, his eyes hard and accusing. 'Where was *your* team, exactly? They were supposed to be on station, ready to prevent this sort of catastrophe.'

'They were,' Hargrove answered. 'They were also under orders to avoid the fallout as much as possible, in keeping with your warning at Fairchild. When the plume first became erratic, I ordered them to hole up at Packwood, but keep their Osprey hot, and head out at the slightest whisper of trouble. By the time *we* suspected a problem, the plume had already come down over Eatonville and the entire search area. My men are good, but they aren't supermen.'

'Then our targets damn well must be,' Flynn shot back. He pointed to the tablet. 'Obviously they had help. That's clear from *this*, and the tracks; we'll get to that. But if what your people say is true, they stayed out a while after the plume fell – and the rads were high enough to deep fry them inside of an hour. A lot sooner, if they headed west or north. If they did, and they're still breathing… that argues for a much larger presence in the CZ. One whose goals are unknown, that's hostile to this country – and has personnel with unheard-of enhancements or equipment, or both.' His look became menacing. 'And unless I'm mistaken, one whose existence you and maybe Mr Costa had an idea of, before you showed up in this diseased shithole part of the world.'

How much had Costa passed on or hinted, to Patrick or Flynn? Not much, Hargrove assessed; otherwise the Air Force officer would have called him out directly. He met the threatening stare with a frosty one of his own. 'You're free to indulge whatever suspicions you like, Colonel. I *can*, however, break you of one of them: Agent Costa and I did speculate on there being some form of group behind the targets' mission, but we had no proof – until now. The others… Having served out here as long and well as you have, I'm sure you know the many ways to avoid or recover from fallout. The targets and their backers may be using all of those, or some new method. If there's anything "unheard-of" in this, that's the likeliest answer.'

Flynn didn't seem convinced, but his anger appeared to be ratcheting down. Hargrove pressed his next point. 'You're correct on one thing. There *is*, or appears to be, an unknown, militant group headquartered somewhere in the CZ. That alone would warrant further investigation, regardless of the manhunt. Now, because of it, they have potential access to information and technology vital to this country – and are showing no qualms about holding onto that access.' He pointed to the tablet. 'Which, from where I'm standing, makes our next course of action crystal clear.'

The Air Force colonel's scowl deepened again. 'True,' he ground out. 'It also makes clear what methods we use, this time around.' He jerked his chin at the window. 'We've held back on constant air patrols in the past: not enough funding, no obvious threats. The only regular sweeps were done from orbit, or along the borders of the less contaminated zones – the likeliest routes any smugglers would take. There wasn't any reason for a more active stance – until now.'

With that, Flynn moved to the door, brushing past Hargrove and the two guards as though they didn't exist. Hargrove trailed after him, his men following. The officer strode toward the end of the corridor, where two guards in Air Force blue flanked a pair of metal doors. Both bore a simple black-white plaque: *Comm Centre.* Hargrove trotted up beside Flynn. 'What are you doing?'

Flynn didn't look at him. 'Calling in more satellite coverage and sending word back to Fairchild and the other bases. Counting my people, we can have half a dozen F-40 squadrons in the air in a matter of minutes, running patrols over the entire CZ. If there's a blade of grass out of place, the bunker-busters come calling. D.C. can squawk all it wants about me pulling pilots off the line, once we've dealt with this steaming pile of—'

Hargrove's hand shot out, grabbing Flynn's arm. A flex of his wrist, and the officer spun around to face him. The other man froze, fist raised, his initial surprise giving way to fury. 'You don't want to do that,' Hargrove said, firm as a teacher correcting a student's error.

Flynn's glare would have melted steel. 'Get your hand off me.'

'Okay,' Hargrove said. He released his grip. A twitch of his left hand told his men to stay back. 'But I'd think you'd realise what you're planning just adds to the pile.'

'What the hell are you talking about?'

'Our targets still have the files stolen from D.C. Whether they're in the hands of the target's *group* now is irrelevant; it only adds more names to our list. My superiors are concerned only about keeping them intact, and undisclosed. Until I hear otherwise, that's *my* concern as well.'

'Good to know,' Flynn replied curtly. 'But the fact is, we are facing a clear military threat – one that's already reared its head, twice. My duty is to neutralise it, by any means. If that includes destroying whatever capabilities or information they've acquired, then it does.'

'No one's questioning that,' Hargrove said. 'However, we both answer to the same boss. And I doubt *he'd* react as calmly to your cluster-bombing the CZ – and the files.'

Flynn's tone was mocking. 'You really think the *President* worries more about some missing memos than a new insurg—'

Hargrove pulled the folded slip of paper from his pocket, and thrust it at the colonel. If he felt like shoving the paper down the other man's throat, nothing in his manner said so. Flynn took it, scanning the pardon rapidly. His mouth twisted, as at a bad taste. 'I... suppose this answers that.'

'Now you understand the pressure I'm under. That we're *all* under.' Hargrove took the paper back and put it away. 'Once we've got the canister back – intact – you'll have all the authorisation you need to scour the whole Sound clean; I promise you that. Until then, we need to keep this a low-key operation, the better to achieve our main objective, and keep the body count to a minimum.'

'A little late for that,' Flynn retorted. Instead of building on that, he went on, 'If you're suggesting we deploy another team of Rangers, or other ground troops, the answer is *no*. Radiation and other dangers aside, I'm *not* sending one more man or vehicle into the Zone. Not until we know one hundred per cent what it is we're up against.'

'Then we're in agreement, Colonel.' When the other man looked perplexed – and suspicious – he continued: 'We can't risk sending in any more of *your* people, or any boots you could pull from other garrisons in the area. Nor can we risk the aircraft we came in with – God knows what other countermeasures the insurgents have, along with what they used on the drone. On top of those, we still have only patchy information about the lay of the land itself. We can write off downtown Seattle and most of the waterfront areas of the Sound – they were in the bullseye, almost, when the Bomb went off, and the radiation's still high enough in some of those spots to kill within an hour, two at the most. But that still leaves between eight and ten thousand square miles to cover. Satellites can give us the general details, but we need ground observation.'

'What *exactly* are you suggesting, then?'

'Just this: me, and the members of my team, will enter the CZ, alone. Once we find the main camp, we hunker down and observe, then infiltrate and recover the canister. If we succeed, we signal for evac or make our way out ourselves, and paint the site for airstrikes. If we fail... We paint it anyway.' Hargrove squared his shoulders. 'Upstairs won't like losing the canister's data – but if destroying it means it stays out of the wrong hands, they'll get behind the idea. And *you'll* have the pleasure of dropping the payload on those that killed Colonel Patrick and his team.'

For a moment, the colonel seemed struck dumb. 'That's... a bold idea,' he said at last. Composing himself, he went on,

'Forgive me if I sound just a bit sceptical. A man of your... years, dropping into the world's largest hot zone, with just four men? Against potentially hundreds of insurgents?' He must not have been fully informed about Hargrove's team in action, then – from Patrick or Costa. *A bonus.*

'I'm not ready for the boneyard yet,' Hargrove replied shortly. 'As for the odds, my men have dealt with worse.' Flynn gave him a querying look. He pretended not to notice, continuing, 'All we need is a Black Hawk, ruggedised comms gear and additional light weapons – we can't be burdened with anything heavy. You provide that – and suitable discretion, of course – we can be in the air within half an hour.'

Flynn studied him, and his guards. At last, he gave a single, abrupt nod. 'Have your people armed up and on the tarmac in fifteen. I'll have the transport ready, and the gear, too.' Without another word, the Air Force officer marched away, heading for the comms centre.

Hargrove nodded back, though Flynn couldn't see him. When he turned back down the hallway, he allowed the relieved grin he'd been holding back to show. The pardon still had its effect, after all – so long as it was used on the right people. Flynn had been a tougher nut to crack; the loyal but suspicious kind of soldier always was. Odds were he *would* get hold of someone back East, in order to get authorisation for the strikes. They would want to know why and how he wanted it – and the colonel didn't seem the subtle type. When he answered, the reaction to *Hargrove* wouldn't take long at all.

His guards came up on both sides. *All team members notified,* his glasses flashed. *Suitably intact water transport located at Tacoma waterfront, through Army satellite recon; additional fuel supplies secured aboard waiting chopper. Request specs as to other appropriate equipment.*

Hargrove thought for a moment. *Standard field gear,* he pulsed back. *Anticipate entering primary irradiated zone: downtown Seattle, and immediate surroundings; anti-rad protection to be kept in reserve. Any renewed signal from team member's stolen comms device?*

Negative. Last activity pinpointed to within 20 miles of suburbs of Olympia. Progression of prior trail suggests targets proceeding to base near waterfront, seeking additional cover from visual and thermal tracking due to lingering secondary radiation and other Bomb effects.

That was Hargrove's impression, too. There was still no clear idea how many rads Golems could take before they bit the dust – although *he* had a good idea himself, he thought, his grin widening a touch. No sane human would come within a hundred miles of the Puget Sound shoreline, not unless they wanted a slow death before seeing the next day's sunrise. Golems were obviously made of stronger stuff, from everything he'd learned and seen, but Hargrove suspected they weren't looking to stay long term in the glowing basin – not without serious protection, at any rate. The canister's theft was confirmation enough. They wanted a shield, be it tech from the Project, or just the threat of its exposure, before things got desperate and they had to migrate – or expand. Armed with its contents, they just might, too.

Hargrove pushed open the doors to the next hallway, brushing past a pair of startled Air Force clerks. One last shot – that was all he had to end this. And this time, he'd damn well pull the trigger himself.

Chapter 17

Longhouse, Old Evergreen State College Campus

Greg paced in measured steps, back and forth, back and forth. The soles of the clinger made only a faint whispering against the concrete floor. Above him, the wooden beams and rafters of the Longhouse creaked in a steady wind coming down out of the north. Most days, the Council handled any issues where they happened – in the field, in the Library, anywhere – and without much formality. Nonetheless, when the Sanctuary was first put together, it had been decided to set the small building aside as a meeting house, to give him and the other members a spot to go over matters in more detail.

A huge, carved wooden eagle, wings rampant and painted in vivid black, white and red, hung over the main doors. The inside was stark and simple – concrete floor, brown wooden walls polished to a high sheen and vaulted ceiling. A round fire pit sat in the middle of the central area, dark and cold. There were wide benches along the wall to the left, and another exit at the end of a short hall. To the right of these, a collapsible wall gave onto a larger assembly area. Three long conference tables had been set up end to end against the far wall and covered with plain forest green cloth. It was this area that Greg paced now.

The main doors opened. A man strode into the Council room, dressed in a brush-patterned clinger; he must have come straight from patrol. His deep black hair was close-cut and swept back from a high forehead. His eyes – a bright brown – were probing and intense. At the sight of the other man present, a pleased smile bloomed across his Asian features, tanned and weathered by sun and wind. 'Greg! Good to have you back.' He extended a hand.

Greg shook, firmly. 'Same to you, Hiroshi. Any trouble on the Kitsap run?'

'No,' Hiroshi replied. 'Nothing really worth salvaging, either, not with the gear we had. The radiation was too high to search closely, either, in some spots.' The smile became fixed, for a moment, before returning to normal. 'We *did* find one interesting thing, or close to it... I'll fill everyone in once they're here.'

As if on cue, the doors opened again. Jorge, Leah and Megan walked in, Jorge carrying the canister in both hands. After everyone had exchanged greetings, Hiroshi beckoned them into the meeting area. He took his place at the centre; Jorge and Megan moved to his left, Greg and Leah on his right. When they were all seated, he held out a hand to Jorge, unspeaking. With infinite care, the engineer placed the canister in his hand. The Council leader stared at the device, eyes raking over every inch. Beneath his ever-present calm exterior, there was a glimmer of excitement. 'This is really it?'

'No question,' Greg replied. 'We still don't know what's on it – but the amount of effort being put to recovering it argues for something *major*.'

Hiroshi nodded. 'Leah gave me the gist of your trip last night, and Jorge has done the same with his work on *this*.' He hefted the canister. 'I'm also told you've brought some guests who can fill in more of the gaps.'

'They're on the way now,' Leah said. 'In fact—'

The doors opened a third time. There was a sound of struggling, followed by a grunt of pain. Three figures entered the Council area. One was Cayden, wearing plain blue coveralls over his clinger. He held two men before him by the collar. Shapeless black hoods were draped over their heads, and their hands were bound in front of them with plasticuffs. One wore an Army Ranger's uniform beneath the tattered remains of his NBC suit; the other wore a plain green coverall.

Cayden pulled the two prisoners to the middle of the room. That done, he released them, and yanked the hoods away. Both squinted at the sudden flash of light. The Ranger sagged, breathing hard, but still alert. The second man shrunk back a little at the sight of the five Council members, but otherwise showed little obvious fear, eyes darting over them and the room in automatic assessment. *Standard Agency,* Greg mused.

Cayden stepped in front of the prisoners, drawing his knife from beneath a flap of his coveralls. He made two sharp swipes, slicing through the cuffs – then he was behind them again, knife sheathed. The prisoners flinched, and edged away. Hiroshi only nodded. 'Thank you, Cayden. Please stay. It seems we have a lot to discuss.' Cayden moved back several paces, keeping himself between the prisoners and the doors. The Ranger faced the Council, back straight and proud. The agent – if he *was* one – did the same, though there was a faint, visible quiver in his legs, as though he were ready to take off at any second.

No one spoke, for several long seconds. Greg glanced at Hiroshi. The other Golem had set the canister at his right hand, and was studying the prisoners, his face unreadable. Greg had been the one to call this meeting, but Hiroshi was still the

Sanctuary's leader. It was he, Jorge and Megan who had first come together in late '51, after straggling in from their mutual assignments in southeast Asia. They'd formed the first group of Project survivors at this campus—'discards' was the term many members used today, in jest and bitterness. When Greg and Leah had joined later that year, they'd started reaching out further, bringing in more members by coded radio, encrypted email and other electronic message drops, and, where possible, face-to-face recruiting. Hiroshi had coordinated all of this, often going out on missions himself, and amassing more knowledge and details than Greg could hope to match. It had taken massive effort and not a small amount of blood, but the Sanctuary had become reality. Now they were on the verge of setting that reality in stone, courtesy of the canister – and these men. It was only fair that its creator should do the honours.

Hiroshi continued to stare at the prisoners. They stared back – one passive, the other edgy. At last, the Council leader spoke, in a quiet, firm voice. 'I suspect that at this point you're expecting some form of interrogation. Sodium pentothal and bright lights, if we were gentle; waterboarding, electro-shock and sleep deprivation if we weren't.' He paused, gauging their reactions. Neither man budged. 'Given the circumstances, however – and some new information that's just come to us – we've decided instead to speak openly with you, in the hope you will do the same.'

The Ranger looked above their heads, at the far wall. 'Patrick, David,' he rapped out. 'Colonel, US Army Rangers.' He fell silent, lips pressed tight.

Unsurprised, Hiroshi turned to the agent. 'And you?'

The agent glanced at each of the Council members in turn, suspicious or nervous. 'Benjamin Costa – Central Intelligence Agency,' he said finally. When none of them showed any reaction, he went on, grudgingly, 'What's this... "new information"?'

Patrick shot him a warning look. Hiroshi gave the agent a polite smile. 'Before I go on, Mr Costa, I—'

'Wait.' Megan's sharp voice cut him off. She leaned forward. Her eyes narrowed. '*Costa*? From Special Activities?'

Costa stared at her. 'How—' He stopped, and set his chin, keeping a careful, studious eye toward Megan, probably gauging whether she'd come at him in the next second. By the way his hands and shoulders tightened, he expected it – and maybe worse.

Leah swivelled to face Megan. 'You *know* him?'

Megan nodded. 'June of '38,' she half-recited, unsmiling. 'The rest of my team was down for recovery, after a clean-up op in Peshawar, so I was attached alone to a SAC operation operating out of the Taurus Mountains. No other Golem presence – just me, two squads each of SEALs and Force Recon, and one guy from the Agency to babysit and cross all the T's. Southern Russia and the various Caucasus republics were tearing themselves apart, and the usual jihadist and smuggling groups were making money hand over fist – guns, heroin, stolen oil, sex trafficking. My group's goal: eliminate the key players, in both cases, and wreck their capacity to fight or ship. When the Russians started moving to "adjust" their border with Ukraine – again – in late July, we switched targets. That's to say, *I* did. By August, their armies were grinding to a halt, and half the terrorist groups in Central Asia were decimated or leaderless.' She pointed at Costa. '*He* was the babysitter. He stayed in his tent so often, I barely saw his face – but the name stuck.'

'Did he know what *you* were?' Greg asked Megan. 'Where you'd been trained?' He looked to Costa once more. He saw

Patrick doing the same, his opaque visage cracking to show dismay. The agent still wouldn't meet any of their eyes.

The other Golem shook her head. 'Doubt it – not at that time, anyway. I was listed as a "highly skilled recon asset"; a lot of us had that label, when we were around non-Project personnel for extended periods. Since then—' She paused. 'Seems he's picked up a few details, or he wouldn't be here.'

Hiroshi folded his hands before him on the table. 'Is that true, Agent Costa?' He showed no anger, only professional calm and curiosity. 'Were you aware of our existence and capabilities, prior to the Turmoil and your assignment to pursue my colleagues?'

Costa remained silent. Patrick edged closer to his fellow prisoner. 'Dammit, Costa,' he growled. 'If you screwed me and my people over some eyes-only bullshit—'

Anger flashed across Costa's face. 'No,' he snapped. 'I—' He hesitated, then sighed. 'I had suspicions, when I first worked with *her*.' He pointed to Megan; she stared stonily in return. 'She always kept to her quarters, except when out in the field or called for briefings. The other teams went out every mission carrying a mini arsenal; she never hefted anything heavier than an MP5, and no other gear besides the knife and "prototype armoured bodysuit" we always saw her wear. At the time, I thought it was part of her training, or maybe just her personality. Minimise contact with others, even allies, in order to maintain necessary distance for operational duties.'

He rattled off the sentence as though reading it from a manual – which he probably had, at some point in the past. 'I thought she was a special project, shared between the Agency and one SF branch or another; all I knew for sure is that she'd been assigned to the operation for reasons way beyond my clearance. It wasn't until I saw some of the after-reports, containing photos of her work in Grozny, Tblisi and Maripol, that I realised there was more to her story – and maybe those from Pakistan and North Korea. But I never heard *anything* about the Project, until I was read into it a short time before the break-in at the Advent facility.'

Patrick's face was turning red. The set of his body showed he wanted to pounce on Costa and beat his brains into the floor. Seeing this, Hiroshi addressed him. 'I'm guessing you've been read into some of these matters yourself, Colonel?'

The colonel's face worked furiously. 'Not as much as some,' he grumbled, sending Costa another glare. 'Up till a day ago, I'd only heard rumours – stories, like he said. Walking patrol in Lahore, Panmunjom and Luzon, I picked up a lot of tales. Huge men, or women, covered in black, coming outta nowhere to slice or snipe, or blow up arms caches or supply convoys. Back then it sounded like just stories, propaganda to pump up the Measured Response idea. At a stretch, I thought it might've been some balls-out Delta Force, or an off-the-books Agency team with classified gear. Nothing ever crossed my mind about… you.' He scowled at the assembled Golems. 'Wasn't until Agent Costa and his "colleagues" showed up that I heard the first about this "Project", either.'

'And who were these colleagues?' Hiroshi asked. The words were polite, but Greg saw the coiled awareness in his old comrade.

Patrick jerked his head at Costa. Hiroshi looked to the agent, silently asking the same question. Costa licked his lips, the first sign of real nervousness he'd shown. *He doesn't know,* Greg realised. *Or he knows – but not enough. And what he knows terrifies him, Agency and all.* The agent cleared his throat. 'He's… a special contractor. My people've kept him around since a couple of years before the Turmoil. From the little background

I was given, he used to be on the staff of half a dozen Pentagon pet projects, and a major shareholder in Advent Tech.'

Greg whipped his head around. He saw the same surprise on Jorge's and Leah's faces. Megan's visage darkened even more. The tiniest edge crept into Hiroshi's voice. 'I see. And you were aware, correct, of Advent's role in the Project?'

'Its initial role, yes. What happened after the Project was separated and became a wholly Pentagon operation, I have no idea. Same with the man I was assigned to, when this all started. He became de facto head of Advent during the Turmoil, when the company *really* started circling the drain. I heard rumours he was putting it to use on other work for the Agency or the brass, but nothing more than that. From what I've seen of his operation and people, there's not much doubt in my mind anymore.'

'Who is he?' Leah demanded. 'The man you're supposed to be supervising?'

Costa didn't reply. Leah was drawing breath to ask again when Patrick's voice cut her short. 'Hargrove. Simon Hargrove.'

The name meant nothing to Greg – at least, not that he could remember. He checked the others' faces, and Cayden's, and saw the same attitude. Something nagged at the back of his mind, but he couldn't place it. Filing it for later, he looked to Patrick once more. 'And?'

The colonel seemed angry and relieved, all at once – as if he'd gotten a huge worry off his chest, and was glad he wasn't facing a bullet for it. 'Like Agent Costa claims, I don't know the man that well. Did seem that he has friends in certain high places, though, back East.'

'Colonel,' Costa said warningly.

Patrick rounded on him. The scorching look in his eyes made Costa's mouth snap shut. Pivoting to face the table again, the Ranger continued, in a robotic monotone. 'When Hargrove and the others on their team arrived on my base, all they told me was that there'd been a break-in at a classified facility in D.C. They said the intruders had nearly been caught, in Chicago, but escaped, and were coming into *my* area of operations. Costa flashed his Agency ID when he showed up at the last minute, but that was all the authorisation I saw from the whole group. With that, and Hargrove's attitude, I pegged it for a covert op from the start, although I had some doubts. When I saw Hargrove's people in action, at Monticello Airfield—'

Patrick fell silent and grim, for a moment. 'No human could take the kind of damage they did. I wasn't the first on scene, so I didn't see the fighting itself – but the Osprey pilots got a few glimpses, and I saw the after-effects. Anyone else – Rangers, Special Forces, Marines, whatever – they'd be on stretchers, if they were lucky. These four looked like they'd gone through a light boxing class, and nothing else. It was then I knew for sure that all this wasn't a manhunt. I didn't know *what* it was, anymore.' He shot another hard look at Costa. 'And after Hargrove and his brown-coat boys came out with the prisoner in a body bag, I was *damn* sure it wasn't going to end with just *one* corpse.'

Greg's fists clenched on the table. A swift look to Leah; she showed the same restrained fury, all the stronger for not being surprised. He realised he wasn't either, and hated it. Caswell had rejected coming with them, so it shouldn't have surprised him whoever was chasing them would dispose of the ex-sergeant if he didn't talk, or out of expediency. That, of course, didn't dampen his anger in the slightest; if anything, it made it hotter.

Features boiling, Cayden took two slow, silent steps toward

the prisoners, the long blade appearing in his hand. One more move would have the older Golem standing over them, throats slit, or stabbed between just the right vertebrae. Greg made a hasty but subtle jerk with one hand: *No.* Cayden stopped, blade still at the ready. His hand quivered, readying itself for a throw. Greg made the same motion, sharper this time. There was still more to be found out, and it wouldn't help if their two best leads were carved up. Cayden had to know that, vengeance or not.

After a few seconds more, Cayden lowered the knife, and stuck it beneath his coverall. Darting a furious look Greg's way, he stepped back into place. His hands clenched once, twice, then lay still at his sides. The bland mask slid back on, incrementally. Greg let out a silent breath. The whole incident had lasted less than a couple of seconds; Patrick and Costa hadn't noticed. Leah sent him a concerned glance, but said nothing.

If the others on the Council had noticed the silent exchange, they showed no sign. Hiroshi pressed on, voice neutral. 'I see. But you stayed with the manhunt; coming all the way out here, in fact, well outside your operating zone. Why is that?'

Patrick sent Costa another glare. 'Orders. From his bosses – and, supposedly, whoever *Hargrove's* were. They came to me and mine acting like a team, but it was pretty obvious who was on top, with them.' Costa reddened with anger, but didn't speak. Patrick continued, 'After Monticello, they were tenser, but all I was told was that I should get together a team of my best, and that we were being added to the hunt for the duration. I could tell Costa wasn't happy dealing with Hargrove, so I thought we could at least work together until it was over – then get as far apart as possible.' He let out a bitter huff of laughter. 'So much for that, as it turned out.'

'That's why you and the team came out here on your own,

then?' Leah asked. 'End the hunt a little quicker, and maybe show up Hargrove for dragging you into it?'

Patrick's jaw ground back and forth. 'Not exactly.' His teeth creaked, audible enough even without Golem hearing. Yet another sharp look at Costa. 'We were there at *his* insistence, as a compromise. The flyboys we were working with on our latest leg, they wanted to recon the Sound by air, get a better idea of the terrain and fallout risks, and maybe follow a route I'd mapped before that avoided the worst in both cases. Hargrove wanted to charge in: just him and whatever his people were, alone. The agent suggested a third option: me, him, and my team, making a general sweep of the area surrounding the site where the plane went down – yours, I'm guessing?' He made a small gesture towards Greg and Leah. When neither of them denied it, he went on, glaring at Costa again: We were airborne for about five minutes, when *he* finally showed his face and ID on my chopper – he'd held back one of my men and dressed in similar gear, so I wouldn't notice right off. I don't know how he made it onto the base – being a spook, it probably wasn't hard.' Costa looked both annoyed and pleased at this. 'I almost threw him out the bay door right then, but we had a mission to complete – and I wanted to know *exactly* who we were chasing.'

Costa paled a little, but kept his mouth shut. Patrick continued, in the same flat recitation. 'We were making a second sweep of the area below Eatonville, when we spotted *him*.' He jerked his chin toward Cayden. The Golem didn't react, continuing to stare balefully at the two men. 'Given the rads in the area, and the likeliest routes west from the crash site, it was obvious it was one of your group.' He flexed his wrists, pushing them against the cuffs. 'We suspected the others were nearby – but we didn't expect other company, not then.' The colonel shifted his shoulders, standing at attention again. 'You obviously know the rest.'

'Yes – to a point,' Hiroshi said. Costa looked surprised; Patrick's brow furrowed, but otherwise he remained still. The Council chair went on, 'When you began this second sweep, did you send out any alerts? Any updates on the search, or fallout spread?'

For maybe ten seconds, Patrick didn't reply. Costa didn't speak, either, although his eyes darted from the colonel to the group, and back, as though gauging who would break – or if *he* should. Hiroshi didn't press them, only staring back with an air of infinite calmness. At last, the colonel spoke. 'We held off on regular check-ins, since we were unaware of what was actually *in* the CZ after ten years. Still, we tried. Right before spotting your group, in fact. We forwarded our readings on the rad dispersal, and our estimated return to base given fuel consumption and wind patterns. No reply ever came – nothing but static.'

He shifted in place, looking ill at ease. 'The choppers were new models, and rad-hardened; there shouldn't have been any issues. I was just about to order us to a higher altitude, see if we could get above any fallout or other interference closer to the ground that might somehow be playing havoc with our gear. That's when we saw *him*'—he gestured in Cayden's direction again—'and decided comms could wait until we had you all tagged and bagged.'

'Instead the opposite happened,' Hiroshi said, without any sign of mockery. 'And when you came under fire from our people, you sent out a distress signal to this backup, like any soldier would?'

Patrick's brow creased again. 'Maybe,' he grunted. 'Why?'

Hiroshi hesitated. Greg stared; he'd never seen the other Golem so uncertain. When the pause had stretched to maybe three seconds, the Council leader gave a clipped nod to Megan. Keeping her eyes fixed on the colonel, she reached down beside her chair, and brought up a plain cardboard box, like the several others sitting around the room. Judging from the size—

His hands gripped the edge of the table in reflex. He could tell where this was going. Her face grim, as of a soldier with an unpleasant duty, Megan pulled the flaps open, reached inside and drew out the battered Ranger helmet. In the blend of harsh indoor and soft outdoor light, the dried blood was easy to see.

The Ranger colonel's face congealed, with shock and anger both. With jerky steps, he approached the table. There was the faintest tremble in his hands as he picked up the helmet, turning it this way and that for a full view. When he saw the name, he froze again. Megan moved a hand out of sight. Hiroshi stopped her with a look.

His movements slow and exaggerated, Patrick set the helmet back on the table. 'Duncan.' His tone was flat, but brimming with fury. 'The kid followed me all through the Turmoil, from his first day out of West Point and straight into Ranger School.' His eyes were bright as blowtorches. 'Where did this come from?' His voice was quiet, and strangled with rage.

'One of our patrols found it this morning,' Hiroshi answered. 'We are still unclear on the details, but it seems someone found your patrol after our departure, and… arranged for their demise. We have theories, and some evidence, but nothing concrete.'

Patrick's hands folded into fists. The muscles in his neck stood out in the overhead lights. 'Survivors?' he bit off. The anger in his gaze brightened, if that was possible. 'Bodies?'

Another round of wary looks went around the table. 'We didn't find any,' Hiroshi replied. 'There were some remains, but we're not sure who they belong to.'

The colonel drew back, confusion now warring with anger.

'What… What do you mean, remains?' His voice rose. 'Where are my men? Where the *fuck* are they?!'

He started forward, hands raised. Cayden was behind him at once, one hand clamped on the shoulder of the Ranger's uniform. Patrick twisted around, fist lashing out. Cayden caught the punch on his jaw, unblinking, then grabbed the officer's arm. Patrick struggled some more, but to no effect.

'Hey, easy! Easy!' Costa stepped up, grabbing Patrick's arms. Bit by bit, the Ranger desisted. At a look from Greg, Cayden released his grip. Patrick's breath came in short, sharp gasps. Savagely, he shook off Costa's hands and stomped away, coming to a halt beside the fire pit. His face was beet-red. He brought both hands to his mouth, breathing deeply. Greg, Leah and the others sat immobile, waiting. When a minute or two had passed, Patrick turned to face the group again. He was calmer, but his eyes were glistening with unshed tears. Mechanically, he approached the table again, holding himself straight as a pillar.

Hiroshi waited until he was a few paces away before speaking. 'I understand your anger, Colonel. We all do, everyone on this Council – and those among the rest of our group who are familiar with the situation. And we also realise that you would have difficulty believing our claims of innocence, given all that's happened. So we can only say that we did not harm your men, in any way, since the events at our first encounter outside Eatonville. We had no reason to then – unless you had persisted in attacking us – and we have even less reason now. We are trying to ascertain how and why your men were dealt with, but at this time, all we have are theories. That is one of the primary reasons the two of you were brought here. To help us, and perhaps come to understand us, and our goals.'

Patrick sucked in a breath, letting it out in a long, quiet

gush. 'Fine,' he said hoarsely. He lashed a finger at Costa. 'Then maybe you should talk to my "colleague" here first. He's been slightly less in the dark than me since this goddamn disaster landed on my doorstep.' Pivoting, he started toward the far end of the Longhouse. His crisp step soon turned into an awkward shuffle-march. He sat down hard on one of the benches, and hunched forward, staring unseeing at the floor, hands clamped on his knees.

Cayden moved a few paces closer, watching him. Patrick didn't appear to notice. Nor did Greg think it was needed. All the vaunted Ranger discipline appeared to have fled, leaving only an angry, confused shell. *Who knows what he saw before this, for him to react that way,* he thought. *Must've been holding that in for a while, even before he got attached to this. All those missions and sweeps, with the same men – they're family by now. Just like us…*

Setting that thought aside, he looked to Costa. The agent was facing the group, eyes darting to meet each of their gazes. He cleared his throat. 'Before I say anything, you mentioned *you* had theories. What, exactly?'

Hiroshi looked down the table at Greg. He nodded, and reached for a flap at the waist of his clinger. When his hand reappeared, it held the vial Megan had brought. He set it on the table. 'What do you know about this?' he asked.

Still wary, Costa picked up the vial, bringing it almost to his nose. His eyes widened when he noted the greyish–white colour. 'Looks like something Patrick's people found, back in Wisconsin. Around the site of a destroyed cabin or house, in an old National Park forest.' He held it away at arm's length, between thumb and finger. 'What is it?'

'It's what we call "Tacitus",' Megan said. She was frowning at the agent, undoubtedly still unsure how much of a threat he posed. 'It's a compound designed to break down the cellular bonds between certain materials – wood, stone, metal – and reduce them, literally, to dust—a desert, in other words, like the old Roman it's named after described. We don't fully understand how it works – we weren't read into the specifics of its design, nor trained to do so. We use it for wrecking buildings or equipment during missions, or when on scorched-earth manoeuvres in retreat.' She nodded in Greg and Leah's direction, and Cayden's. 'They used a small amount to destroy a safehouse in Chequamegon; your searchers probably came across some trace of it that hadn't fully decomposed. Other than that, all the existing stocks are in our care – or so we were led to believe.'

She gestured at the vial. '*That* is an un-decomposed sample taken from the site where we found the helmet, and a few other traces of the Ranger patrol you were with. Judging from what we found, somebody arrived at the site, killed the patrol on the spot, then dragged them to another area and doused them in the powder. They would've been broken down into ashes within minutes – and given how undisturbed the site was, we've pinpointed it to within a few hours ago.'

Costa made a gagging noise. After gulping once or twice, he mastered himself, slipping the Agency mask back on, and set the vial on the table. 'You know who that somebody is?' he asked woodenly.

Greg nodded. 'Those brown-coat friends of yours, and Hargrove's. They've been tracking us since D.C. They have similar skills and equipment to our own – and possibly the same form of regeneration ability.' He paused, giving Costa a chance to confirm or deny. The agent didn't, which was an answer in itself. 'Our theory at this time is they're another black-ops outfit, possibly some attempt at building off the Project template. We have no idea *who* they're working for, other than

Hargrove, or what they are. The only thing we're certain of is that they aren't from our ranks – and they wanted the canister and its contents.'

Costa looked at each one of them in turn, the mask back on. 'And they had something else special up their sleeves, right? Something that might've given them an edge – maybe slowed the two of you down?'

The room temperature seemed to plummet ten degrees. Leah and Jorge exchanged concerned looks. Greg stood up, slowly. 'What makes you say that?' he asked, wary again.

Costa looked him in the eye. 'Because I found a piece of that something at the scene in Chicago. Something that, given what I was told about you, would have to be the ultimate ace-in-the-hole – and yet somehow it didn't work.'

The Council members stared hard at him. He bore these glares with a growing show of strength. 'Before I was assigned to the manhunt, I was given a rundown on all the strengths and capabilities of your type, along with any potential weaknesses; a more detailed version of the material I was given. With everything the files I had access to described, I was curious as to why there wouldn't be an off switch somewhere, under the Project's control or D.C.'s.'

Costa bent down, reaching for his right boot. Greg tensed, but no weapon emerged. Instead, he straightened, his right thumb and forefinger pressed together. Between these digits glinted a tiny shard of metal, hardly bigger than a sewing needle. He set in the palm of his other hand, holding it out for them all to see. 'When word came in about what happened in Chicago, I was sent out to secure the scene. Going through the evidence gathered, I found this.' He held the metal fragment out closer. 'It's a trank dart – with a serum specifically designed to take down Golems. Hargrove referred to it as the Pax Contingency—something *not* in the files, despite his claiming it was part of the Project. And if it worked the way it was supposed to, it would've put both of you'—he waved at Greg and Leah—'in deep coma on the spot, instead of only slowing you down and then wearing off. I doubt the Pentagon would've thrown so much talent and money away on a failed ultimate muzzle for their ultimate soldier. All that – plus Hargrove's man on the spot already up and about after a near-miss car crash, and who knows what other shit – led me to realise he was either grossly out of the loop on what we were chasing, or he had something else in the works, besides recovering the canister.'

He set the fragment on the table, near Hiroshi's hand, and backed away. 'I should've brought it in for Agency techs to evaluate, but the trail was already getting cold – and something about Hargrove being ahead of us in following it didn't exactly fill my bosses with joy. So I saved it.'

The five members all glanced at each other. Greg felt his chest tighten in anticipation. If they had this, they could find a way to build up protection – and maybe another, crucial clue to *why* this Hargrove was after them. If *it's legit*, he reminded himself.

Hiroshi was first to speak, again. 'Interesting. Assuming it's true, what was your purpose, in taking such evidence? And why hand it over now?'

'Insurance, to start with,' Costa said. He sent a glance in Patrick's direction. 'No matter what the colonel says, I had doubts about the nature of Hargrove's activities from the start. Langley's always kept certain projects or people under watch, no matter what their success rate. With Hargrove, it became gradually clear he wasn't on the leash we thought we had him on – anyone's, in fact, except maybe what he *claims* to have.' Instead of expanding on this, he continued, in a grimmer tone, 'Then after what I saw and learned when I got to Monticello,

I *knew* he wasn't going to end this any way but his own – and that scared the *hell* out of me.'

He cast his eyes down for a moment, perhaps in shame at such an admission. When he raised them, though, any sign of this was gone. 'I also knew I didn't have a chance of stopping him and his team – not on my own, and not without backup from Langley, which would take too long in coming.' He made a little wave, taking in the Longhouse, and the campus. 'Given who we were chasing, I had to get to the bottom of this, and report to Langley, before Hargrove finished whatever he's got in mind. So I got ahead of him by Agency jet, got on base, and observed from there. Once I saw what he was planning, I pushed the insertion option, as a way to get eyes on what we might be facing, and act accordingly.' His mouth thinned in an angry grimace. 'Apparently Hargrove guessed that, too.' He pulled himself straight. 'Which leaves me here – something I suspect you won't take lightly.'

Quiet fell again. Greg looked to Leah, and the others. They looked back, and at each other, none of them showing any obvious signs of communicating. To any other Golems, though, they were practically shouting, trying to decide at the top of their lungs what to do with all that had just been dropped on them. Greg didn't know, himself – only that he wasn't sure how much he trusted from this story, and that they didn't have long to decide. The other were likewise divided: Megan coming down on 'shoot-em and dump-em' side, Jorge for the 'dig deeper' approach, Leah somewhere close to his views. Only the undercurrent of indecision united them all.

All except Hiroshi, that was. He sat motionless amid this silent discussion, darting his gaze this way and that to follow what was being shared. When at last Greg and the others stopped 'eye-talking', he broke the stillness. 'Thank you for being so... frank with us, Agent Costa.' The Council leader rolled back his sleeve, touching a command on his clinger's holo-display. 'We will return you and Colonel Patrick to your quarters, while we discuss what you've both shared with us. Once we've reached a decision, we'll proceed from there.'

The Longhouse doors opened. Two Golems in clingers beneath civilian camo jackets and pants, their hoods up, strode into the assembly area. One of them marched up beside Costa, while the other walked over to where Patrick was still sitting, staring emptily at the floor. The agent didn't flinch as a new black bag went over his head. Patrick stood up slowly, also letting the cloth cover his eyes without a word or move.

When they were gone, Megan rounded on Hiroshi. 'I may have only worked a short time with Costa – but ten minutes was enough. He never shared more than he had to, even when lives or missions were at stake, and never hesitated to lie if it served the Agency; it's Day One classwork for them. And Patrick's trained to resist interrogation, practically to our *level*. What's stopping him, *and* Costa, from stringing us along, or just flat-out lying?' She picked up the helmet, almost waving it in Hiroshi's face. 'And how did *this* help, except to piss off one of them?'

'They gain nothing by lying,' Hiroshi said calmly, not bothered at all by Megan's challenging demeanour. 'Costa might, if the matter wasn't as urgent. But if he's as well-trained and connected as he seems – and to be briefed even in general for Project Golem, he'd have to be – he knows he can't prevaricate for long, not with us. And he has to find out what *we* know and are planning, and soon – his bosses won't accept anything less. That means he has to see this through to the end, wherever it takes him – which entails sharing as much as he can about the mission at hand. His training might say otherwise, but so long as he keeps anything *else* potentially sensitive to

himself, he poses no risk to himself or the Agency by talking.'
A momentary smile. 'Especially since he's now at the heart of
something more "sensitive" than anything else on the planet.'

'And Patrick?' Megan inquired, less confrontationally. She'd
long been good at easing off the anger, and more so for Hiroshi
than anyone else – though that could change in a microsecond.
She hefted the helmet again. 'You saw his reaction to *this*. Even
if he has anything worth sharing, what are the odds he'll do so
now, with the state he's in?'

'He may have thought about holding back at the start, given
his skills, and how much in the dark he's been kept by Costa,'
Hiroshi replied. But the sight of *that*' —he pointed to the
helmet—'was enough to provoke a response he couldn't
suppress – far from it. He and his people, they're just following
orders. Orders he doesn't understand, and now hates even
more for getting them killed. And by his behaviour towards
Costa, I'd judge he wants revenge. Not necessarily on the
agent, although that's still a possibility. On the person that
brought him out here in the first place – and who, as his
behaviour and the facts suggest, left them to face us alone,
expecting them to be killed or in a state where they could be,
not long after.'

'You mean this Hargrove,' Jorge cut in. He frowned, more
in thought than annoyance. 'I've scoured every conceivable
nook and cranny of the NeoNet, and done the same in every
older Web archive and classified trove I could think of in
D.C. and around the world, government, military, covert, and
corporate. Not a trace of this guy ever came up in any search
relating to the smallest element of the Project. The Pulse *could*
have affected the files pointing to him – but there would still
be *something*.'

'Unless there was nothing to begin with,' Greg said. '*We*

never existed, from day one. No names, no faces, no background on the families we came from. Not a single hint of the lives we might have had, if we hadn't been picked for the Project. Nobody gets erased *that* completely.' He paused. 'Not without serious help – or *serious* clearance.' Almost of themselves, his eyes slid to the canister. 'Only a few reasons someone would get that kind of makeover.'

Leah followed his gaze. Her eyes widened a fraction, but otherwise showed no reaction. Jorge looked puzzled, while Hiroshi stayed inscrutable. Megan appeared confused, too – then understanding flared in her eyes. 'You mean – one of *us?*' she asked softly. 'You think Hargrove's another *Golem?*'

The others' eyes all locked onto him. Greg met them each in turn, taking a slow breath, before going on. 'Maybe. Maybe not. It's like we talked about before: All we *do* know is that it's somebody who knows enough – about us, or the Project – to stay on our trail practically from the start, and to come up with a few new tricks, based on what it created.' He pointed to the needle fragment. 'This "Pax Contingency". The blades at Chicago and Monticello. The Tacitus. The AllSpec glasses. The *ARC* abilities – faster and more comprehensive than ours. That kind of ability only existed in one place – or so *I* thought, before seeing those brown-coat bastards.'

He nodded at the far wall, toward the north and the Sound. 'I didn't recognise any of them, from the Project.' A moment's glance at Leah showed she hadn't, either; Cayden's look was similar, though like before, it was difficult to tell. 'But that doesn't mean a thing; anyone with the Project's kind of tech and money can easily alter faces. And from the looks of them, they had *serious* surgery, beyond anything we had.' He held out his arm, turning it so the clinger's fabric shimmered in the light. 'We were all improved the same way: speed and strength from the training, with ARC for regeneration and enhancement. The surgeries weren't gentle, but they weren't invasive, or excessive.' For a moment, the memory of the white-clad figures rose up. Forcing it down, he resumed. 'The attackers... they'd had *far* more work done than any of us. Muscle enhancement, strike plate and other skeletal implants; almost anything, from the scars we saw.' He let his arm drop. 'The only thing they *didn't* have were clingers – and if they had, I seriously doubt we'd have the whole Council here, right now.'

No else spoke. He took another breath. 'Thanks to the Bomb, there's no way of digging up the Project – even if we knew where to look to begin with. The dreams, or flashes, don't yield any clues, and the Pulse made sure of any records.' Megan scowled at the mention of the 'dreams'; she'd long been edgier about them than anyone else. Jorge looked uneasy; Hiroshi rigid. Greg stole a look at Cayden, to see the same neutral expression from before, after the plane crash. 'The only way we're going to find *anything* like the answers we want – on the Project, ourselves, *all* of this – is if we work every piece of the puzzle we have. Patrick and Costa are two. The Brown Coats and Hargrove, another two.' He pointed to the canister. 'And the biggest one, connecting all of them, is *that*. Once we know what's on it, and how it's being protected' —he stole yet another look at Cayden, whose neutral look had slid away a tad, revealing wary disquiet not unlike that back at the cabin—'we can find a way to use that info to protect the Sanctuary – against these new enemies, D.C., anybody.'

Greg looked to Leah, and the others, all in turn; none of them showed anything. It was nearly half a minute before Jorge spoke up. 'How do you propose we do that, Greg?' He pointed to the canister himself. 'We've tried everything, and it spat that back at us every time. Even if we had the Project's equipment, there's still no guarantee; with what we have, we're basically beating at it with flint knives. And if this Hargrove and his outfit are so set on recovering it, then we don't have even a fraction of the time needed to keep prodding at it.'

'Then maybe we need to pursue other options,' Hiroshi broke in. The other Council members turned to him. He set his hands in front of him, in the same style as when he began questioning Costa and Patrick. 'As you all know, I took a team up to the Bremerton area, in search of possible supplies – rations, weapon and ammunition stocks, spare parts, anything that the US Navy might have been unable to salvage after the Bomb, and that we might have missed on our other sweeps. The odds were slim, but the drift and hotspots were lower at the start. And with Greg and Leah's mission, it's become even more important to check all possible approaches to the Sanctuary.'

His arms were statue-still. 'We were perhaps a third of the way there, when our equipment began picking up traces of an energy source. Although it had nuclear elements, it was nothing like a fallout deposit; too stable, and the signature didn't immediately register as anything known – to most, that is. We continued north and east; the source got stronger. Based on our pre-Turmoil maps and information, and the Overwatch scans, there was nothing in the area that could produce such a signal. On a hunch, I checked my clinger's scanners for any transmissions or Net connections in the area. No communication frequencies came up – but there was a faint indication of a Net signal, further to the north. Somewhere between the old Navy Yard City, and the northern edge of the Kitsap-Bangor Naval Base.' Hiroshi's features, already stoic, became stiffer. 'What's more, as we came more into range, the systems in our suits recognised elements of the frequency... as similar to those used in our own missions and internal comms.'

Greg sat up, straight as a ramrod. Cayden and Leah stared: the latter's eyes huge, the former's contracted in alertness or suspicion. Megan had gone even paler; Jorge merely gaped, his jaw hanging open. Eventually, Greg made himself speak, in a rough whisper. 'You – you found the *Project*?'

Hiroshi's chin went back and forth, in two small movements. 'I don't know *what* we found – only what it *suggested*.' He brought his hands to his lap. 'And we couldn't get any closer to find out, after those initial findings. The rad count was rising fast – likely hot vapour from the Sound itself, where the Bomb blast was concentrated – and we couldn't risk going any further. So I marked where we'd come to a stop, and ordered the team back.' He nodded to the door. 'Serge and Imran were with me, as part of their familiarisation; they joined us last week, from Morocco and the Caucasus. They took samples from the ground and water, while I attempted to record the frequency for Jorge to examine.' The stoic look came back. 'The moment I tried, however, the signal disappeared – and much of my clinger's scanning equipment was rendered useless, for several minutes.'

'Like what happened with the canister,' Jorge murmured. His initial shock was almost gone, wonder and calculation taking its place. 'So whatever's protecting *that*, is protecting what you came near?'

'Based on what you told me before the meeting, it's a safe assumption,' Hiroshi said. 'What that is—' A shadowy, uncertain look flickered across his face, before he rearranged it into solemn lines, and looked around at the entire Council. 'I'd planned to bring this to you all the second I got back. If the signal and readings point to the Project's site, or even the smallest evidence of it, then we need to pursue it at once. Once

I heard you were bringing in prisoners, however – and after hearing your descriptions of these pursuers – I chose to wait, until we had a better assessment of the threats facing us.'

'The assessment's pretty damn clear from where I sit,' Megan cut in. *Her* shock had faded, too, giving way to anger – some at Hiroshi, the rest at the general situation. 'If those things killed the Rangers, then they're already inside our perimeter by now, or watching it at best, probing for weaknesses. We don't have the manpower to watch every square foot, or the gear and vehicles to get to incursion sites fast enough. And Overwatch is only useful so long as it remains hidden; we use it to alter a satellite's orbit, to give us a better view, it sets off every alarm between here and the Atlantic.' She darted a look at Jorge, seeking confirmation or daring him to tell her otherwise. When the other Golem gave back a grudging nod, she went on, 'So unless we want to wait for them to start knifing us in our sleep, we need to start beating the bushes – and find out just *what* it is we're sitting on before *it* comes at us, too.' Now it was her turn to glance at the far wall, then at the canister.

'That would be the wisest move – the latter, I mean,' Hiroshi said. When Megan looked at him, confused, he elaborated. 'We *do* need to get a clearer idea of what this'—he touched a finger to the canister—'and the signal mean for us here. But as you pointed out, we don't have the numbers to adequately maintain the perimeter or respond to attacks fast enough, beyond our core area. Should we risk sending out all but a skeleton crew – or *everyone*, even, if the situation demands – to hunt down these attackers, spreading out over hundreds of square miles and numerous hotspots, in the hope of flushing out an enemy that, by Greg and Leah's reports, are equal to two or three of *us?* We still don't fully know their capabilities, or weapons. Dispersed, even with full gear and heavy weapons, we run an unacceptable risk of being picked off, or distracted long enough for them to do serious damage to the Sanctuary itself – and grabbing the canister in the process.'

Megan glowered. 'We can't just sit here, either,' she returned. 'If – and it's a damn big *if* – the signal somehow points to the Project, and to what's on the canister's drive, then we *need* to pursue it. But doing *that* means sending a team into the centre of the CZ, roaming around through dead cities and rad deposits for the source. The attackers are bound to see that, and move to intercept. *That* also exposes our location and potential resources, and leads to us risking getting picked off in a single, contained zone, instead of in patrols, where we have greater freedom of movement and present more difficult, less obvious targets.' She stabbed a finger at the table. 'We're facing *two* threats here: one internal, one external. The *external* threat is immediate, and known; the internal, unclear in both respects – and therefore even more dangerous. We have to prioritise, and fast – otherwise one or the other'll decide for us.'

'There's another threat to consider,' Greg added. The others looked to him. 'A Ranger colonel and a squad of his best – plus a CIA agent – are off the grid, as far D.C. is concerned. The CZ's unpredictable, and the units manning the perimeter have a measure of freedom to deal with any sudden events – spills, storms, terror cells, and so on – so occasional lapses in or difficulties staying in contact won't be unusual right away. But Patrick's operating well beyond his original zone. And they had to have had help from FOB Yakima; Wraith-upgraded Black Hawks still aren't common, and only assigned to the largest commands. The loss of those alone is bound to draw notice, if it hasn't already. Add in the missing personnel, and Patrick's "reassignment", and it's only a matter of time –

hours, maybe – before a major response is launched, by the CZ commands on their own, or with heavy support from Washington. And if they find evidence of *us...*'

He paused, letting the implication hang: if D.C. found them, Second Reconstruction or not, the cluster and smart bombs wouldn't take long to reach them. Even nukes were a possibility, despite the hair-trigger fears during and since the Turmoil. Given the military's mad scramble to abandon the bases in the Sound, another mushroom cloud could always be explained as a malfunctioning, forgotten device, or a terrorist cell attempting to steal one and setting it off by accident. Either would serve two key purposes: eliminating an embarrassing, deadly secret from the Vanguard days, and keeping the current government in power.

Hiroshi nodded, unperturbed – in fact, he even wore a little smile. 'All good points, the both of you.' He folded his hands in front of him. 'So the central issue is: how do we solve all three threats, with what we have, and with a minimum of losses or exposure? What's the best option that'll let us avoid prematurely broadcasting our existence, preventing an attack on our people or the Sanctuary – and perhaps, at last, finding the root answers to how *both* came about?'

One of the Council leader's eyebrows made the tiniest quirk at the last question. Greg felt his lips turn up an inch. 'And I'm guessing you already have some idea how to do all that?' he ventured.

Hiroshi's smirk was downright conspiratorial. 'I might.' As soon as he spoke, though, the smirk vanished. 'There are still risks involved – and at least one part of it would prove more dangerous than anything else, it if tanks.' He let out a little sigh. 'But, when set against everything else, it's still the one with the best likelihood of success.'

'We're *already* all at risk,' Megan returned, looking less and less patient. 'Just lay it out, and *we'll* decide if it works – or if we need to add a certain smartass to the threat list.' This last came out warningly, but with an undercurrent of exasperated amusement.

Hiroshi's smile returned, broader. 'Very well, then.' He laid out the details in a few curt sentences. Greg felt his astonishment grow as the pieces of the plan fell into place, buttressed by a slower-rising sense of amazement at its audacity. Judging by Leah's stare, Megan's calculated look, and Jorge's sagging jaw, their impressions marched with his. A quick glance to Cayden showed the older Golem watching them all, face stolid, perfectly still but for the faint rise and fall of his chest.

When the Council leader was finished, Leah spoke up first. 'Well, when you said risks—' She broke off. Rallying, she went on in a different tack, pointing in turn to the front doors, 'You honestly think we can get those two to go along with this – even at gunpoint, if it comes to it?'

'If there was a chance of that, I wouldn't be proposing this,' Hiroshi replied, now looking completely serious. 'Too many things would potentially go wrong if we had to drag them to get this done, and everyone here would suffer for it. But after seeing that'—he pointed to the helmet—'and learning everything he has from us, and his "partner", I have the feeling Patrick isn't much in the mood to play at spooks anymore. Whether or not he believes *we* weren't responsible is moot; all he'll want is the chance to make known that his men were thrown away, and over a threat that some of the spooks kept from the others, and his superiors.'

He picked up the canister, palm flat as if weighing it. 'As for Costa, personal attitudes aside, it all comes down to whether he wants everything – this, the Sanctuary, the Rangers, *Hargrove* – to come out. Any agent with sense – and he'd have to be, to have become part of the Special Activities Division – would want the chance to report in before an operation went *completely* out of control. Especially if he was attached to it as just a minder, and lost control from the start. In which case, *his* superiors would be next up for the axe – which gives him, and them, some room to manoeuvre. Assuming they're informed quickly, ahead of whatever Hargrove and his team have planned. *That* happens, we have room ourselves.'

He looked at each of the Council members. A fierce resolve burned in his eyes; more emotion than Greg had ever seen him show before. 'However quickly the Agency gets word of us, it will still take time for them to organise the right response. Even more so, if they have to devise the right spin for the new government to excuse or authorise their move; doing otherwise only amplifies the risk to them.' His fingers snapped closed around the canister. 'By the time they have both in place, *we'll* have already probed the source of the signal, and, possibly, dealt with Hargrove and his people. With both of those achieved, and the information and capabilities on *this*' —he shook the canister once, for emphasis—'finally revealed, we have leverage enough to hold off *any* retaliation.'

He shook the canister again. 'Possible rally points and hideouts of the other surviving Golems. Locations of hidden Project weapons caches, here and around the world – perhaps even nuclear. Specs of the ARC design process, and possible improvements. Info pointing to the methods for another Pulse; there's still no consensus on how it happened, and everyone would fear the capability in hands not theirs.' He paused. 'At the top of it all: the truth of our origins. The families and people who gave us up: where they came from, if they knew what we were headed for, *why* they did it. How we were modified into what we are, and what we've done over the past twenty years and more. Any one of these would be enough to give D.C. and the world pause, for a time… but *that* would freeze them all in their tracks. And *we* would have the chance not merely to survive, but to live. To build a home for ourselves – and to make it last.'

He set the canister down. No one else in the room made a sound. Hiroshi sat straight, and pushed himself back a little from the table, the picture of self-control again. 'Of course, given the dangers if I'm wrong, I can't and won't force anyone on this Council, or joining in'—he gave Cayden a polite nod—'to approve my proposal. If we go with this, then it's a unanimous decision – no holdouts. At the slightest sign that the Sanctuary is threatened, we pull the plug and evacuate. Were more time available, I'd put the matter to a vote from the whole population. This threat encompasses *everyone*, along with those who haven't arrived, and we were chosen based on original rank, skills and the simpler fact that we arrived first, more than for any real skills.' He let a deprecatory smirk cross his features. 'Since there isn't, I can only put the idea to the Council – and let *you* decide if I warrant a *different* kind of suit than a clinger.' He folded his arms, resting elbows on the table's edge in a style reminiscent of a straitjacket.

None of them laughed. Greg looked at Leah, then at Megan, Jorge, and Cayden. Leah still appeared uncertain, but less so than before. Megan's face was solemn, with a hint of awed respect beneath the surface as she studied Hiroshi; a sign she'd already made up her mind. Cayden still showed nothing, but there was a new set in his legs and frame, indicating he was ready to leave now. Jorge's dumbfounded expression was gone, but the tech looked even less sure than Leah; no doubt he'd already run through all the variables, and didn't like the odds.

Greg already had himself, with barely the smallest portion of Jorge's skills and knowledge, and hated them, too.

How bad will they be if we do nothing? *Or try to handle either threat, by itself, and fail?* The answers were clear there – brutally so, after their tangles with the Boys in Brown. But those creatures were coming any way the Council voted. *Then the question's simple, like Hiroshi laid out. What's the option with risks* and *'the best likelihood of success'?*

The answer to *that* was plain. Turning to look at Leah, he saw the same impression in her eyes, shot through with a greater apprehension than his – but also a growing resolve. He turned to Megan, and Jorge; they each had the same look, now. Bringing his gaze to meet Hiroshi's, he lowered his head, in a slow nod. The Council leader made the same gesture, equally grave. One by one, the others on the Council did the same. They all looked to Cayden. The older Golem didn't speak, or nod, or give any sign, yet the readiness was palpable in his frame. Greg's sigh was almost soundless. *So: Decided.* Of their own will, his eyes slid to the far wall once again. *Now we see what 'success' it leads us to.*

Chapter 18

Approaching Bainbridge Island, eastern shore

Choppy waves lashed the motorboat, throwing up cold spray. The sky was overcast, unlike that above the Evergreen campus. The darkest clouds loomed several miles to the northeast, over the downtown Seattle area. The Geiger counter at the boat's dashboard was clicking faster and faster with every yard, until the sounds almost began to blur together.

Staring ahead, Greg held the scanner to his ear again. The *ping* of the signal Hiroshi had pinpointed had increased again, in volume and frequency. They had left Gig Harbour behind them a few minutes before and were now squarely between Vashon Island and the Kitsap Peninsula. He watched the patchy acres of tumbled suburban beach homes and regrown forest go by on both sides with disinterest for a moment, before facing ahead again. Within ten minutes, twenty at the most, they would be past Blake Island, and approaching Seattle Harbour: the heart of the Bomb's detonation, and the hottest zone anywhere on the planet outside of Hong Kong, Karachi or Lake Balkash. Already, before entering the inlet, he had been able to make out the lines of the city's half-ruined and decaying skyscrapers and waterfront, and the tiny, tilted pinnacle of the Space Needle, all poking through a shroud of distance and late-morning fog.

The threat of rads wasn't the only one on his mind, though. His eyes shifted right, to the east. He couldn't see the Cascades from where he was, of course – but he didn't need to, not to wonder about what might be coming. *They should be getting close to the CZ perimeter, by now. Another hour, maybe two, they'll be able to reach the base. Quicker, maybe, with Jorge relaying perimeter security, route and fallout info through Overwatch – and looking into that 'Pax' deal, if it's real – Hiroshi coordinating the patrols, and Megan at the wheel.*

What would happen *then*, Greg could only guess – and didn't like any of the guesses that came to mind. The idea itself flew in the face of everything he'd trained for – but there was a big enough kernel of logic at the centre that still kept him from objecting, as it had at the Longhouse. Costa had come around to it first, when it was laid out to him; maybe he was enough of a newbie that he hadn't considered the idea of betrayal – or he just saw it as a better chance of survival. Patrick had taken a bit more time, but in the end had agreed, and more emphatically than the Agency man. From his look, the Ranger colonel was set on revenge above anything else, and relished any chance that gave him close to the freedom he needed for it. After that, the nuts and bolts were easy: weapons, rad-hardened transport and radios, profile scramblers for any satellites passing over. The Cascades were the biggest obstacle, coming and going. Once Costa and Patrick were gone, there was no telling what would return.

Hiroshi's got to be crazy, or brilliant, Greg thought. With the other Golem's record, either was possible; the proposal had certainly shown such. And the Urumqi mission was evidence enough already. *No one else would've thought to just walk up to that People's Liberation Army press office, in broad daylight, and just drop the flash drives and memory cards off, like any other military courier.* Through his doing so, the Xinjiang-based terror group behind the Hong Kong and Shanghai attacks had been exposed and destroyed, and World War III averted. But Greg still shuddered at the thought, if they'd screwed up, of having to fight their way through four armoured divisions and several hundred miles of mountains and steppes – and *then* getting to the South China coast, through even *more* troops and cities.

He spared a moment to look back at the other two in the group. Cayden sat to port, fully suited, an XM10 in his lap. Leah was opposite him, likewise equipped. The three of them had hardly spoken since departing Eld Inlet. Cayden's silence was the most unnerving. He had gone through the packing and other prep for the mission without complaint, and without any sign of how he viewed Hiroshi's idea from the start, or thought about what they might find or learn before all this ended. Not knowing what to say, nobody else had said a word to him the entire time. From his blank, stolid demeanour, though, Greg suspected he was more unsettled and anxious to have this done with than any of them. The best, whether Golem or human, always crawled inside themselves before an assignment. Of course, Cayden had worn such a mask since their meeting at the cabin – and all the more after what had been hinted there. Who could say what that would lead to – most of all with one of the 'First Five', unknown to virtually all the later generations?

A new smudge appeared on the horizon: Blake Island. Instead of speeding up, Greg throttled back a bit. He cast his eyes to both sides, behind the clinger hood's protective lenses.

A light crackling sounded in his ears, resolving into Leah's voice. 'Problem?'

'Not yet.' He pointed to starboard, at the tip of Vashon Island, then to port towards the ruins of the Southworth ferry port. 'Perfect spots for an ambush. Just making sure we don't gun right into it.'

They passed through the outlet less than a minute later. He squinted at both points. The clinger's lenses magnified, bringing them into sharp relief. There was a rusting, half-collapsed ferry dock on side, and two lines of abandoned shorefront houses, many of them likewise decrepit or overgrown. He turned the wheel, bringing Blake Island to their starboard side. Soon they'd be inside Rich Passage, the inlet between Bainbridge and Kitsap. At that point, they'd be closing in on the likely cleanest spots to put ashore on the latter island; Keysport was an option, or further up in Liberty Bay. After that, it was a few short miles to the origin point of whatever Hiroshi had picked up.

Greg let his attention drift a little, thinking back. He couldn't *clearly* remember ever staging through Naval Base Kitsap, though it was possible. Golems had always travelled in blacked-out vehicles and aircraft when outside the Facility, as an added security measure, and did not speak to anyone until on-site for their mission. Before the Bomb, it had been the third-largest naval facility in the USA, and a major submarine and strategic nuclear weapon base. The subs and nukes had all gone to sea or been scattered to other bases at the time of the Turmoil, given the still-high tensions with China and fears of domestic terror attacks. This had left only a handful of smaller surface ships and Coast Guard patrols, but the Army and Guard presence in Seattle and the air wing at Lewis-McChord had probably seemed like enough protection.

Until the Bomb proved otherwise. From the Overwatch sweeps before their departure, Greg and the rest of the Council had gotten a general but still striking impression of where the blast had occurred, and how it had affected the entire Sound area. The radioactivity readings from the piggybacked satellite had hit their highest point in the waters between Shoreline and the uppermost part of the Kitsap peninsula, a little south of Indianola. This indicated the Bomb had most likely been set off aboard a ship: a trawler, or small commercial craft, given how closely watched freighter traffic was, then and now. Why the blast hadn't happened dead-centre in the Seattle harbour was unclear. Maybe security had prevented the ship from getting so close, or the device had detonated early – or it *had* been set off in the intended spot. Probably no one would ever know.

The explosion had sent out a shockwave of energy and radioactive water rippling across the Sound, striking every coast from Lakewood to Camano Island. In the downtown Seattle area, these had reached somewhere between fifty and a hundred feet, washing up more almost a mile inland, killing, injuring and irradiating who knew how many in addition to the untold number already affected by the initial burst; the Space Needle had taken the most starkly obvious damage in this. Bainbridge Island, Bremerton, and most of the other coastal urban spots were also wrecked, sowing more chaos and death.

Within an hour, the mushroom cloud had dissipated – into a deadly shroud of hot mist, covering Seattle, the Kitsap region, all the islands in between, and as far inland to the west as Bellevue and Redmond. Olympia and other areas at the fringe had taken it on the chin as well, but days later, and in lesser amounts; prevailing winds had blown much of the post-blast drift to the east and southeast. The Army and Navy had tried to establish a cordon, while they salvaged what they could from Seattle and Kitsap, but the pressure of refugees and radiation had soon outweighed these plans, and they pulled back across the Cascades and the Columbia River, leaving the region to burn and decay.

When Greg, Leah and the other first arrivals had come, there had been almost no sign of regular human presence, and nature had made serious inroads over the flooded and burned-out cities and stretches of suburbia. A few brave or stupid smugglers and looters had combed through the remains – some still did, further south – but the radcount was still too high for even the most daring to travel north of Olympia. The towns and villages west of the Olympic Mountains – Aberdeen, Westport, and others – still existed, but on life-support; kind estimates put their population decline at half, maybe more, with spotty power and food, and little to no real economy. Rads aside, no one seemed to want to live next to a giant mass grave.

Except for those who're already in it, for all intents and purposes. Greg shook his head, trying to get free of the thought; difficult to do, with the sights around him. From a purely tactical sense, it was perfect: where better to hide than in the one place no *humans* could enter and live in? Golems weren't immune to rads – the image of Taylor swam up, an instant before he slapped it down – but they could live in lesser-affected areas for months and years longer than any other being on the planet. *Whatever the Doc put into us growing up, he made it to work, and last.* A new glance to the northwest. *If there is something to be found here, maybe it'll shed light on that – and where we got it, and why.*

He was reaching for the throttle when the bullet snapped past his ear. He dropped flat to the deck before he fully realised what it was. More shots whipped overhead, shattering the speedboat's windshield and punching into the dashboard.

M281s – at least two, his mind calculated automatically. Gripping the wheel from the bottom handles, he twisted it first hard left, then right, throwing the boat into a ragged zigzag.

Fresh automatic fire broke out behind him. He lifted his head to see Cayden and Leah squeezing off short bursts at a craft some 600 yards behind them. Zooming in with the hood, he saw three figures standing in the vessel, clad in dark green coveralls. The boat's wake pointed to its hideout in the tiny inlet just past the ferry port.

Their friends in brown; it couldn't be anyone else. He pulled himself up to a crouch, still holding the wheel. *Should've pulled closer to the rad zone; then they wouldn't have risked it – maybe.* Tossing the self-reproach overboard, he punched the throttle. The engine roared, and the craft launched forward, climbing to 120mph. He clung to the wheel with all his strength, nearly tearing it from the panel. A quick glance back: the other speedboat was falling back steadily. That wouldn't last – the craft had to be less waterlogged, and the engine less taxed.

Both Cayden and Leah squeezed off a round or two more, before pausing to reload. She looked his way. Her voice, automatically amplified over the engine, boomed in his ears. 'What now?'

'We keep going!' She cocked her head, and he went on. 'We gotta limit their movement, force them up against the shoreline. Then we'll have a clean shot!' *And so will they,* he added to himself. *But if we make a run for shore, now, they'll just do the same to us.*

Leah said nothing, only slotted in a fresh magazine. Greg poked his head above the panel, still looping the boat back and forth at random. He spotted the loading docks that marked the eastern corner of Clam Bay. Rich Passage lay immediately beyond. He turned the wheel to port, angling for the inlet.

Another volley ricocheted off the panel's edge, and he ducked flat again, keeping his hand on the throttle as far as it would go. The deck vibrated under his feet, causing his teeth to chatter despite his clenched jaw.

He kept up the zigzag pattern, hoping it wouldn't cost too much of their lead. He looked back again. The pursuing boat was still a good distance behind, but gaining. They'd also become cagier with their ammo; only when Greg held in one direction for longer than two seconds did a spate of rounds zip over his head, or punch into the hull. One tugged at his shoulder; the clinger kept it out. A shout from Leah made him whip around. She was fetched up against the side, clenching a hand to her left shoulder, now a mass of red – but the clinger fabric was already returning to normal. *Long as nothing heavier gets aimed our way, we're fine.*

His head snapped up. *Nothing heavier...* Behind the hood, his lips skinned back in a smile. It was crazy, but... He yanked the wheel hard right, bringing the boat into a wide arc. The eastern shore of the Sound passed in a blur. Another volley zipped over and around him; none struck. He held the wheel all the way over, then brought it straight again. His free hand yanked down on the throttle again. The engine rose to a roar, lifting the bow momentarily clear of the water. When it slammed back down, Greg scanned the water. The attacking boat was still some distance away, maybe three or four hundred yards, but it had peeled off in the same direction, probably hoping for a clear broadside angle: 'crossing the T', in other words. Now it was slowing, righting itself for another charge – and lined up almost perfectly with his craft, bow to bow.

Gripping the siderail, Leah pulled herself up beside him. 'What are you *doing?*' she bawled in his ear.

'Remember that ride we took?' he shouted back. He shot her a knowing look. 'In Atlanta?'

She stiffened. Her eyes flicked to the enemy boat, and back to him. Her mouth shaped a word: *No.* He stared at her for a second, then turned back to the controls. 'You can't – you gotta be fucking *kidding* me!' she yelled.

Instead of answering, Greg leaned back. Leah shouted something else, but more gunfire made her duck and roll, hunching low at the stern next to Cayden. The older Golem shot a quick look at Greg, then widened his stance, grasping the edges of the boat with both massive hands.

Greg chanced another glance above the dashboard. The boat was still bearing straight for them. Three figures were standing near the motor, SAWs in their hands. Bullets tore into the hull, sending chips and chunks whirling. A single round at extremely close range – or several all at once, in the same spot – and the clinger wouldn't help much.

Two hundred yards... One-seventy-five... A fist-sized piece of fibreglass struck Greg in the face and glanced off. He hardly noticed, staring straight ahead. The distance shrank, more and more. The other boat showed no signs of wavering. He was close enough to see the faces of four men now, and make out their hair: two black, one brown – and one blonde, at the controls. The other pilot's eyes – a cloudy green – locked with Greg's. His three partners kept firing in steady bursts, their legs spread wide apart for balance. More shots buzzed around his face and shoulders; amazingly, not one found its mark. The engines and gunfire merged in his ears, becoming an insane cacophony. Seventy-five... Fifty... Twenty-five... Fifteen... He girded himself, knowing it wouldn't help.

Without warning, the other boat's bow jinked left, trying to evade; the pilot wasn't up for 'chicken.' Another two seconds, and it would be right alongside, giving the gunners a perfect shot. Except there weren't two seconds – because Greg had already swung *his* boat straight for the other's flank.

There was an almighty crunch of tearing metal and fibreglass. The bow of Greg's craft splintered as it ploughed through the attacker's stern. He had a brief, vague image of the three shooters rising several feet into the air, as though by levitation, still firing. A heartbeat later, the bow struck the engine, and the tank of reserve fuel beside it.

The fireball swallowed him in an instant. Heat and blast tore at his arms, wrenching him off the wheel. He felt the hood rip back from his face and screamed as the skin of his face flash-burned. Two human-shaped forms flew past him, vanishing into the haze of smoke, fire and debris. He tumbled backwards, bouncing off the deck. Something snapped in his chest and back, sending lances of stinging fire through his torso. His hands scrabbled for something, anything to grab hold of.

Suddenly, he found himself pawing air. Dazed from the pain, he could only focus on ahead of him. All he could see were clouds, grey and forbidding. *Strange; shouldn't they be white?* he wondered idly. Then he struck the water, headfirst, and all was cold and darkness.

Soft white light beamed down, pressing through his eyelids. Bit by bit, he felt other senses returning. He was lying on something soft, giving and wet. Cold water was lapping back and forth over his lower legs. His ears were filled with a dull ringing sound. He could smell damp, smoke, and burning oil. A thick layer of salt caked his lips.

He drew a shallow breath. A dozen cold knives stabbed into his chest from both sides. He hissed in and out through his teeth, struggling to ride out the agony. When it began to ease, he inched his head back and forth, looking this way and that. The light was beginning to fade, bringing new shapes, sounds and images into focus all around him. Grey-black sand, stretching in all directions. The soft roar of surf. The rustling of stunted, dark green bushes, growing near the edge of the sand. A beachfront house in the far distance, its walls sagging inward, its porch a tangle of decaying wooden planks.

The light was nearly gone now, leaving a general blurriness over everything he saw. The pain was receding with each passing second, supplanted by a paralysing weakness – one he hadn't felt in years. The ARC was obviously kicking in by now, so he must have done even more damage than he'd thought. Squinting, he looked harder at his surroundings. Two human-sized lumps were curled up a few yards away, unmoving. They were garbed in clingers, covered with clumping sand. The closer one had close-cut dark hair; he could see a serious gash to its temple closing. The other's hair was similarly dusky, and longer, thrown about in a wild, soaked fan, like a woman's. Its face was smeared with sand, muck and watery blood, half- hiding a gruesome mask of cuts and a shattered nose.

A shadow fell over his vision. Looking up, he could see the dark, blurry outline of a human-shaped figure. It was clad in some sort of shiny, dark green material; when it leaned closer, a pig-snouted gas mask resolved into view. He tried to call out to the others but could only manage a hoarse croak. The figure stooped, extending both hands. One grasped his neck, gently rubbing at the carotid. The other moved to the figure's side, reappearing with a pen-shaped object. When Greg saw the needle extend, he struggled harder to move away. Nothing responded. With surgical precision, the figure stuck the syringe into his neck, pressing a button at the top.

Cool tingling rushed out from the injection, spreading over his body in waves. He braced himself, expecting his breathing to stop in the next second. Instead, the feeling sank deep into his bones. He felt his fingers twitch, and his legs begin to shift at his brain's commands. Every movement was still agony, and the weakness was still pressing down like a straitjacket – but the pain in his chest and sides was vanishing all the faster.

The coolness began to fade. A deep fatigue seeped in to replace it, weighing him down like he'd been draped in lead-lined blankets. Above him, the figure stood upright, moving out of Greg's sight. he angled his head to follow, and saw he was making for the next body. His eyelids were drooping lower and lower, but he fought to stay awake.

The figure turned over the closer body, revealing Cayden's mud-smeared, burn-scarred features. His motions assured yet careful, the figure brought forth another pen-syringe, and pressed it to the older Golem's neck. Just before Greg's eyes closed, he saw the stranger withdraw the pen – and gently stroke Cayden's cheek, with a strange sort of affection.

Sound was the first to return. Cocking his ears, he picked up the soft *drip – drip – drip* of water nearby, from a pipe or faucet. There was a faint pinging noise – an EKG machine; he'd heard them plenty of times. Next was smell: gauze and harsh antiseptic, mixed with latex, dried blood and other, less recognisable odours lingering beneath. Then touch: hard padding beneath his hands and body, swathed in cloth, and the softer, yielding feel of the pillow under his head and neck. He seemed to be partly propped up, starting from the waist. There was a light pressing sensation on both sides of his head, which he couldn't identify. His eyes stayed closed, held down as though by lead weights.

Taking all this in, Greg wiggled his fingers and toes. All of them responded. He rotated his ankles, and his hands at the wrist: same story. The weakness and fatigue from before were gone; now he just felt tired, and content to lie where he was, maybe for hours. He relaxed a little, letting his back flatten against the padding. A much-needed rest, after that insane trick out on the Sound.

The Sound – the boats – Cayden – *Leah*.

His eyes snapped open. Everything was dark and blurry, though starting to come into focus. He sat up, arms out in defensive posture. The room spiralled around him, and he shot out a hand, grabbing the nearest object – a surgical tray table, by the feel of it – to keep from crashing off the bed. He sucked in breath after breath, waiting for the world to right itself.

When it had settled into a tepid rocking, and his vision had cleared to normal, he let go, and looked down at himself. His clinger was gone, along with his undershorts. He felt at his face: no sign of burns. A set of remote lead pads, each the size of a quarter, were pasted to his chest, and an IV lead ran to the crook of his right arm. Reaching up, he gingerly felt two more leads at his temples. Tracking the pinging with his ears, he spotted the EKG machine behind his bed. Two other slim, boxy devices were set up on his left, their displays turned away from him. He couldn't guess what their purpose might be.

He looked around the room. To even the trained eye, it was a standard hospital exam room. A set of light-blue curtains, pulled back, hung around his bed. A plain black clock above the door said it had been nearly two hours since the attack, give or take. There was a set of grey metal cabinets not far from his bed, and a sink. Tiny drops fell from the tap in a slow rhythm. The light above was subdued, flickering every now and then. There was a bare metal door a couple of metres in front of him, closed. Above the frame was a domed glass bulb, with a dull blue light at its centre. A security camera, or something like it.

Two other beds were to his left, both occupied. Leah lay in the nearest one. She was likewise undressed, the sheet pulled up to her shoulders; he saw no sign of any injuries. The same

EKG and IV leads as his were attached to her temples and arm. Cayden lay in the third bed, also unconscious and hooked up. Looking past his companions, Greg saw another counter, covered with scalpels, other instruments, and cloth bandages. Most of these were soaked or speckled with blood.

On a metal table beside this display, he spotted their clingers, neatly folded, with a set of fresh undershirts and shorts beside each. Their knives and pistols had been placed atop all three outfits, cleaned and prepped. He even spotted an extra clip of ammo for each of the guns. *Argues against this being a prison. Or else it's one so tight there's no point in using them.* There was no sign of the canister.

Cautiously, Greg pulled out the IV lead, ignoring the spike of pain from the healing injection. He lifted his legs out from under the sheet and stood up. The dizziness surged, before fading away completely. Still cautious, he yanked the sheet off the bed and wrapped it around himself one-handed. Reaching out with the other, he gently shook Leah by the shoulder. 'Wake up.' He hesitated, for a second. 'Hey, babe, come on. Wake up.'

Leah shifted, groaning. Her arms and legs jerked a few times. Her face twitched, as if stuck by multiple tics, before settling back to serenity. Eyes still closed, she murmured, 'Greg?' She reached out a hand, groping blindly. 'I can't see, my eyes won't—'

'Easy, easy.' He took her hand in his, gripping it tight. 'It'll pass in a second – keep them closed for a little longer. Can you move everything else?'

She wiggled all limbs and extremities again. 'I think so… Yeah.' Her head turned his way. Her eyes fluttered for several seconds, then opened. They locked onto his at once. The grip squeezed all the tighter. She started to scan the room, gently lifting herself up at the waist – maybe she'd managed to get past the vertigo quicker. 'Where—?'

'No idea,' Greg answered. He looked around again himself. 'All of us are here; same with our equipment. No clue how long we were out, either – I'd guess a few hours.'

Leah looked around the room, taking everything in. When she was done, she gave Greg a new look: half furious, half admiring. 'You just *had* to do it? The same trick on that op in Atlanta, when we were tracking a gunrunner to the militias springing up all over the state. Guy was cornered in an alley, right by a gas station, on a cycle; we'd been chasing him almost an hour on our own rides. He decided to play chicken – and so did *you*.' She punched Greg's arm, hard, bringing a wince from them both. 'Only goddamn luck the whole block didn't go up then – and that we didn't get charbroiled *now*.'

'They'd have cut us to shreds in seconds, if I hadn't,' Greg replied, seriously. 'If I'd tried to bolt anywhere, they'd have just run us down, or kept us away from land until we ran out of fuel, then picked us off from a distance.'

'Fair enough,' Leah said. 'Whoever those guys were, they obviously hadn't seen you try it – or expected to.' She bent down to rub at her knees, and check her lower legs and ankles. Only at that moment did she notice the IV in her arm. Pulling the lead free, she studied it, and the bag of liquid. 'What's *this*? Boosters?'

'Maybe,' Greg said, cautiously. He gave the bag a harder look. He'd never seen *what* the boosters really looked like, in any form. Why should he have? With the ARC already in his system, he'd never paid attention to the shots received after more gruelling missions. He held each arm out in front of him and looked over his chest and torso. No residual trauma. Aside from the aches and vertigo – now almost faded completely away – he felt perfectly normal.

That was a surprise, and a concern. No matter how quick or well the ARC worked every time it kicked in, and the boosters when they were needed, every Golem went through anywhere from one to three hours – commonly the latter – of fatigue and general weakness, before they were fully up and running again. Training, instinct and sheer will could compensate at times; it certainly had for the two of them. But neither he nor any of the Golems he'd ever worked with could be back on their feet so fast, after an encounter like that on the Sound, even with multiple boosters – not without prompt help. That argued for a new kind of booster, one that they'd never encountered, and acted faster and went deeper – or something completely different, altering their ARC and physiologies in unknown ways.

A new groan brought him back. Cayden's head was shifting back and forth, face creased mildly in pain. He moved his arms and legs, sliding the sheet down to his waist. Gradually, his eyes opened. At the sight of Greg and Leah, he grunted in surprise, and sat up, which made him wince and grab his head with both hands. When the spasm passed, he looked hard at the two of them. 'What's going on?' he growled. His gaze moved about in all directions, like a trapped animal. 'What is this place?'

Before Greg could answer, a new voice cut in. 'Don't worry, Cayden.' The voice was female, soft and melodious. 'All of you are safe, and in good hands.'

Cayden froze, looking about in every direction. Greg was rooted to the spot. *That voice.* A chill dropped down his spine like a waterfall. *But that would mean—*

'I know you,' Leah murmured. Both men looked at her. Her eyes were wide, and perplexed. She climbed delicately out of bed, clasping the sheet to her body. 'You – you were always there. At the Facility, all through the Project. When we were training… when we came back… all the time.'

The voice chuckled – nostalgically? 'Yes, Leah. I was entrusted with your care, from the very first days. You, and Gregory, and Cayden – all of those who passed through the Project. All of you proved beyond extraordinary. I can't express how much it pleases me to see you here, whole and recovering.'

'Where's that?' Greg asked. Casting about again, he traced the voice's source – the security camera, if it *was* that. 'I went through every room at the Project, and I *know* this isn't one of them. So what is it?' He stepped closer, squinting at the blue-lit glass. 'Who's holding us here? *Why* are we being held? Who the hell are *you?*'

The voice went silent, as if hesitant. When it spoke again, its tone was the same mix of pleasant and soothing as before. 'My name is Gaia, Gregory. And everything will be explained, and soon. First, though, there are some things you'll need to see.'

A low buzzing sounded from the direction of the door. All four of them turned their eyes to it. The heavy metal slab swung open, hinges squeaking. Beyond it was a dimly-lit corridor, turning out of sight at a sharp right angle.

None of the three Golems made a move. Leah's body was outwardly relaxed, but her eyes were wide with astonishment, one hand inched toward the wheeled tray table at her bedside, ready to grab it as a weapon. Cayden sat stock-still, lips pressed tight. Greg hardly dared to breathe. At last, he let the sheet fall to the floor, and reached for the clothes and his clinger.

Chapter 19

Point Defiance Marina

Outskirts of Tacoma, WA

Hargrove stood at the railing of the pier platform, staring out at the water. Desolation and fallout aside, the view was spectacular. The clouds from yesterday had mostly drifted away, letting him fully enjoy the sight of the bay, the low forested landscape of the islands and the mainland shore, and if he turned around, the towering magnificence of Mt Rainier. He inhaled, trying to take in as much of the air as he could. As usual, the taste of it was sterile, harsh, and tinged with soot and salt. The filters on his face mask were good, but they couldn't keep out everything. Still, it was satisfying, in a way. If nothing else, it gave him a hint of what everything would turn to, assuming anything else went wrong.

Like yesterday. His grip on the railing tightened, working back and forth. Tiny flakes and splinters fell from the weathered wood. With a supreme effort, he made himself stop, and turn slowly around. The three 'associates' stood in a loose line, several feet away. Their green coveralls were ripped and charred in many places, and smeared with mud and fuel oil, but they bore no visible injury, other than their original scars at neck and hands, and elsewhere hidden from sight. Behind the silver-framed glasses – saved through no small effort, after the previous day's *debacle* – their faces were as blank as ever.

Hargrove took a step or two back and forth, marshalling his thoughts, and his temper. Finally, he faced the three men again. *Repeat summary of events,* he pulsed.

One of the agents – J-003, his brown hair a mess of short, singed curls – pulsed back immediately: *All assets departed as instructed, upon alert of movement from suspected enemy base west of Olympia, through satellite thermal monitoring of entire Sound region. Movement rapidly determined to be single water transport, with two or more occupants, rounding Kitsap Peninsula. Assets took up position at northernmost tip of Vashon Island, per interception strategy. Engaged target vessel upon its entrance into Rich Passage, where manoeuvrability would be restricted, and likelihood of capture greatest before targets reached anticipated destination.*

The scrolling text stopped, for a second or two, before resuming: *Likelihood proved incorrect. After brief exchange of fire, target vessel rammed asset's transport, resulting in destruction of both craft, and significant injuries to all parties. Lacking transport, hardened radiation gear, and precise knowledge of targets' location, assets swam to rally point at present location.* A second stop. *Target group's location still unknown – as is T-001's, after separation from main force. Locator signal inactive, or masked. No indication of T-001's status, or that of target group.*

Hargrove had been furious before. Now, watching the words move across the lens, he was almost incandescent with rage. Long training and innate self-control kept this mostly out of his face and posture, except for the bone-white clench in both his fists, the knife-slash tightness of his mouth, and a mere flicker of heat in his eyes. In some ways, maybe, he was becoming more and more like his 'associates' than even he had thought was possible. A disturbing thought, but one that held a certain attraction – and one which was keeping him from smashing the assets and the pier to dust, out of sheer rage.

Dismissing these meditations, he pulsed: *Last confirmed position of target group?*

Nearest to southwestern shore of Bainbridge Island; between Lytle Beach and Fort Ward Park, J-003 returned. *No sightings since engagement, and no noticeable movement detected, on Bainbridge or Kitsap – or from suspected base to the south. Currents not fully known; possibility high that target group was swept farther, west or east. No civilian or military facilities of note indicated on island, based on satellite and ground recon. Also no evidence yet found of serviceable transport from Bainbridge, by water, air or land. Sole land connection, Agate Pass Bridge, under continuous observation.*

Growling under his breath, Hargrove turned away, looking across the water again. *Makes sense, however much I hate it.* After literally running into their pursuers, the targets would want to disappear again, fast, and under the nearest possible shelter. And being back at their starting point – in every sense of the word – they now had more options; all the more so with a base undoubtedly manned by others of their kind, with an unknown amount of weapons, gear and transport. It made Hargrove nervous, leaving a place like that at his back while he chased the main objective, but he didn't have the manpower or resources to deal with it. *For the time being, that is.*

Nor would the targets stay in one place for too long. Moving was risky, but kept them from being pinned, as it had so far. He shifted his gaze northwest, toward Kitsap. *And with the* Facility – *or what's left of it* – so close, they'll want to move even sooner.

There *had* to be something of value at the old site. The fact that the targets were trying for it argued they couldn't crack the canister, or its contents, and were seeking out tech they believed – or *knew* – might do so. And if *one* of the targets was who he was beginning to suspect, after re-watching the Monticello footage... *It'd be a hell of a shock, if it was. But then again, the only way to be sure a* Golem's *dead is to have one at your feet – in pieces. Airstrikes sound good to most, but tend to overshoot.* Assuming that thought was correct, the chances were good they'd have info on exactly *where* to look in the Facility – and how to bring it back to their base, or use it on-site. *That happens, I might as well swallow Tacitus, save Costa and his crowd the trouble.*

He stared at the Vashon shoreline, as if he could see through it all the way to Kitsap. There was nothing in that area that could hide them for long, from visual, thermal or any of the other sensors on the now-geosynced satellites. Weather and fallout – and the Golems' clingers – made it difficult to pinpoint exact movements of anything in the entire Sound area, but traces of these were still easy to pick up, with the right amount of effort. So where could they hunker down, away from *all* prying eyes, right on the Project's front porch? He looked off toward the horizon, not really seeing it. *Has to be something* connected *to it. Question is: How do they expect to get in, Golem or not? The Facility was tougher to enter than Fort Knox, Langley, NORAD, and all the CIA's black sites put together.* So what –

He stopped. A slow, cunning smile stretched across his face, the first open one he'd worn in days. It was a slim chance, but the only one that was possible. The smile grew wider as he turned to face his 'associates'. *If it is, then this little road trip just became a* whole *lot more interesting – and* fun. He laughed aloud at the thought. The sound echoed over the isolated spot.

Chapter 20

Naval Base Kitsap

Site of Project Golem

On the surface, the hallway was mostly unremarkable. The walls and floor were grey-white, and lit by soft fluorescents, giving it the look of an ordinary hospital corridor. The lack of doors or windows made clear it was anything but, however; the sight reminded Greg of temporary and permanent negative pressure passageways used to isolate patients with contagious disease. *Or radiation.* He crushed that thought back, and kept moving forward, one eye checking every inch of the walls, the other trained on the door ahead. Like the one to their 'recovery room', it was almost vault-like, with a keypad where the door handle would normally be. When he was within a couple of yards, the lights on the pad changed from red to green. Another buzzing alarm, a series of sharp clunks followed by the hiss of escaping air, and the door popped open, sliding back.

The others behind him stopped at once. Glancing back to check the rear, he saw Cayden and Leah mimicking his pose, hands at the weapons flaps of their clingers. *Till we know for sure what's ahead, this is all enemy territory. Even more so, after what we've heard already – and whatever's waiting ahead.*

He stepped through the door, and found himself in another hallway. This one had several long, wide windows stretching in either direction, with heavy metal shutters drawn down. There was thick dust on the floor; traces of grime and mould decorated the walls. Other than a pair of grubby, unmade hospital beds against the wall, there was no sign anybody or anything had been in the place for years. *Almost* no sign; glancing down, he spotted a set of tracks, standing out starkly against the filth. Human tracks, made with hiking or military boots – and running from the door and down the hallway, disappearing around another corner. Greg gripped the pistol even harder. *Someone* had saved them, then, and patched them up – but what the hell *for*?

'Turn right, then straight ahead,' Gaia's voice said. Greg looked to Leah and Cayden again, and lifted his free hand, making a V-sign with the first two fingers. At their nods, he hefted the pistol again, crouched lower, then sprang out around the corner. In a flash, he was across, and back in cover. Two dark blurs followed a heartbeat after: one to his right (Leah), the other to his left (Cayden), both disappearing almost as he registered them.

Other than a creak or two from the building settling, or from the wind outside, nothing happened. When this had lasted for maybe ten seconds, Greg spoke, keeping his voice to a murmur. 'Where are we – exactly?'

'The main hospital, in the southwest area of Kitsap Base,' the voice responded. 'Right at the edge of the old PX zone.' A pause. 'The entrance to the Project's heart, for all intents and purposes.'

Greg looked to Cayden and Leah. They each made a small wave, telling him it was his call. Pistol raised, he rose, and padded almost soundlessly down the hall. He kept glancing around him as they walked, taking in every sight, sound, and smell. There was still no sign anyone had come near the place in years – but since there was no idea exactly *what* was waiting for them, he wasn't taking chances.

A trio of doors, spaced wide apart, came up on the wall to his left. He was halfway past the second when he stopped: the light coming through the frosted glass was softer than it should be, with fluorescents. He raised a hand, motioning the others back, and gently grasped the door handle. Finding it turned easily, he pulled the door open – and froze. 'What?' Leah whispered.

Greg didn't respond. He took several steps forward, until he was standing before the uncovered window. From the height of a line of far-off trees, he judged they were on the building's third floor. The view was westward: the sun was setting, almost hidden behind the treeline, but still strong enough to reveal plenty of the surrounding terrain. A short distance away, through a thick fan of brush and trees, he saw the edges of a block-shaped building, its white paint dulled to a washed-out grey. A blacktop road, weathered almost to the same colour, formed a loop between both buildings, before stretching off in opposite directions. Bringing his face almost to the glass, Greg saw the nearer branch was shorter, curving under the trees to an open field 200 yards further on, then splitting again. He could just make out traces of white lines on both branches: track lanes.

Déjà vu washed over him in waves. He didn't recognise any of the scenery – and yet, somehow, he *did*. *Did I do laps on that road, when in the Project? Was that field a firing range, or where I practiced empty-handed combat?* Incoherent, hazy images played through his head: all he had, when it came to memories. *Did I ever see* anyone *not in a clinger, or a uniform –*

Something brushed at his sleeve. He started to whirl around, only to see Leah at his side again, and Cayden just behind her. They stared out at the view themselves, wearing looks probably much like his own: confused, unsettled, barely comprehending. Finally, Cayden seemed to shake himself free of the spell, and moved back toward the door, though keeping his body turned partway in the window's direction. Greg followed him, checking all sightlines before stepping back out into the hallway; Leah brought up the rear.

Farther down, a pair of doors – plain polished wood now, with small windows – was almost in sight. Greg made a V-sign to the others, and started forward again, moving farther out in front. His step was a tad quicker, but still made only the barest rustling against the tiled floor. He told himself it was just the urge to get inside, and not the thrill of *finally* seeing 'home.' Part of him even listened. He searched his memory, trying to remember any previous time he'd seen this place. Nothing came; other than the 'dreams,' and the scattered snapshots – the training field, the labs, the barracks – everything was blank. *Or scrubbed.* The pistol came up higher. *And maybe here's the answer as to* why.

Another blue lens gleamed above the doors as the three Golems came close. Keeping one eye on it, Greg tugged lightly at one door handle, then jumped back – he'd lost count of how many rigged entrances he'd cleared. When nothing happened, he pulled at it again, extending his gun hand through the gap. Beyond was a darkened lobby and reception area, also painted white, with green trim. Despite what he'd expected in the wake of the Bomb, there were almost no signs of a hurried evacuation: no scattered papers, no dropped or missing computers, not even a stray wheelchair or stretcher. *More proof.*

Leah and Cayden fanned out to both sides, checking the adjoining hallways. No response of any kind came. Greg swept the reception desk, and looked up to the ceiling. No cameras, and no easy sightlines. If they moved further into the place, who knew what traps or other surprises were waiting.

He started to turn, to check the next move with Leah, then stopped. Above the centremost elevator, almost out of sight from the door, he could see a round white disc set into the wall – with a blue lens in the centre. He moved closer, nerves singing with tension. Leah and Cayden came next, keeping their eyes and guns moving over the front doors and all other access points.

He halted before the centre elevator, which had a yellow and black *Out of Order* sign taped to one door. As he stood there, there was a cheery *ding*, and the doors slid open. He jumped back, and turned around, looking to Leah and Cayden. They were every bit as tense – but neither made a move to run, or looked about to suggest it. Taking one last look around the room, Greg got in, moving aside to the corner to let Leah and Cayden follow. Once everyone was aboard, the doors closed. The car started – heading downward, and silently, without any bumps or jolts that would indicate constant usage, or neglect-related wear.

After perhaps five seconds, it stopped. The doors didn't open. 'Press 3, please,' the voice said, now emanating from the car's overhead speaker. Sharing a wary look with the others, Greg stepped forward, and put his thumb to the button. A soft buzzer sounded from somewhere. Above the row of buttons, the small, square light panel suddenly changed colour, becoming bright red: a palm-scanner. Cautiously, he placed his hand flat against this.

The panel changed again, to light green. There was the faintest crackle from the ceiling, then Gaia's smooth, calm voice. 'Access confirmed.' The voice paused, for hardly more than two seconds. Greg heard a faint set of clunking sounds, somewhere above them. 'Surface entry points secured. All detection systems functioning. Stand by for final descent.'

With no other warning, the elevator dropped again. Greg's ears popped, making him cringe. He grabbed for the wall handhold but had hardly grasped it when the car slowed again. Another *clunk* from above; a hatch, or security door, for added protection. *Wonder how they built the whole set-up, if the building was already there. Or maybe the whole structure was a fake to begin with.* He pulled his mind away from these thoughts. *Concentrate on how they built the real surprises – and whatever those are.*

The car came to another halt. This time, the doors slid open. Instead of a hospital floor, there was a grim, harshly lit concrete room, and a wheeled, blue metal rail platform, sitting on a set of tracks. Following these with his eyes, Greg saw that the tracks extended into a tunnel, similarly lined with concrete and metal support beams. He looked up at the ceiling, where he could almost see another blue-eyed lens through the frosted lighting panels. 'Where's this lead?' he demanded.

'To the answers you wanted,' Gaia replied, still in that smooth tone. When none of the Golems made a move, her – its? – voice went on. 'Please believe me, Gregory; I do not intend to harm you, or Leah, or Cayden. I am only here to show you what you came here for: the truth.'

The three Golems shared another look. Finally, Greg went first, pulling open a section of the metal railing and letting Leah and Cayden climb in first. Stepping onto it himself, he went to the small control box at the front, where he spotted a joystick, and another palm scanner. When he put his hand to it, a low thrumming sound made the platform rattle, before settling into a barely noticeable vibration. Face expressionless as Cayden's now, he grasped the small joystick at the top of the box, and pushed it forward.

The platform started forward, gliding down the tracks. Greg took hold of the railing, but soon discovered he didn't need to; the platform was moving at a steady but slow clip, without so much as a bump. Chancing a look over the side, he saw maybe six inches of space between the bottom of the platform and the tracks: maglevs. Lights came on in the ceiling as the platform passed beneath them and shut off once it was past. They made one smooth, wide curve at one point; other than this, the ride stayed almost perfectly straight. From this, Greg guessed they were following an existing surface road, or maybe even tracks; some other bases he'd seen in the course of his duties had them, to move heavy equipment or supplies when trucks or forklifts wouldn't do. He tried to calculate how far they'd come, from what he remembered of the satellite readouts of the Kitsap base area. Nothing was certain, but he was willing to guess they were somewhere close to the centre, where the Trident missile storage and main base complex were set – and getting closer by the second.

He eased the joystick back. The platform began to slow. Ahead, more lights came on, illuminating a loading area like the one they'd started from – except for one glaring difference: A pair of massive metal doors, set what Greg guessed to be a metre deep into the wall. They loomed over the bay like brooding giants, the light reflecting off them with a dull, harsh glare. There was a keypad and scanner identical to the elevator's on the left-hand side, and another of Gaia's blue eyes in the ceiling above; other than this, the area was as unadorned and severely functional as the walls of the tunnel they'd just come through.

The platform halted, smooth and silent. Greg climbed off first, and walked to the keypad, his pace quick yet somehow mechanical. Leah and Cayden stepped down onto the loading floor, pistols at their side. He studied their surroundings again as he put his left hand to the scanner. *Multi-storey underground location, maglev transport, multi-layered security at start and finish… and all beneath the third-largest base in the country.* He closed his hand tighter around the butt of his own weapon. *The answers* have *to be here.*

A heavy *thunk* sounded from the doors. Two more followed, accompanied by a grinding squeal of metal on metal. Deadbolts the size of girders, by the sound. A line of light appeared between the doors, and began to widen, inch by inch, as the gargantuan slabs pulled apart. Tiny sparks and bits of rock flew from the runners in the floor. Leah and Cayden came up next to him. She had her weapon out, though in a more relaxed way. He wore his perpetual taciturn look, and carried nothing, though both hands were set in a ready position.

The doors halted with another screech and clank, leaving a gap just wide enough for an old M1 tank to pass through. Past this opening, a long, bare metal ramp sloped downward maybe a dozen metres, to a second set of doors – plain, blacked-out, likely bulletproof glass this time, with no sign of a lock. This puzzled Greg for a moment, before he turned his eyes up to check for cameras and saw two more frames in the ceiling. *Extra blast doors. Not as thick as the first defences, but enough to delay a serious attack in a pinch.* He felt a moment's hesitation. Not fear – more an undefinable unease. *I should remember this. The inhibitors, surgeries, and all the rest, they couldn't have erased every memory – could they?* He didn't see how – but he didn't see any other explanation.

He went first down the ramp, stepping carefully. Print scans or no, they could still trip some security measure, this deep inside a place so secure and buried. Nothing happened. Stopping at the bottom of the ramp, he motioned the others to stay back, and moved to the door, in tiny steps. Bringing the pistol to bear, he put his hand on the door handle, a plain metal rod. It was warm to the touch, another sign of the power and temp control. He took a deep breath, and made his fingers close around it. Conscious of the others' eyes on him, he flexed his arm, and pulled.

The door slid open – so easily, he had to take a step back, to keep from slipping backward from the momentum. He pulled the door open to its fullest, and pushed once against it to secure the maglock at the corner. Ahead, all he could see was blackness, and the outlines of a staircase directly before him. Were his clinger hood up, he could have used night-vision. Instead, he took another breath, and stepped over the threshold.

A click sounded. Strong light flashed on overhead. Greg whirled around, gun raised, but no shots or other threats came. He spotted another blue lens on the ceiling right above his head; no doubt it served as a motion sensor, along with surveillance. More lights activated, one after the other, stretching in long rows down the ceiling.

He turned, following these – and stopped. Before him, a single chamber was laid out – half a football field, at the very least. He was standing on a wide, stainless steel walkway, running along the walls. with numbered doors of like material every several metres. On the lower floor, a large rectangle of space was occupied by towering computer servers, enclosed by half a dozen holo-screen desk terminals. He spotted more computer equipment against the walls: printers, scanners, and 3-D displays. Additional doors gave onto this space, some of them open; he saw a break area, and a conference room. To even the trained eye, it was no different from any workspace in the world.

This sight wasn't what had jolted him, however. At the far back of the room, at the walkway level, two large, square windows looked out onto another space beyond – much bigger than the 'office area', from the way the light extended. Something about them, the way someone might look standing at them, looking down at what and who was beyond...

He strode toward this view, following the right-hand side of the walkway. When he came to the windows, he stopped again. The gun fell to his side; he had to make a conscious effort not to drop it. The view extended a lot further than he'd thought; a full football field's worth this time, maybe more. Most of the area closest to the windows was taken up by exercise equipment: mats, treadmills, bikes, elliptical machines, free-weights of every size, even a G-force simulator. Various personal combat gear hung from racks on the walls: padded chest armour, gloves, helmets – and blunted knives, metal and polished wood clubs, staffs, and dummy rifles.

Another glass divider – thicker and stronger, suggesting more layers of tempering – split this zone off from the rest of the area. Through this, Greg saw rows of gunmetal-grey tables and benches, perfectly aligned, situated before a short, closed-up kitchen counter in the farthest wall. Several doors led out from this space, all closed. He saw a label on the closest one: *Hall 12*. He knew that, from somewhere. Was that where his room was, or a way to another spot?

He stepped up to the window, putting his hand to the glass. It felt cold, even through the clinger. *I know this place,* the back of his mind whispered. He strained to take it all in. Everything was familiar – and yet as new as if he were seeing it for the first time. Images and sensations flashed behind his eyes, like snapshots. Ducking low to avoid a strike from a shaven-headed man in a grey jumpsuit, much like the one he wore – and smelling the hard rubber of the mat when he was slammed down. The greasy taste of powdered eggs and sloppy oatmeal: the same breakfast every morning, without fail. The shrill buzzer that woke him for it, and during random drills, night or day. The ever-present odours: old sweat, antiseptic, deodorant, other cleaning solutions, sometimes shot through with scents from the day's meals. The eyes always watching: Gaia's, Caswell's, the Doctor's – and others. Ones which he never saw, but knew they were there, behind the glass, or around the next corner, even hovering above him somehow.

He squeezed his eyes tight, trying to call it all back. *It was here. All of it. Every day, from the first.* So why was it all so strange, so alien? Nothing came, beyond the same fragments. He opened his eyes, and stared at what lay before him, even harder. At the far end of the space, another bank of windows – one-way glass – was set higher in the wall, about the height he was watching from, looking out over both sections. He suspected the spot they were in now had the same shielding, hiding anyone behind from the view of those below. Observation areas – or something different? Was that where the unseen eyes had watched from, his whole time here? He suddenly realised he'd never learned just how *big* the Facility was: how many floors, how many rooms, how far underground. It made no sense; he'd lived here his whole life. *Why can't I remember?*

Leah came close to his side. He looked to her, not saying a word. Her face bore the same mix of wonder, apprehension and uncertainty that must be on his own. Cayden joined them, still showing absolutely nothing – although his stance, and the blade and pistol in hand, said how hunted he felt, and showed how ready he was to fight at the slightest whisper of a threat.

'I see you remember your old rooms,' Gaia said, breaking the silence. The sober tone of her – its? – words couldn't quite hide the maternal pride beneath them.

'Something like that,' Greg said. Try as he might, he couldn't keep the puzzlement from his voice. He kept staring, almost fixedly. 'It's all there – and not, at the same time.' He made himself turn aside from the view, and scan the room, until he spotted another blue lens to the group's right, where another pair of elevator doors stood waiting. 'And you're going to fill in the blanks.' It wasn't a question, or a statement.

'Yes,' Gaia replied. 'And given what we're dealing with – perhaps it'd be best if we start with the most recent ones.' The elevator's doors slid open before the reply had faded. This time, the three of them headed for it without hesitation.

Chapter 21

The ride down this time was much slower – or so Greg's ears told him. The elevator car was certainly much wider than the ones aboveground. Instead of floor buttons, the call panel consisted of a palm, retina, voice and heartbeat monitor; only when one of them – Leah, this time – had stood before these had the car started into motion. Gaia's blue eye stared down from the ceiling. The bulkiness of the metal door and walls suggested enough shielding to stop a rocket launcher; it was almost like riding in a safe. They certainly looked strong enough that Greg doubted he'd be able to pull or punch them apart, as he had with the vault at Advent Tech. He couldn't remember ever riding in them – but the same familiarity remained. *Maybe that's what they were built for. So many like us, all in one place, all needing to be kept under wraps until the time came – they'd want the place securable against* anything. The idea didn't anger him; in fact, it gave him a rush, of anticipation and grim eagerness. The cafeteria, the barracks, the gym, the offices were typical of any base, covert or not. Now they were approaching the heart.

The car shuddered to a halt. The doors slid open, eerily quiet. A white-panelled room lay on the other side. The smell of antiseptic was strong enough to make Greg want to draw his hood up. Directly across the room was a pair of plain metal doors, sealed shut, with a sign above it in bold red letters *Emergency Operations*. The only disruptions in the scene were a curving desk of the same colour, set well out of the way against the wall, Gaia's all-seeing lens above the doors – and a hospital stretcher close to them, the kind with automated linkups that allowed a hospital computer to route critical patients to the right rooms when the staff were swamped. When Greg looked closer, he noticed the stretcher's cushion seemed damp – and was lightly stained with dirt, and brownish-red spots.

His gun hand snapped up. Leah and Cayden matched his move. 'Wait,' Gaia said, still peaceful; she/it might've been asking him to pause and tie his boots before running. 'There's no threat here, not so long as we're careful.'

'Careful about what?' Leah demanded. 'What's down here?' She pointed her weapon at the stretcher. 'Who else is here? Are there casualties? Did someone breach the place?'

'They would have, I'm sure, if they had been aware of it,' Gaia replied. A short pause. 'Following your firefight on the Sound, another survivor was brought here for treatment and observation. I have gotten acquainted with it as best *I* can, and so I think the first order of business is for you to do the same.'

Cayden saw what the voice was driving at first. 'You've got one of them in there,' he rumbled. 'One of the Brown Coats.'

Greg tensed again. His gun hand started to rise again, before he stopped it. 'Yes – although there wasn't much in the way of clothing, brown or otherwise, when he was found,' Gaia said, without a trace of humour. 'That manoeuvre of yours did quite a number on him, and his friends. Enough to kill any ordinary special ops assassin, and to put the three of you out of commission for a while.'

'That *was* the plan,' Greg said tightly. He made himself

holster the gun, keeping the other hand close to his knife. 'I'm assuming he's in there, confined somehow? Otherwise, he'd probably be tearing his way out looking for us – and *you*.'

'Very possibly,' Gaia said. 'He is under heavy sedation, however, and is not expected to reawaken for some time. As for confinement – you will see for yourself.' As though cued, the *Operations* doors slid open.

Greg took the first step, then another. He drew his knife; guns were more of a risk, with such close quarters. Leah was at his shoulder, Cayden right behind. That alone was more comforting than any weapon. Some of the others in their 'class,' to use the Doctor's term, were repeatedly handpicked for solo missions, but he had always found his best work came from team efforts. *It'd better, if this goes sideways.*

The doors slid open when he was a foot from them. Inside was what appeared to be a standard ER set–up, not too different from the clinic they'd woken up in. A wide room, enough to easily accommodate eight stretchers, partitioned into smaller sections by cloth curtains – all of which except one were drawn back. Instead of stretchers, however, the spaces were occupied by stationary beds: stiff-looking white pallets, on sculpted metal frames that looked welded to the floor. Steel cabinets and readout screens lined the walls, along with wheeled carts of surgical and emergency gear. Another blue lens overlooked all this from the centre of the ceiling. There was a new smell in the air, partially faded and buried beneath the harsher hospital scents: a sour-sweet odour, as of an overdone pot roast.

Greg looked over everything, knife hand still at the ready. The unsettling familiarity rose again. He'd been here before, or someplace very like it. There had been plenty of checkups, all through his time with the Project, and a lesser number of injuries – like the slow cook of the Balkash mission – that needed ER care. Yet he still couldn't nail down where, when, or *how*, beyond the by-now typical fragments.

He halted before the sole curtained section, hefting his knife. Before he could reach for the cloth, Gaia spoke again. 'He is no threat, not the way he is now. He was in much worse shape on arrival – it is amazing he's recovered at all, much less so quickly. Although you might not think so, once you see for yourselves.'

Greg hesitated a moment longer, then drew the curtain aside, pulling it all the way to the wall. Leah couldn't quite hide a gag: a major display of revulsion. Cayden didn't, although there was a momentarily greater tint of grey in his features. Greg just stared, somewhere between fascinated and repulsed. He hadn't known exactly what he'd see, although the smell should have given him some hint – *should have* being the key term. This, though... He knew the inhibitors were almost gone by now; the medics at the Sanctuary were reasonably sure of that. Right then, though, he was grateful for any that might be keeping his reactions muted.

The man on the bed before them lay on his back, naked. The slow, minute rise and fall of his chest was the only movement he made. His head might once have been covered in blonde hair, before it was burned almost completely away, and the remainder shaved off in a haphazard style. He was shackled at the arms, ankles and legs; the cuffs looked wide and strong enough to restrain an elephant. An IV and several readout leads were plugged into and patched onto his left arm and upper chest.

Except for this, and most of his face, seemingly every inch of the man was covered in lines of mottled, red-white scar tissue. Much tinier scars, the size of a paper clip or smaller, dotted the edges of his long, angular features, suggesting plastic surgery, or a much gentler form of whatever kind had been worked on the rest of him. Greg hadn't noticed them before; now, up close, he saw how they made the man's visage look older, more worn. It was definitely one of the team from the attack at Caswell's airfield – the one he'd nearly killed. He studied the face, more closely, then shook his head. Nothing about it clicked, despite the nagging in his mind.

He looked over the rest of the prisoner. The cleanest, thinnest cuts connected and spread out across his chest and stomach, traced over and along his collar and shoulders, and extended down his arms to his wrists and the backs of his hands. The most obvious and gruesome looked irregularly placed, or so Greg could tell, dotting the man's scalp, biceps, and forearms, and more below his rib cage and along his waistline. A large, circular scar covered most of his throat. More incisions lanced down his thighs and lower legs, bunching up around the knees and pelvic area, and even reaching to the base of his toes. And there were probably even *more* such mutilations all over his back, and his calves and the backs of his knees. Nobody could take so much surgery – *if* that was what it was – and live. *Maybe not even us.* Yet these creatures *could*, somehow.

He stepped up to the side of the bed, beside the sleeping man's shoulder. He reached for the man's left arm, then stopped, looking at Leah and Cayden. They nodded, shifting to defensive stances. Hiding a shudder – another first, for him – he grasped the man's wrist, and lifted it higher, bending in for a better look. Up close, the incisions were older and more precise than they looked; done with surgical tools, not hacksaws, and quite some time ago.

He peered closer at the sleeping man's chest and shoulders, confirming his theory. Every one of them was precisely situated over a critical muscle, organ, or bone. The work wasn't reparative, then, or done for torture or someone's sick pleasure. Although a *true* surgeon wouldn't have left the incisions to heal so haphazardly, risking more infection or worse scarring; even ones without access to the reparative effects of ARC had others to at least minimise the latter. Someone with skills and the right tools had done this; someone who didn't care what the effects were, only the results.

He straightened, and looked up to the lens. 'You said he recovered. How, exactly?' He paused, a heartbeat's worth. 'Like *us*?'

'Not quite in the same manner or speed – but yes,' Gaia replied. 'He was found almost a mile south of where the three of you washed up, still unconscious. Given his associates still being at large, and the slow healing consistent with ARC noted in his case, it was decided to bring him here for containment as well as treatment.'

'Decided by whom?' Leah demanded.

Instead of answering, Gaia continued, in a kind of litany. 'Severe burns over close to fifty per cent of his body, most of them third-degree, along with additional lacerations and multiple broken bones from what's believed to be debris from the two boats involved.' The voice turned reproachful at that for an instant, before going on. 'The cuts and breaks were healing even as he was discovered; the burns took longer, but were gone by the time clean-up and initial analysis were finished. He remained unconscious through this, and the ride back to the Facility; perhaps a natural, built-in response to the pain he *had* to be feeling, as the wounds and burns closed.' A significant pause. 'Similar reactions were noted in other Golems, after excessive trauma. Based on this, and preliminary facial reconstruction, I think the four of you may already be acquainted.'

Greg looked to the others, puzzled. They all wore the same baffled expression. He stepped closer to the bed, angling his head, trying to see the Brown Coat's face from different sides.

Then he stopped, frozen in place. Cold shock washed over him. His mouth opened, but couldn't form any words. At last, he finally managed, '*Taylor?*'

Chapter 22

Leah's face went white. She crowded close herself, to confirm or deny. Cayden didn't, but the older Golem was watching more intently than ever; maybe he recognised the name as well. Greg snapped his eyes back to Gaia's lens. 'How?' he whispered. 'How – He's dead. I *saw* him, at the end.'

He scanned the room, in quick little jolts of his neck. 'It was *here* – right here.' The images of that day cascaded through his mind: the first fully coherent, tied-together memory. 'I was recovering, but he wasn't. The ARC was working, but that only made him worse; the rads kept cooking him while he healed, and re-healed. They wheeled him out, to someplace else; the morgue, I thought. He couldn't have... he *shouldn't*—' He trailed off, unable to continue. He stared again at the ravaged body and altered face. The basic features he remembered were still there: the slim eyebrows, the stubby nose, the mole at the back of his left jawline. In every other way, the man was unrecognisable as the same one who'd gone through the hell of the Balkash breach.

'No, he shouldn't,' Gaia replied. 'And according to my own records, he didn't.' Beside the bed, one of the monitors changed, showing a set of files. They scrolled quickly through several pages, before finally stopping. 'These are casualty lists for the period immediately following your operation at Lake Balkash.' The voice began to read. 'Golem ID T-305/339; given name, Taylor. Severely wounded from unexpected secondary blasts during mission, and major subsequent radiation exposure. Blast wounds healed en route to Facility, but irradiation proved too extensive, causing reopening and exacerbation of wounds during attempted ER procedures, and total body shutdown approximately twenty-four hours following return. Pronounced KIA shortly after; body removed from Facility for appropriate interment.'

The screen returned to its previous readouts. 'This was the standard procedure for "appropriate interment" of Golems killed in action, intended to be simple, and discreet. First they went to the Facility morgue, until a full confidential report on their deaths was completed; when the casualty rates rose somewhat just before the end, sometimes they would temporarily go to the cooler at the naval base proper. Once the report was received by Langley, they would be brought up to the surface in temp-controlled cargo containers, shipped across the bay to Lewis-McChord by military ferry, and put aboard the next flight to D.C. Upon arrival, the Agency would take charge of the remains, perform a last autopsy to confirm the report, and deliver the bodies to a cremation facility it maintained in the area.'

'Looks like they missed a few,' Cayden growled. He was studying Taylor with an almost morbid fascination, despite his by-now standard dispassionate manner. 'Nobody raised a fuss so long as we did our jobs in the dark – not you, the brass, or anybody else. Doubt they'd do any more once we were in a box.'

'Very possibly, Cayden,' Gaia said, without obvious praise or rebuke. 'In this case, however, unlike many others before and then, the Agency appears to have taken extra precautions.' More files appeared on the monitor, scrolling almost too fast to read. 'All Golems who passed away at any time during the Project went through the same process – at least, so the records indicate. No video footage of the bodies was kept anywhere in the Agency's digital files, and obviously hard copy clips are inaccessible if stored in a cold vault, which would be standard procedure. And that leaves aside the fact that, apart from the ARC compound, the bodies would have very little value. The Agency would nonetheless want them destroyed for that exact reason, but there would be little need or point to altering the paperwork anymore than they had.'

'No *obvious* point,' Greg corrected. He wanted to focus his attention and anger on Gaia, but couldn't keep from stealing glances at Taylor's carved-up form. The sight gave new impetus to a question he'd wanted to ask since first waking up that day – since they'd first come together in the Sanctuary, in fact. He looked up at the lens again. 'There was no one else who had any sort of ties to the Project, outside the Agency and D.C.? No other groups, or personnel?' He pushed a little more. 'No *families*?'

'None that I am aware of, Gregory.' The blue light blinked once, or maybe it was his imagination. 'The Project was meant to be a sealed operation, from the beginning. Only I and the people on the ground here knew its innermost workings. The Agency Director and his representatives, as well as the Pentagon and the President, knew the general details only, and weren't wholly informed of those, either, or even tried to become so, due to compartmentalisation concerns.'

'Then it was done from inside,' Leah said. 'If the Project was so airtight that not even *families*'—she stressed the word herself, trying to boost Greg's probing—'were informed when somebody sneezed wrong in this place, then only the people who knew *anything* about it would have the resources to make changes in the process.' She stopped, palpably debating whether to continue. 'Along with going after the ones in the know who stood a chance of stopping them.'

'Please explain what you mean, Leah,' Gaia said. Leah laid out the details of their escape from Chicago – including the Pax effects, though she left out the name – and the encounter at the airfield: the Brown Coats' arrival, Caswell's likely death, and the backup that had shown up at the very end. When she finished, Gaia didn't immediately respond. After several seconds, she – it – asked another question. 'What happened after you were airborne?'

'Plenty,' Greg replied, unable to keep the ice from his tone. He described the battle with the drone, and the response team – leaving out Costa and Patrick – along with their and Jorge's summary of the tech they'd faced with the Brown Coats: the blades, the glasses, and the ARC-like talent. *No sense in revealing everything, until we start learning* something.

Once Greg was done, Gaia was silent again. 'Your recovering the canister would bring a strong response – the Agency would not let it go without one. The choppers, the troops, the drones are standard for a retrieval operation where the targets are presumed to have backup of some kind. If the staff of the Project are being targeted as well, along with its records, and believed or confirmed survivors, this would suggest a larger operation, to erase everything related to it – including the canister.'

Greg nodded; the explanation fitted with what the Sanctuary Council had discussed. 'So where does *he* fit in?' He moved back to Taylor's bedside, looking over the scars even more closely. 'If he *didn't* die, somehow, how and why'd he end up like *this*?'

Before Gaia could answer, he spotted a slim black device the size of a hole-puncher, sitting on the bedside table with a short cord running to a tablet computer: a portable medscanner. Grabbing the device, he powered it up, and brought it to Taylor's sternum, holding it several inches above his mangled flesh.

The screen showed an image – holographic? Modified CAT-scan? – of the sleeping man's ribcage, albeit with false, shifting colours to differentiate between organs and bones. Greg could distantly recall seeing similar equipment in his other visits to the ER but hadn't ever found out what they were. Cayden and Leah gathered around him. Right away, he spotted a line of grey material, following the length of one of Taylor's ribs, connecting to a larger mass of the same, in the dead centre of his chest. The colour stood out clearly against the backdrop of multiple tints and the white of the skeleton. As his eyes adjusted to this, he saw more and more grey lines, along the other ribs. With slow, careful moves, he held the tablet to Taylor's shoulders and collarbone, down across his stomach and waist, and over both arms and legs. Everywhere, the same kind of implants were present, inserted within bones or running along their exterior. In some places – the knees, the shoulders, both elbows and hands, even several vertebrae – entirely artificial versions had replaced the original bones. The sight was grotesque and awe-inducing. 'What… the hell *is* this?' Greg managed to whisper at last.

'Multiple forms of surgical implantation,' Gaia said. 'The current implant count is estimated at 150. The types of implants include intramedullary rods in the legs and arms, internal fixations at these same areas, various forms of joint replacement. Cursory examination indicates no discernable medical need for such operations, due to the presence of ARC. Present theory is that the implantations were made as a means of providing additional reinforcement and strength to the individual, alongside that provided by ARC and other pre-existing augmentation.'

'Who made the implantations?' Cayden asked, not taking his eyes from the body.

'Unknown,' Gaia replied. 'All catalogued implants have no serial number, or other form of identification commonly used in medical implants. However, whoever performed the procedures had to have known the patients were given the ARC compound. No normal human could withstand the trauma of so many surgeries, all at once or over a certain period. Infection, shock, blood loss, or some combination of the three would kill them in short order – yet this individual went through every single one. Including some with no discernible medical need, in the oesophageal region.'

Greg held the scanner over the designated spot. He leaned in for a better view – and flinched back. Leah sucked in a breath; Cayden muttered something low and sulphurous. He looked to the lens himself. 'They cut out his *tongue?*'

Another possible blink of the light. 'Professionally, after a fashion. There is no clear reason for the operation, unless tongue cancer been detected – which, despite the effects of your mission, is doubtful. The reason for the implant in the oesophagus is also unclear.'

What? Far from sure he wanted to, Greg looked where the voice indicated. Nestled in the middle of Taylor's throat – right about the same place as the circular scar he'd noted before – was a grey lump, about as big as an eraser. 'What's *that* supposed to be?' he asked, more to himself than Gaia or the others.

'Unknown,' Gaia said, her – its – maternal tone unchanged. 'Earlier examination suggests a vocalisation device of some kind; closer scans indicate connections to the speech centres of the brain, and perhaps to another apparatus outside the body.

The removal of the tongue, however, indicates speech would be impossible, or at best difficult, with or without the device.'

'That's putting it mildly,' Leah said. She stared hard at the image of the implant. 'Doesn't make sense, either, for a covert ops team; they *have* to communicate, every way possible. So—' She cut off, shock and understanding blooming on her face. 'AllSpec,' she murmured.

Greg frowned, not following – and then, suddenly, he did. Every soldier or operative had to talk sometimes: to give and respond to orders, or identify for superiors or security measures, or any of a hundred other, basic reasons. *But what if someone weren't interested in vocalisation – in speech of any kind? What if they just wanted the AllSpec to issue orders, without being overheard – or getting unnecessary backtalk?* He tapped the screen, zooming in on the device. 'Where's this thing placed, *exactly*?' he demanded.

'The implant is situated in the exact site of the vocal cords,' Gaia replied. 'The cords themselves were surgically altered to accommodate it a long time ago, and somehow have not regenerated; this was confirmed by scan, and an endoscopy.'

'Right,' Greg said tightly. Instead of asking who'd done those procedures – *one mystery at a time* – he brought the image even closer in on the object. Extending from the top and bottom were several extremely fine filaments; to Greg's eye, they couldn't be thicker than spider's silk.

Leah reached past his shoulder, pointing to the objects. 'These have to connect directly to the nerves controlling the vocal cords, and from there to the other, similar implants in various parts of the brain, including the speech centre. It doesn't only detect the movement of the cords, relaying them to the AllSpec, and the target person with the same tech; it actually *receives* the words, as thought by the user.' She moved back, eyeing the image and the body in a new, disgusted fascination. 'An ideal set–up for covert communications, like Jorge said. Add the tongue removal, and the other surgeries, and the desired result is a lot clearer.'

'A new version,' Greg half-muttered. He was unable to keep his eyes from following the twists and intertwining of every scar. 'An upgrade, maybe, the way they saw it. A mute hit squad, with Golem training and abilities, controlled with a blink or a texted word.' The idea sickened him at the same time it made perfect sense, from a purely tactical stance. *Real-time direction from anywhere, and quicker than any. No need for shouted orders, or any words at all. No need for the boss to be on site, either, not with the cameras and mikes. And the surgeries would make them near-invulnerable, paired with the ARC.* It explained almost everything about the Brown Coats, from their surviving car crashes and killshots to the 'accident' on the Sound. He couldn't understand, though, why *Taylor* had wound up being part of this bizarre experiment. The 'kid' had believed in the Project and his duties, same as the rest of them. There was no way he'd have willingly stayed, even after being revived by it. *He was forced, somehow. And if the ones who did it had access to other bodies, once they went up the chain…*

The train of thought came to a sharp halt, replaced by a new, more unnerving one. It didn't click, not at first – but as more pieces fit together, there were fewer and fewer other answers. He spun to face Cayden. 'The others in the "First Five". Did you work with them *at all*, after the North Korea mission?'

'Not even then, for very long,' Cayden replied. 'We were *supposed* to operate solo; it allowed us to cover larger stretches of territory, and more potential targets. We only cooperated when the targets were higher-profile, or more complex than a one-person strike could bring down. We were shipped home as a team, but separated soon as we landed at Lewis, for debriefing. *I* never worked with any of them again; it was solo missions only for me, from that point on. Don't think I spotted them when I was here for—'

The older Golem cut off. His slowly whitening features – from anger or shock – said he understood where Greg's line of thinking was headed. A quick look Leah's way showed the same reaction. Greg turned back to the lens. 'What *did* happen to the other four?' he demanded. 'They never showed at the Sanctuary, and we've never found or heard any hints about them anywhere.'

'After the mission to Korea, they were sent on other individual assignments, as Cayden said,' Gaia replied at once. 'They were the first, and therefore unique in that sense, but not for very long.' The tablet image changed, bringing up four files at once. The voice became a steady monotone. 'M2 – Michael – listed as killed August 2037, in a raid against a terror cell along the Iranian-Pakistan border; remains shipped from Persian Gulf to D.C., rather than by the usual route. D4 – Drake – killed accidentally in an airstrike in Indonesia, January 2039; body delivered via normal process, despite Turmoil-related delays. J3 – Joey – killed in raid on narco-terror compound in the Sierra Madre, September 2041; body sent directly to D.C. F5 – Fred – killed during op in Yunnan, China, July 2038; body delayed due to still-elevated tensions in the region, but processed according to standard procedure.'

Cayden leaned in, staring at the documents for a time. Then he looked at Greg again. 'You think they're the others,' he said, in an equally flat tone. 'The other four you encountered.'

'Until every body's accounted for, that's the theory,' Greg said. 'If you're looking for the best candidates for this'—he waved at Taylor—'then the first ones off the line would top the list. You weren't just the first, either; you were the best.

Every class after them was great, with its own specific talents – but *nobody* tops the ones who set the standard. Modifying members of the "First Five" would give the ones behind it serious prestige, in Agency and Pentagon circles. A chance to improve on the perfect soldier... plenty of brass and spooks would be drooling at the chance.'

He flipped the tablet around, showing it to the others. 'And think about when the bodies were delayed, or went by different routes. Check the *exact* dates for each one.' He did so himself. 'All of them died in ops well after any threats – obvious or subtle – that needed Golem attention were over, or reduced to manageable levels. The Hong Kong and Quetta bombings, the revolutions in Southeast Asia, the cartel conflicts that spilled into the Southwest. Millions of people on the move or tearing each other apart for living space or resources. The governments and spooks involved just wanted to get a handle on the situation and start rebuilding. They wouldn't think twice about authorising more covert ops to help that along, or worry when bodies started coming back.'

'Or if they came back in delayed or off ways,' Leah put in. Her nod was reluctant, but conceding. 'People stopped paying attention to flag-draped coffins fast in the old War on Terror; very few would do the same for bodies that never existed in the first place. Perfect cover for moving them to some other site, once they got back to the States. List them as KIA, and anything becomes possible – even this.' She motioned to the insensate Golem.

'Except there's *no* idea how *he*, or the others, could be brought back – in every sense of the word,' Cayden growled. 'I worked with every one of the First Five, from the beginning. They wouldn't consent to *any* of this, and would fight like hell to break free if they were shipped back in chains. So either they had to have been kept under the whole way – no easy feat, for people with only the barest idea of what they're dealing with – or they were dead to begin with, and were somehow revived.'

He fell silent, looking deeply troubled. Greg didn't blame him. *He* wouldn't mind coming back from a sure kill, if it meant getting on with the mission; he'd faced plenty in his time. But if the Brown Coats had that ability, along with all the others...

Greg swallowed the unnerving thought. His voice slightly unsteady, he said, 'The other question is how he was so... *altered*, once he was at whichever site inflicted this work on him.' He pointed to one batch of incisions, then another. 'None of these are prior wounds from the Balkash mission, and no part of the Project involved this kind of destructive modification. His ARC ability should have allowed him to heal – not without marks, in certain *serious* cases, but nothing *this* extensive.'

'And even assuming he *could* be revived, after what he endured, why wouldn't he have recognised *you*?' Leah asked. 'I didn't know *every* Golem in each class personally, by the end – but he wouldn't have attacked you. Not after what you'd both gone through, in that mission and before.'

Cayden paced along the side of the bed, visually probing every inch of Taylor's form. 'There has to be another form of control involved, beyond the AllSpec and the surgeries. Maybe some kind of conditioning, related to the cranial implants, although I doubt it; the procedures would be damaging, possibly fatally so, and he's obviously not lobotomised or dead.'

'Right.' Greg touched the IV, then addressed Gaia. 'What is all this, exactly?'

'A precautionary detox programme, begun after his arrival,' Gaia answered. 'Nothing has appeared on any of the tox tests, although there are plenty of masking agents which would prevent such detection. It would, however, take years to create the proper mixture, without killing the subject or rendering them comatose.'

Detox. The word clicked in Greg's head. Looking to the others, he saw the same slow, disturbed realisation. 'What does the detox cover?' he asked. He moved a step towards the lens. Cold anticipation – and not a little dread – seeped into his veins. 'Maybe the inhibitors – and boosters and other injections he got, and us, when we joined the Project. The ones that none of us recall ever getting the whole story on? The shots that might have had some other effects, besides vaccinations and "recharging" the ARC – like memory loss and plenty more?' He made a sharp gesture in Cayden's direction. 'A *lot* more, in certain cases – maybe *all*?'

Gaia didn't respond. Leah and Cayden came around the bed, forming up on either side of him. Leah's look was direct, like his must be. Cayden's was even more opaque, but with intent, searching eyes; he knew what Greg had been driving at, and wanted the same answer. Greg took another step, and another, until he was directly below the lens. In a polite but iron tone, he said, 'I think we've gotten what answers we can here, for now. Maybe it's time we got fully reacquainted with the Facility – and find out the *rest*.'

The lens stared back at him. He stayed mute for a full minute, gaze never wavering. Finally, Gaia spoke. 'Very well.'

Chapter 23

They entered the elevator, filing in silently one after the other. Instead of starting a descent or rise, a flap popped open beneath the keypad, revealing a small compartment. Inside, a tiny needle jutted from a circular black base. Gaia's voice came from above. 'This area of the Facility requires your DNA to unlock the security measures. You recall the aboveground areas well, judging by all the signs. And you recall most of what you've seen on this level, and the living and training sections several floors up. Those were the Project's primary use areas; the limbs and a good part of the brain, so to speak. The heart is where we're headed now – something you've never seen. You may hate what you learn there. My hope is that you'll come to understand, once you see everything there is to see.'

Not trusting himself to speak, Greg kept quiet. Leah and Cayden made no sound or move, either. Greg faced the controls, and stuck an index finger into the open panel. The needle jerked up, almost too fast to see; he winced as it bit the tip of the extended digit, drawing a large drop of blood. There was a dull chime, and the panel swung closed. Ignoring the still-welling blood, Greg went through the rest of the scanner process.

The elevator shuddered to life, beginning a descent even slower than the ones they'd taken so far. Greg felt his heart pumping harder, enough to make him feel short of breath. He stayed almost at attention, eyes on the doors – though he couldn't stop them from making infinitesimal glances in the direction of Gaia's lens. Anticipation and dread wrestled in his gut. For the first time since they'd entered the place, he wondered if it wouldn't be better to head back upstairs, take what they'd learned so far to Hiroshi and the rest of the Council, and leave whatever was below them buried, where it—

The elevator stopped with a jolt, so hard and unexpected Greg almost lost his footing. He grabbed the nearest handrail for support, one hand moving from knife to pistol, and back. Leah and Cayden backed against the walls, with similar motions. The doors slid back, revealing a second set: heavy metal slabs, three feet thick at Greg's guess. A white plaque was pinned to each. The letters, written in blood-red ink, spelled out several curt warnings:

Project Golem Lab Wing

Restricted Area

Visible ID Required At All Times

Lethal Force Authorised

'There is no need to worry about the last two warnings,' Gaia informed them. 'All the guards left with the rest of the staff before the Bomb, and the whole sector locked down. There is a backup measure designed to suck all the air out of the room, in the event of a breach, but that is deactivated as well.'

Greg held himself to a nod, not sure how else to reply. Somewhere outside, a buzzer sounded, soft and echoing. With a deep groaning noise, the second set of doors began to slide back. Directly above the doorframe, a yellow alert light was whirling, cutting out when he stepped over the threshold. A short white-walled foyer, almost identical to the one in the ER, sat beyond the elevators. At the other end, two glassed-in booths – bulletproof, Greg could tell from the way they caught the light – flanked a pair of similarly tempered doors, secured by a state-of-the-art biometric lock. The glass was frosted, hiding what lay ahead, with no label or markings of any kind. When Greg leaned out, keeping most of his body in the car, he saw two more booths, next to the elevator, and a fire exit doorway; he wondered if it reached all the way to the surface, or just to the next level. Checking one of the booths, he saw four assault rifles secured to a stand beneath the desks within, and an array of body armour parts, Taser wands, stun grenades and CS canisters. Perfect for any potential breaches – yet somehow he had the feeling that wasn't their *main* purpose.

The three Golems went up to the frosted doors. The lock itself was outwardly unexceptional: a concave impression in the shape of a hand, lit blood-red, a dark readout screen, and three small, blinking lights beside it. After glancing at the others, Greg stepped up and placed his hand in the space. The impression changed to a bright green. Half a dozen needles – one each for the palm, the thumb, and four fingers – stabbed out, making him yank away. Before he could do anything else, the lights beside the readout spat out three long rainbow-tinged beams, raking over his entire body. *3-D scan*, he realised, right as the beams shut off. 'Voiceprint required,' a flat, mechanical voice demanded.

Nonplussed, Greg hesitated. There'd been any number of passwords when he was in the field, but he couldn't recall ever needing one at the Facility. He looked to Leah and Cayden, only to see the same confusion and uncertainty. Deciding to take a chance, he faced the door again, and spoke the first phrases he'd usually given, when asked for ID on missions. 'Gregory, G-250/228.'

His voice played back to him from a tiny speaker, shifting in pitch, tone, volume and frequency. Then the readout blinked on, flashing two words in green: *Access Granted.* There was the clunk of deadbolts retracting, from every side of the doorway. When nothing happened after that, Greg started to reach for the silver door handle, but Leah beat him to it. Grasping it, she tugged, the cords standing out on her neck. The door slid open, slowly. At last, she managed to get it all the way open, and stood beside it, panting a little. *Bulletproof* and *reinforced*, Greg observed. *Overkill, maybe, with everything else keeping this base hidden and protected, but probably extra peace of mind for D.C.* Plenty of other military complexes and secure zones he'd passed through had had similar protections. So why did it feel like he was stepping farther into a prison, rather than a base?

Past the doorway, Greg saw a walkway like the ones upstairs, with a glass barrier between it and the chamber below. Seeing the others' caution, he took the lead, managing to keep his hands away from his weapons, with an effort. The first thing he noted was the size of the place: close to that of the training and mess areas above them. Unlike them, though, the chamber was white as snow, with heavy support columns snaking up the walls to meet and form an intricate double-helix symbol. A larger version of Gaia's lens sat in the very centre, like an electric-blue gem.

There was a wide metal staircase leading down to the chamber floor, behind another secured door. Greg ignored this for the moment, and approached the railing, scanning the chamber. He hadn't known what to expect when they'd started down – and now that he was here, he wasn't sure whether to be disappointed or suspicious. Two sections of darkened offices –

or so he guessed them to be, since they were made of the same misty glass partitions – stretched down the length of the room, their ceilings extended to the walkway. Some were larger than their neighbours, but otherwise the design was uniform. The light from the ceiling bulbs was softer than those upstairs, but not by much; it gave the place a weird mixed feeling of hospital and warehouse. The space between the offices was wide – the size of a soccer field, maybe a little bigger – but completely empty. The white linoleum sparkled in the light, like the cleaners had come through just that morning. When he looked at it from certain angles, he could see the same helix design, patterned in miniature, interlacing style, across the entire floor.

Greg started down the stairs. The sound of his boots echoed through the room, though he was treading as softly as possible. Leah and Cayden came next: she curious, he wary, as before. Greg peered at each of the rooms as he descended. Nothing could be discerned, except for several shadowy shapes that could be desks, or anything else. When he reached the bottom, he looked to the ceiling again. They hadn't come very much further down from the ER, but he still had no clear idea of the complex's size. From the support columns, it was possible this area had been the starting point, with the other levels added as the Project got on its feet. *But if we were brought to the Project when fresh boots or whatever else we were, they'd want the barracks and everything else ready first – wouldn't they?*

More lights sprang on, in each of the rooms. Though not enough to pierce the cloudy glass, it still allowed Greg to parse out more objects: a desk here, a lamp or chair there. The ones farther away seemed empty, although that meant little; he resolved to check those first. Somewhere, he heard the soft whir of servers starting up, and the beeps and chirps of other equipment.

'These are the main offices, for administration, and some of the higher-level trainers, like Sergeant Caswell,' Gaia declared. Greg clenched a fist at this, but otherwise kept his cool. 'We – the Doctor, and I, and the other high-ranking trainers – were working so often, monitoring your training and other aspects of the Project, they were hardly ever occupied.'

'We can tell,' Leah said neutrally. Greg nodded; Cayden, still staring around the room, didn't show any reaction. Leah motioned to the rest of the rooms. 'And all *that*?'

Instead of speaking, Gaia's light blinked once – Greg was sure of it, this time. One of the doors in the larger, still-dark sections, set centremost in the row, popped open – with a click and rush of purified air. *Pressurised*, Greg recognised. He couldn't remember any of the rooms upstairs being so, and none so far on the 'tour'. He moved to the entry, letting some of his eagerness propel him ahead of the others.

In the first glance, he saw nothing unusual. A standard operating table, the cushion flat and starched white like everything else on the level. An array of wheeled monitor screens set in a semicircle around it. Gleaming white cabinets, holding who knew what. A bank of lights, extending down from the ceiling above the table. All typical OR fare—

He stopped, frowning. Stepping farther into the room, he studied the table more closely. Something was tucked below the mattress at head height, almost hidden from view. He moved up and pulled it free. A grey cloth strap, not much different from a seatbelt, but wide as a man's hand, and thicker than two fingers. Checking down the table, he found four more, at spots that corresponded to the shoulders, sternum, waist, knees and ankles. He was puzzled. Restraints for uncooperative or unstable patients, or—

He was in another place, lying on his back on a slab of cold metal.

His head, arms and legs were held down by cloth straps. He jerked against them, but they didn't yield. The walls around him were a dazzling pure white, with soft light shining down. He could hear the faint beeping of machines, and thought he could see screens of some sort to either side. Human figures moved in and out of sight – ghostly white suits, without faces. One of them approached from his right, a syringe at the ready –

He gasped, letting the belt fall. The memory receded as fast as it had come, leaving a cold, tingling residue of impact. His knees wobbled for a second, enough for him to grab the bed to keep from toppling. 'What is it?' Leah's voice came to him as though from far away – and then she was right beside him. Her hands gripped his arm and shoulder. 'Greg? What's wrong?'

Those words brought him the rest of the way back. Legs steady again, he let go of the bed, and turned around. Cayden and Leah were both in front of him, watching closely. 'It was here,' he murmured. 'The operations, the exams, the ones we've all dreamed of in some way – they were *here*. I never knew what was happening – *why* it was happening. Every time was the same: one minute I'm somewhere else, on the base or in the Facility – then here.' He gestured in a half-dreamy way at his chest and arms. 'I'm always tied down, can't move an inch. People in white coats and gowns, coming at me with needles – or scalpels.' His voice faltered. 'But I wasn't a recruit, or anything – I was too *young* to be—'

Leah and Cayden stared at him, unable to speak or react, or not knowing how. Without a look to the Doctor or the others, he strode back out into the main chamber. His mind was churning, still trying to wrap itself around the memory and what it meant. He looked around the space, in short, probing glances. *If* that *was here, then what came next had to be* – His eyes fell on the other large 'office', in the opposite row. *There.*

He crossed the space to it in a near-leap. He heard Leah call out to him, and Cayden; none of it registered. He wasted a moment tugging on the door handle before he punched the keypad, crumpling the apparatus with a shower of sparks. An alarm began beeping from the ceiling above him; he ignored it, wrenching at the handle again. This time it yielded, smoothly.

The room inside was less brightly lit than its counterparts, creating an almost relaxing feel. Unlike the chamber, the floor was carpeted in plush dark green. The walls and glass were tinted sky-blue, with a pattern of white fluffy clouds, dotted with images of planes, jets, and all kinds of birds. Bins of kids' toys and stuffed animals stood in one corner, along with a pair of worn beanbag chairs. A stack of yoga or athletic mats was arranged against the far wall. Five of these were laid out in the centre of the room, forming a neat row right beneath another Gaia lens. Greg went to the closest of these. Kneeling, he felt at its sticky, weave-patterned surface. Near the top, about where the head would rest, there was a sprinkle of brown droplets, almost invisible in the lighting.

'We came here,' Leah said. Greg got slowly to his feet, not turning around. She moved beside him, staring at the mats. 'After the operations.' She spoke with detached calm. 'When we were done with… whatever they'd done to us, and had to recover.' She looked at her stomach, brushing her hands over each other and her arms. 'Nothing was different about me, not that I could see. But everything hurt; I couldn't move, and I was afraid to even breathe. People were crying around me, every time; little kids. Then the men in white came again, for new… work. I always tried to turn away, to get up, to *run* – but nothing.'

She cut off, edging away from the mats with fear in her eyes. Slowly, it faded, and she looked up at the lens. '*You* sang to us,' she half-whispered. 'All the time, while we were lying here.

Lullabies, happy songs, to help us sleep or calm down.' She began to sing herself. *'Sleep, my child, and peace attend thee… All through the night…'*

A shadow fell across them. Jerkily, Greg turned. Cayden was standing in the door, feet on the threshold like he was afraid to come any closer. Gradually, that fear seemed to erode, and he took one step into the room, then another. He went to the wall, raising a slightly quivering hand to stroke at some of the painted images: a biplane, a soaring owl, a fighter jet, a bald eagle. He walked along its length, legs stiff and jerky, brushing fingers over more images, and the stack of mats. Only when he'd made a full circuit of the room did he stop, and look around, taking everything in. A sea of emotion warred over his features: anger, agony, confusion, hatred. *What did he endure, in this room and the others? Had he been a recruit like them – if that's what* they'd *been?*

He brushed at another image, then let his hand fall. As though this were a signal, Cayden's reverie shattered. He pushed past Greg and Leah, grabbing one of the mats. He took one long look at the dried blood spatter, then stomped up to the Gaia lens; Greg felt the vibration through the floorboards. Eyes burning, he shoved the mat against the blue eye. 'Explain,' the older Golem growled.

'I will, Cayden,' Gaia replied. Greg couldn't detect any condescension or deception; just a mother's patient tones. Somehow, that made it all the more eerie. Cayden let the mat drop to the floor and stalked out. Once Greg and Leah had done the same, he slammed the door to the – nursery? play area? recovery room? – closed, and marched toward the large Gaia eye, halting in the centre of the room. The other two Golems formed a V behind him: partly team instinct, partly deliberate. Gaia didn't blink or show any other evidence of processing – or intelligence or emotion, if it was it was capable of such. Instead, she – it – only said, 'You may want to stand near the walls.'

Leah looked to Greg, puzzled. He shrugged, and glanced to Cayden. Glowering, Cayden shrugged in turn, and stepped to the side, back near the room they'd come from. Greg and Leah moved in the opposite direction, toward the surgery; Greg kept his head turned away from it, and noticed Leah doing the same.

A low rumbling started up. Greg looked down, in time to see two large sections of the floor sink almost a foot, and slide back, revealing a pitch-black space beneath that could be four feet deep, or 400. He shifted further back, one arm out to shield Leah, the other going for his pistol. Across the room, Cayden was also alert, machete-like knife half drawn. Greg started to speak to him – and suddenly noticed two panels of the nearby wall had slid back as well, almost soundlessly. Beneath these, a huge holographic screen blinked into life, showing Gaia's blue eye, as large as the wheel on a carousel, against a black background and overlain by scrolling streams of code. *Her system core?* Nothing else made sense, so far as he could tell.

The rumbling got louder. Now Greg could pick out other sounds beneath it: grinding moan of gears, and the scrap of metal on concrete. He edged closer, peering over the lip of the hole. At that same moment, a square of searing lights flashed on inside the space, momentarily blinding him. When he'd blinked the spots out of his eyes, he saw a platform rising up through the lit space – on which stood five man-sized cylinders.

He backed away again, in trepidation as much as caution. The two platforms rose up to the floor's level and halted with a shuddering groan. Sharing an edgy look with Leah, he moved onto the platform. The cylinders were composed of gleaming metal – steel or titanium, he couldn't tell, although he had a sense it might be a stronger material, one that perhaps he'd never heard of. Each one was as tall as the Golems, and nearly as wide. The only break in the metal was a darkened, tablet-sized screen. Tentatively, he reached out a hand towards the closest one.

The screen blinked on before his fingers were halfway to it. It beeped shrilly, turning blue, then showing a series of readout graphs, like the kind on medical monitors: heart rate, BP, EKG. He retreated, startled – then stepped close again, squinting to read them. All they showed were zeros, and a long, flat white line.

'They have been that way since the Facility closed.' Gaia's voice made him jerk up again. 'When the Bomb detonated in the harbour, the EMP that followed was actually the greater threat – to us. The Facility was shielded against blast effects by its very construction, and the ruggedised power system prevented a total shutdown. What no one accounted for in construction was that the system required a reboot to bring certain specific systems back online from protective shutdowns and connect to the shielded main generators. These had to be done manually, from an on-site terminal with a backup power supply supposedly proof against any level of EMP.'

Leah was first to find her voice. 'So, how did *you* stay... alive?'

'Every section of the Facility has its own separate generator batch, to keep the power going if an attack somehow did knock out the overall system,' Gaia replied. 'These are designed to kick in automatically when the main power cuts out, and they have strong shielding of their own, though not quite up to the same standard as the primary. Unfortunately, they were not intended for use longer than twelve hours, and focused only on critical systems: internal and external communications, wi-fi and hardline connections, air filtration, emergency lighting, security doors, locks and refrigeration of any hazardous materials. Anything else was... left out. And since some were already damaged from the EMP, or their connections, with no one around to make repairs, the generators did not remain online for long.'

None of the three Golems dared speak. Finally, Leah did. 'I thought there were still recruits here, going through training when you packed up.' She sounded confused, and not a little suspicious. 'What happened to *them*? Why couldn't *they* handle the reboots, if the comms still worked and you could give them the codes?'

Gaia's eye dimmed in brightness, like it was half-closing – or maybe Greg was imagining it. 'I perceived this problem first, when I powered back up after the Pulse faded. There were no protocols established for me to implement the reboots and reconnects myself and no way around the need for someone to be physically at the terminal. I alerted the Doctor at once when the process failed and made every effort to fix the problem – the priority being the lab wing. He laboured to repair the damage, alone. Nothing worked. The auxiliary generators shut down, one after another, and their sections with them. The Project data was still intact and saved, and the Facility itself was sealed off and mostly unharmed. Nonetheless, the damage was already done.'

'*What* damage?' Greg demanded. He'd listened to the voice's ramblings for hours and was finally at the end of his patience. 'What's down here that was worth taking *that* kind of risk?'

Gaia didn't speak for a time. At long last, she – it – responded, in a completely new vein. 'You asked whether there were any recruits on site, when the Bomb went off. I think it is time you met them – and who has been watching over them, as with you.'

Greg felt a new surge of irritation; why couldn't she – it – just *tell* them what they wanted, without the show-and-tell routine? Then the words really registered, and the remark died in his throat. The sharp hiss of escaping air made him turn. White plumes were escaping from a small gap that had suddenly appeared at the tops of each cylinder. He jumped back, off the platform. *Now what?* Leah was watching the scene with nervousness and curiosity both. On the other side, Cayden had backed farther away, and was walking carefully around the lip of the platform, knife now in hand.

The white gas sank, forming a dense, cold fog that covered most of the space around the cylinders. As it began to dissipate, a loud clunk sounded. The fronts of the cylinders slid down, back into the floor. Beneath was a glass compartment – tank – nearly as wide, sitting atop a metal base studded with more readouts and keypads. The compartment was filled with a cloudy tan-white fluid, nearly opaque.

The covers retracted fully, with a thud that reverberated through the room. Mystified, Greg took a hesitant step toward the nearest tank. As he looked more closely, he saw several thin wires of different colours trailing into the liquid from the tank's cover, and a larger, clear tube. He also began to see little bits of darker material, floating near the top of the liquid or drifting at random throughout it. He bent even nearer, until he was almost pressing the tip of nose to the glass. The bulk of the fragments seemed to be nearly the same colour as the fluid, and clustered in the middle. The wires led down to this mass, too; in fact, they seemed to be tethered or otherwise connected to it. Tentatively, he put his hand to the tank. The glass was cold to the touch, too much for standard refrigeration. *Liquid nitrogen.* It made sense, given the fog. *What needs that, and all the other security, down here?* He wiped his clinger-clad hand across it, clearing away the thin film of dust that had accumulated, and rocking the tank a bit.

The fragments began to swirl, like debris in a tornado. Greg moved away, startled. He shot a quick look at Gaia, irrationally expecting a rebuke. The blue eye only continued to watch him, and the others. He turned back to the tank – and stopped dead. *Fitting way to put it,* a tiny part of his brain said. Everything else – his mind, his eyes, his body – was petrified, focused on the sight in front of him.

Most of the fragments had begun to settle at the bottom of the tank, or waft to the top, leaving a cloudy but clearer gap. In the centre, supported by the fluid and the wires, was a mass of some kind: pale, yellowish grey, with more bits of material breaking off and floating away as Greg leaned in for a better look. It was about the size of a football, but much lumpier, more misshapen. Gradually, he began to discern more details: the smaller lump at one end, the short, clubbed appendages at the other. Focusing on the former, he made out two small depressions, and a stubby growth jutting out between them. Together, they almost made…

He flinched his face away, staggering backward. The heel of his clinger caught on the tiny gap between the platform and floor, and he tumbled over, landing on his back so hard the wind rushed out of him. 'Greg!' Leah cried. She rushed to his side, but he was already recovered, getting back to his feet – and still moving away from the grisly sight. 'What is' – She followed his transfixed gaze. Her mouth dropped open in a horrified gasp. Cayden came up on Greg's other side. His face, already pale, was as white as the walls around them.

The eyeless baby stared out at them, drifting back and forth in the decay-filled liquid. Most of the face had long rotted away, leaving softer tissue and half-formed bone beneath. The flesh of its body was similarly ragged and disintegrating. Its hands and feet were mere nubs, not fully formed. At a wild guess, it had died somewhere around four or five months; Greg couldn't tell, and did *not* want to look any closer. The wires from the tank's ceiling connected to leads inserted in the baby's arms, legs, head, chest and groin. The clear tube ran to where the umbilical cord would normally be, in a *naturally* conceived baby – or so the few bits of biology he recalled said.

Artificial womb. The words made only an abstract sense to Greg, as he stared at the blob of decomposing organic material. In the corner of his vision, he saw more remains, in every tank. Some were less far gone, still hanging by wires; others were practically bone, or had sunk to the bottom in separate, flaking clumps. *What... How... why...*

Lost in this sickened incomprehension, he almost missed the sound of a heavy deadbolt lock sliding back. The swish of a door snapped him fully back to himself, and he twisted on his heel, gun up and clasped tight in both hands to stop them from shaking. One of the office doors, directly across from the platform, was opening. A tall figure in a white lab coat stood at the threshold, his face in shadow. One hand gripped a cane of polished wood, tooled with intricate, interwoven designs. When the door was fully open, the figure took one step forward, then another. More features appeared: A jutting jaw, fringed with day-old stubble. A strong, aquiline nose, crooked and bent by some long-ago strike or accident. Combed brown hair, streaked with grey and cut awkwardly. Lined, dark blue eyes, gleaming behind dark-rimmed glasses.

The man approached the three Golems, his step slow and sure. He halted a pace or two away, looking at the gruesome show with a new, grim regret. The look remained when he faced them. The silence stretched. Then the newcomer coughed raspily, 'I see you've all recovered.' His voice was a sober baritone. 'Better and faster than I imagined, in fact. When I brought you here, it was touch and go, even with your abilities, and the tools I had here. But it looks like the compound did its work, as always – along with your own tenacity and stamina.'

He paused, leaning slightly on his cane. The three of them continued to stare, silent. The older man let out a soft sigh. 'I imagine how strange this must be for you all,' he said. His manner was collected, with something else – a mournful pride, mixed with deep regret – beneath this. 'Like you've seen a ghost, maybe, or something worse.'

Greg drew himself up. He met the man's eyes, unflinching. 'You could say that – Doctor.'

Dr Richard Garrett's smile was sad, pleased and bleak, all at once. He spread his hands. 'Welcome to Project Golem, Greg, Leah – Cayden,' he intoned, in a low, funereal tone. 'Welcome home.'

Chapter 24

The lab was silent. Time passed – seconds, minutes, hours, it was impossible to tell. Greg stared at the Doctor, then inch by inch, turned back to the platform. He wanted to tear his eyes away, to cover them, to run away and scrub them clean – yet he stood rooted to the spot. Leah's hands were so tight on his arm, the bones were creaking; they might break soon, if she kept it up. He didn't feel a thing. He just kept staring, watching as more of the dead foetus's flesh flaked away, or broke apart as it sank or rose. The body itself wasn't a shock; he'd seen plenty like it and worse, on a hundred different assignments and battlefields. It was the way it *floated,* sitting amid its own decay. And the way the long-gone eyes seemed to bore into him, following every twitch –

Something broke, in his mind or chest. He tore his arm free of Leah's grasp, and stormed towards Garrett. The Doctor's lips opened, to speak or sigh – and then he was dangling in the air, hoisted by the front of his shirt. Glaring, Greg slammed him up against the closest wall, hard enough to drive the air from the older man's lungs in a great *whuff.* He gasped a bit for more as Greg pressed his grip harder, but didn't try to fight or pull free. Leah and Cayden moved behind Greg, to watch, join in or pull him away. If they'd tried it in that moment, Greg would have hurled them across the room. Instead, he let Garrett slide down, until they were eye to eye, then leaned close. '*What – is – this?*' he ground out.

Slowly, Garrett recovered most of his breath. He looked at Greg, still unafraid – and the regret and suffering still churning behind his calm façade. 'It's what I said. What it's always been, from the very beginning. For you, for all three of you, for everyone you fought with, who came before them – and would have come after.' His eyes moved around the room. 'It's home. From the start, *this* is where you were conceived, born, raised, taught, and trained. Nothing more, and nothing less.'

'Born,' Greg rasped. In the wall's reflection, he could see the outline of the tank, and its... contents. The sight almost made him want to crush the Doctor's windpipe, or draw his knife and spill his innards across the spotless floor, like the floating detritus in the cylinder. 'Born *here?*' He almost couldn't get the word out.

Garrett nodded, grimly or sadly, maybe both. Greg's hands shook, though he managed to keep his grip. Bits and pieces of memory – the ones from his dreams, and a thousand other snippets he could only catch a glimpse of, before they flew off again – flashed through his head. Mastering himself – or as close as he could get – he uttered, 'You told us. Whenever we asked, in training or studies—' His voice cracked. 'Adopted kids. Foster kids. All given up by family, to the country, and giving back, in the service.' The crack widened. 'We had families. We didn't know them – but they were *real*. Parents, brothers, sisters – *families*, out there.' He shook the older man like a rag doll, in a sudden burst of new anger. 'You *told* us!'

Instead of getting dazed or angry, Garrett only smiled, in the same sad manner. 'In a way, you did.' He raised a finger, pointing to himself, and, more slowly, in the direction of Gaia's screen. 'Your parents were always here, watching over you while you grew, learned, trained, fought – and were the first to see you through what healing was needed.'

'What... *is* she?' Leah asked. She stared up at the lens with a wary intensity. 'I heard her all the time in training. She woke us up for training each day, oversaw our progress, laid out additional points for missions—' She trailed off. Her mouth thinned. 'She sang to us. At night, after lights-out – and in recovery, after the augmentations.' The frown deepened. 'I used to think she sounded like a mother would, if I were still living with mine – or remembered her face, and her voice.'

The Doctor's nod was slow, still without obvious emotion. 'That was part of her purpose, from the beginning.' He looked at the lens himself. 'The full name, starting when the first subroutines were put together, was Greatly Advanced Intelligence Authority. Given the tasks she had, GAIA – after the mother deity of all the Greek gods – was fitting. An artificial intelligence like none other in the world – then or since, from all that I've seen and heard. Its – *her* – task was to monitor your training and surgeries, and safeguard the Project's systems from outside attack or unauthorised internal access, whether against its mainframe or the geothermal power systems that kept it independent. Initially, she was intended as a closed system – an intranet, of sorts, to make hacking all the harder. Later, as the number of missions and threats increased, I saw to it she had wider access, to evaluate and in some cases predict likely and certain trouble spots. By the time the Turmoil really got rolling, she almost had more eyes and ears than there were humans – including those here, set up on my own time.'

A soft smile. 'Didn't expect to rely on her so much – but she's kept me safe and secure, since the Bomb. As for siblings—'

He made a hesitant half-wave, in Leah and Cayden's direction, and the tanks. 'Every brother or sister you could ever want was here, whenever you needed them. When the time was ready, they joined you in training, at meals, in class – and your family became that much bigger, and stronger.'

The world began to blur in front of Greg's eyes. Forcing it away, he focused on the Doctor's face again. He squeezed the other man's shirt so hard his fingers began to dig through the tough fabric – then suddenly let go. Garrett dropped to the floor, landing hard enough to draw a gasp of pain, but he didn't get angry, or fearful. Greg's stare bored into him. 'Talk,' he growled. Leah and Cayden came to his side, the same order in their poses.

Garrett levered himself up with his cane, bringing it in front of him as a brace. His eyes drifted over the three Golems, and beyond them to the tanks of horrors. He took a step forward. When none of the three stopped him, he walked between them, and up to the platform. They followed, keeping a rough triangle around him. He studied the closest tank, his back to them. 'Some of this you know, from before – or guessed, from what I can tell.' He paused, perhaps expecting a rebuke, or a blow. After neither came, he went on. 'When the ARC was fully realised, and I was finished with tests on cultured tissue and crippled vets, the Pentagon asked what the chances were of implanting the ARC *directly* into adult test subjects, making it part of their physiology, along with certain other chemical enhancers – thereby turning them into supersoldiers.'

An angry shadow flitted over his face. 'I told them it was impossible, something only a rabid sci-fi reader would think of. It didn't matter. They kept pressing me, demanding I perform *some* form of adult testing. I kept resisting, pointing out the million different unknowns: the possible psychological effects, the unclear longevity of the compound in adult subjects, the eventual breakdown of tissue due to constant regeneration. None of it registered – or it did, and they ignored it.

'Finally, word came that unless I went forward with the testing, not only would DARPA confiscate all my research and facilities and proceed with the work, but I would likely be tossed into Leavenworth or the just-rebuilt Gitmo, as a safeguard against taking my worries public.' The flash of anger came again, stronger, mixed with helplessness. 'I couldn't allow them to go forward, creating even more cripples for the sake of a policy – but I also couldn't face prison.' He turned to them. 'In the end, I agreed, on the condition that *I* would handle every second of organising, administrating, and assessing the tests, with minimal oversight.'

He stared off into the distance, hands folded on the head of his cane. 'The injections were only the first step, and the easiest: administer the ARC, and monitor for adverse reactions. Most of the subjects didn't show any changes at all as I'd told their superiors, countless times. No measurable increases in strength, no improvements in vision, speed or agility; everything they'd expected, and exactly what *didn't* happen. Unless they were injured in some way, there wasn't any way of knowing if the ARC even worked – and there were many, when the physical element of the tests started. Lifting 200-pound weights for hours at a stretch, thirty-mile nonstop sprints, even more hours swimming in the Sound or pool treadmills, breaking through or scaling walls with no more support than standard combat loads—'

He paused. 'It was a nightmare, those four years. So many left with severe injuries in their first week: broken arms, legs, necks; a few left as para- or quadriplegics. No one died, or went insane from the injections – that was a minor concern of mine, from the first tests years before. And it did its job, when the injuries were minor or life-threatening; subjects who cursed me for putting them through it would prostrate in thanks in between. But every time another of them went down screaming…'

Another pause, a longer one. When he resumed, it was with a new undercurrent of anger – and self-hatred. 'I compiled all the data, and sent it on as required. I thought that by itself would show the sick, twisted fools mistakenly called generals that ARC was useless as a weapon, that its only use was in restoring those *they* sent out to be killed or crippled. Instead, a week after the final test wrapped up, I received orders to continue research, with *positive* results expected in no less than three months. Snyder had taken over fully by then, and I suppose he wanted to move the process along even faster, to bolster the "Measured Response" policy.

'I objected, the moment I saw the email. I'd have done better shouting at an avalanche, or in outer space. And the same threats were still attached: work, or jail. By then, I was almost ready to demand they slap on the cuffs and hood, or destroy my research and go underground. I'd had enough of seeing young men and women broken for policy, and my work made into a tool of war.'

'But you didn't,' Leah said. She stared at the Doctor, as though afraid to come closer – or holding back from charging, knife in hand. Her voice was shaking, from lingering shock and growing anger. 'You stayed – and kept working.' She stabbed a finger at the tanks. 'How long before you got to *this*, whatever the *fuck*'—she drew the curse out—'it is?'

Garrett kept staring at the gruesome display. It was some time before he began again, in a more set tone. 'I wanted to quit – with all my soul. I'd already sacrificed my family; I wasn't about to do the same for so many more. But I knew it wouldn't end if I quit, or died. There would only be more experiments, more projects, more searches for the ultimate warrior, at the cost of dozens, hundreds, *thousands* of lesser ones. And *my* work would help advance that, with or without me. Without, I'd go to my grave a spineless coward, giving up everything in the name of pride, or a principle that no one would believe when set against what I'd helped create. With, I had the smallest chance of keeping the death and cripple rate to a minimum – and maybe even advancing humanity, a little bit further.'

Cayden moved up to the platform. Seeing his expression, Greg started to do the same; enraged as he was, he didn't want the older Golem losing it, either. Cayden made no move for a weapon, or any of the Doctor's vital spots. Instead, he stood close to the man, looming over him. 'How?' he rumbled.

Garrett faced him, and Greg and Leah. His face had changed again, becoming more reflective, analytical. In a half-musing tone, he said, 'Most people in this country – in the *world* – don't really understand how *vital* the donation process is for the world of medicine. Kidneys, corneas, livers, hearts, lungs, bone marrow, sperm, eggs, blood, glands. Millions of people – no, *billions*, I'm sure by now – have gotten a transplant of some kind with one or more of these, or donated them at death or to make quick cash, willingly and not. Every day, before and since the Turmoil, somebody keels over from a stroke, or dies in an accident, or goes into an exam room with a specialist or a cup. And every day, somebody ends up in a hospital needing something from these donations to live, whether it's one year more, or fifty.'

The dark, determined look re–emerged. 'Plenty of the recruits who went through the first ARC tests needed many of both, even with the compound to accelerate tissue healing. When I finally decided to heed D.C.'s demands, I made it *very* clear that I would *not* allow anyone else to endure the tests – and what would certainly come later – unless *I* had total control of *every* part of the process. Oversight would continue, and I would obey the core directives, but only the President or the Joint Chiefs could make or suggest changes.' A bitter, knowing smirk. 'And since neither wanted *too* much involvement, beyond the end results, for the usual political reasons, I had the closest thing to autonomy I would ever have.' The smirk died, returning his features to complete solemnity. 'Enough to take the Project to a new stage – one where its graduates would not only be able to endure its demands – but have that endurance within their very selves, from the beginning.'

'*What* new stage? Greg demanded. Leah edged up next to him. She looked as impatient and edgy as he felt, although she was keeping her hands in the open, away from any weapons or sure killing blows. 'How could—'

He stopped. His eyes went from the Doctor to the tanks, and back again. A sickening, penetrating coldness spread from his head to his toes. A sudden lightheadedness followed hard on its heels; it took all his energy to keep steady. Leah, sensing this, took his arm. He looked at her, mutely; the words were clear enough in his stare. Her face drained of what little colour it had regained. Her eyes went wide: so much, the pupils almost seemed to disappear. Her mouth shaped a silent word: *No.* Unable to hold her gaze, he looked to Cayden. The other Golem's features were bone-white; more from fury than horror, by his judgement. His hands were trembling, as though itching to rip the Doctor to pieces, and the room next.

Numb with his own shock, disbelief, and fury, Greg turned back to Garrett. The Doctor was regarding them all with sad sympathy. Greg almost lashed out at him then; that was the *last* emotion he wanted. Before he could, the older man began to speak once more. 'I knew from the first test results that ARC could never work in adults, other than in the hospitals. Testing on children was obviously impossible, for countless reasons, and not just my own revulsion.' He swallowed, and straightened, balancing himself more evenly with minimal help from the cane. 'So I decided to start even earlier.'

He looked to the closest tank, watching the little corpse sway in the dense liquid with an eerie detachment. 'When I was at CellWorx, there was a joint project that never got much beyond the planning stage; an idea that Sam and I bounced around in a few bull sessions, before he… left. We'd worked with patients and tissue continuing some of the most debilitating inherited and acquired afflictions known to man, often with little more than painkillers to help those enduring them, or their children. The latter resonated with me most of all; how many millions of people who knowingly or unknowingly carried the genes for these tortures had to watch their offspring manifest and suffer them? We wanted to do something more. Create a means to prevent the most harmful effects of a person or couple's genes from being realised, while still giving them a child that was wholly theirs.'

His arm moved out, to take in all the tanks. 'So many eggs and sperm sit around the country, waiting for their turn in the testing lab or procedure. And the final design for the artificial womb – what we simply called the NeoMater, in the planning stage, and it stuck – was relatively simple, for myself and Sam. Between the two of us, we had more background, knowledge, and training in genetics, micro- and neurobiology and surgery than probably ninety-five per cent of the medical field at the time, and we had access to other specialists and labs of similar calibre to fill in the blanks. The only thing we needed was an Everest of funding, and permission to set up a facility that turned out babies on demand, free of whatever faults the parents didn't want.'

He grunted, in irony or black humour. 'Needless to say, D.C. wasn't inclined to waste money on what they and the more... devout factions backing them already considered a potentially blasphemous idea. And there were plenty of doctors and professionals with perfectly good arguments against it, moral and legal. We shelved the plan, and soon after Sam went his own way. I didn't even recall it – until the "continue" order came in.' The Doctor studied the dead foetus again. 'When it did, I realised I had a way of controlling the Project, literally from birth to death. Nothing else was acceptable. If the Pentagon wanted a breed of supersoldier so badly, they'd get it – and *I* would see it done right, without needless deaths or lifelong pain.'

He put a hand to the tank's glass, gently. 'I pulled the NeoMater design out of the files, and presented it to DARPA and the Joint Chiefs along with an outline of my intended process. They agreed without too much discussion; "Measured Response" was in full swing by then, and the demands for boots on the ground were multiplying every day. With the blank cheque I now had, there was little to no trouble building the first five devices.' His eyes flicked in Cayden's direction. The older Golem's chin went up and down an inch in acknowledgement, without a change in his fixed, tense look. Garrett turned to face Greg and Leah again. 'After that, it was an even simpler matter to get access to the right DNA – and begin the gestational process.'

'The right DNA.' Leah's voice was hollow, almost devoid of emotion. 'From where?'

Garrett's sober look said he understood the *real* question. 'Most of the sperm and eggs I requested came from the NIH, through acquisitions by shell foundations and labs. Others came from the Army Medical Research and Material Command; the crises and weekly bioweapon scares at that time meant they were frequently acquiring the bodies of soldiers after death, for experimentation. There were no names attached to the donations, when they came to me. The military didn't want any chance of their being traced to me – and I didn't want to know who had given them up.'

Leah's eyes shone, in anger and grief. Greg felt a tickling in his own eyes. Blinking it away as best he could, he moved another step closer. 'What about these?' He made himself look to the tanks, and point to them. 'They weren't just wombs, were they?' He had to force the words out. 'There was something else – otherwise we'd never have become... this.' He waved at the decaying sights before them.

Garrett inclined his head in assent. He brushed his hand against the screens on the nearest tank. 'The most important work was done well before these were necessary – but they were still a vital part of the procedure.' The hand shifted, pointing to one of the rooms on the opposite side, which was a bit larger than the rest. 'That was the lab, where it started, with the assessment and selection step. We – or rather *I* – had access to almost every kind of sperm and egg material in the country, but it wouldn't work to just bring two of any kind together and make changes as it grew. Days or weeks would be wasted, to say nothing of material.

'Screening was necessary. First for inheritable diseases or conditions, such as predispositions for stroke, heart disease, diabetes, brain tumours, mental disease where possible – the list was near-endless, and plenty of samples were set aside for later work, or destroyed; less of a paper trail. Then there was a battery of checks, for any undesirable traits.' He touched at his glasses. 'Myopia and farsightedness, to start with. Every one of you was gifted with 20/20 vision from birth, and you'll have it till the day you pass.' He squinted a little at each of their faces. 'The glow in your irises is a side effect of that, apparently. I've never been able to pin down the exact cause, only that it's related.' He adjusted the glasses again, then continued. 'Deafness and muteness were next, and a shorter list of others after that. Much of these first two rounds was done by the NIH or Army facilities sending the material, and based off donor histories, yet I still performed many myself to be sure.

'By then, the number of samples *least* in need of modification was small – but still well into the hundreds. At that stage, it was time to move from analysis to alteration.' His finger moved, to the next room down. 'That was the lab where the samples were fertilised, and then modified. In my few light moments, I slipped and referred to it as the Backseat.' Garrett showed no sign of lightness now, although he seemed to take some mild professional pleasure in the recollection. 'The first changes eliminated any hints of… deficiencies that slipped through. Next came the improvements the Pentagon wanted: increased height, muscle mass, agility.' He looked at each of the three Golems. 'The implantation of the ARC capability was easy, from a purely technical standpoint. Insert the coded gene into the fertilised egg's DNA, and monitor for any adverse changes elsewhere; a first-year geneticist can do it.

'The problem was, the gene, while still ultimately composed from human tissue and sequences, was still an *artificial* component. Hundreds if not thousands of replacement organs get rejected every year by the bodies they're implanted in; the risk was no less great here. And there was always the chance of unexpected consequences with the egg, or later foetus, once the gene was implanted. Very little of what was being done in this lab had even gotten past the debate stage, not to mention the technology. The potential for mistakes and rejects was huge.'

'What happened to *them*?' Leah asked. 'The mistakes, and the rejects?' She'd blinked away the angry sheen in her eyes, but the faint tremble in her otherwise empty voice told how affected she was. 'Did they get tossed out, like the "unwanted" ones at the start?'

Garrett regarded her kindly. 'Very few did, I'm relieved to say. When they did, most often at the earliest stages of growth... I saw to it they were ended, painlessly.' A wispy chuckle. 'Something the pro-lifers would gnash their teeth over, I'm sure.' He became sober again at once. 'I knew I was playing with lives, on a slide and when grown. The technology for the entire process *was* new but *I* had designed the bulk of it, and I knew where to look first when there were problems. In a matter of months, these were gone from the tech itself, and down to almost none in the fertilisation and alteration parts of the process. Once the ARC was inserted, and the other genes tailored as needed, I moved on to the next, most important stage.'

He stepped down from the platform, moving back several paces to take in the entire display – yet still in easy reach of any of his guests. 'The theory for workable artificial wombs had existed for close to a century. Money, ethics, and the nagging workability questions kept it a theory for all that time, before Sam and I dreamed up our rough version. Here, it was even harder. It wasn't simply designing a device that could sustain an embryo, then a foetus, then a fully-grown infant. Technology already existed for each of those stages: some crude, some state-of-the-art.'

The Doctor paused. His look became more wary, apprehensive. Not for himself, Greg judged, or not completely; more for them, as if he were worried they couldn't handle it. He choked back a caustic laugh. *I've come this far without crushing his head like an egg, and* he's *worried about* me? Keeping this to himself, he gave Garrett a brusque nod. The Doctor nodded back, seemingly reassured, and continued. 'As I said, the technology and technique was there, for each part of the gestation period up to birth. Umbilical nutrition, growth monitoring and enhancement, general health – everything. I had a working prototype here within six months, and all ten you see here in a little over twelve. But the *natural* birthing process takes nine months, in a healthy woman, and another eighteen years for the infant to come close to maturity. D.C. wanted the... final specimens the day before yesterday, despite my warnings about the need for more testing and observation.' He looked at the floor. 'So I went back to the drawing board. In less than a month, I found a way to redesign the prototype to not only shorten the time between creation and birth – but also to accelerate the growth of every child born.'

Greg's mouth was dry as a desert. 'How much?' he managed to croak.

The Doctor spread his hands, keeping his cane to the floor. 'It varied for a little while. The system didn't have every kink worked out, not until the "First Five" were already grown.' He cast a look Cayden's way; the older Golem returned it coldly. 'The average was within three years, although some developed quicker or slower. Even after the last bug was solved, though, and the... batches were coming smoothly off the line, I watched every one of you, every step of the process. From the day you left the tank, through all the surgeries and tests. From your first day of training, with the clingers and other weapons, to your last mission as adults. I'd done all I could to give you the best possible start, before you even drew breath, and I wasn't about to send the power-mad idiots in D.C. anything but the best.' He looked at the three Golems with the same infuriating little smile. 'It looks like I did, in the end.'

Batches. Off the line. The words tolled in Greg's mind, with a new, morbid understanding. He glanced down at his arm, to the site of the tattoo he'd borne since birth – or whenever it had *actually* been done. One eye swung to the tanks, then just as quickly away. How long had he spent in his, unconscious and unaware of the life already planned for him? How many of the others had gone to their graves – or nearly, in Taylor's case – without ever knowing the *truth?*

'What about the memories?' Cayden's growl yanked him from these thoughts. He was now only a foot or so away from the Doctor, the fingertips of one hand perilously close to the butt of his pistol. 'We went through all this' – he jabbed his free hand at the tanks, and the entire Facility—'but we can't remember *any* of it. *How?*' His sudden, sharp grip on the pistol said the answer had better be good.

Garrett didn't seem fazed. 'One of the slightly brighter bulbs in DARPA raised the very same issue, midway through yours and the other Five's gestation,' he replied. 'The worry was that, if any of you were told the truth about your origins, whether from the tanks or the petri dish, you would react dangerously. Enough that you could potentially wreck the Project, or break out and go "freelance", for any of the at-home terror and militia groups, or the highest bidding enemy nation.' He scowled. 'They whispered in the right ears at the Pentagon, and the Chiefs demanded safeguards. Some I was already implementing, as basic security measures: keeping you in small groups, out of any unauthorised eyesight, and plenty of guards and other measures.' The scowl grew – aimed at himself, it appeared, along with the long-gone overseers. 'That wasn't enough – not for those who'd demanded the perfect soldier, and now rightly feared them. They wanted more ways to keep you caged and docile when not on assignment, preferably unaware of the bars. And others to bring you down quickly, should those bars break open.'

Leah's face coloured, a furious pale red. 'The Pax Contingency,' she ground out.

'You know the name?' For the first time, Garrett looked honestly surprised. 'I never did, even when I submitted it to the DARPA watchdogs. To me it was simply a modified tranquiliser, meant for those with your genetic makeup. I honestly thought it had been lost in the coup against Snyder; the anti-Vanguard mobs went after every federal agency they could, and the transition government's still doing the same from what I hear, albeit more surgically.'

He made the merest twitch of a shrug. 'It didn't matter what they called it, in the end. I shared some concerns regarding your learning the full story – but I also wasn't about to become a jailer as well as a scientist.' His scowl took on a craftier edge. 'So I sent the earliest version of the Pax to the Army, with a working model of the delivery system. What I may have failed to include was a warning about the estimated *longevity* of any effects. They never tested it, or even asked – and I never got around to clarifying the matter.'

'Thanks,' Greg bit off, in a voice that was anything but grateful. 'Except we didn't forget anything after getting hit with the "effects." And none of what we've remembered is gone either; hell, it's gotten clearer every second we've been in this place.' He came closer to Garrett himself, almost shoulder-to-shoulder with Cayden. 'What "other measures" were there?' The urge to take the Doctor by the head and plough him through every tank and window in the room was stronger than ever.

Garrett didn't answer, at first. Instead of nervous or sombre, he now seemed resigned, almost relieved – even pleased. Before Greg could speak again, or *make* him talk somehow, the Doctor reached out and took him by the left wrist. He started to draw back, then desisted; he could snap the older man like a twig at the first sign of trouble. Garrett turned the arm over, feeling gently along the clinger sleeve until he reached the crook of the elbow. He probed with his thumb, a little harder. 'There,' he murmured. Seeing Greg and the others' puzzlement, he let go, that strange vague pleasure still on his face. 'You recall the shots you received, as adults? The ones that came mainly at the start of and during your training, but also after missions, and other points?'

'ARC boosters,' Leah said, with an unwilling nod. 'Megavitamins, for when we weren't sure of eating for days or weeks. Vaccines, too, for specific disease hotspots. And what you kept calling all-purpose inhibitors, to suppress certain... urges or suspected conditions we might have picked up on past assignments – or inherited – that might be problematic in the field.' She looked to Greg, her lip curling up in a real smile for the briefest of seconds. He found himself returning the look, though still not entirely sure *what* they were smiling about. Then she faced Garrett again, and it was gone, back to grim, angry purpose. 'They were more than that, though – weren't they?' Now she came closer, hand to her pistol. 'A *lot* more.'

The Doctor took no obvious notice of this. 'Some *were* boosters. The ARC was part of you from the very beginning – but there were times when it needed help. *More* acceleration, in short.' He pointed to the next room down from the 'Backseat' lab. 'When I saw how some of you were returning with still-healing wounds, I cobbled together a stimulant that would boost the regeneration process, several times over. The drawback was a spike in pain reception – more so if the damage was neurological along with everything else – but it meant a much shorter recovery period.'

Greg nodded; he remembered some of the quick repairs others had gone through in the field – and his own, after Lake Balkash. Taylor must not have received any, that time… or it had only made his injuries *worse*. 'And the others?' he asked, woodenly. 'What help were *they* supposed to be?'

Garrett stayed quiet, for another long moment. When he did speak, it was in that same mingling of pleasure and relieved resignation. 'You were already perfect, in nearly every respect. Regenerative capability, up to near-fatal injury. Genetically improved strength, vision, hearing and speed. Immune to most diseases, thanks to the ARC or the work in the labs and in utero. The best possible soldiers, in D.C.'s eyes – and the world's greatest threat, should you go AWOL or worse.' He looked each of them in the eye again, his gaze regretful and stoic. 'They wanted you to be the new face of the American military, crushing any and all threats – but they also wanted protections. Not just the locks and weapons upstairs, or the Pax, both of which only kept you contained physically. Methods that would keep you tame, wouldn't affect your skills – and which you wouldn't think twice about.'

He held up his own arm. 'The inhibitors, as you call them – they were exactly that. A cocktail of hormone and psychotropic suppressants, like those in standard uppers or downers. These controlled emotional responses that might endanger a mission or your training – and other, natural progressions in your growth, keeping them low-key or blocking them altogether. There were hints of longer-lasting effects, such as sterility, or increased growth rate for tumours or other conditions; nothing ever came to light, though. Long story short, they remained in your system longer than the ARC boosters and other injections you received; still, it was decided to combine them into one procedure, to be administered immediately prior to missions, and following, if injuries occurred. If not, the injections were delayed until your next weekly physical. You'd remain focused, and battle-ready, without any desire to find out anything beyond the day's lesson, or expected threats and mission resistance.'

He lowered the proffered limb. 'I could see the basic wisdom in this policy, though I still hated it, and its secrecy. It was an unnecessary extra control, given *other* options being considered for dealing with potential leaks or desertions, and it threw grit into every part of the Project's mission.' The resignation grew stronger, alongside a new surge of self-reproach. 'Except I didn't know *all* of that grit's impact, until it was much too late.'

Cayden took another step toward the Doctor, almost closing the distance between them. He didn't draw or reach for a weapon or make any other moves; he just stood stock-still, waiting. Greg and Leah joined him. Garrett didn't back away, but his body sagged, shrinking in on itself. All at once, he truly looked *old*. 'Every drug has side effects, alone or in combination,' he said softly. 'You were supposed to be proof against the more conventional ones, and those from deliberate poisonings. I had a small part in the initial design of the inhibitors, to ensure against either, and so I believed – or was led to – that they were just what they claimed to be.' Garrett raised his head, meeting Cayden's eyes. 'It wasn't until you and the rest of the First Five came back from the Korea mission that I saw what was wrong – and that I wouldn't be able to stop it from becoming standard policy, for you and all the others.'

Cayden didn't press him aloud, though his posture screamed for the Doctor to go on. Garrett's words came out even lower. 'When you came back... you barely recognised me, or the Facility. You knew who I was, who you were, and the details of your mission – but everything else was gone. And not from any blows to the head, or some unknown agent exposure.

The only agents present in your system, apart from the ARC, were the inhibitors. When I examined samples of these, and observed the effects on you more closely, I found that the combination contained markers for a side effect I hadn't known was possible, during the development process.'

His head drooped again. 'I didn't want to believe it at first. That anyone would even *try* something so grotesque, or that I would be such a key, unwitting and unwilling part—' He let out a raspy sigh. 'The cocktail interfered with or outright blocked memory formation, at all levels: long, short, intermediate. Over time, every one of you would gradually forget almost *everything* about your service and time in the Project, apart from selective or immediate details. Nor did any of you show any signs of wondering about this, or trying to figure it out; the memories faded too rapidly, and the other cocktails stifled any discontent. Certain memories formed before the injections remained partly intact, or simply buried. The operations you went through as children, for example, to reinforce bone and strengthen muscle mass where the gene therapy hadn't – and your recovery afterward. Your basic recall was also left intact: place and person names, your training and other education, certain noteworthy missions, and other memories of that kind. Everything else… '

He trailed off. When he began again, there was a newer strength in his manner – and a greater self-hatred. 'I fought with them. DARPA, the Pentagon – even Snyder, when he finally realised the danger in putting off the man behind the linchpin for "Measured Response". His hands squeezed tighter on the head of the cane. 'I tried to make them see the inhumanity of the "safeguards", the threats they posed not just to the health of all the Project's offspring, but to them, if it ever came out. None of them budged.' His grip relaxed, but the bitter tone only got stronger. 'I couldn't quit by then, or go public. I'd already sold my soul, by agreeing to stay before, and there was even less chance of going public to force their hand.' His face became even more deeply lined. 'The only choice I had was to go back to work – and hope that one day *someone* would see the danger.'

'But they didn't,' Cayden said. His voice was shaking now. 'They kept us dosed, brainwashed – *docile*. And you helped them.' He slid in front of the two other Golems. 'You *made* us, for them. From day one, we existed for them – and for *you*. *That's* why you never backed out; not at the start, and not then – not during *any* part of the Project.'

His hands were clenching and opening, his fingers like claws. 'Because we were *your* greatest work. We belonged to *you*, and no one else. And when the time came that somebody finally tried to destroy it all, to wipe this place out, and every one of the "graduates" you'd made… you scattered us to the winds, without a clue of what happened, or how to find out. All to protect your best *experiment*.'

He snatched the canister out of Garrett's grip, holding it accusingly in front of the Doctor's eyes. Garrett held still, not speaking. Greg's blood hammered in his ears. Everything they'd seen and heard kept washing over him, like waves against rock – and a little more control washed away, each time. Anger, shock, hatred, grief – all these fused into a roiling sea inside him. Leah's stricken, tormented face said the same struggle was tearing at her. He didn't know which of them wanted more badly to reach out and crush the life out of the old man – only that the other would be half a step behind.

The tomblike quiet stretched. Garrett made no move to run; he seemed to have turned to stone, his eyes fixed on Cayden. Jerkily, Cayden lowered the canister. His expression was completely flat, a mask like none other. 'Just one answer left, after all the rest,' he said, in a similarly empty tone. He lifted the canister again, balancing it in the palm of his hand. 'When *they* showed up my door with this'—he made a tiny jerk of his head toward the other two Golems—'they walked me through the security. Said what was in here was the key to the Project, and that only you had the key. You – or somebody with a similar bio-signature. A genetic match, or enough of a *connection* to equal one.' His breath came in quicker, nearly silent puffs through his nose.

He pressed his thumb against the aperture. In the deathly silence, the *snick* of the needle was almost like a gunshot. When the top unsealed, he flipped it back hard enough to nearly snap it off, and jammed his hand inside. The tiny flash drive winked in the light when he pulled it free.

He pushed it into the Doctor's face. 'I was more than just the First,' he ground out. 'More than the first one in the field, out of the tube, or slapped together in the petri dish.' There was a new sheen in his eyes, unlike anything Greg had seen: grief, anger, disbelief. 'You made me – from *you*. Your first experiment, with some random eggs and your own swimmers – all to make your very own, pet Golem.' He held the drive even closer. '*That's* why you made me. *That's* why you always favoured me, with the best gear and assignments. I remember *that* much, and never knew why – till now. To see if the Project worked – and to have a *son* as proof. Isn't it?' The drive was a millimetre before Garrett's right eye. 'Isn't it?' he whispered again. The Doctor said nothing. *'Isn't it!?'* Cayden roared.

The echo rolled and reverberated across the chamber. Still Garrett made no sound or movement. The look on his face was somewhere between grief and hate – of himself, Greg judged, and a deeper kind than any other. Finally, when the quiet had returned, a murmur escaped his lips, almost too soft to hear. 'Yes.'

Leah let out a choked sob. Cayden withdrew his hand. The drive fell from his fingers, landing with a clatter on the linoleum. His entire body was quaking. Greg had a vivid image of him seizing the Doctor by the neck and tearing his head from his shoulders, or hurling him into the blue-eyed screen. Instead, with a roar of inarticulate fury, he hurled the canister at the nearest tank. It punched through the tempered glass, throwing shards in all directions, and smashed into the one next to it, breaking that capsule as well. Twin floods of milky, tan liquid splashed across the floor, spraying the three Golems' clothes. Bits of watery dead flesh floated in the mire… and two larger misshapen lumps.

The sight and sound broke something inside Greg. He lashed out with his fist, aiming for Garrett's mournful face. He pulled the punch at the last millisecond – or had the Doctor managed to duck most of it? – but it was still enough to hurl the old man backwards, into the far wall, his glasses flying away in two separate chunks. Not stopping or caring to see what the damage was, he spun and charged at the closest tank still standing. His shoulder bashed into the readout monitors; the force of the hit wrenched the tank free from its base, and smashing into its neighbour, toppling them like dominoes. More fluids and decayed matter spattered over his arms and chest. He barely noticed, swinging out for his next target. The world became a blur of noise and motion, with burst of pain as his foot or fist struck something harder than expected, before breaking through and collapsing it to pieces. Somewhere nearby, he heard Leah screaming like a banshee, and the sound of heavy glass crashing to the floor. In one of his few half-sane instants, he saw her standing in the gap of a shattered opaque office window, an office chair in both hands. She hurled it through the next-door wall as he turned away, bringing another cacophony of breaking glass, then tore at the bare metal frame, screaming still.

At last, he paused, breathing in great, sucking gasps. This brought his other senses rushing back, including a steadily decreasing pain in his hands and heels. He looked around. Every one of the five tanks were toppled over and broken open, their grisly contents spread over almost the entire floor. Liquid dripped in a cheerful patter from the broken edges, forming tan-white puddles. The labs and offices stood open to each other, and the main floor, their walls now jagged holes, or empty, sagging frames; slivers of glass still hung or dropped from some of these. Spiralling cracks at random spots on the wall told of fists or feet punching at full speed and strength. Greg had little doubt they'd come from him. Looking up, he saw the jagged edge of a tank's lid, protruding from Gaia's main screen. The blue-eye image flickered and danced over the fractured screen, laced with corrupted data; maybe the whole program was damaged beyond repair. *Good.*

Leah was standing in the door to the operating room, her chest heaving as hard as his. The stand of lights from the table dangled from her hand, still tossing sparks. Cayden was standing in the middle of the tank display, his machete-like knife in hand. From the slash marks on the walls, and the cut patterns in some of the tanks and the glass front of the 'recovery ward', he'd found plenty of use for it. Like his two 'brethren', he was covered almost head to toe in womb fluid and viscera. Unlike them, however, his breathing and posture were completely calm, even normal. He didn't seem to register their presence, only kept staring at the Doctor. Garrett had gotten back to his feet, one hand pressed to the wall while he held a handkerchief to his face with the other – but showed no sign of wanting to run or beg.

None of the four spoke. Then Cayden blinked once, apparently bringing himself out of his trance – or the last of his rage. He strode up to the Doctor, who had by now put the bloody cloth away, and was standing erect again, without the cane, meeting the older Golem's hard stare with a steady one of his own. Cayden halted a step or two short, blade still in hand. Greg readied himself for the swing that would take the Doctor's head off, or spill his guts over the floor to join the other bits of flesh. Instead, in one quick, smooth move, Cayden's arm came up. The blade shot past Garrett's head, burying itself almost halfway in the concrete.

Garrett didn't flinch, or even blink. With the same sharpness of motion, Cayden turned his back on the man who had created him – created *all* of them – and marched toward the stairs. Not looking back once, he climbed up to the next level, and went out into the foyer beyond. Greg heard more glass breaking, and other objects being hurled to the floor or walls – then the slam of a door, hard enough to dislodge more bits of glass from the destroyed office façades. Greg sensed the older Golem wouldn't stop walking until he reached the surface – maybe not for hours, days, weeks. Not until he'd put everything – the Facility, the Project, the *Doctor* – far, far behind him.

And us? Leah came up to him. She didn't speak, but her haunted, tear-filled eyes held the same question. He had no answer; he couldn't even form a single word. Everything was hazy, like his mind was filled with weighted fog. To give him *some* focus, he looked toward Garrett. The Doctor was standing without aid now, hands folded atop his cane. There was no sign of any bruise or blood from the hit he'd taken; Greg guessed he must have pulled back more than he'd thought. The pain and torment in his dark blue eyes were real, however.

Seeing it made Greg's fists clench again. The hot rage rekindled. He hadn't known a sensation could reach such heights – until a few moments ago. He's *feeling pain?* Him? The anger burned hotter. *All the nights of agony, from the operations to recovering; all the friends I watched die, or wish they had; all the lies that kept us here, and sent us out to suffer and die – And he's the one in pain?*

He took a step forward, fist half-raised. Garrett watched him, unmoving. Another step, the fist rising higher – then suddenly slackening, falling back to his side. The heat inside died down to embers, replaced by a cold, burnt-out numbness. *What's the point?* He could pound Garrett's face into the wall until it turned to paste, rip apart the lab and everything above down the foundations – none of it changed a thing. *And you pushed for this. You wanted to know what lay at the heart of this place. For the team, for the Sanctuary – and for you.* Now he did.

He tried to make himself focus. Only one task remained at that moment, as he saw it: To warn Hiroshi and the others. To scrap the plan, or as much as could be, and *get away.* The Sanctuary could hold out against the remaining Brown Coats, though they might take losses. Against the entire Army, and Air Force? No. Better to break up and scatter, like they'd lived before. With Overwatch, they stood a good chance of staying ahead of any pursuit, and maybe even holing up in a slew of isolated, well-hidden spots, out of sight and mind. It'd be a life spent on the run, looking over their shoulders for drones or bombers or men in brown coats, but it would be theirs – and one well away from *this.*

These half-formed plans came to him as if from a distance, unimportant and uninteresting. *I should've died at Balkash, or a hundred times before. I should've stayed in the mountains, when the Air Force hit – or let the Brown Coats put one between my eyes.* Any of these would've done the trick – and spared him from the here and now.

Slowly, robotically, Greg turned away from the mournful gaze of the Doctor. Leah watched him, her look almost that of a scared, uncomprehending little girl. Avoiding her gaze, he started for the steps himself. He didn't know *where* he was going, or what he'd do next – and didn't care in the slightest.

A flash of reflected light winked in his eye when he passed the Doctor's office. He didn't stop, or slow his stride, but he still caught a glimpse of the source. A framed picture lay against a toppled, splintered metal desk. The glass was cracked, but the photo – a smiling woman and grinning young boy, both with dark hair – was easy to see even in a second's glance. *He lost them, so he made us. A perfect, all-powerful* 'family', *leashed and drugged – and never knowing or wondering* why.

The anger tried to flare again. Instead of letting it, Greg kept walking, up the stairs and into the foyer. The security booths were pulverised, turned to heaps of tempered glass; the weapons, armour and gas grenades were tossed every which way. The fire door stood partway open, one hinge nearly broken. He nudged it open. The staircase wound up and up the shaft, until he couldn't see it any longer. He didn't care. He put one foot on the first step, the other on the next. Soon enough he'd be back on the levels he'd known his whole life – and yet never known at all.

Chapter 25

Later That Night

Greg sat at the edge of his cot. He stared at the bland, white linoleum floor, seeing nothing. The mattress was stiff, unyielding: one step above wood or stone. He'd been sitting since he'd come across the room, hours ago; he didn't remember how long ago, or care. It might've been his at one point, or not; they were all the same. The space was small and cramped, with only bare metal panelling for walls, a lone bulb directly overhead, and Gaia's ubiquitous eye above the door. The blue lens was dimmed, almost unnoticeable. Perhaps she – it – was still online after all, and giving him a measure of privacy. *Another first.*

He'd passed through this room and any number of its kind more times than he could count – between training, surgeries, missions, recoveries. The memories were still unclear, but he could remember *that* much. And since a few hours ago, they'd been coming back in a steady torrent, some fragmentary, others hazy but nearly whole. The missions were the clearest; perhaps the inhibitors had been arranged somehow to leave those intact, for debriefings. Endless laps around the track.

Just as many rounds in the wrestling and empty-hand rooms, the weights and exercise machines, the flight simulators, and on the firing ranges – above and below ground – practicing with everything from pistols to Stingers. Classes where he sat ramrod-stiff in unyielding metal chairs, typing out notes, or listening to or watching lecture after lecture: tactics, science, first-aid, and so many other subjects he soaked up for their possible use in the field. One tasteless meal after another in the cafeteria. Passing other Golems in the halls, mess and gym, never talking unless they had to work together – or so he could recall, thus far.

The constant replay didn't help. If anything, it made him wish he *hadn't* held back from a killing blow. The Doctor's face seemed to hang behind every memory and image, like a half-faded afterimage. More than once, Greg could almost *see* him in the background, watching him in every session, assignment or recovery. Yet he couldn't stop it – and wasn't sure he wanted to. One thing was clear from it, at least: He had never been intended as anything other than a weapon. Leah, Cayden, Taylor, the others on the Council and in the Sanctuary, the ones who were still out there or already dead – *they* weren't intended for anything else. The inhibitors, the surgeries, the ARC – from day one, it had all aimed toward the same result.

He could see now why they'd been kept so isolated and regimented, from their first conscious days. No distractions of any kind, or potential leaks or embarrassing questions. Any free time that came up, he was training, or in a room like this, staring at the ceiling for hours on end or reading through whatever files he might be given on the next assignments. He hadn't thought anything of it, or not much; thanks to the inhibitors and the training, he hadn't *needed* to. There'd been nothing else, all his life.

Bitterness rose like a geyser. He let out a bark of harsh laughter. *What life?* He wasn't even supposed to exist, officially or unofficially. None of his 'kind' were. He, Leah, Cayden, the Council, the other Sanctuary survivors – they weren't soldiers, or heroes, or orphans. They weren't even *human*: they were *rejects*. Discards, pure and simple. Scraps of unwanted DNA, cobbled together to make something more, something *else*. Something to be controlled, trained, *inhibited*, until the right moment. Something with *one* purpose, and only one: Killing.

A snippet from one of his classes suddenly came to him – history, or maybe strategy, he couldn't remember, and it didn't matter now. In ancient Greece, it had been common to 'expose' infants who were deemed unfit to live, due to some real or perceived physical or mental deformity. Too small, too sickly, a club foot or a tendency to cry or shit too often – any of these earned a spot on some lonely hillside, left to the elements or hungry predators. The tough, grim, militaristic Spartans had done this more than others, according to the sources. For them, it was the only way to cull themselves of inferior genes, and mould those who were spared into the perfect soldiers, the ancestors of the 'best of the best' today.

On some occasions, the books also claimed, someone would find the abandoned infants, and take them in as their own, sometimes even raising them in a way that overcame any deformities or afflictions. *The Doc must've loved that story.* And he'd done it one better, too. Everyone in the Project had been abandoned even before birth. Garrett had taken them, turned them into soldiers – and then left them to the world's harsh mercies anyway, when he was done with them.

Greg stared down at his hands, watching the light shift over the clinger's surface. The fingers closed, knotting into fists so tight the fabric creaked. What would he have done, if he'd been born? Not grown, but *born*? What would his life have been? Would these hands have been put to other uses, besides wielding knives or snapping necks? His vision began to cloud, with tears, anger, or both. Would he, maybe, have been *loved*?

A light tap came at the door. Greg didn't speak, or budge. The tap came again, louder. Still he did nothing. There was a brief pause. The door handle began to turn, slowly, hesitantly. Greg made no move to grab it, or block the way.

With a soft creak, the door swung open. Leah stood in the hallway outside. She'd stripped away the rags of her civilian garb, leaving her in just the clinger. Silent as a shadow, she stepped in. She sat beside him on the bed, her movements stiff and creaky. She stared at the wall, unseeing. Her face was wet, but no new tears were falling.

Neither of them spoke, for what seemed an eternity. Leah's lips began to move, but no sound emerged. Gradually, they formed a whisper. 'All this. All our lives…'

Greg brought his chin up and down, mechanically. There was nothing he could say. Nothing *to* be said. Everything they had done – it had all been for *this*. The surgeries, the missions; the agony, the bloodshed, the losses; the *Sanctuary* – it was just 'part of the plan.' In the end they had had no existence, beyond these walls. They weren't *people* – only survivors.

A soft grip closed over his hand. He looked up, into Leah's bright, shimmering brown eyes. They leaned close, bringing their foreheads together. He felt Leah's pulse, beating in time with his own, and the tremors beneath her veneer of controlled grief.

He lifted his head. She mirrored the motion, bringing his gaze level with hers. They stared at each other. Her lips parted.

Slowly, ever so slowly, they shifted closer to each other. He brought his arms around her waist. Their lips met, pressing tenderly. He squeezed her tighter; she did the same for him. Their hands moved as though by instinct, searching and knowing in equal measure. Those first stirrings, when the inhibitors began to flush out, they'd seemed too strange, too foreign to act on – though he hadn't hated them, either. Now... Neither of them fully knew what they were doing – only that they *had* to.

Abruptly, Leah shifted away, breaking free of his grasp. With the same smooth slowness, she stood up, bringing her hands to the neck of her clinger. The zipper parted, sliding down to her navel. After a moment's hesitation, she peeled the garment away, pulling her arms free of the sleeves, and sliding it down to the floor. Her bare, brown-skinned body gleamed in the light above.

Greg's breath failed at the sight. Trancelike, he got to his feet. His hands went to his collar, pulling the clinger from his shoulders. In moments, he stood before Leah, as bare as she. She smiled, the expression sad and lovely.

They drew to each other. He kissed her, harder and stronger. She matched him, holding his head to hers. As one, they lay back down on the cot, side by side. They stroked and kissed one another, letting the caresses speak for them.

Greg turned over, so that he lay above. He looked at her, asking with his eyes. Leah gave the smallest of nods. He shifted, bringing his weight on his arms. Leah's hands caressed his spine from neck to navel, sending shivers across his frame. Gently, he pushed forward. Leah's mouth parted in a slow gasp, of pain and pleasure mixed. Greg felt her hips rise to meet his, matching his slow, rocking rhythm. Her ankles wrapped together, pulling him tight against her.

He buried his face in her neck, inhaling the scent of her

sweat – of *her*. He began to rock faster. Beneath him, Leah's gasps and moans came quicker, merging with his. She tightened her grip, making his ribs creak. He ignored the pain, and sped up, making the cot rattle in its frame. Her short nails dug into his back, drawing tiny drops of blood.

At last, he threw his head back, plunging his hardest yet. He let out a short, huffing groan, staring at the ceiling, seeing nothing. At the same time, Leah cried out, softly, eyes screwed shut. A pink flush rose in her face, spreading across her body. Warmth trickled down his thigh, and hers. Waves of bliss crashed over him, filling him to the brim.

When Greg looked down again, he saw Leah staring back at him, solemn and blissful. She stroked his face, with infinite tenderness. Then she brought one hand to his shoulder. A gentle push made her request clear. Carefully, Greg slid off, lying on his back. With similar smoothness, Leah swung a leg over his waist, sitting astride him. She stared down at him, hands brushing over his chest. He lay still, holding her gently at the waist.

One of her hands wandered, behind her. Greg shuddered with pleasure at her touch. That same intense look on her face, Leah leaned back. She stiffened for an instant, before relaxing, mouth half-open. He groaned, gripping her waist tighter.

She planted both hands on his shoulders, pinning him to the bed. Her hips began to grind, gyrating with a dancer's grace and skill. Greg's hands roved over her sculpted body, making her quiver even more. The cot shook and rattled beneath them.

Finally, Greg's waist lifted, as if of its own will. A new torrent of ecstasy washed through him. In that same moment, Leah froze, and let out another trembling cry, loud enough to almost rattle the walls. Gasping, she seized both his hands in hers, squeezing with all her strength. Greg matched her, sucking in great breaths himself.

Little by little, the pleasure began to ebb. Their breathing slowed, becoming steadier and calmer. Still astride him, Leah lay down, resting her head on Greg's sweat-covered chest. He inched onto his side, so that they lay together, face to face. Their eyes met, never straying even an inch. The only sound in the room was their breathing, and the soft tick of the clock above the bed.

A shrill, blaring note sounded. Greg sat up and swung his feet to the floor, grabbing for his clinger. The sound died away as he stepped into the suit. He was halfway dressed before his eyes opened all the way. Then his brain kicked fully into high gear, and he stopped, hand on the auto-zipper, darting his gaze around the room to track the source. Naked from the waist up, he padded up to the door, staring directly into the blue lens. 'What is it?' he demanded.

Gaia's soft tones came through at once. 'A possible breach of the sensor net was detected moments ago, Greg. With the storm and stirred fallout, readings are understandably difficult, and thus suspect. Regardless, Dr Garrett insisted you be alerted. He requests you and Leah come to the main training and observation floor immediately, to assess the information. All real-time data is being routed to his tablet, via my servers on that level.'

Greg closed his eyes. *All that's happened, and the sick, lying bastard expects our help?* His hands twitched, almost clenching as they would around a throat. His throat felt swollen with rage, too much to even whisper. A wild urge hit him. If the storm was bad enough, maybe—

'We'll be right there,' Leah said from behind. He spun around to see her climbing out of bed, holding the sheet to her body. She looked to the lens herself, every inch the soldier in her stance. 'Where's Cayden? Has he been warned?'

The voice seemed to hesitate. 'Cayden does not appear to be present in the Facility, Leah. He may have engaged his clinger's stealth options – my sensors are limited in those instances. Or he may have left the area altogether. I have sent warnings to his system, but there has been no reply.'

'I wouldn't reply, either,' Leah sighed, almost too low to hear – though probably not too much for Gaia. She straightened, back to business. 'Tell the Doctor we'll be out shortly.'

The lens blinked once, presumably in affirmation, then dimmed again. Leah faced Greg, one hand already lifted. 'I know what you're going to say,' she said, still direct and calm. 'You're going to say we need to leave, before this gets any worse. That we have to get back and get everyone evacuating. That we should leave this'—she waved at their surroundings—'to the Brown Coats, and whoever's running them – along with Garrett.' She lowered her hand, bringing it to the other that clasped the sheet. 'How'd I do?'

'Three for three,' Greg said, resisting a small smile. Even after everything they'd found here, she still knew him best. The mild pleasure died. 'Although to clarify, I wasn't set on leaving him for them – *alive*, that is. And Cayden might have us beat there, soon enough.'

'You'll both have to wait your turn, then,' Leah replied coolly. 'Until we're done with Taylor's… friends, though'—she grimaced, in disgust or remembered horror—'it's better we deal with him later. Otherwise they'll do worse – to all of us here. Then it'll be Hiroshi's turn, then Megan's, then Jorge's – then the whole Sanctuary. If we've got any kind of mission now, it's stopping *that*.' She came closer, glowing eyes drilling into him. 'Can you handle it?'

Can YOU? Greg almost asked. He bit it down, and managed

a nod. Seeing her scepticism, he nodded again, more vigorously, and zipped up his clinger. He pulled his knife free, twirling it once to test his grip, then sheathed it and drew his pistol, checking the load. Leah nodded herself, convinced, and moved to grab her own clinger from where it lay wadded in the corner. The sheet slipped to the floor as she laid the garment out and stepped into it. Just for a moment, Greg's breath faltered at the view. He still felt confused, unsure – and not a little thrilled. Leah looked over her bare shoulder. Her smile showed the same emotions. He found himself returning it, almost by reflex. *Something* else *to sort out, when all is said and done.* He finished the weapons check, and moved to the door. Unlike what they faced now, though, the thought didn't anger or scare him in the slightest.

The hallway outside was silent. Greg checked both directions regardless, keeping his body out of easy sightline, before emerging and starting for the main workout and mess areas. Leah matched his clip, crisp and businesslike. The hallway was one of twelve, as he'd seen when they arrived, with around fifty rooms. Each one's door was shaped like the hatches on a ship: small, thick, with multiple outside locks. *More safeguards*, Greg thought. He clenched his teeth. *Not now. Soon enough, though – that's a* promise.

They came out into the main exercise area. Most of the gear had a thick layer of dust, proving no one had come through in months, more likely years, proving *one* part of the Doc's story. He glanced up toward the mirrored glass – and saw that it had changed, showing the room within: a bank of servers and screens, with a large Gaia lens suspended over them all. Garrett was standing at one window, hand flying over his tablet. He looked up at the motion, and waved: *Come up.* Swallowing a last bit of anger, Greg climbed the stairs to the walkway, Leah following. He glanced at the other gallery, where they'd first come in. The multi–ton doors were sealed, yellow emergency lights whirling. If Cayden *had* left the Facility, he wasn't getting back in that way.

The door to the gallery – a larger version of those in the dorm area, and far heavier – popped open with a loud hiss at the Golems' approach. Greg pushed it open farther, and strode in. 'What's going on?' he demanded.

Garrett didn't look up from his tablet. 'Perimeter sensors detected movement thirty seconds ago,' he said. The mournful resignation from before was gone; the Doctor spoke in clipped, steady tones, and carried himself the same way. 'It's storming hard outside, and the fallout coming down or being stirred up tends to play havoc with the net.' A half-second's pause. 'Except the havoc never registered as anything larger than a deer or rabbit, and *never* already well inside the line.'

'How far inside?' Leah asked. She looked sharply over the computer banks, and out at the main entrance, searching for any threats. 'What showed, when it *did* register?'

The Doctor tapped once at the tablet. 'The perimeter covers everything between Liberty Bay and the Hood Canal, and extends from Dyes Inlet to Lofall.' Another tap. 'The blip popped up on Kegley Road, near where we came in – moving west, before it vanished again.' The older man's face grew grimmer. 'It came up as one object, possibly human-sized, but the scan was too fuzzy to be sure.'

'So it could be more than one,' Greg said. He arced a half-mocking eyebrow. 'Maybe two – three, even? Looking for a friend they lost around these parts?' Garrett ignored his tone, still typing. Deciding to let it be – for now – Greg continued, less abrasively. 'How soon till they're into the base itself?'

'Three minutes,' Garrett answered. 'Assuming they're at their peak, despite the storm, and no serious obstacles.' Now he *did* look up, to them, then to the main entrance. 'There's no way to breach *those*, short of a dozen armour-piercing rounds from an M1 tank. They're locked and sealed, along with every other section down here. Only other way in is digging – not even a ground-penetrating nuke would get through.'

'So we've seen,' Leah said, no mockery in *her* words; just fact. 'What about the fire exits? Where are they?' She went to the window, looking over the room below. 'Do any lead to the surface?'

Garrett frowned. 'Only one, from this level.' The pain entered his words, for the briefest moment. He pointed out the window to a single vault door, set into the east-facing wall of the training and mess area. 'Cayden used it earlier, when he left.' He tapped and swiped again, more forcefully, then paused. 'Leads up to one of the hospital outbuildings. It's sealed, same as the other section exits and entrances. Still a weaker point, if they try a breach, but one we can manage.'

'We?' Greg demanded. Leah elbowed him in the side. A little less belligerently, he went on. 'Assuming they do, hopefully you've got more than the standard mission gear lying around somewhere?' He let some acid back in. 'Because it seems the First Five – and Taylor – turned out better than expected, when they left the tanks.'

'So it would seem,' Garrett said, outwardly unbothered by the caustic words. 'Even assuming they broke through the first layer, they'd still have to breach the second – at which point a secondary door will engage to reseal the passage, and the oxygen depletion will have already kicked in.' He didn't show any pleasure or distaste at this prospect. 'As for gear—' He nodded to the back of the room. Following this look, Greg spotted a thin black case, sitting atop another, larger crate. On the surface, it was the same as the countless others they'd seen and used, when in the Project. Greg approached it cautiously, nevertheless, flipped the clasps up, and threw back the lid.

Instead of assault rifles or heavy weapons, as he'd expected, the case held two sheathed machete-length blades, nestled in packaging foam, and the empty space for a third, in between. He pulled one of them free, and drew the blade. The metal shone brightly. The edge itself was razor-sharp, and had a strange, near-imperceptible sheen; almost like a rainbow, when he tilted it the right way. He swung it once or twice, impressed with its balance and weight. He wasn't much of a fencer, but he could handle any blade given him – like everyone in his class, he'd trained with knife and empty-hand skill above all else, even firearms. *Not much help against a* bullet, *of course. Still, a longer reach can't hurt.* He pressed it flat against his hip experimentally. The clinger fabric closed over it at once. 'Nice,' he grunted in modest approval. 'Anything else?'

'Not unless you want to try the arsenal, three levels down, for which the whole system would have to be unlocked.' Garrett shrugged at Greg's hard look. 'Fail-safe, built in when Gaia came online and the Facility was completed. Every room and level locked down and cut off from the other, except for a single comm line, and all entries, movement and Wi-Fi/radio usage controlled by the higher-ups.' He spread his hands, indicating who that was supposed to be. 'Supposed to be a way to keep any unauthorised types from getting to weapons, sensitive files or the lab wing – including any from the Project's ranks.' The Doctor held up the tablet again. 'So long as remote access stays with me, no one inside goes anywhere, or reaches anybody outside, and no one outside gets in, unless they—'

A strident beeping interrupted him. He checked his tablet, stiffened, and dashed to the nearest terminal. The light from the holo-screen showed his face losing its colour. 'Shit,' he whispered. 'Shit!' He typed some more, rapid-fire.

Greg and Leah joined him. 'What's wrong?' Greg demanded. Multiple dialogue and code windows were opening and closing on the screen, too fast for him to see.

Garrett kept his eyes to the terminal. 'Someone uploaded a Golem access code to unlock the fire exit passage to this level. Soon as that code went through, another that was piggybacking came in as well. Door locks, Wi-Fi, internal/external comms – it's spreading to every part of the system, crashing what it doesn't take over.' His hands became near-blurs as they typed. 'Gaia's mainframe's shielded, physically and electronically, but that won't last once they're through, and can just *walk* into the server areas.'

'Which code was it?' Leah demanded, moving to look over the Doctor's shoulder. Greg joined them, trying and failing again to read the pop-ups and scrolling digits. *Maybe it's Hiroshi, or one of the others?* The chances were dim, but if the Council leader had gotten close to the Kitsap area before, he might have again, pinpointing the source of Gaia's signal, and thus the entrance. There wasn't much else to hope for; if the comms were cut or hijacked, they wouldn't be able to reach the Sanctuary – or Cayden, if he was still out there.

Garrett opened yet another window. He frowned. 'One of the first ones to be issued. Came with higher priority tags, too, which is why it wasn't kicked back, or—' He stopped. His hands stilled over the keyboard, mid-type. 'Christ,' he whispered. 'It's—'

The roar of the explosion drowned him out. Blast knocked Greg off his feet, throwing him into the far wall. In the dazed moment before the windows burst, he saw the last of the fireball pouring through the gaping fire exit door, and chunks of the ceiling crashing down. He threw his arms up, protecting his face from a glittering blizzard of supposedly blastproof shards – then leapt to his feet, drawing the new blade and yanking the clinger hood over his face before the spray had fully subsided. Whatever the blast had come from, the Brown Coats would be right behind it.

He stood in the open window frame, assessing the view. The level was already full of smoke. He blinked once, activating the infrared filters in the hood's eyes. Most of the mess area and exercise gear was scattered all across the room, or crushed in place beneath ceiling fragments or other wreckage. Several small fires burned in the fringes of the wrecked doorway, and smaller spurts rose from amid the debris, already dying fast; nothing else.

He jumped down from the gallery, landing easily and almost without sound, and started into the greyish-white fog. A whispery thud made him turn: Leah rose up from a crouch behind him, blade hefted and pistol ready. He considered drawing his, before raising his own sword, and kept moving toward the door, stepping delicately over the piles of rubble. For the close quarters they were in, the blade would be better.

A low hum started somewhere above him. The smoke began to clear, wafting up to the ceiling. The filters, by Garrett's command or their guests'. He moved to the right of the door, keeping back far enough to avoid any potential fire. Leah made the same move, to the left. He pressed up to the cracked wall, coiled and tense. *They should be hitting* now. Every second counted, after a breach; infinitely more, for Golems. *Why're they holding—*

Three loud pops sounded from the stairwell within, before his mind formed the word *back*. He went rigid as a trio of smoke trails shot through the opening, landing with a clatter amid the ruined training gear. A thick grey-blue cloud rose up, expanding and replacing the smoke in seconds. The clinger's mouth sealed shut automatically, the lips of the breathing filter poking between Greg's lips. He didn't recognise the stuff; a low beeping in his ear said the clinger's system didn't either. *CS? Sarin?* The filter was proof against both, and plenty of other gases. *Another delaying tactic; keeps us tense and off-balance, even if it doesn't kill.* He took a slow sip of air, readying himself for the first Brown Coat to charge through.

Suddenly he felt a tingling pain spread through his chest. He gasped and stumbled, coughing and hacking. This only made the pain spread further, down his torso and into his limbs. On its heels came a cold numbness – one he remembered vividly. *Pax,* his mind wheezed, in between coughs. He tried to straighten up, to shout it to Leah. She was half-sitting against a knocked-over table, weapons at her feet, retching as badly as he. When she looked up, searching for him, Greg could see the same terrified realisation in her eyes.

He slumped to his knees, then to all fours, still gasping and coughing. The sword fell from his senseless fingers. The numbness had spread over his entire body; it seemed a miracle he wasn't flat on his face. From somewhere above or behind him, he heard a man's voice, muffled and shouting like he was speaking through a wall of gauze. Very soon, it faded away; he wasn't even sure it was real.

His elbows gave way, dropping him to the floor. His eyesight grew darker and blurrier. He forced his head up, and looked to the door. Three dark-clad figures were stepping through the exit, wearing gas masks, blades shining in their hands. They fanned out, one each to the fallen Golems for a split second, then farther into the room. A fourth figure stepped inside after them, wearing a gas mask like the others, but dressed in a plain blue coverall. It ambled over to where Greg lay, and stood over him, eyes watching in curiosity or amusement through the mask's goggles. They were dark green – and with a tinge of light that seemed somehow familiar.

New motion made the watcher turn his head, and step away. Greg struggled to squint through the blurriness. The two other men were approaching, dragging a third man between them: Garrett, his mask hanging askew, head lolling. The leader yanked the mask away. Garrett coughed, then looked up, mouthing words Greg couldn't make out. With a more ceremonial air, the leader lifted his own mask back. the Doctor's eyes went wide. His mouth formed a single, slurred word: *Sam.*

Just before everything went completely black, Greg tried to reach for the blade again. Nothing worked; he could barely make his fingers wriggle. The leader swung a fist, cracking Garrett across the jaw. The Doctor slumped forward, dead or knocked out. Greg made one last lunge, fingers quivering for the hilt. A boot stomped down on his wrist; he felt the crack of bone, but no pain. Before he could blink, a second hard blow smashed into his own temple, and the blackness dropped over him in full.

Chapter 26

A jarring thud made Greg's eyes crack open. He squinted at the light overhead; the clinger's hood was off, letting it shine right in his face. He tried to lift his arm and found he could only raise it an inch or so – the limb felt weighted down by little sacks of cement at the joints and shoulder. He was seated, his back against some hard surface. Every inch of him ached in some way, though it seemed to be fading. Whatever they'd inhaled, it was losing its effect, or most of it.

Inhaled... *Pax...* He tried to stand, but his body wrenched itself painfully, and he sank back down, gasping through his teeth. With another painful effort, he turned his head, blinking away the spots and haziness as he gauged the surroundings. The walls around him were pure white, and he felt a sticky, half-dried fluid beneath the footpads of his clinger. *The lab wing.* He heard a crashing sound, rock on metal, and footsteps. Looking to the right, he saw the Doctor, seated in an office chair below the broken Gaia screen. His arms and legs were ziptied to the chair; his head was tilted into his shoulder, apparently in unconsciousness or stupor. Greg could see the tension in his shoulders, however, showing he was awake and aware. *Much good it'll do* him, *unless* we *get the chance.*

Looking past the older man, he saw Taylor, clad in white hospital shorts and nothing else. The garish scars on his chest and limbs shone in the light. He was sporting the same silver eyewear, and two of the ultra-thin blades the Brown Coats had carried before. Unlike before, however, he seemed ill at ease, or still not fully out of the semi-coma he'd been in on arrival. He was standing beside another clinger-clad form, also propped up by the wall, unmoving. *Leah.* He tried to speak, call out, but only a croaky whisper emerged.

Somebody stepped in front of him. 'He lives,' a cool voice said. Looking up, he saw the blue overalls, and a pair of vivid green eyes, behind silver glasses. The face wasn't one he recognised. Nearly as old as the Doctor's, with sharper features, and more grey lacing the dark blonde hair. 'Wasn't a sure bet on my old access code working, so you can imagine how I felt reconfiguring that Pax stuff to gas form, with the extra trank to pierce any mask. Always the risk it would've turned out to be fatal.' He paused, leaning in closer. Greg thought he could see the edge of a white-red scar, below the collar of the overalls. His breath was hot on the Golem's face. 'Of course, with all the trouble running the three of you to ground, that was one risk I didn't mind.'

Greg glared. His arm twitched again, trying to come up in a swing; no luck. The stranger smirked, and moved away, toward Garrett and Leah. Greg watched, running a silent check on himself. Still no lift in any limbs, but the aching was nearly gone, and he could sense the strength building again in the rest of his body. They hadn't been brought here long ago; several minutes, at the most. Soon enough, the right moment would come.

Keeping the movement slow, he swivelled to the left. In the 'recovery room', he saw a shadow moving back and forth, and heard heavy thuds, from objects thrown or from someone punching the wall – maybe through it, too, looking for hollows. He'd hardly noted this when two of the men in green stepped out from the room, and halted in front of the door, arms crossed. Another did the same from the office closest to Greg. His hands and the front of his coveralls were covered in dust. Greg's knife – he recognised the small chip in the carbon-ceramic hilt, below the grip – Cayden's blade, pulled from the wall, and the new blade Garrett had given him hung from clips at his waist. His hair, probably once black, was singed close to his head, almost gone in places. That, the silver glasses he also wore, and the thin, almost-healed white line across his throat, brought back Greg's memory.

And we're *supposed to be tough.* With what he'd seen of Cayden, and learned since, he hadn't thought even the 'First Five' could take the kind of punishment dished out at the airfield, and still be standing. He wondered randomly which one *this* guy was, and whether Cayden would recognise him, after so many years. The thought of Cayden made him glance around again. No sign the older Golem was present, meaning he was long since gone – or long since dead.

The leader walked past Greg with only a side glance. Greg saw his throat was pulsing, as if he were speaking – except no words came out. Each of the men in green made the same motions, more succinctly. The leader pulsed something back, then turned to face the three captives. There was dark amusement in his look, but the anger was plain behind it. 'Seems my people are having trouble finding the item you lifted from D.C.' He started a slow pace around the tank platform, kicking aside chunks of glass and flesh. 'Nice work, bringing it all the way back home. Smart, too; most wouldn't consider the hottest zone in the States the best spot to go under. Especially not with such a valuable haul.'

The leader stopped; something cracked under his heel.

'Now, though, the triathlon's over – and it's time for the trophies.' He bent forward from the waist, at Greg. 'Since the Doctor's still out of it, how about you save us some more digging?' He jerked his head in Leah's direction, smiling harder. 'She's been no help so far, so maybe you'd like to save *her* another round with your old squadmate, too.'

He cast a look around at the destroyed NeoMater equipment, and the chipped and scarred walls. 'Although it looks like there've been a few rounds already – and it seems we're missing one of the team. He take off, or you bury him somewhere? Family squabble, maybe?' His eyes glittered in amusement. 'Saves us the trouble, if so.'

Rage ripped through Greg's chest, drowning out the aches and weight. It took all his effort not to grab for the other man's throat; the move would be too weak, and he'd probably end up with another gassing – *if* he was lucky. 'Who – are – you?' he spat.

The leader's eyes widened in mock astonishment. 'You mean he *never* once mentioned me?' He looked over to the Doctor, and shook his head, tsking. 'It's never pretty when a partnership ends – but I'd have thought he'd still *think* of me now and again.' His chuckle was anything but humorous. He made a mocking half-bow. 'Sam Hunter, MD, PhD, and a few others. Formerly of CellWorx Labs, and the start-up process for Project Golem – now freelance.'

Greg fought not to let his shock show. He must have failed, for Hunter laughed. 'Oh, you *do* recognise me – or the name, anyway. I've had a few others over the past couple decades, so it's understandable. Living off the grid, and all that, except when needed.' A mirthless smile. 'Like now.'

He ambled over to Garrett's chair. The Doctor was shifting in the chair – feigning waking up, Greg could tell. Judging by his grin, Hunter knew this, too. He leaned in, and swatted Garrett lightly over the head – though it was still enough to rap him hard against the headrest. 'Hey, Rich!' He shook him by the shoulder, none too gently. 'Still with us? Can't have a proper reunion, otherwise!'

Garrett groaned, slowly pulling himself up and wincing. When he lifted his eyes to Hunter's, however, there wasn't a trace of pain, just dismayed anger. 'What the hell is this, Sam?' he growled.

'A whole lot of things,' Hunter said airily. With that same attitude, his fist shot out in a quick jab, knocking Garrett backwards and almost toppling him. Hunter grabbed the chair's arm and righted him before it was halfway over. A little sharper now, he went on. 'We could start with all that you pulled at the end of your most recent job. Theft and or destruction of government property – specifically, the *Project*, and everything attached to it. Add to that aiding and abetting a known arms trafficker who snuck in the Seattle Bomb, and actually *triggering* the blast by forcing interdiction. Plenty of reasons right there to stick the needle in.' The sharpness grew stronger. 'Or we could take it all the way back to the beginning – when you forced me out of what we'd spent *years* putting together, ruining *everything* I'd done, all the work with you, and solo. Then taking the whole thing to the Army anyway, after I'd almost begged on bended knee for the same idea.' He yanked the chair closer to him, so that they were inches apart. 'Your choice,' he said, voice dangerously soft.

Garrett wasn't cowed. 'I took it to them because I had no choice. You just wanted to cash in, sell ARC and everything else to whoever paid the highest – without even *thinking* about what it was capable of. What ends it would be turned to.' He glared. 'And by the looks of it, you weren't ruined for long.'

'Oh, I knew right from the start, *Dad*,' Hunter said, mockingly. 'All those hours spent watching skin cells regrow, or muscles re-knit – that was penny-ante *bullshit*, not even first-year work. You knew it, I knew it, the brass and Vanguard bunch knew it, too.'

He began to pace around the chair. 'But no, there were always more tests, more observations, more *concerns*. No chance of ARC reaching its *full* potential. If we'd waited even half the extra time you kept pushing for, we wouldn't have come *close* to anything like *this*.' He waved at the lab. 'Then, right when the offer of a lifetime drops in *our* lap, you—' Hunter stopped in mid-rant. 'Doesn't matter. Not now, that is.'

He came around in front of the Doctor again. 'And you're right; I had a few friends left in D.C., even after you tanked CellWorx and practically blackballed me on your way out.' His smile came back, almost wolfish. 'Governments never throw away new toys they like – or their makers. Especially not the more covert branches. Once they saw how flaky you were getting over the first round of tests for the Project, they decided they wanted a backup. Somebody who could keep the Project going – or take it in a new direction.'

'That's where they come in, isn't it?' Greg said. His voice was hoarse, but came out clearly enough. Hunter and Garrett looked his way. Past them, he saw Leah's head rise. Groggy at first, her eyes went wide at the scene. Her arm started to rise; the gas must have worn off quicker, or she was just stronger. He blinked rapid-fire, in Morse: *N-O*. To his relief, she halted, hand on her chest. They'd taken her weapons along with his, but that hardly mattered, with the right strike.

Hoping he hadn't paused too long, he jerked his chin in Taylor's direction. 'Probably took half the Pentagon's budget just to get the Project off the ground. So they took a few shortcuts, didn't they?' His mind was still foggy – but with Hunter's name, and his own anger, everything was falling together clearly enough. 'No one pays attention to flag-draped coffins anymore, so they wouldn't for Golem bodies in shipping crates. They wind up in D.C., signed for and ready for the furnace – and then get rerouted to a black site, for *deeper* work. Maybe one that was part of a contractor, for the very same Project that produced the bodies – and their gear.'

Hunter made that scornful bow again. 'Good to see the "all brawn, no brain" image isn't *all* true, with your type.' Seeing Greg's eyes flick to Taylor, he chuckled. 'Can't say the same for him, unfortunately. The ARC upgrades I designed did the trick, when it came to getting him and the rest up and about. Unfortunately, they could only go that far, in the best cases. Had to send the rest on to the furnace after all; they were too far gone, or the upgrades didn't take for other reasons. *This* one was a rare exception, although it took a while to straighten him out – and will again, looks like. Then came the endless implantations, the neurosurgeries – a whole lot of shit needing to be done, and a lot of on-the-job learning, so to speak.' His voice was rueful. 'Course, wasn't as bad for *them,* since I had the technique down pat. Those first few tries, solo—'

He tugged at the end of one sleeve, drawing it partway back. This let Greg see the long, jagged incisions, running along the inner and outer forearm. Hunter smirked at his recognition. 'These were a *bitch*, I can tell you. Decades of surgical experience, and plenty of local anaesthetic – and I *still* kept slipping up because some nerve ending or other wasn't *completely* shut off. Not to mention the *look* of me, once these and the rest were done.'

He began strolling back and forth between the Doctor and Greg, never quite taking his eyes from them as he mused.

'The rest weren't *that* hard, by comparison. God bless the occasional Agency medical team, to make sure I didn't slice the wrong way.' He rubbed at his neck. 'Still can't get used to the transmitter implants; feels like somebody's always got their fingers in my throat. Compared to the work done on *them*, though'—he waved absently to Taylor, and to the men in green—'I suppose I should count my blessings.' A crooked smile. 'A little hard, seeing how many I had.'

Garrett was sitting board-stiff, arms tense against the ties. He didn't – or couldn't – take his eyes from the scars. 'How in God's name—' He stopped. His features drained of colour, from shock as much as anger. 'The day you left.' he growled.

Smiling still, Hunter moved a hand to his belt, reappearing with a short combat knife. He placed the blade in the palm of his other hand and jerked it down. Blood dripped to the floor, mixing in with the half-dried tank fluids. With no sign of pain, he held out the wounded hand to Garrett and the two Golems. The slash was already half-closed when Greg got his glimpse; *much* faster than any ARC should work. *No. Just the ones* you *know.*

Nonchalant, Hunter reached into another pocket, drawing out a handkerchief. His eyes – set and hard – didn't leave Garrett's as he wiped the blood off his hands. 'So many months slaving away over the greatest medical advance in human history – you didn't think I'd leave without taking *something* besides a last paycheque?' He tossed the bloody cloth in among the tank wreckage and looked to the green-clad guards. His throat flexed, once. They stepped back into the rooms they'd come from; the sounds of the search rose again. Hunter faced the Doctor again. 'Wasn't hard, either, given how trashed you still were after Gwen and Aidan. It was the early version, the first one you'd tested and put aside for destruction or modification – and then forgot about.'

He looked momentarily annoyed. 'Hadn't planned on using it *myself*, not at first. The Pentagon already *owned* ARC, in every way except for some paperwork – and had a copy locked away in the DARPA archives. The way you were headed at the time, it was reasonable to assume they'd want another option, and soon. So I went to them – and they said since it's a prototype, a rough draft, they had "doubts as to its viability". They didn't mind *how* it showed up at their front door, just that it might be a day past the sell-by date.' The annoyance vanished, replaced by a cold pleasure. 'I showed them *exactly* how viable it still is – and got approval for *my* work inside of an hour.'

'Without a thought for the consequences, as usual,' Garrett ground out. He seemed to be keeping himself from lunging only by sheer force of will; Greg could see the deep creases in his arms where the ties were digging in. 'You didn't even *see* the field tests, I'll bet. The poor fuckers who'd signed up for a chance to be *more* – and were lucky if they wound up brain-dead, shitting in bags the rest of their lives. The ones your "friends" in D.C. threw away, for some mirage of power.'

Hunter spread his arms, taking in the room. 'Not just a mirage in the end, though, right?' he asked, rhetorically. 'The excess strength took some getting used to, I'll admit; still can't grab anything without crushing it, if I'm not careful. But the other perks...' His left leg lifted a few inches – then shot out with lightning speed. It struck one of the toppled NeoMaters, which had to weigh close to 300 pounds, and sent it skidding off the platform and into the wall with a rending crash.

His guards came running out at the sound. Grinning, Hunter waved them away, then addressed Garrett again. 'That first batch was flawed, true enough. But you didn't see how or whether it could be improved – only that it didn't work. Same with the prototype for the ARC-retarding compound, I'll bet.' Greg's head whipped up at that. Hunter didn't notice. 'Another "containment measure" I'm sure you had a gun to your head to make, for the brass. Luckily, there wasn't any need for that on my end. So much left sitting around, waiting for the right brain and set of hands...' He tsked again. 'And you say *I* don't consider the consequences.'

He gestured to the tanks, and to Greg and Leah, his smile more cutting. 'Something I'm sure your *kids*'—the word came out almost as a hiss—'know more than a bit about now, I'd say.' He set his hands on his hips. 'All the effort and tricks to keep them in the dark, and you let them see *every* part of the old homestead. Getting soft in your old age? Or you get them confused with a *family*, and figured they were owed the "truth"?' He snorted. 'A little late to grow a conscience, if it was the second one. Way you handled the Project's ops when the Turmoil started, it was like watching somebody else. Somebody who'd finally gotten the message – and was taking it to new levels.'

Garrett didn't make a sound. Most of the anger had drained out of him, leaving behind a grim, resigned mask. Hunter clapped his hands together, rubbing them in an appearance of briskness. 'Well! Enough catching up for right now, I think! Time to get down to business – starting with the hottest.' He walked up to Garrett. 'Where's the canister? None of your *kids* here have it, and we would've seen soon enough if your third one had it on him when he took off – not that you'd be so stupid as to let him run with it.' He crossed his arms, like an impatient teacher or parent. 'So – where is it?'

The Doctor stayed quiet. Hunter didn't look disappointed;

in fact, he seemed pleased. He drew the knife again, letting the blade catch the light as he walked to the side of Garrett's chair. He weighed it in his hand, tossed it up and down once, then slashed in a short, downward arc. The upper sleeve of Garrett's shirt parted in a spurt of red. The Doctor grunted and cringed away in pain, teeth clenched. Blood soaked through the dark fabric, turning it almost black. Greg couldn't see the wound from his angle, but it had to be deep, maybe down to the bone.

Still smirking, Hunter bent close again. 'There's somewhere between 600 and 800 muscles in the human body, *Doctor*. That was at least one.' He checked the blade, now dappled in red. 'Two or three, best guess; these diamond edges cut deeper than you'd expect, sometimes.'

Garrett breathed steadily through his nose, facing straight ahead. Hunter moved back into his line of vision. Some of the other man's humour vanished. 'Every ten seconds you keep up this vow of silence, another muscle parts – maybe some tendons and bone with them. In less than five minutes, I can cripple you for life. In ten, they'll need to identify you by your teeth – assuming any are left, by then.' He brought the blade to the tip of Garrett's nose. 'Talk, and maybe you'll leave here in just a wheelchair.' When Garrett still made no move or sound, Hunter grunted. 'Fine. One. Two. Three.'

Greg shifted into a better sitting position, keeping up his outward slump. He'd thought he was furious and shocked before; now he was almost incandescent with anger. It was a cold fury, though, hard and focused. He checked the guards; they were all focused on Hunter and Garrett – Taylor, too, in a more befuddled way. Leah's lower lip was trembling – in rage, not shock or grief. She blinked once, showing she was ready. He braced his hands and back against the concrete. *Go for Black*

Hair first; arm, then neck. Then second guard; Leah takes Taylor.
Five, six seconds; then—

Something beeped, interrupting his assessment. The Gaia screen, from which the tank lid Greg had hurled earlier still protruded, blinked into life, showing a map: The Sound, centred on the Facility. Hunter paused in his countdown, looking irritated, and backed up. A red dot suddenly appeared at the corner of the map as he did so – moving westward, tiny lines of tracking data appearing and extending from it. His brows knotted in perplexity. 'What the hell's—'

Greg launched up from the floor before the words were half-spoken. Leah catapulted to her feet as well, moving almost too fast for Taylor to see. One of Greg's hands fastened on Black Hair's right wrist, twisting it behind him in the same move, while his left arm wrapped around the guard's throat. A quick flex with either would snap his arm in three places and twist his neck halfway around, something no ARC could repair, or not fast enough even with 'upgrades'. Then draw the knife and hurl it in the second guard's face before he took even a step in Greg's direction. He'd be throttling Hunter four seconds later, max.

The Pax effects must still have been lingering, however. His arm shot out for Black Hair's throat – and missed, by less than an inch. The guard ducked low to avoid the grab, and spun in Greg's grip, pulling the Golem's own arm with him. He tried to rip free, but the momentum was already carrying him forward. He brought his arm to block a punch, grasping for the wrist again, and took a booted foot squarely in the abdomen. It only slowed him for a heartbeat – but that was enough for the guard to land a second punch, across his jaw.

Stars flashed in Greg's eyes. Momentarily staggered, he felt the guard slip behind him, pulling his trapped arm along, and raised his free hand to stop the armlock he expected. Instead of that, however, Black Hair stomped hard on the inside of his right leg, dropping him to his knees. The trapped arm drove up into his back, almost wrenched from its socket. A hand grasped his hair, pulling his head back; a boot slammed down on his left ankle, pinning it to the floor. In less than twenty seconds, he was immobilised.

He wrenched painfully against the grips; nothing yielded. Beneath the screen, Leah stood trapped as well, struggling against the other two green-clad guards, their arms pinning hers to her side and wrapped across her chest. One of them sprouted a thin blade from his shirt, and held it to her throat, finally making her desist. Taylor stayed in place, with the same foggy look; he didn't seem to be taking any pleasure in the capture, professional or otherwise.

Hunter had sprung back at Greg's lunge, letting the guards move between him and the fight. When neither Golem broke free, he stepped forward again, looking even more pleased. 'Well – up and about again! I was starting to wonder if I could keep turning my back.' The genial air faded fast. 'I'm guessing that'—he pointed to the screen, where the dot was now approaching the Sound's eastern rim, near Tacoma—'is something you were waiting for? Backup from your friends down south, maybe?' When Greg and Leah stayed silent, he moved back to Garrett's side, wordlessly placing the knife at the Doctor's throat.

Despite the pain and situation, Greg felt a chuckle forming in his chest. 'You might as well cut our throats,' he growled instead. 'Not going to help, any which way.'

'How's that, exactly?' Hunter asked, dubious but also curious. 'Even assuming your friends know where to look – and they don't, since we've had enough time to confirm you're not carrying trackers, or anything else readable through the storm – they'll never get inside. The storm'll take care of them, or make them easy meat when we leave.'

'Didn't say they needed trackers,' Greg replied. 'And I never said they were friends.' Now his lips began to quirk, in a vestige of a smile. 'Although given what Costa's probably shared with Colonel Flynn, by now, I'm sure they'll consider this a working partnership.'

Hunter narrowed his eyes. 'Costa?' The eyes went wide, then shrank to slits. 'No bodies,' he muttered, half to himself. He shook his head, letting the blade drop a bit. 'Knew from the start that little shit'd be a problem. Hadn't figured he'd turn, if you *did* grab him – or just not so fast.' He eyed Greg with a touch more respect. 'Patrick turned, too, after he saw the details you must've gotten on his men, I'll bet.' His head shook again, in annoyance. 'Never send a Ranger to do an Agency job; they're always bound to let conscience get the way, somehow.' He craned his head around, studying the dots again. 'And unless I miss my guess, a whole company of that bunch's flying out here, complete with air support. Flynn didn't strike me as the type to do things halfway, and Costa's whispering in his ear would only add to that. A terror cell, with top-level classified data and unknown weapons, hiding in the world's biggest rad-zone; anybody would buy it.'

Slowly, his anger faded. A new, cold pleasure replaced it. Still watching the screen, his neck fluttered. One of the guards let go of Leah, made an about-face, and walked to the end of the row of offices. Disappearing around the corner, he returned a moment later with a large, boxy black case: the one from the training room gallery, Greg realised, when it came into his line of sight. He set it on the platform, between Greg and Garrett, then stood not far away, hands crossed in front of him.

Hunter knelt before the case. He snapped open the clasps, and lifted the lid back, almost reverently. With his back to

Greg, the Golem couldn't tell what was inside. The other man let out a slow whistle. He looked to Garrett, with momentary respect. 'Still can't figure how you kept *this* quiet, even with the Turmoil. Guess Barsamin went native, after so long liaising between you and the Agency.'

Barsamin… The name clued Greg in right before Hunter stood up, giving him a clear view. A bulky cylinder, about three times the size of the canister they'd carried from D.C., sat in the middle of a foam inset. A tiny keypad and readout screen were fixed in the middle of its shiny metal surface, and several cords and other accessories – including what looked like a remote trigger – were placed around it. A small symbol was painted above the keypad, in yellow and black: the symbol for radiation.

Absorbed in this, he almost missed Garrett's voice. 'He left it because there was nowhere else.' The Doctor shifted against his bonds, more in unease than pain, although he tried to hide it. 'He knew how chaotic things were Upstairs, even better than me. When the order to disperse came through, he obeyed – but he didn't trust it. He suspected somebody would try to hijack the bombs en route, or that the order *was* the hijack. So he left one with the most secure operation on earth – the only one he thought he could trust, to equalise any threat.'

'Very sweet,' Hunter jeered. 'I'm sure D.C. would've *loved* to hear that excuse for clinging to a WMD, once the operation was done.' He stepped closer. 'And you never came forward, did you? Not even once you heard about Drew's demise – and *theirs*, supposedly.' He waved to Greg and Leah. 'No; you just went ahead with the programme.'

Garrett remained silent. Hunter's grin became frigid and shark-toothed. 'And when you *knew* the other bomb was in play – when you *knew* it was bound to be coming straight for

Seattle – you still didn't do anything. You didn't call in the threat, or warn anybody local – and by the time you did, it was halfway set off. Instead, you abandoned your post, and pulled the dirt in after you – just before burning every digital bridge on the *planet*.'

Greg grasped his words a heartbeat before Garrett did. His chest constricted, making him draw breath in sharper gusts. By the dawning shock in Leah's face, she saw the same. The Doctor's eyes narrowed, to black spots of fury. Hunter smiled, even wider. 'The Pulse was a smart move; that one's, I'm assuming?' He waved to the Gaia screen. '"Greatly Advanced" is right, if it managed to crash the planet *and* bury the Project, all under the cover of the largest nuclear terrorist attack in history. Have to see about makin' my own, when everything here's said and done, thanks to *this*.'

He nudged the case with his foot. 'Didn't take much to get hold of the right group to raid the transport – a little discretionary cash waved around, and you got guns aplenty, when the Turmoil was at full steam. Then a call or two here and there, and every trace gets cleaned up by the ones you ripped off.' He sighed, in annoyance that didn't hide the simmering anger beneath. 'But Barsamin turns out to be a bit more suspicious than expected – and here we are.'

Garrett's fists were almost bone-white. The tendons stood out on his neck like knotted cables. The chair creaked; he must be nearer the snapping point than ever. 'What the hell are you after, Sam?' he said, in a rage-choked whisper. 'What the *fuck* is all this *for*?'

Hunter pursed his lips, in a parody of deep thought. 'Payback's a big one, like we've already talked about. But that's a little cliché, all on its own. Money's no object; Agency pays well, even when it's waist-deep in the red – and those Advent shares they doled out are still worth a fair amount.' He bent forward, placing both hands on Garrett's wrists, bringing his face less than an inch from the Doctor's face. 'So what else could it be?' he half-whispered. 'Come on, Rich. It's staring you right in the face. Has been since the day you and I started working on it – and you've kept your eyes closed to it the whole time.'

Garrett just glared back. Hunter smiled again, plainly expecting nothing else. He backed away, hand on one chin like he was studying the tableau in front of him. His gaze suddenly turned to Greg. 'How did it feel, when you were out there?' he asked, out of the blue. 'When you were on missions, doing recon or right in the middle of killing somebody? How'd it feel, watching every enemy go down, or even just stroll by, knowing they were *less* than you?'

Greg didn't answer. *Where's he going with this?* His mind was still tipsy with all he'd heard, but the confused thought rose above it. 'Powerful,' Hunter answered himself. A strange sort of glow came into his eyes – not too different from the kind Greg saw in every mirror. 'Not just the kind of power that comes from any battle rush, or to a predator when it hunts and kills prey. The kind that only comes when you, a superior being, tracks and takes down a lesser one. The ones have the smallest chance of getting away or fighting back, they're the best of all. But *any* time you use that skill, any chance you have to prove it – *that's* true power.'

Greg didn't say anything; he couldn't think of anything *to* say. Hunter faced Garrett now. 'You did good work on this pair, and all the others, once you got the process right,' he said. 'But like I've said – here, and a thousand times before – you never wanted to go farther. To find out just *how much better* you could do. Not just with the Project – with *all* humans.'

He walked in a slow ring around the Doctor's chair. 'Think about a world with ARC set free – *truly* free, and truly utilised. No serious injury, anywhere in the world, and hardly any death. Minds and bodies raised to new heights of strength, and intelligence. Every human finally equal, and more powerful than they've ever been in the whole history of humanity.' He paused, significantly. The glow in his green eyes grew stronger. 'And the ones with the greatest knowledge and strength, previously held back… *they'll* be sitting in the halls of *true* power.'

Hunter let out a dramatic, peeved sigh. 'But you didn't think of that. Or you plain refused, thanks to *ethics*. So I had to take steps, to show the people who supposedly glimpsed this new world that it *could* be realised.' He waved to his men, who were watching with the same dour expressions, though Taylor still looked vaguely confused. 'Obviously I didn't go far enough in opening their eyes.'

Irritation flashed in his look, and a deeper hatred. 'First my work is sidelined, "kept in reserve" as they loved to call it. So I arrange for one of these, to drive home my point'—a wave to the nuke—'and show them how halfhearted your pet Project really was. It does exactly that for about a day – and then *you* unleash the Pulse. I try to get ahead, make the new, blind idiots in power see the value of everything I'd done – and I'm dumped on the sidelines a second time. When the canister comes up, I set out to try a third time – and here we are.' He looked to the screen. The glow in his eyes was burning hot now. 'With plenty more of the nearsighted crowd soon to be dropping in. Ready and willing – eager – to make sure a new world *never* sees the light of day.' After a short pause, his smile bloomed again, in the same cold manner. 'So I suppose we'll have to let the light in some other way.'

Garrett's glare bored into Hunter's. 'You're insane,' he ground out.

Hunter shrugged. He knelt and pressed the main power button on the nuke's keypad. The little screen lit up at once. Hunter spared a look back to his long-ago colleague. His smile was calmer, almost regretful. 'I'm sure *some* back East'll wonder about a second nuke going off in an already-contaminated zone. But the *confirmed* destruction of the Project – along with a number of Rangers – should convince the new crowd in the Pentagon and the White House of the threats still out there.' The coldness returned. 'Threats for which they'll need the best brainpower and tools. Ones their predecessors shunned, but now stand the best chance of saving them, and the country – and will bring about the changes the *world* needs.'

He stood up again. His blade danced from hand to hand, and spun in circles too fast to see. 'In order for *that*, of course, *all* the tools have to be accounted for.' The hilt smacked into his palm, and his fingers wrapped around it, tight. He held out the knife, caressing it against Garrett's jaw. 'One last time.' He pressed the tip deeper, drawing a bead of blood. '*Where – is – the – canister?*'

Garrett didn't respond. The only sound in the room was the beeping of the tracker program: the dot was now past Tacoma and over the Sound, though slowing – perhaps due to the storms. When close to half a minute had passed, Hunter lowered the blade. 'Fine,' he growled. He turned and nodded to the guards holding Greg and Leah. They shoved the two Golems several feet closer – enough for arm's reach, if either of them could pull free long enough for it.

Hunter stood between them. Raising the knife, he pointed it first at Greg, then Leah, then back and forth. His lips moved silently: *Eenie – meenie – minie –* At *moe*, he stopped, the knife aimed at Leah. Smiling, he took a step closer – and slashed downward, with one sharp stroke.

The fabric at Leah's collar parted at once. Red splashed the front of her clinger. She shrieked in pain, and tried to tear loose, but the guard held her down. Greg lunged, only to be yanked back to his knees. Garrett pulled against his bonds, with the same lack of result. Leah tried to tug free one more time, then subsided, panting and grimacing, eying Hunter with new hatred. The wound stretched from her collarbone to the right breast. Not deep – but the edges were barely closing, and the clinger along with it.

Still smiling, Hunter faced Greg now, the blade dripping. He paused, as if in consideration – then made a swift jab, aimed at the Golem's left shoulder. Agony tore through his frame, from head to toe; he tried and failed to keep a scream from escaping. Gradually, the pain died to a slow burn. He made a subtle flex of his arm, and was rewarded with a new, deeper jolt; the blade must have reached nearly to the bone. Angling it up for a better view, he saw the same splatter of blood, the same slow closing, and the even slower clinger repair. A few more cuts and stabs in the right places, and he wouldn't be able to lift his arm more than an inch, much less fight.

Less amused now, Hunter turned to Garrett. The Doctor stared back with a burning rage, hotter than any Greg had ever considered he had in him. Hunter held the knife out at his old partner. 'New rules,' he said, even colder than before. 'Every second *you* stay quiet, starting in the next five, *they*'—he twitched the point in the Golems' direction—'go through more of the same. You try to help them, *you* take the cut, and double for them. I'd prefer to be leaving *now*, everything wrapped up and ready to fly – but some things you never leave without making sure of them.' He put the point to Garrett's face, between his eyes. 'Your choice, *Doctor*.'

'Not much chance of flying.' The words echoed in the vast chamber. 'Weather's a bitch out there.' Hunter was on his feet in less time than it took to blink, knife at the ready. The guards spun toward the sound almost as quick; Greg was wrenched around, so that he faced the stairway. Blinking away the sudden jolt of pain from this, he refocused – and saw a single figure, standing at the top of the stairs. Hope flared in his aching frame. Cayden's voice rang out again, flat and purposeful. 'Step away from them. Now.'

Chapter 27

Greg could barely breathe. The pain in his shoulder was a distant thrum, and growing more remote. He stole a quick look behind him. Leah was watching Cayden with the same hope – though not without tiny glances at her captors, and Greg's. Garrett was staring up at the older Golem with an odd look. Pride, definitely – yet also a deep sadness. The kind of look a father would have, watching a son in his prime going into danger.

Hunter's bemused chuckle broke the silence. 'Ah. *Now* it's a proper reunion!' He let his blade hand drop, and stepped forward, though still within reach of the Doctor. His face gleamed with admiration. 'It's Cayden, isn't it? The *first* one, in every way. I'd always hoped we'd have the chance to meet.'

Instead of answering, Cayden moved down a step. Hunter was behind Garrett's chair again before he took the next, knife at the Doctor's throat. 'Careful,' he warned, back to business. 'Too close, and the party gets a lot rougher.'

Cayden didn't appear to be listening. He came down the rest of the stairs, halting at the bottom, and looked to the guards. Something like warmth cracked through the unreadable mask. 'Hello, guys,' he rumbled. 'Been a while.' He sounded almost sad, not angry. 'Thought Michael would've made it, too; nothing ever seemed to stop him.' His gaze shifted, to Black Hair. 'Had my doubts you'd go down that easily at the airfield, Drake. Nice to see I was wrong.' The older Golem's look moved to the two holding Leah. 'Same goes for you, Joey, and you, Fred. We all went through worse, right from the start; not surprised to see you coming out the other side. Didn't expect you to wind up like *this*, though, once you did.'

The guards stared back, hostile and primed. Hunter chuckled again, with a nastier edge. 'Don't waste your breath. They don't answer to you – or to *him*.' He pressed the blade to Garrett's collar. 'And unless you want that to be permanent, *keep back*.' His smile grew wider and harder. 'Although if the rumours way back were true, I'd think you actually *would*.'

'I don't care about him,' Cayden didn't sound angry, only certain. His fingers were slightly clenched, the sole sign of his tension. 'Tried just walking away before – it wasn't enough. Now… I just want *all* this over and done with. Doesn't matter how.'

One of Hunter's brows cocked. 'Really?' He moved the knife away. 'Then allow me.' With no further warning, he twirled the knife once, and stabbed it into Garrett's right thigh. The Doctor jerked and shouted in agony. Before he could draw breath to scream again, Hunter pulled the blade free, bringing a spurt of red – thankfully not the fountain that would've meant a severed femoral – and slashed it across the older man's chest in a short, vicious cut, spattering more blood over the front of his shirt.

Greg pulled against his captors' grip, but only wrenched his arms painfully. 'Stop it!' Leah shouted. Hunter ignored her, slicing another wound in the Doctor's stomach. He kept up a steady rhythm of slices and jabs, drawing blood almost every second, the cuts alternating from shallow to deep, from collar to waist to wrist. Garrett was panting hard, grunting or moaning with each strike, crying out when they cut deeper. Cayden's face was rigid, though his eyes twitched at every cut, as if he were taking all of them himself. He took an instinctive step forward. One of Leah's guards – Joey, at a guess – let go and blocked his path, the double blades dropping from both sleeves. He halted, never taking his eyes from the gruesome scene. The faint tremble at the tips of his weapons was his only movement.

After maybe a minute of this torture, Hunter stopped, and brought the knife back to Garrett's throat. The Doctor's breathing was ominously slow, although his eyes stayed partway open, moving from Hunter to the others in the room, and back. He was practically drenched in blood from the neck down; his shirt, now in red tatters, barely hid a quarter of the abuse. Greg tried not to look, and failed. He couldn't understand how the old man was still alive, let alone conscious. Cayden was a statue, without even the faintest twitch. Greg could see the readiness in his poise, though, and the hatred and anguish behind his eyes.

His voice now pure iron, Hunter addressed the two captive Golems. 'That was just a taste. He keeps fucking around, and we start again – with *all* of you.' Keeping his eyes on Cayden, he hissed in the Doctor's ear. 'He tries to interfere, or make any kind of move, and one of *them* takes the hit – yours *and* theirs.' He pressed the knife against Garrett's carotid. 'Come on, Rich. Everything they've been through for you, and you still want *them* to take on *more* of *your* shit? Give me the canister, and they'll never have to again – I can promise *that* much.'

Garrett's head lowered, chin almost touching his chest. Like he was falling asleep – or into a more permanent state. Hunter pulled his head back by his hair. When the older man didn't even blink, he rabbit-punched him in the gut with his knife hand. Garrett doubled over far as he could, coughing up blood-streaked saliva. The fit ended fast, however – faster than Greg would have expected, with so much injury. Still bent over, the Doctor whispered, 'All right... All right.'

Greg's shoulders slumped. He turned his head aside, not wanting to see or listen. A glance Leah's way showed the same stricken, defeated look he had to be wearing. Cayden didn't show a thing.

Hunter smiled, in real pleasure this time. As he held the blade under Garrett's chin one more time, the older man spoke again, a little louder. 'Just one thing you should probably know... if you want the *whole* story.'

'Make it quick,' Hunter said curtly. He mimed looking at his watch, and glanced at the Gaia screen. 'Time's running short – and I doubt *you've* got much to waste.'

Garrett took no notice of this. He stayed hunched forward, in pain or shame. 'You and I, we both hammered away at the ARC formula, day and night. So many changes, so many samples – there were times I lost track which version was which, and where. Sometimes... I had to comb through every freezer or file, to find just one.' His head began to rise, inch by inch. 'But there was *one* I always knew where to find. The very first – the one you *thought* you took.'

Hunter's frown was puzzled and annoyed. 'What the hell kind of crap is *that?*'

Somehow, Garrett managed to lever himself up. Blood coated his chest and torn-up shirt, dripping in streams to the floor – yet he was still conscious, and aware. The blade at his throat didn't seem to faze him anymore, either. His voice was a dull murmur. 'I knew from the first day what I was creating.

What it could become – and would, because of me, or others. I tried to forget it, to tell myself I was paranoid, or afraid of progress. But the truth stared me in the face, with every test – and would again in worse ways, when the trials began. I couldn't allow that – not without knowing *all* the dangers.' He lifted his head a little higher. His smile was sad – and oddly, without self-hatred, for the first time. 'So I found out.'

Hunter stared at the old man. Greg stared, too, with slowly growing wonder. Something was *different*, he realised. Not only was the Doctor's posture stable, but it was *better*, shedding years of hunching from lab work and simple age. His chest was swelling inch by inch, looking stronger and more muscular with every slow breath; so were his upper arms, and legs. The flow of blood from his wounds hadn't just reduced; it had *ceased*. And beneath the rags and sheen of red, the cuts themselves seemed different – almost *smaller*.

Hunter's face was slack with disbelief. His knife hand wavered. 'No,' he whispered.

'Oh, *please*, Sam,' Garrett said. '*You* know the first rule of any theory.' He paused, still smiling – but now with a knife-hard edge. 'You *test* it.'

Hunter snarled with shock and rage. He swung the knife back, to stab into Garrett's chest or throat. In that moment, the Doctor flexed his arms. The zipties tore away like paper, and his hands came together, catching Hunter's fist between them. The other man yelled in fury, then in startled pain as Garrett's foot slammed into his abdomen. He sailed backward, crashing amid the tank wreckage.

Features hard and determined, the Doctor sprang up. Every one of the knife wounds was gone, as if they'd never been. His entire body seemed to glow and pulse with energy. He paused a half-second to flip his cane into the air with a jerk of his foot, and catch it one-handed. A sword blade – the same as that of Cayden's and the Brown Coats, by its gleam – flashed when he twisted the head free.

Taylor rushed at him, blade twirling. With unearthly speed, the Doctor spun away out of reach, and slashed at the ex-Golem's back, following with a sharp swing of the sword hilt to the other man's head. Taylor convulsed and staggered, but stayed upright, already whirling to block the next attack. This let Greg see the long, deep gash that gaped open across his back, from shoulder to waist – and which was just starting to close. *More anti-regen,* he thought, wonderingly. *He had it. All this time, he –*

Hunter jumped to his feet. Face contorted with fury, he shot out a hand to one of the guards holding Leah. The guard – Fred – made a short jerk of one arm, tossing him the thin sword. Hunter caught it easily, not taking his eyes from Garrett – then charged, blade spinning like a marshal's baton. Garrett braced his feet against the floor, bringing up his own weapons. With a roar, Hunter crashed into him, hard and fast enough to topple a young tree. A burst of sparks flew from the connecting blades. The Doctor barely retreated a step, pushing back with all his strength. The two old men grappled at each other, straining and grunting. Then, Garrett suddenly toppled over, bringing Hunter with as he somersaulted backward. He slammed into the wall with a startled squawk, hard enough to leave a deep circle of cracks in the concrete – though he had enough time to tuck in his head and shoulders, avoiding a snapped neck. He landed on his ass, momentarily dazed – then sprang up again, matching Garrett's move.

Taylor and Joey started forward, blades up. That broke the spell of shock that hung over Greg. Ignoring the wrenching pain this brought in his leg, shoulders and scalp, he pushed off the floor with his knees, jamming his head into Drake's stomach with all the strength he could manage. Drake wasn't completely distracted – he thrust his hips back, avoiding a blow that would've broken all his lower ribs, at full speed – but the hit was enough to knock the wind from him with a loud '*Oooff!*' His hold on Greg's hair loosened. That was all Greg needed. He yanked his left arm free at last – shouting in relief as feeling returned to it – and spinning around into a fighting stance, while yanking his other hand across the ex-Golem's belt.

His knife, new blade, and Cayden's machete tore free from their clips. In less than three seconds he had flipped the machete to Cayden as the other Golem charged into the fight, and was up and ready, both other weapons in hand. He glanced to the right; Leah had broken out of her captors' hold as well with a deft twist and roll, pulling her own sword free from his waist. She back–flipped to Greg's side, coming up in a combat stance.

Scowling, Drake snapped his arms out, drawing his two blades. With no further heads-up, he rushed them, the two thin weapons stabbing out. Greg bent backwards at the waist, just missing a stab to the chest, slashing at Drake's arm and face even as he dodged. The ex-Golem ducked both easily, and drew back from Leah's follow-up cut with equal grace. Greg advanced, hacking downward with his sword and slicing up with the knife. Drake brought his weapons across his body, blocking both, and kicked out with his right leg. It missed Greg's crotch, but still managed a glancing hit on his partially–numb left leg, making him stumble. The ex-Golem stabbed at him again, aiming for his face, but Leah's blade parried it away. She forced him back, knife and sword glittering blurs.

This gave Greg a moment to regain his footing, and assess the fight. Beyond the wrecked tank platform, Cayden was fighting Taylor and Joey both at once, dancing, ducking and leaping out of the way of one's strikes as he parried or sliced at the other, with the same grace and speed he'd shown at the airfield. His clinger was rent at chest and arms. Blood flew in droplets when he moved, but he showed not a hint of pain, or lethargy. Joey's coverall was in red-soaked rags, from collar to cuff. Taylor's scarred frame was even more ripped up, with blood loss to match the Doctor's running down his frame and staining the cheap shorts he wore. Neither of *them* was slowing down, either.

A blurred, writhing shape shot across his vision as he processed this. It smashed into the platform's tangle of glass and metal, throwing chunks of both in all directions – and blood and viscera, too. He swung toward it, in time to see Hunter and Garrett rise to their feet, panting and wheezing. He watched, transfixed. Both men's clothes were shredded, and turned almost black with blood. Then their figures blurred, and smashed together again.

Greg felt the impact through the soles of his clinger. More fragments flew; he ducked to avoid one the size of a trashcan lid. He snapped out of the funk once more, and sprinted to rejoin Leah, who was just holding her own against Joey and Drake. The latter spun to block Greg's stab at his ribcage, then swung scythe-like at the Golem's head. He ducked – then, in the half-second before Drake could swing again, leapt forward and slammed his knife into the ex-Golem's gut with all his strength.

A red geyser drenched his arm. Drake grunted like he'd only been punched low. His backhand swing was slower than before, but still fast enough that Greg took a deep cut to the forehead ducking it. Instead of letting go and rolling away, however, he hurled his body into Drake's. Both men crashed to the ground, with such force that their blades were torn from their grips. Rather than scrabble for his, Greg tore his knife free, and lunged up at his enemy's face, scrambling atop him with one pull of his free hand. Drake blocked his stab, drawing a long slice along his left arm, and swung a knife-hand at Greg's head as he tried to sit up and grab for the Golem's throat with the other. Greg knocked the grab aside with his knife hand, and shifted sharply in the same move, taking the blow on his other arm hard enough to bring a *crack* of breaking bone – several, by the feel.

Agony lanced up to his shoulder. He ignored it and pushed farther up, so that he was almost sitting on Drake's chest. The ex-Golem brought his arms up again, to punch or block. Before he could do either, Greg swung the knife in a short, tight arc. The blade punched into the left side of Drake's throat, protruding from the other. He gobbled and choked, fists flailing against Greg's chest like bricks. The Golem ignored these, bearing down harder with the knife. Blood spewed from the wounds and Drake's mouth; both carotids must have been hit. His struggles grew less and less. Greg pulled the knife free, raised it above his head, then brought it plunging down with all his strength.

The point pierced clean through Drake's throat. Greg felt the tear and crack of muscle and bone, and a harder thunk when it struck the concrete below, embedding itself several inches. Drake's thrashing abruptly stopped. His limbs dropped to the floor, twitching. He let out one last, soundless choke, then went still, eyes staring emptily into Greg's own.

A thunderous crash of metal and glass on concrete reverberated through the room. Breathing hard, Greg yanked the knife out a second time, and scrambled to his feet – and stopped, momentarily stunned. Badly damaged before, the entire right-hand block of offices and rooms was now gutted. Piles of rubble were heaped in the doorways and what was left of the glass partitions; some were still settling. More spiralling impacts starred the walls beyond, and the floor.

As he processed this, another crash sounded from the surgery room – what was left of it. Two struggling forms, grappling at each other, thudded into one of the larger heaps of metal and glass. Before Greg could tell who was who, one of them shot out a knee, knocking the other back into the room. Leaping to his feet, he charged after his enemy. More crashes and shattering noises rose, along with grunts of pain and effort. For a moment, Greg could only stare, watching the destruction. Even *he*, at his worse or more desperate, hadn't come close to this kind of strength – or rage. *How can* they?

New shouts broke him from this wonder. He spun, flipping his dropped blade into the air with a jerk of his foot and catching it, all in a single move. Leah was driving Fred back toward the stairs, their blades slashing and parrying so quickly he couldn't see the strikes. Cayden was still battling both Joey and Taylor, still with barely any wounds – but they'd backed him farther into the space between the last left-hand office and the far wall. Every time he made a slash or dodge that would break from the trap, one of his opponents always blocked the way. He was still fast, not showing any exhaustion, but he couldn't last.

Almost without thinking, Greg sprinted toward the three of them. He leapt at one of the tumbled tanks, and sprang off it into the air, new blade carving down at the closest target: Taylor, whose back was still to him. His old partner must have sensed him, however. Rather than lunging in for a new attack on Cayden, he spun and slashed up with a double-bladed strike at Greg's legs.

Greg caught the swing on his blade, right as his feet ploughed into Taylor's carved-up stomach. Hardly winded, the ex-Golem let the strike knock him free of the block, and rebounded off the wall, one blade thrusting out in a stab, the other swinging down at Greg's head. He dodged the stab, deflecting it with his knife, and blocked the swing; the blow made him drop halfway to one knee. Still vague-eyed but determined, Taylor pirouetted away, out of reach of an answering stab, then charged in again, slashing with both blades – first horizontally, then vertically, creating a near-impenetrable shield for the several seconds it would take to get close enough for a killing strike.

Greg fell back before this onslaught, then parried the last vertical swing and stabbed at Taylor's face with the knife. His ex-partner jerked his head back awkwardly as he made his own parry, slicing a new furrow in Greg's bad shoulder. Hissing with the pain, Greg slashed again, at Taylor's face, making him bring both swords up to catch it, then pushed with every ounce of strength he had. Taylor stumbled back with the force of the shove, arms raising above his head for a split second as he fought to stay balanced. That was all Greg needed. He pushed hard one more time on his sword arm, forcing Taylor back another inch – then leapt forward, knife outstretched.

The blade plunged into Taylor's chest, burying itself to the hilt below his sternum. Red droplets sprayed into Greg's eyes, enough to blind him momentarily. Taylor flinched, grunting. The swords slid from his grip, falling with a clatter amid the rubble. Still burning with adrenaline, Greg gave him one last shove, pinning him to the wall below the Gaia screen, and twisting the knife deeper, up into his chest cavity. Taylor didn't make a sound, or try to fight; in fact, he'd gone nearly limp.

He brought up the sword, to stab into Taylor's head or neck – then stopped. His ex-partner was staring at him, in a new way. Almost as if he were *awake*, for the first time in days, months, *aeons* – and had seen all that had happened, while he was out. He looked down at the knife in his chest, as though surprised – and yet, also, not. When his eyes lifted, there was a deep gratitude in them. Tears formed at their corners; two slid down his cadaverous, bony cheeks. His mouth opened, dribbling blood; a faint grunting rose from his throat. Greg leaned closer, trying to hear better. His ex-partner's mouth formed three words, or as close as he could get: '*Thank... you... Greg.*'

Greg stared back, too startled to speak. Taylor's legs wobbled, then gave way. Greg released his grip on the knife, and Taylor sagged to his knees, still propped up. Slowly, the vivid light in his gaze died. Greg felt a sting in his own eyes. How long had his ex-partner endured his role, after literally coming back from the dead? Had his mind watched, trapped, as his body acted and fought under Hunter's control? Garrett had said he'd started flushing the inhibitors and all other compounds from him; maybe that had accounted for Taylor's slowness, and halfhearted skill. Had he been coming back, right up to Greg's killing strike? He'd never know now.

Blinking away the wetness, he reached down and jerked the knife free. When he straightened, they were dry – and hard as stone. The pain from his wounds was gone; only an icy numbness remained, filling him from head to toe. *Time to end this.*

Off to his left, Joey had finally managed to block Cayden into a corner on his own. He feinted and jabbed constantly with both weapons, forcing the older Golem to block every time before he could make any strike of his own. Greg pivoted on one heel, priming to charge the ex-Golem. In that same instant, Cayden dropped his guard a fraction – long enough for Joey to score a deep stab to his left abdomen, below the ribcage. Cayden slumped to one knee – and seized the other man's arm. Before Joey could draw back the sword or swing the other, he pulled him in deeper, and swung his own blade down in a tight, cleaving arc.

There was a thick crunching sound. Joey froze, staring cross-eyed at the blade now embedded in his forehead. He let out a couple of hitching grunts, then collapsed. Cayden wrenched the blade out as he fell, bringing a splash of blood and grey matter. Moving stiffly, he stood, and yanked out the sword still embedded in his side with a stifled wince. He let it drop to the rubble-strewn floor, staring at Joey's blank, greying face with no expression of his own. Greg was sure, though, that the older Golem was as shaken as he.

He spun on his heel, knife and sword ready. *Three down.* A heavy pall of dust hung over the scene, shot through with tendrils of greyish smoke; something had caught fire in one of the offices near the stairway. More crashing metal and stone came from the same direction; Greg spotted two human-shaped forms grabbing at each other through the cloud, but couldn't tell which was which.

On the other side of the platform, Leah was now retreating, being pressed back toward the 'recovery area'. Her arms still moved quicksilver-fast, but Greg could see the fatigue in her shoulders – and the several glancing cuts to her arms where that had already cost her. She parried another strike and tried to counter with an underhand stab. Fred was quicker, however; the ex-Golem crossed his blade with hers before the stab was halfway up, then bulled forward with all his strength, locking them at the hilt. Before Leah could dig in, he hurled her backwards into the 'recovery area's' teetering frame, hard enough to tear through the support pylon and send her flying into the mirrored far wall. There was a crash of glass; Leah screamed, more in pain than fury, a sound that abruptly cut off.

Greg leapt onto the nearest higher object – one of the destroyed tanks – and propelled himself into a flying leap. Fred was spinning to face him as his sword came slashing down. He ducked aside rather than block, then stabbed at Greg's head with his own weapon. Greg beat it aside, and leapt back to give himself room for a strike of his own. To his right, he saw Cayden advancing on Fred's flank more slowly, waiting for his chance – or still not recovered from the earlier stab.

Fred caught this, and shifted his stance, steely eyes flicking back and forth behind the silver lenses. Before any of the three men could make a move, there was a crinkle of glass from behind Fred. He twisted at the waist, blades dropping to block – but not fast enough. There was a sharp punching sound. The point of a sword tore out through his back, dead-centre and dripping. He let out a strange choking sound, standing stock-still in mid-swing.

Panting grimly, Leah pushed him hard with one hand. Her sword slid out as he dropped onto a small pile of wreckage, weapons falling from nerveless fingers. Blood seeped copiously over his chest and pooled on the rubble beneath him. His eyes fixed on Cayden. He raised a hand toward the older Golem, in supplication or one last grab. Cayden didn't make a move. Slowly, Fred's eyes dimmed, staring into emptiness. His hand dropped limply to the floor, twitched once, then was still.

Leah limped forward, fully out into the room. She coughed once, spitting a mouthful of red. 'Finally,' she croaked. Her teeth shone with blood, in a cold, exhausted grin. 'Thought he'd never—' She faltered at Greg's look. 'What?' It was then she looked down at herself – and saw the two jagged glass shards, protruding from her left pectoral and waist, extending out her back. She looked up, more dumbfounded than frightened. 'Shit.' With no more than that, she crumpled to her knees.

Greg was at her side before she'd finished falling. Cayden joined him half a second after, moving behind Leah and gripping her under the arms to keep her upright. She was still conscious, eyes shut tight and biting her lip against the pain. 'Keep still. Just keep still,' Greg half-babbled. It was all he could do to keep his hands steady; adrenaline and fear were running neck-and-neck. He brushed at the glass, and the wounds themselves; Leah flinched, though he'd kept his touch light. He'd seen his share of stabs, even treated a few, on the rare occasions he worked with a non-Golem team. This was worse – and he had no idea if her earlier cuts meant the anti-regen compound had seeped into her system. If it had, the wounds might not close no matter what he did – and probably would mean death if he pulled the shards out.

He grabbed her wrist, checking her pulse while he scanned her arms. Cayden kept her steady, face grave. The gashes *looked* to be healing, but the blood and dust made it impossible to tell – although the clinger was taking its time, a bad sign. There was no pink froth around either shard wound, so the lung wasn't punctured. He looked around, for a kit or even just a piece of relatively clean cloth. It was then he realised the sounds of battle had ceased – no smashing rubble or furniture, no grunts or shouts. The whole right-hand side of the room was practically covered in a dust cloud. His eyes smarted, making him squint, and reach for the hood of his clinger.

A shadowed, hunched figure loomed out of the murk before his hand had reached halfway. As he shifted in front of Leah, knife raised, a second figure rose behind the first. After a heartbeat's pause, it lunged forward, crashing into its rival. The two of them spun out of the cloud, hands gripped at each other's shoulders like grappling wrestlers. Hunter's teeth were gritted in a snarl of hatred; Garrett's face was tight with effort, but devoid of emotion. Both men were caked in dirt and powdered concrete, making them look like aged statues. Filthy, crusted rags hung from their waists and shoulders.

Bloody cuts and gashes – some paper cut-sized, many foot-long or more – decorated almost every inch of their bodies and faces.

They strained at each other for a long, slow moment. Hunter's stance began to slacken – then pitched forward in an almighty shove. The two old men tumbled to the floor, clawing and gasping. Chunks of debris spiralled in all directions wherever they rolled and struck. Something soft struck Greg in the face – a piece of cushion, maybe – though still hard enough to knock him off-balance. When he'd regained it, he saw Hunter rise, sitting astride the Doctor's waist. Panting like an animal, he raised both fists high above his head, and brought them down with all his strength.

The ground seemed to shake with the impact. Garrett let out a choking gargle. His body convulsed, limbs flinging upwards, then went slack. Roaring now, Hunter swung again, and again. Greg stared, frozen. Puffs of dust rose, tinged with red. The third blow brought a dull crackling sound, like twigs splintering. Ribs, or maybe the sternum. One more blow would send fragments of bone into the heart and lungs – and ARC wasn't a sure bet to help *that*.

Time slowed to a crawl. Hunter's arms rose again, fists fused together. As they passed behind his head, the ice shattered in Greg's mind. The knife flipped around in his hand, tip of the blade between thumb and two fingers. He rose to his feet, with dreamy slowness. His arm came back, then whipped forward in a sudden rush of speed – or maybe it was the world returning to normal.

The knife flashed across the intervening space. Hunter bellowed in pain. His swing halted, and he grabbed at his side, where the hilt of the knife now sprouted from between two ribs – instead of the neck, as Greg had intended. He lurched up, pulling the knife out with only a mild grimace. Snarling, he started toward the three of them, movements slow and jerky but gaining speed.

Greg looked around for some other weapon: the new blade, a girder, a chunk of concrete. His eyes fell on something at his feet: a plastic bag, maybe a lab sample flung out from one of the destroyed labs. He started to look away – then stopped. He was still a little woozy, and the still-floating dust made his eyes smart, but…

Cayden recognised the object sooner than he did. The older Golem pushed him aside with a swift jab of his elbow, and scooped up the bag, all in nearly the same motion. He stepped between them and Hunter, unarmed, the bag now open in the palm of one hand. The older man fixed on him. His smile ice-cold, he raised the bloodstained knife, and charged. Instead of dodging, or grabbing for a weapon, Cayden arced his arm back like a pitcher, and hurled the bag in a short, overhand throw.

The bag struck Hunter in the upper chest, below his neck. The grey powder within exploded into a cloud. He staggered back, coughing harshly and waving an arm to clear it. When he finally regained control, he faced Cayden again. The powder had settled over almost his entire near-naked frame, making him look more statue-like than ever. Greg hardly dared breathe. *If it was* –

Scowling, Hunter began to advance again. Cayden made no move to defend himself, hands at his sides. The older man hefted the knife, to stab or slash – and stopped. His hateful expression became more confused – then agonised. Some of the powder began to slough off, revealing the bare flesh of his chest and face – and the deep, spreading reddish circles as the 'Tacitus' ate its way through.

Hunter began to scream, a steady, drawn-out sound that made even Greg wince. He didn't look away, though – nothing would have made him. Still shrieking, Hunter fell to his knees. He writhed and twisted, in almost impossible contortions. The knife dropped from his hand as he clutched at his face, scrubbing and tearing at it. Bits of flesh broke off, landing on the floor with little grotesque splats. More inactive powder sprinkled away, showing more wounds. They spread with unbelievable speed over his entire body, exposing the reddish underside of the man's flesh, going deeper to the muscle, sinew, tendons, even bone – and breaking every one of these apart. Greg kept watching, grimly satisfied.

Bit by bit, Hunter's screams died down to a steady heaving. With perhaps the last of his prodigious strength, he forced himself back up on his knees. His face was a shredded, gory mask. Dissolving flesh and tissue dangled in shreds, showing wrecked muscles, flaking bone – and a skeletal grin. He started to rise, hands clenched and reaching for Cayden. He was dying even as he moved – he *had* to be – yet he didn't falter. The older Golem showed no reaction. Greg's mind screamed at him to grab a weapon, to *finish* it – or for *him* to do it himself. No part of his body responded; it was as though he were cemented to the floor.

As Hunter got one leg under him, a clattering of rubble came from behind. He stopped, and made an awkward, ungainly turn. A hunched form came up from the ground, and stumbled out of the settling dust. Garrett's face was almost obscured by blood and gashes – some healed, others still gaping. His chest was a solid purple-black colour, just beginning to fade; every move or jerk brought a grimace. Nevertheless, he shambled forward, dragging a long, thin object behind him – something that caught the light with a cold gleam.

Hunter stared, panting, heedless of the pain and dripping gore. The Doctor halted a foot away, staring back down at him, breathing in steady, measured gusts. Before Greg or any of the others could speak or act, his hand whipped up in a brutally short jab. The sword cane pierced Hunter's forehead, dead centre between the eyes. The point sprouted from the back of his head, fragments of brain and bone hanging from its edge. Hunter made a low gasp, like he'd been shocked. His eyes crossed, following the blade to Garrett's hand.

Garrett tore the blade loose, letting the tip rest against the floor. Blood and brain matter trickled from the wound, into Hunter's staring, empty eyes and mixing with the accelerating decay. He didn't register it. Without a sound or gesture, he dropped. His head cracked open when it struck the ground, spilling more red and grey detritus – but the entire skull was already crumbling, as well. The rest of his body was breaking down even faster. In moments, there was nothing but a misshapen sludge of red and pink, all lightly dusted with a whitish powder. Soon, there would be almost nothing left.

Garrett stared down at the grey-red mass at his feet, breath coming slower now, and more halting. When he turned to face the three Golems, there was the tiniest trace of triumph in his grim, bloodstained visage. His eyes, glowing a brighter blue than ever, found Cayden's. 'Thank you,' he whispered.

Cayden bent his head in acknowledgement, still as impassive as ever. The Doctor took a step toward them. He'd hardly taken the next when his knees began to shake. He started to prop himself up with his sword – but his arms and shoulders were already trembling, too. In less than a breath, his entire frame was shaking, in rapid-fire jerks and spasms. 'Doc?' Leah whispered. She pulled out of Cayden's grasp, got unsteadily to her feet and moved closer. Greg and Cayden were inches behind her.

Still stolid, Garrett waved her back. Just then, his legs gave out, and he dropped against the wall. There was a crackle of something breaking in his skull, or neck. 'Doc!' Leah shouted.

Ignoring the agony this had to bring, she grasped both shards and ripped them out, then rushed to the Doctor's side, grabbing him by the shoulders. A massive tremor tore him free of her grip. His limbs jerked and spasmed wildly, wringing themselves in random, painful contortions. His head flailed back and forth like a rag doll's, bouncing against the floor. His eyes rolled up, showing only white. His mouth opened and closed rapid-fire, letting out a bizarre, animal-like keening.

Too shocked to do anything but gape at first, Greg pulled himself from this dismay, and knelt by Garrett's side, trying to bring one hand beneath the Doctor's head and stabilise his waist with the other. He knew almost nothing about seizures and their symptoms; maybe this was an episode? Leah, her face as scared and confused as his must be, tried to turn Garrett on his side, to aid his breathing. Cayden grabbed the Doctor's ankles, just avoiding kicks to the face and chest.

Finally, the spasms or whatever they were died down to intermittent, random spurts. The Doctor's head rose. His face was contorted, frozen in a half-snarl as though by a stroke – but the eyes were refocused, and alert. 'I'm sorry… for this,' he managed to croak. 'Came on… sooner than expected.' The unfrozen part of his mouth turned up in a momentary bitter smile. 'Bonus of growing old – with some changes.'

'What's happening?' Cayden demanded. His normally impassive look was gone, replaced by the same fear as theirs – and a deeper kind, below it. 'Where's the worst hit? What can we do?'

Garrett let out a rasping chuckle, which ending in a choked cough. 'Nothing… that hasn't happened… before,' he managed at last. 'Wasn't that bad, the first time. Must not have been anything serious enough.' Another choking laugh. 'Still left its mark, more ways than one – all thanks to me.'

'*What* did?' Greg pressed him. He kept the fear from his own voice, but only just. 'What's doing this?'

The bitter humour left the Doctor's mangled face. He tilted it in Greg's direction. 'Just like I said, before. Wasn't going to let… anybody go through the ARC, and the tests. Not until I *knew* what it could do.'

He took a long, deep breath, gathering himself. 'First version – *very* first – had more add-ons. More 'roids, more compounds… to amp up strength and speed, when ARC kicked in. Thought they'd be permanent, or long lasting. Enough to get our people out of tight spots – or make them the demigods the Pentagon wanted.'

A second breath, even deeper. 'But I didn't know – *couldn't* know – the strain.' His arm, still twitching, lifted a few inches. 'Everything wears out: muscle, bone, other tissue. Natural progression, or caused by outside stimuli.' The smirk returned, for an instant. 'ARC… certainly was *outside*. Every time the body repaired itself, and amped up in response… it was dying faster, in some other way.' His hand lowered, resting on his once-bad leg, now still. 'Nerve damage. Muscular degeneration. Bone decalcification. Anything could start failing, when strained by healing – and it did.' He barked bleakly. 'Dying by healing: the ultimate irony.'

'No,' Leah said, flatly. She seized Garrett's arm. 'Not happening. We're *not*—'

'Stop,' Garrett interrupted. With one superhuman push of his legs, he brought himself to a half-seated position, propped up against one of the destroyed NeoMaters. 'You need to go. Get back to the Sanctuary… away from here.'

A new, steady beeping sounded, as though in agreement. Startled and alert, Greg looked up. The image on the Gaia screen had changed; it now showed only the Kitsap Peninsula, centred on the base itself. In the right-hand corner, to the southeast, the red dot appeared, coming closer. *Patrick and Costa,* he remembered, tardily. The storm must have lessened, giving them a clearer, slightly less hot flight – or they were hauling ass even faster. As he watched the image, a new window appeared at the top, showing a timer: 00:15:00:00.

Startled, he looked to the Doctor, who was watching with a faint smile. 'Thermobaric devices,' he said, even more softly. 'Several dozen, placed on every level, but concentrated here. Enough to incinerate everything classified… and collapse the whole Facility.' A faint note of urgency rose. 'Leave… now.'

'But why?' Greg demanded. He knew, of course, on a certain level – which didn't stop him from asking. His voice was growing rougher – but he didn't care. 'They're coming for *us*. They know what Hunter did, and why. They can get us out – get *you* out, to a hospital…'

Garrett nodded. '*They* can, maybe. But D.C.—' His face hardened. He cast a look around at their wrecked surroundings. 'They can't find this, intact – they *can't*. They do, it starts all over again. A new Project. The kind Hunter wanted.' A quiet, reflective look came over his contorted face. 'Without any qualms, or sane restraints, and no chance to let them loose. As I did.'

'Like the Pax,' Leah said, softly. She studied the Doctor with a new, dubious respect. 'It was supposed to be one restraint – but it never worked from the start. Because of *you*.'

A twitch of Garrett's chin: the only nod he could make. Greg found himself nodding as well. It fit – and yet there was more that didn't. He leaned in. 'What else?' Part of him was shouting to be gone, to leave everything here behind, to be destroyed in whatever measure the timer controlled – but he had to know *this*. 'What other controls didn't work?'

Garrett's eyes – now considerably dimmer – met his. The old man's eyelids flitted halfway down, like he was going to sleep, or into a trance. His words came out in a low, croaking voice. 'The inhibitors...' He halted, swallowing back pain or blood. When he resumed, his tone was a hair stronger. 'They weren't only for... what I said.'

'What were they for?' Cayden asked. He was still less reverential than the two other Golems, but the directness made up for this.

Garrett's eyes, still half-lidded, rolled to each of them in turn. His enigmatic smile returned. 'Not enough to create a supersoldier. You have to watch him grow, and channel that growth... or suppress it.' The smile faded. 'I saw the point, in this – but that didn't stop my hating it, day and night, like all the others. So I vowed to change what I could... and see what could come out of it, when and if they faded from you.' He coughed once more, spitting up more red. When he'd cleared the last of it, he met their eyes again. 'Some kinds of growth are the hardest kinds. Can't be channelled, so you bury them. Some involve memory; I told you as much. But the biggest one...'

He faltered; not from pain or shame this time, or so Greg guessed. With one abrupt lunge, he slapped his hand on Greg's. Fingers clasped tight, he dragged it to Leah's. He smiled – or tried to – at their mutual confusion. 'You had a small taste of it. Last night.' A deep, shuddering breath; he was mastering every ounce of control he had. 'What the people behind Golem feared, most of all. And what it could lead to, not long after.'

For a split second, Greg didn't follow him – then he did. The unspoken meaning struck him like a freight train. The world turned grey and hazy at the edges; he had to plant his hand flat on the ground to keep stable. The control returned, a fragment at a time. His pulse sped up to a jackhammer, pounding at all parts of his body. He glanced at Leah. She was staring back at him, ghostly-white from shock. Cayden was staring at Garrett – but in a different way. Almost satisfied – like he'd had a question he'd carried for years, *decades*, and finally had his answer.

Greg forced his gaze back to Garrett. The Doctor was watching him and Leah, a sad yet proud tinge to his smile. His face was becoming steadily greyer: the colour of 'Tacitus'. 'Now you know,' he murmured. 'All the secrets, all the truths.' His hand leapt out again, grabbing both of theirs. 'Go. Take them, *all* of them – and *live*.'

Dreamlike, Greg slowly climbed to his feet. Leah matched his move. In a small, halting voice, she asked, 'Where's… the canister?'

Garrett's smile returned, relieved and pleased. One finger made a jerking motion, toward the platform. Looking to it, Greg saw the case containing the second nuke, resting top down on a nearby wreckage pile, battered but intact. Head still whirling, he went to it, turning it right side up. The nuke was intact when he raised the lid; nothing looked out of place. At first he didn't understand – then he saw the tiny, almost invisible gap between the padding and the sides of the case. He wedged his fingers underneath this, and lifted the entire chunk of packaging away. The nuke was lighter than he'd thought; forty pounds, not much more than the heaviest equipment load he'd ever carried. Beneath this was a mesh of canvas webbing, and another space, nearly empty – except for a small metal stand. Even in the bad light, Greg could tell it was the same as the one back at the Advent Tech vault. The canister rested atop this, secure and undamaged.

He tore away the webbing and pulled the canister free. The faintest rattle from inside said it held the thumb drive. Stiff and precise, he handed it to Leah. She looked at it, her expression somewhere between terrified and awed, then put it to her waist, below the small of her back. The clinger clasp snapped into place over it.

The two of them looked to Garrett again. The Doctor nodded at their unspoken question. 'Everything you need, it's on there,' he rasped. 'All Project details, from names, to tools – to the ARC itself.' He tried to make another finger twitch, toward the blue-eyed screen, and only partly succeeded. 'Along with a full backup of *her*. Jorge shouldn't have any trouble opening the files now, with her help.' A third twitch, to the nuke. 'All the knowledge you need – and all the protection for it.'

For the first time in his life, Greg could find no words. He knelt by Garrett's side, and squeezed the older man's gnarled hand in his, gently. Garrett's hand gripped back. He held it for perhaps an eternity, then got up, not taking his eyes from the Doctor's. Leah knelt and held Garrett's hand in turn. New tears were dripping down her cheeks. He smiled, grasping her hand even tighter. Cayden made no move to join the silent homage. The satisfaction from before was gone. His new expression now was strangely knowing – and shot through with an odd finality.

A new alarm sounded. On the screen, the timer started counting down: 14:59, 14:58, 14:57. Snapping out of his funk, Greg grabbed his knife and new blade, plastering them to the clinger sheaths. Then he carefully lifted the nuke back into the case, and locked the lid closed. Leah moved to help him, but he motioned her away, grabbed one of the handles, and swung the case onto one shoulder. She nodded, and went to retrieve her own weapons, hiding a wince from the pain of her wounds, which were almost closed. He wouldn't have any trouble hefting the case to the surface, or through the forest. What they'd do with it afterward…

This thought came to a halt when he saw Cayden, standing

in the same spot as though rooted to it. He was staring intently at Garrett, still emotionless. In a low, serious tone, he said, 'We all weren't just soldiers, were we? We were family, after the first one was gone. From birth through training, all the way to the end – we were the closest thing you had to a second chance.'

He paused. 'But it was closer with me, wasn't it? Right from the start, I could tell there was something different – about me. It made you look at me different, every day; made you act different, too. Always the best gear – and the most challenging missions. Whenever I came back in a team, you always went straight to me, even when I wasn't leader. When I went out solo, you were the first face on the helipad, or coming off the elevator. Didn't think much of it at the time; you were Project head, and I was the best of the First Five. Made perfect sense, on that alone. More so, when you finally owned up. But there was more to it. Even when I was out there, trying to decide between running away, staying behind – or jumping off a cliff or drowning myself – I knew there was more.' Another weighty pause. 'Now I'm sure of it.'

Garrett was silent, save for his slow, heaving breaths – which were growing ominously slower. Keeping eye contact with him, Cayden reached down beside him, and pried an object from the rubble. It was a warped, broken picture frame; at a guess, it had been on the Doctor's desk in his lab office. When Cayden wiped away the dust, Greg saw a pair of faces staring up through the broken glass: A woman, and a young boy. The boy's face was closer to the camera, and turned slightly to the left. When the older Golem held it up, Greg saw them in profile, side by side. It was only for the briefest of seconds – but that was all the time in the world, for him.

Someone's hand dug into his arm, nails cutting like knives even through the clinger: Leah. The shock vibrated into him through this grip. He hardly noticed; he couldn't tell if he was still breathing. If someone had pushed even a little, he would have tipped over, and maybe shattered like a porcelain figure. Cayden bent closer, bringing the picture and his own impassive face within inches of the Doctor's. The same calm gravity laced his next word. 'How?'

Garrett remained silent for a time. There was a new, stranger peace in his features – that of a last burden being lifted away, after years or decades. Finally, he drew in a long, powerful breath, as though saving up to get out every needed word. 'Gwen and I, we'd tried for years, the natural way,' he said, in a voice as hoarse as sandpaper. 'Nothing happened. We went to every kind of specialist… they said nothing was wrong. We wanted it to happen, so badly. I could have done it myself, but Gwen… didn't want my work to be part of it.'

The unaffected part of his mouth turned down, in a self-reproaching way. 'I couldn't take the waiting, and the constant failure. So one day, I… acquired some of Gwen's eggs… from one of the specialists' offices, and brought them to my lab. When I was sure they were healthy, I implanted my sperm and started the test regimen. One way or another… *I* was going to succeed.'

His mouth turned up, in a smile both pleased and rueful. 'Then, the very next day, Gwen calls me at work. Seems the last time turned out to be the charm.' The smile grew; even the paralysed half seemed to be responding. His right hand, still dotted with half-healed cuts, lifted high enough to brush the bottom edge of the photo, then fell back to the floor. 'Nine months later, we had Aidan. A perfect, healthy son – the natural way, like she'd wanted.' The smile faded, back to a sober look. 'The day after we came home, I hid the eggs, in the deepest part of the CellWorx freezers. We were both getting older, so naturally wasn't certain, if we wanted to try again. Until then... she couldn't know.'

The Doctor stopped to draw another breath. None of the three Golems spoke, their breathing near-silent. On the screen, the numbers kept ticking down: 13:45, 13:44. 'I'd almost forgotten about them, even after the Project started. I had my work, and a family to get me through.' Bleakness spread across his still-working features. 'Then came the accident...' His eyes found Cayden, who was staring back intently. 'That night – the other man, the one responsible, walked away.' A bleak grief like none other entered his voice. 'When it happened, though... he couldn't. Not at first.' His head sagged. 'He was left scarred, limping, for the rest of his life, though he should have died, that night... along with them.'

He went quiet. Greg could only stare, dumbfounded. Leah's eyes were wet and glimmering. Cayden's face was rigid, with the tiniest hint of shock and fear. A tear beaded in the Doctor's good eye. When he resumed, the words came out in a near-inaudible whisper. 'I couldn't bear the loss – the loss *I* caused.' His hand formed the shape of a gun. 'I was staring down into God knows which number bottle, hoping the next would be enough... to do the trick.' The hand relaxed. 'Then I remembered the lab – and what I'd saved.'

The reproach came back. 'I hated myself for *thinking* it. Part of me wanted to pull the trigger, just for that. The only thing that stopped me was wanting back the life I'd destroyed.' He locked eyes with Cayden. 'So I chose to remake it, in body – and give it a strength I would never have. The Project might be its purpose – but the mind, and soul, would be all its own.' His smile returned, warmer, prouder and happier than at any time since their arrival. 'And it has been.'

Cayden set the picture down. He didn't look angry. There was almost no emotion in his look at all, in fact, a one-eighty from the near-insane rage not that long ago. Rather he looked... satisfied. Like he'd gone his entire life with a question hanging over him, too afraid or too unwilling to explore it – and had finally gotten the answer, which counted for more than any pain or joy it brought. He brushed aside several bits and pieces of concrete and metal, and knelt down beside the Doctor. Watching this, Greg could suddenly see the telltale signs: the hair, the jawline, the shape of the skull. Even the facial muscles moved in much the same way. The effect was dumbfounding – and mesmerising. *All this time...* One quick flick of the eyes, to the Gaia screen. *And where else could* that *voice have come from, if not from* her?

This look made him see the countdown timer again: 12:30, 12:29. He stole a glance at Leah. She was still crying – but the set of her body was firm, and ready. She stepped up to the two men, and knelt before them. Delicately, she leaned forward and kissed Garrett on the forehead. The Doctor smiled in thanks, eyes also wet. She rose, made a slow about-face, and began walking to the stairs. A faint trembling rippled in her shoulders; other than this, she gave no sign of any emotion.

Greg looked to the two other men himself, the unspoken question plain. Garrett's disfigured visage dipped in silent reply. Cayden made the same wordless motion, and got to his feet. One hand moved to the grip of his knife, still in its clinger sheath. He slid it free, studying the well-worn hilt and near-pristine blade. Instead of hurling it away, as before, he let it fall from his grip, to land with a clatter amidst the rubble. Looking quietly pleased, he held his hands out in front of him. Greg glanced at his own as well. He understood perfectly what Cayden saw. For the first time, they felt truly empty. Like they were finally *free*, to do far more than they'd been made for.

Cayden lowered his hands. He looked to the old man – *in*

every *way*, Greg thought with an inward smile. 'I found the cabin,' he said, almost out of the blue. 'Wasn't sure I would, at the time – wasn't sure of a lot of things, then. It was rough, some ways – but it was happy, in most.'

Garrett nodded, the only movement he could manage. 'Found it on a trip with Gwen, not long before we got the news. She loved to hike, more than anything; said she wanted to hit every park in the country, before… ' He fell silent. When he resumed, it was in a more plaintive voice. 'I would like to see her there, one more time. Her, and… ' He broke off again, from shame or grief.

One of Cayden's hands drifted. It found the Doctor's still-working right, and squeezed. He shifted, turning his head in Garrett's direction. The Doctor's look locked with his, tears welling. A low rumble reached up through the floor. Cayden didn't close his eyes, or look away. He felt no sadness, no fear, no anger, nothing – just a profound peace. Softly, he said, 'We all will, one day… *Dad*.'

The intact side of Garrett's face bloomed in a smile. Cayden smiled back; his first *real* smile. He held out his hand to the Doctor. Straining with effort, Garrett managed to bring his arm up, and grasped it. The moment stretched; even the countdown seemed to pause. Then Garrett let go, swinging his arm in Greg's direction. Greg seized his hand in turn, gripping tight. The world blurred in front of him. He blinked hard, until a semblance of clarity came back. Slowly, stiffly, he released his grip. He, Cayden and Garrett all stared at each other, without sound or movement. Then Cayden turned, and started after Leah. The set of his shoulders showed how hard he was keeping himself from looking back. Greg followed, trying to match the poise. His legs wobbled, now and again, but he stayed upright, and moving. The nuke case, impressively light before, now seemed to weigh him down more and more with each step.

Leah was waiting beside the elevator, standing at perfect attention. Before they stepped into the car, she took one last look toward the lab. Greg and Cayden mimicked her. The Doctor was out of sight, of course, but he could still sense the man's eyes on the lobby – and them. On the screen, the timer showed a little over ten minutes left. Plenty of time to get to the surface, get clear of the compound, and back to the beach, with the right speed.

Leah moved into the car, and pivoted, finger hovering over the button. Greg followed suit. He stared at the lights above, keeping himself from one final look by sheer force of will. Just for a microsecond, his foot twitched, ready to propel him back out and drag the Doctor along with them. He'd have gladly carried him, along with the nuke. All that'd been said, and done, before Hunter and his crew showed up – all that he'd learned, and come to hate, since coming here… it all seemed distant. Not unimportant, by far – but far more different than anything he could have imagined.

The closing of the doors cut this impulse short. The lift shuddered into motion, rising up at a rapid clip. He lowered the case from his shoulder, carrying it by the handle. His arm seemed to sag under the weight, to where it almost touched the ground. Illusion – for the most part. *He was right,* the Golem reflected, with a new flare of sadness. The canister – and the nuke – were the keys to the Sanctuary's future, and that of every other Golem, still out there, in hiding or on the run, completely in the dark on *why. After tonight, the doors'll open – for all of them.* What would come next, he couldn't even begin to guess. His eyes went to the floor. *Thanks to him, we'll have the chance to see it.*

The darkened forest began to thin out: fewer trees, more ferns, tall grass and other brush. Up ahead, Greg could just make out the shoreline. Out over the glittering waves of the Sound, he spotted a trio of blinking lights, and heard the soft humming of 'Wraith'-upgraded rotors. He slowed his pace, until he was down to a brisk walk. They were already far enough; no need to force it, not anymore. He didn't look back, only tightened his arm around the case on his shoulder, stepping or hopping over the occasional root, stone or fold in the ground. Leah kept up the same pace, hands floating above her weapons. Her face was calm, and dry of any tears – though the hurt was easy to see in her eyes.

The humming grew louder; the Black Hawks must be at full throttle, sacrificing stealth for speed. Greg walked past the treeline, into the clearing that fronted the beach. The centremost set of lights grew larger and brighter, aiming for the same spot. The other two branched off to north and south, likely to set down at flanking sites. Greg halted, ignoring the steady wind off the Sound and the gusts from the chopper buffeting at him. Leah did likewise, watching the approaching lights impassively. Cayden didn't even glance up, only stared straight ahead, not registering anything.

Twin searchlights stabbed out, focusing on them. Greg didn't blink, or pull his hood. Gracefully, the Black Hawk set down on the flat stretch of earth and grass, beams still trained. Half a dozen men in NBC suits tumbled out, laser markers already centred on the three Golems' heads and chests. They fanned out in a semicircle, keeping a fair distance. When neither Greg nor Leah made any moves, one of them put a hand to his ear, then waved to the chopper. Three more figures climbed down at once. Two were in the same NBC gear, masks off; the third wore a clinger, hood thrown back.

Even through the glare, Greg had no trouble discerning Costa, Patrick and Hiroshi's faces.

The three new arrivals stepped past the firing line. Costa looked pleased; Patrick and Hiroshi determined. 'You made it!' Costa called over the whirring chopper engines. His smile grew when he saw the case in Greg's grip, and spotted the canister on Leah's belt. 'Looks like you found some answers, too!' When neither Golem said a word, he gestured, a little awkwardly, to his companions. 'Managed to convince D.C. to have us be the military and Agency point men for the Zone, given the sensitive aspects! Shouldn't have any trouble sorting this fucking mess out for good, soon enough!' He pointed behind him, eastward. 'Sanctuary's got the word; they're prepped to help in any way! More choppers are inbound from Yakima and near Portland, to assist in securing the area! Soon as that's done, we'll—'

A crackling roar to the west cut him short. A bright flash of yellow-orange light burst through the clearing, rising and expanding in all directions. Costa and Patrick each threw up an arm; Hiroshi pulled his clinger hood up for a few moments, then let it drop again. The Rangers flinched away, cursing and grabbing at their night vision goggles. Greg didn't move; nor did Leah or Cayden.

Two or three seconds after, the shockwave rippled over the scene: strong enough to rock him a little, and make the new arrivals stagger and reel. In the Black Hawk's main window, he saw a spreading cloud of fire, dust and smoke. The blast had surely levelled the entire Facility, as promised – and incinerated the naval base, and all the land for miles around it, too. How many thermobaric bombs had there been? Plenty – that was all that mattered. *Burning bridges… every last one.* Now they were on the other side for good – and for better or worse.

Costa recovered quicker than the others. He goggled at

the spreading inferno, watching it spread farther and farther – and gradually begin to subside, becoming a low burning wildfire. The agent pointed. 'What the hell was that?!' Patrick and Hiroshi stared with him: the former alert, the other calm – and understanding.

Instead of answering, Greg slid the case off his shoulder, went to one knee, and set it on the ground between them. Costa and Patrick watched him, careful and puzzled. He flipped the catches up, turned it around, and lifted the lid. Both men's eyes almost bugged out at the sight of the radiation sign. They stepped back a pace; the rest of the Ranger team imitated them. Hiroshi looked startled himself, but stayed still, and calm.

As Greg stood up, Leah stepped forward in turn. Her face was dry now, no tears in her eyes – even the pain was gone. She reached behind her back. Half a dozen guns trained on her. Barely noticing this, she brought the hand forth again. The canister rested flat in her palm. She let the two men stare at it for a full ten seconds, then, still wooden-faced, returned it to the clasps. Greg moved a step in front of her, resting a hand on the lid. 'We've got some things to discuss,' he said, voice flat, and purposeful.

The agent and the Ranger officer looked at each other, then the four Golems, then the blaze. Neither one seemed able to speak, or move. Finally, Costa stepped up. He couldn't quite take his eyes off the nuke. 'Looks like we do,' he said, uneasily – but with a growing purpose to match Greg's. He held out his hand. Solemnly, Greg took it.

Epilogue

The Brothers Mountains, Washington State

Four Months Later

Pulling hard with both hands, Greg hauled himself up onto the rocky ledge. He got to his feet, and sucked in a great breath, letting it out slowly. The summer air was smooth and clean, with a taste of salt from the Sound. A gentle breeze wafted around him, making his blue T-shirt ripple. The feel of the clinger was only a memory now, and growing more distant – a fact he was happier with by the day.

Trees were sparse all around his current spot, but those few there were – mostly evergreen – were strong and healthy. Below him, the entire landscape was bedecked in vibrant green, with a few dead, grey patches near the beach from the Bomb's radiation washing ashore. At this height and distance, he could make out the two small watch sites still occupied on the shoreline. A vessel – a trawler or small freighter – cruised on the Hood Canal, making its way deeper into the Zone from the intro point at Bangor. Samir was reportedly on this trip, along with several others; another reason for his hike.

Up to almost 400 now, coming in from all over, he reflected. *If Hiroshi's right, the rest of the 'lost tribe' will be here by October: 200, maybe more.* With those, they would come close to accounting for nearly all the Golem population – those that still lived, anyway. Some of the new arrivals had been distrustful, keeping to themselves; all too natural after years underground, often in conditions that made the Sahara or the Arctic look like the pre-flooded Bahamas. Almost all of them, however, had been curious enough to explore further – and had quickly fallen in love with the thick forests and secluded bays of the place. Whatever the numbers, they would have no trouble finding room for them. Cayden was helping with their acclimatisation, often volunteering to go out solo to find any who were still holed up. Possibly he was onboard the freighter, shepherding in the next batch before heading out again. Eventually, everyone would be found, and he would choose a permanent spot for himself in the Enclave – still part of it, though on his own terms. Till then… till then, he acclimated in his own way, on his own terms.

Greg shifted his gaze southward, past the end of the Canal. If he felt like it, he could lift the binoculars around his neck, and just be able to spot the next convoy of troops being deployed outside the demarcation line. The border along I-5 and 101 was de facto in place, even with Patrick and the Sanctuary negotiators not yet done hammering out the Seattle sector, around Mercer Island and I-405. From all the signs, Costa – and the rest of his negotiating team, sent out from D.C. – were willing to concede them.

The westernmost area was still undecided, too – hence today's combination of survey and afternoon hike. Backup supplies were still coming in, thanks to Patrick's insistence and Costa's heft; there was almost no need for the smuggling routes out the south, anymore. The croplands and greenhouses around Olympia were already showing signs of a bumper yield, and the first surveys and clearing of suitable land were proceeding apace on McNeil, Anderson, Hartsine, and the cleaner areas of the Kitsap Peninsula.

Tentative surveys had revealed Vashon and easternmost Bainbridge and Kitsap to be still too contaminated for reliable growth or permanent settlement, even by Golems. But the levels were decreasing; another decade, and they would probably be habitable. The same couldn't be said for Seattle itself. Cautious sweeps of the region, after what was already being called the 'Facility Incident', or the 'Battle of Bangor' by some of the others, had shown it would be between twenty and thirty years before the radiation was low enough for long-term human settlement, augmented and otherwise. The firebomb hadn't helped, either; much of the un-decayed but settled fallout in and around the Facility was now free-floating again, mixing in with the downtown deposits.

Then there were the hints Patrick had dropped from his conversations back East, about some hardliners – who'd pointedly looked the other way when it came to the Golems at their height, and Hunter at his worst – making noise over yielding Seattle, and so much other abandoned valuable land and infrastructure, no matter how contaminated. Their turning over the second stolen nuke hadn't lessened the clamour by much; indeed, some of the politicos and military brass were pointing to it as further proof of the Sanctuary's hostile intent.

Doesn't really matter, Greg reflected. *Long as we've got Gaia, and the canister, we've got the proof – and another Pulse, if need be.* Despite Garrett's final gift, they had no need for nukes, with that kind of power. It was the perfect defence against anyone, anywhere in the world, who saw them as a threat. *Hopefully the message'll stick for a while, giving us time to build a new home, and set it in stone.*

Looking around, he spotted a small boulder, a few feet away. Part of the surface was marred in odd lines, almost like writing. He peered closer. His eyes widened, then crinkled in humour, amazement, and not a little melancholy. With a furtive look over one shoulder, he knelt beside the rock. Pulling out his knife – he was getting less and less used to carrying it, nowadays, with hardly anyone in the Sanctuary wearing clingers except on patrol or guard duty – he set it in a little crevasse between the rock and the mountaintop, well out of sight. He sat back on his haunches, bemused and, in a way, saddened – but without regret.

A *huff* of exertion broke his reverie. Getting to his feet, he saw Leah's face appear over the edge of the rock, reddened and straining. He moved closer, one arm out, but she yanked hard with both hands, and pulled her chest above the edge of the rock. Lying on her side, she crawled one-handed the rest of the way. After a pause for breath, she brought her knees underneath her and stood up. Her eyes glowed. 'Still got the moves,' she remarked, with hardly a pant.

'Always have and always will.' Greg's answering smile showed a hint of mockery. 'But, of course, I made it to the top first – as always.'

With a growl, Leah sprang forward, grabbing both his arms and pushing him toward the ledge. Laughing, he pivoted hard on one heel, spinning her around. They pushed and wrestled at each other like mountain rams. Then Greg let his legs give way, and they collapsed in a heap. Rolling on top of him, Leah pretended to clamp both hands around his throat. He fended her off easily, seizing both her hands in his. She desisted, gasping and laughing, and leaned forward. Her lips pressed against his. He wrapped both arms around her waist, squeezing tight.

Eventually, Leah slid off, and sat down beside him, one hand still gripping his. With the other, she pointed eastward. 'Almost no fog; you can almost see the Needle today.' Her gesture shifted to the south. 'Same with the new camps at Belfair, and Victor.' She glanced at him. 'I'm still surprised you didn't push the Committee to relocate somewhere else. Olympia's cleaner, but right on the new border. We *will* need an HQ deeper in the CZ at some point, and one that's not as potentially exposed.'

Greg shrugged. 'Didn't see any real need to. Besides, it's a good spot: small, on the water, without most of the rebuilding problems in the rest of the Sound. We'll need Seattle and the other sites later, for salvage, and maybe more space. In the meantime, we can keep the place secure – and we shouldn't have any serious threats against it.'

Leah's gaze turned east again. 'You think *they'll* ever change their minds?' Her voice held a touch of worry. 'That they'll work up the nerve to try and end *this* experiment, and come back around to making something more… more like *Hunter's*?'

'Maybe. Maybe not.' Greg peered east himself. 'The radcount'll keep them out for another decade, at the periphery. After the Doc's last act, and the work with Costa and Patrick, I'd say we've got a good while after that, before they'll be in any shape to come here.' A little conspiratorial smirk. 'Plus there's the little worry about a certain package, still missing from D.C., and still not confirmed as lost in the Facility. Long as that's still out there, they'll be watchful, but won't want to come knocking.'

Letting go of Leah's hand, he let his rest on her stomach. The swelling was just noticeable now, despite her loose white shirt and khaki shorts. His voice went softer. 'Well before then, we'll be settled – and there'll be plenty more of us to deal with.'

Leah's mouth curved in a soft smile. Taking his arm in both hands, she reclined against the rock, closing her eyes. Greg smiled back, though she didn't see it. He looked at the boulder once more. A crude heart was carved into its face, much faded by sun and weathering. Two names were chipped within the image, along with a date: *Rich + Gwen, 7/15/00.*

He lay on his back, free hand behind his head. The sky was a brilliant blue, with hardly a cloud to be seen. His eyes fell half-closed. All around them was the wind, the rustling of leaves and pine needles, and faintly, the whisper of water lapping against the shoreline, far below. *Best place to build a home,* he thought dimly, as sleep crept over him. *For ourselves – and for whatever comes next.*

FIN

Unbound is the world's first crowdfunding publisher, established in 2011.

We believe that wonderful things can happen when you clear a path for people who share a passion. That's why we've built a platform that brings together readers and authors to crowdfund books they believe in – and give fresh ideas that don't fit the traditional mould the chance they deserve.

This book is in your hands because readers made it possible. Everyone who pledged their support is listed at the front of the book and below. Join them by visiting unbound.com and supporting a book today.

The Birthday Fairy
Gail Blundon
G.E. Gallas
Emma Grae
Grace Helmer
Simon Ingram
Dan Kieran

Sue Knox
Amy Lord
Courteney MacKuen
John Mitchinson
Carlo Navato
Justin Pollard
Sobia Quazi